THE DAMNED

THE COVEN OF BONES SERIES

The Coven
The Cursed
The Damned

THE DAMNED

HARPER L. WOODS

BRAMBLE

TOR PUBLISHING GROUP
NEW YORK

This is a work of fiction. All of the characters, organizations, and events portrayed in this novel are either products of the author's imagination or are used fictitiously.

THE DAMNED

Copyright © 2025 by Harper L. Woods

All rights reserved.

A Bramble Book
Published by Tom Doherty Associates / Tor Publishing Group
120 Broadway
New York, NY 10271

www.torpublishinggroup.com

Bramble™ is a trademark of Macmillan Publishing Group, LLC.

EU Representative: Macmillan Publishers Ireland Ltd, 1st Floor, The Liffey Trust Centre, 117–126 Sheriff Street Upper, Dublin 1, D01 YC43

The Library of Congress Cataloging-in-Publication Data is available upon request.

ISBN 978-1-250-36523-1 (hardcover)
ISBN 978-1-250-36524-8 (ebook)

The publisher of this book does not authorize the use or reproduction of any part of this book in any manner for the purpose of training artificial intelligence technologies or systems. The publisher of this book expressly reserves this book from the Text and Data Mining exception in accordance with Article 4(3) of the European Union Digital Single Market Directive 2019/790.

Our books may be purchased in bulk for specialty retail/wholesale, literacy, corporate/premium, educational, and subscription box use. Please contact MacmillanSpecialMarkets@macmillan.com.

First Edition: 2025

Printed in the United States of America

10 9 8 7 6 5 4 3 2 1

For those who weren't believed

TRIGGER WARNINGS

The Damned is a dark paranormal romance that takes place in Hell between a witch and an archdemon, and due to the nature of that dynamic, features content that may be triggering for some readers. Most importantly, our heroine, Margot, is a survivor of childhood sexual assault and the story centers around her emotional and physical journey to healing her trauma. Please read at your own discretion.

Triggers include:
- Dubious consent
- Force-feeding
- Graphic on-page violence and torture
- Rough and explicit sexual content
- Forced proximity and captive scenarios
- Betrayal
- References to past abuse and traumatic reactions to triggering stimuli
- Knife violence
- Graphic depictions of blood
- Physical harm inflicted upon the main character
- Ritualistic murder
- Rape of a minor by an adult (off-page, historical context)
- Self-harm / cutting for magical purposes
- Blood magic

LEGACIES OF CRYSTAL HOLLOW

Crystal Witches (also known as Whites)
House Petra
House Beltran

Cosmic Witches (also known as Purples)
House Realta
House Amar

Earth Witches (also known as Greens)
House Madizza
House Bray

Air Witches (also known as Grays)
House Aurai
House Devoe

Water Witches (also known as Blues)
House Tethys
House Hawthorne

Sex/Desire Witches (also known as Reds)
House Erotes
House Peabody

FIRE WITCHES (also known as Yellows)
House Collins
House Madlock

NECROMANCY WITCHES (also known as Blacks)
House Hecate

PART I

1

BEELZEBUB

Before

It was fucking cold.

Lucifer had promised us a haven, and we'd gotten a half-frozen tundra where frost covered the grass in the morning. I'd never thought to miss the heat of Helfyre lingering nearby, but would it kill them to have the fireplaces lit in a place this cold and damp?

My black leather wings brushed against the archway as I crossed through one of the narrower hallways, forcing me to tuck them in tight and duck my head down low so I could fit through. Scraping my wings against the stone walls might not have caused any damage, but it sure as fuck would serve a single purpose.

Pissing me the Hell off.

Lucifer was out of His mind giving that much of His blood to His consort, and I'd left them at the boundary of the woods, feeling entirely unsettled, after she'd clearly attempted to escape. I didn't know how she'd managed to wrap Him around her finger so efficiently; it wasn't like she was a Red witch and had corrupted Him with the addictive nature of sex.

She was *nothing* special, just another human. He'd seen countless others who would have been willing to warm His bed and been far less complicated in the end.

I'd seen demons and lost souls fawn over Him in Hell, and I could only imagine the way they went for Him in the plane of the living, especially at a time when they hadn't known how dangerous He truly was.

I strode through the hallways, heading toward the rooms Lucifer had given to the archangels in the meantime. It was a tiny, secluded hallway just off the Tribunal rooms and the courtyard that was crawling with plants that practically writhed with life.

Whatever the witches had done, that part of the world oozed with power in a way that the rest of Hollow's Grove didn't.

I'd spent the rest of my day after leaving them tending to the business that Lucifer *should* have been handling Himself. Keeping the archdemons in line, teaching them not to eat the witches for their lunch.

To keep their hands off until Lucifer worked out how He saw all this going down. Ruling over them had always been His intent, and where our visions for this world differed. He saw them as wayward children, as beings He could bring to heel and live alongside.

I saw them as the reason Lucifer had abandoned us in Hell, and it stood to reason that they should know how that solitude felt for themselves. They didn't seem to appreciate having Him walk among them for all these centuries, not the way His faithful demons would have been overjoyed to have Him return to us.

To *choose* us.

Him having a witch for a wife—a complication none of the archdemons had seen coming—wasn't part of the plan.

I faltered in my steps, hearing the soft sound of an innocent melody ringing through the night as I went about my patrols. All the witches had retreated to bed before dark, as if they feared what the archdemons might do to them if they were caught out of their rooms at night. It was a wholly foolish endeavor. They should have known, as well as anyone could, that evil wasn't relegated to darkness.

We could kill them just as easily under the shining sun of day.

The plants in the courtyard swayed in place in tune with the soft melody. The woman's voice was husky and low. I glided forward on steady, sure feet, unable to resist the call of that tone. I couldn't see her, not with the way the plants shielded her from view.

Muffling her song, I realized. Keeping it private in an area that might have otherwise been occupied if not for the witches' fear of us. The very notion that one of them was brave enough to come out alone when the others weren't would have been enough to pique my curiosity as it was. But the heartbreaking beauty in that song tugged at the place a heart would have been, had I believed myself to have one.

A smarter male would have turned away for that reason. While I'd never heard the song of a witch before, I knew of the power they held for all who heard them—the way some witches used them to ensnare their victims so they could feed from the lust they crafted.

I moved forward anyway, drawn to that sound in ways I couldn't otherwise explain, enraptured like a moth to the flame. I approached the stone wall at the side of the courtyard, stepping over it with ease to approach my captor. The roses formed an archway in the center of the garden, almost like a walkway that was created for me, leading me down the path to temptation.

A woman lingered at the end of the tunnel they formed, her back to me. Wavy blond hair fell to just above her shoulders in layers, making it look fluffy and softer than anything I'd ever felt. The sudden need to touch it overcame me, making me take another step as my gaze trailed down over the smooth expanse of her shoulders. Her deep red top dipped low in the back, revealing the curve of her spine. She'd tattooed music notes up the center, the ink billowing out into wisps as it met the defined lines of muscle that ran down either side.

Her plaid skirt was short, and the white thigh-high stockings hugged her long legs and the smooth definition of them. There wasn't a lump in sight where the top of the stocking met her thigh. I could already imagine the strength I would find in those legs if I ran my fingers up the length of them, immediately making me want to know more about her vice of choice—the exercise she used to gain such obsessive control over her body.

There wasn't a hair out of place on her head, not a speck of dirt or lint anywhere to be found on her clothing.

She was careful and meticulous about her appearance, but something in it felt more forced than natural, the tattoo up her spine the only hint of the real woman who lingered beneath that careful external control.

I took another step, wincing at the sound of a stick cracking beneath my boot. The plants ceased to move as they sensed my presence, the swaying roses and vines of ivy stilling in a way that only made my misstep feel louder in the silence that followed.

The woman spun suddenly, her song stopping as her hair flipped to reveal her pretty, shocked face.

No, *pretty* wasn't a strong enough word.

She was an angel, her mahogany eyes wide and her perfect bowed lips parted in shock. Her eyes drifted closed as she took in the sight of me and sighed, and I couldn't stop the growl that rumbled in my chest.

Didn't she recognize the predator in her midst?

I stalked forward, pausing only when she stumbled back a step in fear. Her cheekbones were high, cut like glass, and her nose the perfect button at the center of her face. Her uniform revealed a line of cleavage, showing breasts ample enough to fill my hands.

"I didn't mean for anyone to hear me," she said, her voice a husky melody tinged with apology. There was a roughness to it that reminded me of passion on a hot summer's night, that made me think of balmy air and sweat-slicked bodies.

"I heard you, songbird," I said, taking another step forward.

The woman winced as if I'd physically struck her. "You'll unhear me soon enough," she said, stepping around me. She kept her head down as she tried to pass me by, her entire body scrambling frantically when I reached for her and my fingers brushed her arm.

I retreated from the touch immediately, unable to understand why I cared enough to respect her wish for space. She was a witch, the very creature I had spent centuries of life despising and plotting for the day I could punish them as I'd been punished. They deserved to know every bit of pain that came with being left behind, to have a life without hope in the darkest of all places.

So why did the very idea that she'd already known such pain fill me with rage I thought myself incapable of after all these years?

My brow furrowed, narrowing down on the look of panic on her face. There was no mistaking the caution there. The fear of being touched.

Who?

I didn't voice the question, shoving my hands into my pants pockets to appease her. She was already so jumpy. She tracked my every movement, her body tense as if waiting for me to attack.

Her feet were shoulder-width apart, braced to fight just as much as to flee. That alone earned my respect, knowing that she would do whatever it took to navigate her way out of danger—that she'd likely vowed to take any would-be attacker down with her.

The muscle tone in her delicate body only confirmed it.

"What's your name?" I asked, watching as she ran her tongue over her lip to wet it. My entire world narrowed down to the movement, my body tensing with the need to feel that wet heat on my lips. I knew it had to be a consequence of her song, this attraction that was so potent and unnatural it could be nothing less than her magic working its way through my body, attempting to twist me into her willing servant.

"My name doesn't matter. You'll forget all about me soon enough," she said, turning on one of her high heels. She moved like a professional in them despite the dirt beneath her feet, easing her way over the stone half-wall border that surrounded the flourishing courtyard. Her heels clicked against the stone floors as she fled quickly, but she didn't run. She didn't give me the privilege of that fear.

Leaving me staring after the mystery woman, wondering how *anyone* could ever forget her.

2

MARGOT

The weight of my mother's gaze never left me during the class that had long ago become the bane of my existence. Growing up under the thumb of my aunt, the Erotes Tribunal member, was no easy task, but it meant that I already knew all the theology surrounding our magic and the ways that it worked. While my aunt was the Erotes Tribunal member, she hadn't had children of her own so she and my mother had taken it upon themselves to work in tandem when it came to my education.

That was knowledge she often used to her advantage, asking me for answers that she knew I had when others wouldn't. While the Reds as a whole were more sexually liberated than many of the families within the Coven, that didn't mean that all of them were quite as encouraging as my mother had been.

She'd known even from a young age that I wasn't like the rest, that my magic had a darker nature than many of the others'. They could control the pull in their songs, having to expend effort and magic in order to allow that magic to seep beneath someone's skin and claim them from the inside, until their body was only an instrument to be used.

I'd never had a choice, never had the option to reject the magic that so easily pulsed at my fingertips. It was in everything I touched, in everything I did, and in every word I sang.

It was the reason I refused all invitations to join the choir that occupied most of the Reds' free time, the reason I often kept to myself in the library instead of spending time with my peers. They didn't understand the weight of that magic and what it meant for me.

They didn't understand how it had come to be my curse.

"Are you even listening, Margot?" my mother asked, forsaking the general understanding that even when teaching their own offspring, they are meant to keep a certain level of distance from their progeny.

Here, I wasn't supposed to be Fritha Erotes's eldest daughter, daughter of the next heir to the Erotes Tribunal seat, as my aunt who currently occupied that seat had no children of her own. Here, I was supposed to be a cool, collected *Miss Erotes,* like so many of the others who occupied the class alongside me—cousins and second cousins and family members who descended from the same line but had merged far enough back that it became impossible to keep track.

The Peabody legacies sat on the other side of the classroom, the divide between the two more evident than ever.

"Yes, ma'am," I said, giving a meek nod of my head as I looked down at the book in front of me. A quick glance to my cousin Belva beside me confirmed that I was six pages behind, lost to my own thoughts. Even before I'd noticed my mother staring at me, it had been a certain red-eyed archdemon who occupied my mind.

Seeing him in the courtyard the night before had kept me awake all night, and I knew half my mother's anger was probably for what she saw as my lackluster appearance in the wake of that. The first rule of Reds was that appearance was everything, and one couldn't use magic to replace a good night's sleep and a few extra moments of care in the morning.

"Then explain to me the exact functioning of the cone of power and the ways that we use that for the ultimate power manifestation," she said, making my cheeks flush with heat as all eyes turned to me.

Goddess, sometimes I wished I had a normal relationship with my mother where discussing these things was uncomfortable for all involved and not just me.

"When utilizing the cone of power, a witch stores all the magic that she has accumulated during sex, from both her and her partner's desire, within her body until the point of climax is reached. At that point, she uses her body as a conduit and sends it into the universe, making her intentions clear as she does and using it to fuel the spell so that her desired outcome can come to pass," I said, the words almost verbatim from the textbook in front of me.

It didn't matter that I wasn't even turned to the proper page, not when those words had been drilled into my brain from the time I turned eighteen and my mother expressed her disappointment that I wasn't showing signs of interest in any of the extracurricular activities my peers had already begun to engage in.

My mother nodded, turning away from me and continuing on about her lesson that I'd already heard countless times. I heaved a sigh of relief the moment her attention was elsewhere, my thoughts immediately returning to the danger waiting for me.

I didn't know how long it would take for the archdemon to show his face in my life, but I knew the song would demand it of him. He wouldn't be able to stay away, and that was the consequence of my taking a moment to sing.

I'd been too afraid to venture out to the outskirts of the school, to run along the edge of the woods until I was far enough from listening ears that I could sing freely. I'd thought the witches had all gone to bed and that maybe I would be safe in that abandoned courtyard so late at night.

Instead, I'd managed to entrap one of the greatest dangers to my well-being. I didn't even know which archdemon he was, having never paid as much attention to my schooling when it came to the history of the Coven. If it had been a few days prior, I might have turned to Willow for advice.

But my friend had enough to worry about with the devil claiming to be her husband. The last thing she needed was to worry about my safety.

The bell rang, sounding the end of the last class of the day. It seemed stupid to continue with our education like our entire world hadn't just turned upside down, like the devil and His archdemons didn't walk the earth for the first time in history.

None of us knew what that meant for the future of the Coven, for the future of the witches who called Hollow's Grove home. For all we knew, this could very well be our last day to live. It felt like a day that should be spent with loved ones, a last opportunity before it was all torn away.

Instead, Hollow's Grove once again forced us to prioritize our education because, as the future of our kind, knowing how our magic worked was of the utmost importance. Yet, if Willow was to be believed, we'd long since lost the true nature of our magic. Her Green magic had brought the plant life around us back in a way I'd never seen; I was so used to the husked and half-dead plants that I'd never even questioned what they were meant to look like.

I moved to pack up my textbook, sliding it into my bag as my mother's lithe form stepped in front of me. She rapped her knuckles on the surface twice, her nails painted a glossy fire-engine red as I froze in place. "I'd like to speak with you before you bolt out of my classroom," she said, turning her back on me quickly and making her way to her desk.

As the other students filed out, I dropped my book bag on top of my desk and rose from my seat carefully, making my way to her. It was another one of her power plays to make me go to her when she'd been standing at my desk only a moment before. Another in a long list of games.

"You look like Hell," she said, not wasting any time before the criticism began. She took her eyes from me as soon as she said the words, picking up a pen from her desk and grading papers while I stood there beneath her judgment. The door hadn't even swung closed yet, meaning that the nosy students who waited just beyond it could hear my ridicule, but my mother didn't care. "Your image is a direct reflection on this family. What have I told you about stepping outside of your room without taking care to make sure you represent us properly?"

The sad reality was that I'd done everything I could to make myself meet her standards. I'd woken up before the sun rose even though I'd only just managed to fall asleep, showered and styled my hair, done my skincare with the ointments the Reds were so proud of producing to keep aging at bay.

But nothing could erase the circles from beneath my eyes.

"I couldn't sleep," I said, even knowing it wouldn't be enough of an excuse in her mind.

"Are you having nightmares again?" she asked, referencing the days when I'd go to her the morning after Itan visited me, telling her about what he'd done.

She'd brushed them off as nightmares, figments of my overactive imagination that were only natural considering the pure volume of magic at my fingertips.

"No," I said, changing the subject quickly. I didn't want another reminder of the reality that my own mother didn't believe me, that she'd sooner believe I had hallucinated my abuse than suspect one of the Tribunal members of being capable of such a crime. "I was afraid. Something happened last night. I made a mistake and—"

Her mahogany gaze that was so like mine met mine suddenly, her pen dropping to the paper as she glared. "What did you do now?" she asked, the words said from between clenched teeth. Her fingers tapped on the surface of the desk impatiently, waiting for me to give the words that she was so certain would be a disappointment to her.

Just like me.

"I sang in the courtyard last night. I needed the release with everything going on and the way that everything feels now that Lucifer is here," I said, referencing the way magic seemed to pulse off of everyone. I didn't know if it was just the increase in tension making people wish for more enjoyable releases or the presence of Him in general, but I felt like magic seeped into my bones no matter where I was or what I did. I'd needed to release some of it the only way I was willing.

"You could have just taken a partner to your bed like the rest of us," my mother said, sighing her disappointment. "You know that Keane would be more than willing to accommodate you in that way before your handfasting." The reminder of the betrothed the Covenant had chosen for me at a young age was like being dropped into an ice bath.

It wasn't even that Keane was unattractive or cruel or any of the things that should have made me dread our union. He was one of the kindest men I'd encountered in the Coven, a Peabody witch who had sacrificed his magic when the Covenant offered to match him with me. The other girls had all fawned over him, telling me how lucky I was to have secured such a match.

For all purposes, I *should* have been thrilled with it. I should have been able to feel the affection for him that he so obviously held for me, following me around like a lovesick puppy for years until he finally began to keep his distance because of my discomfort.

But I didn't feel it. I had long since begun to suspect that I *couldn't* feel anything more than a general knowledge that someone was attractive. Something so important was just missing within me, making me incapable of feelings of desire and love and all the warmth that I could have potentially gained from the nature of my magic.

"Well, I didn't," I snapped, immediately regretting the tone when my mother's gaze hardened into the one that threatened punishment for my attitude. In our world, it didn't matter that I was twenty years old and a grown-ass woman, she would always be my elder as a future Tribunal member and matriarch of our line.

"Who heard you?" she asked, preparing to do damage control if I'd accidentally spelled someone within the Coven. While it wasn't illegal, it was frowned upon to use our magic against those in higher positions of authority than us.

I swallowed. "One of the archdemons . . ." I said, letting the words trail off as her head tilted to the side in thought.

Her face was carefully blank as she studied me, all traces of anger gone from her features. "Do you know which one?" she asked, and I shook my head.

I didn't know his name. Didn't know which of the creatures I'd bound to myself. "The winged one with the Enochian tattoos on his chest. Red eyes," I said, offering the simplest explanation I could. I didn't think my mother would have noted the way his deep brown hair was the same length as mine, pulled back into a bun at the back of his head. I didn't think she would have noted the strength in his square jaw, the way the harsh lines of his features were brutal and beautiful all at once, his eyebrows two angry slashes that had softened for me.

"Beelzebub," she said, picking up her pen and using it to draw Enochian symbols on her notepad. They were the same ones I'd seen on the archdemon's chest the night before, and I nodded when I recognized them. "Did he seem affected by your song?" She lowered her pen slowly, as if she didn't dare to move too quickly.

I thought back to the night before, wondering if I'd misread the situation. If I had merely assumed that he was under my spell when he wasn't affected, but the memory of him calling me *songbird* was a whisper in my mind, the sound of his deep, guttural voice like a caress on my skin.

I shivered in response to the sound of it, remembering the way it had felt in that moment. I'd never felt such a thing in my life, never heard a voice so deep and harsh but somehow gentle before. The way he'd reached for me when I tried to leave, seeming at war with himself for a moment, before he respected my wishes.

He'd let me leave.

"I think so," I said, answering her question as best as I could. I couldn't make myself share the nickname with her, feeling as if that was something better kept between he and I for the time being. It felt intimate, like something he hadn't given freely but that I'd stolen from him with the magic in my voice.

A name I hadn't earned, that didn't need to be claimed.

My mother's face spread into a broad grin the likes of which I'd never seen, making her face transform into the beauty I knew she was capable of when she was surrounded by people she liked.

I just wasn't among them.

"Oh, Margot, that's wonderful!" she said, standing and stepping around the side of her desk. She came to me, cupping my face in gentle, soft hands so tenderly that everything within me clenched. I wanted to retreat from the unnatural touch, from the glee and pride in her face.

I'd done something horrible, and *that* was the thing that made my mother happy.

"It is?" I asked, swallowing back the venom in my words. Arguing with her that it was monstrous would do me no good, not with the way she stared at me like I'd given her hope.

"You've ensnared Lucifer's second-in-command. If you and Willow can work together, then this could give us an edge. You'll have Beelzebub wrapped around your finger in no time if you keep singing for him now that you have him on the hook. I'll be sure to let the other Reds know that the song works, and maybe we can pull the others under our control as well," she said, trailing off as she left me to return to the papers she needed to grade, the moment passed.

"But that's horrible," I said, thinking of how dangerous the situation was. If Beelzebub became too addicted to my magic, if I brought him further under my spell, it was only a matter of time before he wanted to *act* on that spell. "You're talking about intentionally taking away their free will. I didn't mean to do this, but if they seek the archdemons out . . ."

"Oh, Margot, don't be so dramatic," she said finally, waving her hand to dismiss me. I'd served my purpose, and now she was done with me. "They're archdemons. They don't have feelings."

I nodded as I grabbed my book bag off my desk, retreating from the room as quickly as I could. My mother might have claimed it didn't matter because they lacked feelings, but I knew well enough to know that even someone broken and devoid of warmth would feel the violation that this was.

I certainly had.

3

MARGOT

I hurried to the right, curving my way up the staircase without so much as glancing at the students who had gathered near the doorway as I passed. I took the stairs more quickly than any of the others, my book bag bouncing where it hung by my hip. I pushed myself to skip steps as my legs spread to accommodate the longer stride, hugging the wall to keep anyone from seeing up my skirt near the railing.

The need to push, to make my muscles strain with the speed that I sprinted up those steps was so overwhelming that I couldn't have hid it if I'd wanted to. Making my body hurt was the only way to make myself *feel* what I knew should have hurt, the reminder of my childhood and the lack of approval from my mother not really striking me in the way they once had.

The numbness was a plague upon my soul, haunting me so much that I wondered what was wrong with me and how I could fix it so often that I'd lost track.

But I couldn't, and the only thing I could do was work my body until I felt like I might give in. The woods and the grounds weren't safe, hadn't been even before the archdemons had come, but now they were even less so and I'd have to risk my life in order to take the chance and find my outlet.

I wasn't at that point yet, so I raced the four flights of stairs up to the library at the top, my lungs heaving by the time I reached it. I paused outside the door, gathering my breath and trying to compose myself for a brief moment. Sweat slicked down my spine, tickling over the place where I knew my tattoo marked me. My mother had been furious the first day I showed up to class with it covered in the sheen of a healing ointment, the ink fresh and skin still a little swollen.

Reds did not participate in body modification of any kind as a rule. Personal expression like that was seen as a diminishing aspect of our objective attractiveness, making it so that our prospective partners would either love it or hate it. Most witches could not create something from nothing, and that meant that remaining attractive to as many people as possible was an advantage in the eyes of our elders.

My mother hated my shorter hair for the same reason, because it was an act I'd done in a direct rebellion of her wishes. I refused to allow it to grow past my shoulders because of how much I knew she hated it. The piercings I hid beneath my top that I'd foolishly done myself were another silent protest against the rules placed upon us by a too-strict Coven that wanted to erase any and all traces of our individuality. It didn't matter to me that no one else would see them if I had my way.

I hadn't done them for anyone but myself.

I sighed, turning to face the library door and stopping suddenly when *he* appeared in front of it and blocked my path.

Beelzebub.

I staggered back a step, desperately seeking the distance between us that he hadn't afforded me. This close, he seemed even larger than he had the night before. I was far from short at five seven and he had to be a foot taller than me anyway. His shoulders were broad, the rippling muscles tense where his arms were crossed over his chest. His wings settled down at his sides as he raised his chin, settling into his place in front of me.

I had to assume he'd flown to the platform that led to the library. The space was narrow and left me with the staircase at my back looming too close. One quick shove and I'd fall, ridding him of the curse I'd placed upon him by allowing him to hear my song.

For a moment, I wondered if he'd do it. For a moment, I hoped he would.

Jaw clenched and red eyes blazing, his gentleness from the night before was gone. His hair was still pulled back into that bun at the back of his head, and I wondered if he ever let it fall free around his face. His golden Enochian tattoos glowed, pulsing with light as he took a step toward me, and my heart raced in anticipation of my coming death.

"What do you want?" I asked, glancing over my shoulder at the staircase behind me.

He didn't respond, studying me intently. He looked at me as if I were a puzzle, reading the lines of tension in my body and whatever he could see in the expression on my face.

I didn't know if it was fear or exhilaration that made my heart race, waiting for him to make the decision we both knew danced behind the evil in that gaze. It would take one quick movement and he'd be able to free himself, and I let my body relax as I waited for it.

He tilted his head to the side, studying me as if I'd surprised him.

"Why do you not sing?" he asked, reaching forward so suddenly I thought he might push me. Instead, he grasped me by the strap on my book bag, tugging me forward sharply, and I toppled into him. My hands planted on his chest, the heat of his skin sinking into me as his mouth parted.

Every song. Every *touch*.

I jolted back as his mouth dropped open in shock, stepping around him to lean my back into the wall beside the library door. It left him with no choice but to swap with me, putting the stairs at his back. He was still too close, leaning his arm against the wall above my head, but he kept his distance enough not to touch me.

That in itself felt like a kindness, given what I knew of the effects of my touch. It felt restrained, where so many lost their self-control entirely under such close proximity to my magic.

"Why did you not sing?" he asked again, his eyes narrowing impatiently.

"Not really feeling the music right now," I said, giving him a bitter half smile. It felt more like Willow than me, a sarcastic response that I hadn't known I had in me. If the archdemon were going to kill me he would have already, and something in that emboldened me.

"I could have killed you, and you just stood there and waited for me to," he said, dropping his arm from the wall. I flinched, waiting for the touch I felt so certain would come, but he only glared down at me.

Waiting for my answer, I realized. Seeing too much, I knew.

"You didn't," I said, shrugging and feigning a casual ease that I did not feel.

He growled, the sound low and vibrating within his chest. It was barely audible, but I heard it. I felt it as if he were touching me, the sound sinking into me. "I should have," he warned, earning a nervous swallow from me. "Would you have stopped me, little siren? Would you have defended yourself if I had tried to snap your pretty neck?"

The bitter smile faded off my face, leaving me slowly as I held that red-eyed stare and tried to find the well of make-believe where all my pretty lies came from. I tried to find the energy to pretend I cared what happened to me beyond never allowing someone to take from my body again.

I spoke the single word quietly, giving him a vulnerability that I hadn't afforded anyone else. I didn't know what possessed me to choose him as the one to receive it; perhaps it was the distinct knowledge that I didn't need to care what he thought of me.

He was an archdemon. He was the enemy.

Let him think me weak.

"No," I said, raising my chin to hold his stare as his glare faded into shock. I let my answer sink in, let him see the truth of it in the emptiness of my eyes for the briefest of moments.

And then I donned my mask once again, forcing a pretty smile to my face before I turned and tugged the door open, retreating into the relative safety of the library.

I made a beeline for the table I always claimed at the back of the library, hanging my book bag on the back of my chair and dropping into it with a sigh. His steps were loud as he approached me, uncaring of the people studying around him as he closed the distance. I hated that he'd followed me, hoped that I'd shocked him into leaving me alone for a little while at least.

He stood on the other side of my table, glaring down at me as I turned my eyes up to meet his. "How long will this fucking spell last?" he asked, yanking the chair out and dropping into it. His wings fluttered behind him, trying to find a comfortable way to rest, and he grunted his frustration when it seemed an impossible task.

"They look inconvenient," I said, watching him struggle.

He glared, seeming uninterested in making small talk with me. "How long?" he asked again, forcing a sigh from me.

"That depends on whether you stay away from me or not. Touch will worsen the pull, so you should avoid touching me at all costs," I said, taking my book out of my book bag. "If you stay away, maybe a couple of weeks at most and then you'll be free."

"Convenient for you that I should avoid touching you given how you recoil in fear when I try, songbird," he said, an arrogant smirk tilting his lips up at the corner.

He thought I was lying, and there was a challenge in those words that I so wanted not to rise to meet.

My pride got the best of me. "I'm not afraid of you," I snapped, dropping my book on the table without a care for the way the thud echoed through the occupied library. I was all too aware of the stares that turned our way, watching our interaction for what it was.

Gossip fodder.

"No?" he asked, reaching out in an attempt to touch my cheek. I flinched back, hating the visceral reaction that I couldn't control any more than he could his pull to me. "That's what I thought."

He pulled his hand back as I looked down at my book on the table, opening it to the next page and getting ready to ignore him in favor of the pages about magical history. "It's not about you. I don't like to be touched," I said, offering the appeasement that I wasn't certain why I felt was needed. It felt like an attempt to be comforting, and maybe it was the play of vulnerability on his face.

Maybe being somewhere new made him feel like a monster, too.

"Why's that?" he asked, snapping my attention back to his face. "Who made you that way?"

My own growl rumbled in my chest, making his brows rise in surprise as something monstrous welled up within me. "You don't get to ask me that," I snapped, baring my teeth in a grimace.

"Easy, songbird. I'm just trying to get to know you," he said, raising his hands placatingly as if to try to convince me he was innocent. Like he hadn't just asked me a very, very personal fucking question. I hated that he saw enough to know that there had been a who, that I wasn't just born hating touch.

There'd been a time when I was physically affectionate as a child, constantly seeking out hugs from my family and friends.

He'd taken that from me, made me despise the very notion of another person's scent on my skin.

"Yeah? Well, don't," I hissed, flipping through the pages of my book to try to find the right page. "It's far better for both of us if we know nothing about each other."

He paused, leaning back in his chair and getting comfortable as he watched me. He crossed his arms over his chest, not in anger but in comfort, as if to say he was planning to stay awhile. "I think I disagree with you on that one."

"Do you *want* to stay stuck under my spell forever? Is that it?" I asked, watching as his smile faded a little.

"No," he said, barking a laugh. "But if you're going to occupy my every fucking thought against my will, then I might as well get to know you so I have something to think about. Besides, you're the most interesting way I've found to occupy my time here."

"I'm not sure if you meant that as a compliment or an insult," I said, leaning back in my chair.

The fucker really wasn't going to smarten up and stay away from me, determined to condemn us both to this misery.

"Maybe it was both," he said, his face lighting up with a playful grin that I felt everywhere as I swallowed, feeling my heart in my throat.

Shit. That Goddess-damned song was going to be the death of me.

4

MARGOT

I'd never seen the Tribunal room so full as the space was typically reserved for Tribunal members and the select few they deemed worthy of their presence when they met. Even I'd only been permitted within the space a handful of times, none of which were memories I wanted to keep.

The day the Covenant deemed me the beauty of my generation of witches. The day they shared the news of my betrothal. The day they brought me in to give me my formal invitation to attend Hollow's Grove. There'd been maybe two other meetings where the children of Tribunal members were all present to be observed by the Covenant, studied for potential placements through our childhood. As much as I might have dreamed of being one of the few Reds with high enough marks to be chosen to work in the apothecary in town, I knew it was an unlikely occurrence. Daughters of Tribunal members were typically more active in the politics surrounding the town and its ordinances, even those who were not chosen to take over their mother's Tribunal seat.

I wanted nothing more than to go play with potions and herbs, spelling them with the whisper of my magic so that I could give something back to those who wanted it, rather than keeping it eternally contained within me because I *didn't*.

I glanced around the room, moving to take up space beside Della. She glanced up at me, smiling softly as she reached down with a cautious hand to take mine in hers. It was one of the first times she'd attempted to touch me, knowing how much I hated it, and I couldn't help the subtle jolt that came with it.

Her skin was cool to the touch, the temperature of a refreshing lake on a hot summer's night. I realized it was my skin that was overheating, my body already stressed from what might occur within these walls for it to be necessary for all of us to be present at once.

"I heard the winged bastard is giving you trouble," she said, leaning sideways so she could whisper in my ear. Della was slightly shorter than me, making the whisper well-placed, and I hoped that no one could hear her.

I swallowed, my gaze immediately going to Beelzebub on the other side of the room. The siren song should have meant that he was pulled to me, that he was the one who sought me out; the reverse wasn't often true. I shouldn't have been able to pick him out in the crowd, shouldn't have been able to sense where he was before my eyes ever found him.

I brushed it off, knowing it was likely just the power that radiated off him. When you combined that with his formidable size, his massive black wings that were so reminiscent of the bats the Vessels were able to call to their aid, he exuded a presence that most of the men I'd encountered before him simply did not have.

"Where did you hear that?" I asked as members of the Coven continued to file into the room behind us, answering the call we'd all felt in our blood.

"Juliet was lurking in the back of the library," Della answered with a blush, more openly discussing the Vessel she'd been involved with for months in secret. With Willow and Headmaster Thorne's relationship being public information now, it hardly seemed to matter what the Covenant had placed on us in terms of rules.

At least my friend was free to be with the woman she loved, even if she was a Vessel and I had concerns for how that would work out in the end. They were eternal and lived forever, whereas we were not and would age and die in time.

The people around us were restless as we waited for something to happen. Lucifer and Willow were nowhere to be found, and I could see the rest of the Tribunal waiting for them within the inner circle of the room. The thrones they occupied formed the outer boundary, the sound within muffled so we could not hear the irritated words they spoke, but their body language conveyed the manner of the conversation.

"She should probably mind her own business," I said, hating the snap within the words. The knowing stares of others on me as I watched Beelzebub said that Juliet wasn't the only one who had seen our interaction, and that the others had been far less discreet in who they told about it.

Beelzebub turned his attention away from the demon at his side, the only one who was bigger than him, with scaled skin on his forearms, and met my stare. I expected a hint of the playfulness he'd shown at the tail end of our conversation in the library, or an arrogant curve of his eyebrow when he found me staring at him unabashedly.

Instead, the archdemon remained completely impassive. His arms were crossed over his chest, his body tense with what I had to assume was impatience. All gentle ease and humor had been erased from him overnight, and his expression was a stern glare as he waited for me to look away.

I did, unable to bear the hatred in that stare. I didn't know if my song had worn off somehow or if it was *because* of the song that his anger toward me seemed to have gotten worse since I'd fled the library for the privacy of my room, to his amusement. I guessed it didn't matter. All that mattered was hoping that his hatred would be enough to encourage him to control his impulses if the song hadn't worn off, keeping him as far from me as possible, to my mother's dismay.

My gaze wandered to her, finding her knowing smile as she watched him and swallowing against the implications of that.

"She was concerned for you. Are you sure you know what you're doing, messing around with an archdemon?" Della asked, her voice gentle. It wasn't judgment I heard, but I couldn't help the incredulous laugh that bubbled in my throat.

"Says the one who's dating a Vessel?" Della's wince was almost enough to make me regret the bitter reprimand, forcing me to continue on. "What makes you think I'm a willing participant in this? He heard my song, so I'm just waiting it out," I said, and Della nodded as if that made sense.

Our conversation was interrupted when Lucifer and Willow stepped into the open doors. A hush descended on the chaos of the room at their appearance. Willow held Lucifer by the elbow, allowing Him to lead her. Something changed on her face as she approached. Where before she'd appeared to be a defiant rebel every time she approached any kind of authority figure she didn't respect, somehow that had shifted.

She no longer appeared the rebel. She held her head high and strode into the Tribunal rooms as if they were hers.

They walked straight up to the boundary that kept most of us from entering the center circle, not even pausing before entering it. The boundary tugged at Willow, slowing her steps into a slow-motion sort of movie as tiny pinpricks of magic grated over her arms. I knew what that felt like, knew the pull of the magic drawing droplets of blood from needlelike wounds. Her blood floated through the magic of the boundary as Lucifer watched her in rapt fixation.

All those individual droplets of blood gathered into a single large tear-shaped droplet, lingering in front of her as she raised a hand to rest beneath it. The boundary released her into the center circle, allowing her to step through and putting her into the middle of the Tribunal's anger.

She ignored them for the briefest moment, turning her body to face where the rest of the Coven waited out of reach. We couldn't hear what was being discussed within the boundary, but Willow smirked and winked at me as she met my stare.

With a sigh, dropping her attention to the droplet of blood within her hold, she whispered something to it, her mouth moving with the intention and incantation before she squished her hands together, splattering her blood along the magic of the boundary.

It burst, exploding in a rush of wind that made it so that sound finally reached my ears. Itan was ranting, his voice immediately putting me into a trauma response. I knew it for what it was, felt the shiver on my skin as I broke out in goose bumps.

I would have given anything to be able to leave that room, to escape his presence as Willow smiled at me reassuringly and turned her attention back to the ranting male witch that someone needed to silence.

Permanently.

I felt Beelzebub move closer to me as if he could sense the shift in my energy, but I couldn't spare a moment of my attention for him. I couldn't tear my eyes off Itan, watching where he lounged in his throne like some kind of savior to our kind when he deserved nothing but pain and suffering.

He deserved justice. He deserved karma, and one day, I wanted to be strong enough to send it all back to him.

"What is the meaning of this? You decorate your whore in the bones of the legacy we *lost* now?" Itan asked, waving a hand toward Willow and the bones lingering at her waist. It was the first moment so many within the Coven were learning the truth of Willow's lineage, of the deception she'd committed when she came here to find the bones that no one thought she should need.

The legacy of the Hecate line had been lost to us for so long, not even the Covenant had seen her for what she was. A prophecy come to pass.

A reckoning come for us all.

Lucifer growled at Itan's words, making Willow take a step forward. She moved toward the abandoned Hecate throne, the bones at her waist clacking together as she walked. It was a sound so reminiscent of the way Susannah and George's feet had clacked against the stone floor that it triggered something in my memory, a parallel I wasn't ready to connect.

They'd been nothing but bones, taking control for a witch who drew power from bones and death itself.

I shook my head, forcing myself to enjoy the moment for my friend as the blood gathered back with her as if it had never left her side. It moved with her toward the throne, following after her like she commanded it.

"What is lost can always be found, Itan," Willow said, raising her chin and giving Itan a glare I wouldn't have wanted to be on the receiving end of.

Itan recoiled from her words, looking as if he'd been struck as he leaned back. He recovered with a shake of his head, his mouth twisting into a snarl. "Bullshit," he said, tilting his face up in an arrogant challenge. He'd left Willow with no choice but to reveal herself, forcing her to do the one thing that she would never be able to undo.

Shed the power that came with her anonymity.

She stepped up in front of the throne and stared down at the aging seat. It was crafted of the bones of those who had come before her, the skeletal remains of the ancestors who had already come and gone. Where the ones that were strapped around her waist were finger and hand bones, the throne had been remade from the femurs and rib cages and skulls of the oldest generations. Willow paused for a moment to appreciate the significance.

She looked over her shoulder at Itan, smirking before she glanced toward Lucifer. She dropped her hand, allowing the blood she'd brought with her to splash all over the aging and yellowing bones.

"Congratulations. You can make a mess as well as any child

attempting to play with the grown-ups. What was that supposed to prove?" Itan asked, his loyal followers barking out a peal of laughter from where they hid behind him, relying on him to protect them, which was a foolish endeavor entirely. He would sooner offer them up as a sacrifice to save himself.

As she turned to face him fully, her lips pulled back over her teeth in a dark, menacing smile that was all power. "Are you completely unfamiliar with foreplay?" she asked, raising her hand and waving it in a lazy motion toward the bones that were now covered in her blood.

Covered in her magic.

The chair groaned, creaking as the bones began to shift, collapsing to the tile floor until the throne was gone.

"I don't understand," someone whispered, lacking the patience necessary to wait out Willow's display of power. She knew better than most that anticipation was half of fear, that keeping them waiting and expecting her big reveal was half the fun.

She didn't so much as look behind her as the bones clacked, their pieces groaning and smacking together as they reassembled themselves, standing on top of one another, into the body of a man, until his figure shifted forward to stand at her side.

Lucifer barked a laugh of pure joy, His enjoyment at the look of shock on Itan's face rivaling my own. I couldn't help the twisted smile that pulled my lips back, revealing all my teeth in a broad grin that felt completely unfamiliar.

"You." Itan paused, looking back and forth between Willow and the creature she'd summoned from the dead. "But you're a Madizza! I've seen it with my own eyes."

Willow turned her attention to the Madizza throne, lifting her dress and stomping a foot upon the floor. The vines of the Madizza throne squirmed instantly, sliding out of places they'd been trapped for centuries. The throne slid along the ground, shifting into nothing but a tangle of roses and vines and thorns as it made its way across the center of the Madizza circle. It climbed the steps of the dais, centering itself where the two thrones of the Covenant had once been.

Willow nodded to the skeleton, earning a wordless nod back before it proceeded to the dais along with the vines. It crumpled to the floor on top of them, and we all watched in fixation and horror as the vines wound around the bones of Willow's ancestors.

Uniting them as one.

They twisted and turned, maneuvering their way into a new throne. A throne of bones and blood and life.

Willow ascended the steps slowly, her flair for the dramatic admirable, and exhaled a single sigh. She turned and looked back at the Coven from her place on the dais, easing down into the seat that only she could occupy. "Anything else, Itan, or are you done questioning me now?"

5

MARGOT

Itan glared at Willow, taking the first step toward the dais. He paused when Lucifer moved to join Willow, acting like her bodyguard rather than the devil Himself. The dynamic was so bizarre, so unexpected that I caught myself holding my breath as He turned His back on the Coven that would have seen Him dead. His eyes were only for Willow, facing the windows behind her as He reached down to capture her chin in a moment that was so heartrendingly sweet something within me throbbed.

It felt as if I missed having that for myself, but you could not miss what you'd never known.

He tilted her face up to His, smiling down at her with lips that tipped up at the sides. I could just make out the pride on His face from where I stood, the pure and undeterred approval of her actions.

He leaned down, kissing her gently for all of us to see. She melted into His touch, the tension leaving her body in a way that made no sense to me.

She'd hated Him. She'd come here to destroy His kind.

And yet . . . the energy between them felt so much warmer than anything I'd seen in all the married couples within the Coven. The matches that were supposedly determined based on compatibility were nothing compared to watching the two of them together.

My skin warmed, the energy of that emotion coasting over

it. It brushed over me and then continued on as if it could not penetrate into me.

As if I wasn't worthy of such warmth.

"Never stop surprising me, witchling," Lucifer said, turning to stand beside her. He allowed her to take the position of power, heeding her in a way that most men would be too insecure to do. Even in our world where the matriarch was the ultimate power, where women were allowed to have it all—magic and a family—the men of our society who clung to their power struggled to give in to the women who challenged them.

Toxic masculinity at its finest.

"You don't deny it then? You've reduced yourself to being a plaything for this asshole?" Itan asked, turning to glare at his nephew Iban, who watched with a face that had paled with shock. I almost felt sorry for the friend who had given in to the Covenant's intentions to marry him to Willow to preserve her magic for her heirs and continue her legacy, but he'd been too stubborn to read the writing on the wall.

"I deny nothing," Willow said, getting more comfortable in her throne, letting her hands rest on the arms and crossing her legs demurely. "Though I think we can agree, I seem to be far more than a plaything. Perhaps the real reason you find Him to be such a threat is because He actually respects women enough to allow me to sit at His side."

"Willow is my wife, and soon we will make it official before your Goddess. At that time, I expect you will all fall in line and accept this union for what it is: the chance for us to start anew. We have the opportunity to come together in truth, our peoples united by marriage," Lucifer said as Willow leaned forward in her seat.

"I must confess though, Itan, you will not be around to witness what becomes of this Coven," Willow said, tapping her finger on the vines of her throne. The words filled me with a rush of hope, my mouth dropping open as Della's hand squeezed mine. I felt her stare on the side of my face, unable to tear my eyes away from Itan as Willow's vines moved forward slowly.

Itan panicked and fought for control of the plant life that should have belonged to him as much as it belonged to Willow, but he'd failed to nourish that relationship the way she had in her short time in Crystal Hollow. He'd chosen to allow the plants to wither and die beneath the pull of his magic upon them, using them for his own self-interest rather than giving any of his blood back to fuel them for future use and generations to come.

Willow had worked to maintain the balance and done exactly as she'd preached, living within the restrictions of her magic and never taking what she wasn't willing to give in turn.

The vines ignored Itan's call, pressed onward and wrapped around his ankles to hold him in place when he attempted to flee. "Willow, stop this!" Iban called, his voice penetrating the eerie silence as none of the watchers dared to draw attention to themselves on Itan's behalf.

He was a waste of life. A bastard that didn't deserve to live freely.

Itan struck out when Willow did not retreat, catching a single vine from the Bray throne. It struck Willow across the chest, tearing the delicate organza at the top of her black dress and ripping into her skin. She stared down at it, looking at the parting of her flesh for a moment in curiosity.

It should have been agonizing to be torn open like that, but Willow only looked at it like it was a scratch. I watched in awe as gold spread over the wound as if it were molten, filling the gap with the color of Lucifer's eyes.

Lucifer was furious, but Willow held up a hand and watched with the same shock I did as the gold receded and the wound healed over for all to see.

Fucking Goddess.

"That's impossible. Only the Covenant is eternal," Itan said, struggling against the bonds of the vines as they spread up his chest and over his shoulders. They dragged him down to his knees, the thump of him striking the stone echoing through the otherwise silent room.

No one dared to speak. No one dared to *move*.

Willow was *immortal*.

"Were they really, though?" Willow asked, scrunching up her nose and offering the sarcastic response that only she could achieve in a moment where she seemed to realize, alongside all of us, the exact ramifications of her bond with Lucifer.

"You backstabbing bitch! She was your grandmother!" Itan yelled, spitting at Willow's feet.

"She was an abomination to this Coven," Willow said, rising to her feet. She descended the steps, stopping directly before Itan as her gaze came to me. She remained silent as she held my stare, sympathy in her face as she watched me.

I didn't know what it was in that stare, but I *knew* what she wanted to do. I knew in that moment what she would reveal if I gave her permission, the secret she would unleash on the world.

It terrified me to think of the same dismissal I'd seen from my mother reflected on the faces of the rest of my Coven. They were meant to be my family, meant to be my kin, and yet I couldn't say if they would care enough to believe me.

If they would support me through my truth.

But Willow would. Willow would stand there and defend me until her last breath, and I knew that in the depths of my soul because it was what was right. Because she always did what she thought was right, no matter what the consequences might be for herself, or what fear she might feel when she did so.

Because she would always stand for women, and she would always help her sisters take back power for themselves.

She made me want to be braver than I was. She made me want to face my own demons head-on instead of cowering in my room at night and hoping they never came back to haunt me again.

So I nodded, even as tears burned my throat. I pulled my hand free from Della's grip, taking a step forward until I stood ever so slightly before the rest of the Coven.

"And you are going to tell them exactly what she conspired with the Tribunal members to do," Willow said, continuing on as she leveled Itan with the full force of her glare.

He had the grace to blanch, staring up at Willow with a furrowed brow. There was a question there, a sincere lack of understanding as he tried to catch up with the trap Willow had laid bare for him.

"How—"

"That's right, Itan. I know what you did to this Coven, and I know what you did to their daughters," Willow said, gesturing to the rest of the Coven as everyone stilled. "And you are going to confess it all."

The vines squeezed tighter around him, making him groan as the creak sounded through the room. "Go to Hell."

"Tell them why the witches are buried in boxes when they should be with their elements. Tell them why you have deprived the Source of our magic when we return it to the balance. Tell them how you starved it and weakened the witches, all with the intent for each and every one of them to be a sacrifice so that you could live free of the Vessels when they were all dead," Willow said, shocking me into silence. I'd known her views of what had happened to the balance and the Coven in the years since her mother left, but I hadn't stopped to think about the depth to that deception—the motivation.

We were all sacrifices to be cast aside so they could live freely when we were gone. I glanced toward my mother and aunt where they stood on the sidelines, my mother's pale face the only confirmation I needed as to what they'd intended and what she'd known of it.

They had children. They had grandchildren.

And they were so lost to their own corruption that they didn't care what their choices meant for them. There was no love to be found in this place, no warmth to be felt.

Only cold, cruel selfishness.

Willow raised a hand, touching a single finger to the front of Itan's throat. One of the vines followed, wrapping around his neck and squeezing as he glared up at her in brutal defiance. He gasped for breath, struggling against the binds that held him tightly secured.

The vindictiveness in my blood was bad karmic energy, and I knew it, but there was no stopping the glee I felt at watching him struggle to breathe the same way I had.

"Willow!" Iban protested, coming to stand closer to Willow. Lucifer moved into his way a moment after, blocking his path and forcing him to keep his distance as his uncle sputtered for breath under Willow's control. As the twenty-year-old witch reminded her elders what power could be gleaned from maintaining the balance of our magic, from returning to the way we were always meant to be.

Willow leaned in close enough that her face filled Itan's vision, making sure it was all he could see. I knew the way his vision narrowed in, the edges of his sight going fuzzy as he fought for breath and oxygen left him. I was all too familiar with that struggle and the way it made a victim focus in on the very last thing they wanted to see.

"Tell your nephew what you did to *her*," Willow said with a sneer. She left my name out of it, but I couldn't help the shocked gasp that flew from my mouth. Even though I'd known it was coming, even though I'd thought I was prepared, *nothing* could prepare me for the moment of reckoning that I'd waited years for.

Willow met my stare, and I watched as Iban followed her gaze right to me. The rest of the Coven hadn't caught on yet, but his mouth dropped open as his brow furrowed, a question in that stare that made me raise my chin even as my bottom lip quivered with my panting breath.

Willow raised her hand, motioning as the vines wound between Itan's legs and put pressure on the part of him that he'd used for violence against me. It had been a weapon to be wielded against me.

Now it was his weakness.

"Uncle," Iban said, but the caution in his voice was heartbreaking. I knew Iban well, had grown up alongside him and knew that the bonds of family were everything to him. He would spend the rest of his days haunted by the reality of what his family member was capable of.

I took a deep breath and closed my eyes for a moment, releasing that breath and letting go of all my fear. My breath shook as I took the first step, my legs trembling as I made my way through the crowd to put myself in the center circle. I stepped up beside Willow, lacing my fingers through hers and offering her my presence. My grip trembled as she squeezed me back, offering a silent reassurance.

I could practically hear her voice in my head when she turned her stare to mine, that same pride I'd seen on Lucifer's face when He looked at her now reflected back at me.

"Enough," I muttered. Willow heeded my request immediately, offering me the power that had been stripped from me for so long without a moment of hesitation. She released the vine from his throat, and I watched him collapse to his chest on the tile. His face smacked against the floor when he couldn't catch himself, his lip splitting beneath the force.

"Margot, thank you," he wheezed, the hoarse sound of his voice barely reaching us even though we stood before him.

The last time he was this close to me, he'd violated me. He'd taken so much from me that I would have *never* given him willingly.

He would never take from me again.

I took a step forward, pressing the toe of my heel to the top of his hand. I ground it down, drawing a scream from his throat as my eyes warmed with the sting of tears that I felt through my glare. "I did not stop her for your sake," I said, squatting down in front of him carefully. I used all the training I'd been forced to undergo at that moment, keeping my mother and my aunt's teachings at the forefront of my mind.

Beauty and grace, always. Even in our darkest moments.

I tucked my dress beneath my knees. "I want to hear you say it," I said.

"Say what?" he sputtered, whimpering when I twisted my foot to cause him more pain.

"Tell them what you did to me," I said, forcing my voice to remain steady. I felt the moisture of tears filling my eyes, but I never allowed them to fall. My entire world narrowed down to Itan's pained face. The only thing penetrating my haze of rage was the presence of a winged archdemon stepping forward.

Lucifer waved him off, but I did not miss the fury written into his face, his body tense and ready for the kill. He froze in place when I ground my foot down harder. I barely managed not to reach out and grasp him by the throat, not to let my power sink into his skin and compel him to give me the confession I wanted.

In the distant haze, I knew his defenders would use that to say I had forced a false confession from him. They'd use my magic against me, blame me for the actions I never deserved.

He groaned as Willow twisted her hand, allowing her vines to wind their way beneath his body and the hem of his shirt, touching the waistband of his pants in a silent threat. It was enough to make him startle, jumping in place as if he could stop it. "I snuck into your room at night," he said suddenly, but still kept his words purposefully vague.

"And did what?" I asked, standing and taking a step back from him. Willow used her vines to force him up from the floor, putting him back onto his knees.

"Touched you."

"No," I spat, leaning into his face. Whatever had existed within me that was quiet and kept to myself was gone for the moment, my actions driven by my rage that it had taken *years* for this moment to come to pass and he still thought to downplay what he had done to me. "You didn't *touch* me. You raped me. Say the word."

"You little bitch—"

"Say the fucking word. Admit what you did to her and what you and the rest of the Tribunal conspired to do to this Coven, and I will give you a swift death. But make no mistake, Itan, you will die either way. I will make sure you suffer for every day you made her have to look at your disgusting face, fearing that it would be the day you came back," Willow said, waiting as he considered his options.

He glanced toward the other Tribunal members, the horror on their faces making me feel like I had finally gotten one tiny piece of justice. They feared the exposure that would come with Itan's confession, but they didn't look as if they questioned the truth of my words, seeming to believe me more than my own mother had. She had the grace and decency not to look at me, not to meet my stare as the truth of what she'd called nightmares and brushed off finally came to light.

I resisted the urge to scream at her.

That was a rage for another day.

"*I raped you,*" Itan said finally, the words making me slump in relief. They crashed into me like a torrent, washing over me like the snapping of a bond I hadn't known existed. I'd been trapped beneath the weight of this secret for so long that the relief of no longer having to bear it in silence made me feel heavy in a new way.

I didn't know how he appeared so quickly or why, but the moment my breathing turned ragged, massive but gentle hands gripped me around the shoulders. I didn't even have the energy to flinch back from that touch as Beelzebub turned me into his chest, offering me a place to cry where they couldn't see.

His bare chest pressed against the side of my face, but I couldn't make myself pull away, not when the tears finally came and poured down my face. Not when silent sobs racked my body and made me tremble.

I couldn't let them see.

"Shhh," he soothed, rubbing those gentle hands over my arm where he held me steady. "I've got you, songbird. Let it out."

"And the rest?" Willow asked, moving on as Lucifer moved forward to take the place I had vacated. Beelzebub shifted me slowly, inching me out of the way and out of the center of attention.

"The Covenant and the Tribunal conspired to rid Crystal Hollow of the Vessels once and for all," he said. I couldn't see anything but Beelzebub, but even I knew that was a half-truth meant to save face.

To make him look like a hero, even now.

"Tell them how you planned to do that," Willow pressed.

He groaned, the sound reaching me. "Don't say another word!" the Petra Tribunal member yelled.

"We were going to starve them. To do that, we were starving the Source. When the magic dies, so do the family lines. Breeding becomes more difficult, witches fall sick. Their blood becomes less potent until . . ."

"Finish it, Itan," Willow snapped.

"Until only the Tribunal remains. The Vessels cannot feed on us without breaking the bargain, and the Vessels would then be weak enough to fade away. The Tribunal members would carry the magic within us then, and we would return the power to the Source. We'd fix it," he said, as if it changed anything. As if it changed any of the reality that they'd been actively attempting to sacrifice all of us so they could have freedom for the rest of their lives.

"You mean after everyone in the Coven was dead, you'd fix it for yourselves," Willow said, always having the words to convey the absolute horror that we all should feel at this secret they'd kept.

"Yes. That's exactly what I mean," Itan agreed.

I pulled my face from Beelzebub's chest to look at him one last time, to commit his weakness and his death to memory as Willow wrapped her vines around his throat once again and twisted, snapping his neck so quickly and efficiently that I wondered if she felt any hint of remorse for her actions.

If she felt as empty inside about it as I did.

The rest of the Coven didn't seem to share my emptiness as Beelzebub tore me out of the center circle, the Coven members descending on the Tribunal members that had betrayed them. He spun me away from the bloodshed, shielding me from it by placing himself between me and the violence.

But I would never unhear my aunt's dying screams.

6

BEELZEBUB

Most of the witches were dining around the grounds, either in the hall or out on the grass, sitting in small groups as if it would offer them safety. It was not lost on me that they kept to their own houses, the colors of their uniforms a dead giveaway to what enabled them to separate. I couldn't say for sure if that had been the case before the archdemons arrived, or if it was a consequence of the bloodshed from the day before.

The memory of my songbird's tears wetting my skin was enough to make me seek her out in every cluster of red I passed. The overwhelming need to check on her was strange to me, a new complication I hadn't anticipated.

I should hate her for everything she stood for, for the lighter side of the magic she'd been gifted by Lucifer when He turned His back on us and left us in Hell to pursue His next adventure on Earth. I should absolutely despise her for the pull of her song on me, for the way it was a constant battle to stay away from her. I hated that I looked for her in every corner, checked the shadows for the gleaming light of her soul that radiated warmth and beauty. That need to seek her out had only gotten worse since the day prior, and even knowing I had been a willing participant in offering her my chest to hide her tears, I couldn't help but feel like there was more to it.

I didn't regret the contact, even as I struggled to stay away from her the next day and finally succumbed to the urge to hunt down the little siren wherever she'd hidden herself away from the rest of her Coven. Being there for someone who needed me felt strangely uplifting, like I'd done a good thing in offering comfort to my enemy.

I'd meant it when I said she was far more interesting than most of those I'd encountered since coming to Hollow's Grove. I fully intended to make the best of the situation and allow her to be my entertainment until Lucifer made sense of His infatuation with His *wife*. The very notion that He'd bound Himself to her willingly was ludicrous, both of us knowing exactly what that meant for Him.

It made Him vulnerable in a way He'd never been, opened Him up to the possibility of death. He'd worked too hard and struggled to find a way to make a new home on Earth just to throw it all away on an ungrateful witchling who didn't even seem to like Him half the time.

I couldn't understand the path He'd taken to come to that choice, and it wasn't like He was willing to discuss it with me. Prying Him away from His wife was near impossible at the present time, getting anything more than a calm assurance to be patient even more difficult. The archdemons were restless, antsy to get started with what we'd all expected to occur when we finally joined Lucifer above the surface, and yet here we were.

Fucking waiting on Lucifer, all over again.

So I sought out my own witchling, scouring the grounds for her. I forced myself to walk rather than fly, knowing that approaching her from above would frighten her too greatly. I didn't know why I cared, not when I should have wanted to toss her to the demons as a plaything. I should have wanted to watch her suffer as I had, for all my centuries in Hell.

But it wasn't with retribution that I sought her out. It was with concern.

She'd bolted from the Tribunal rooms as soon as she was able, escaping the bloodshed as a woman I had to assume was her mother screamed for her dead sister and tried to get *Margot* to come with her to lay her to rest. Margot hadn't been able to do that, retreating from the situation and leaving the former Tribunal member who must have been her aunt to her fate.

As she deserved for what she'd tried to do to her own kind, for what she had done to the witches who had already passed.

A blur of red raced in front of the tree line at the edge of the woods, moving faster than I'd thought possible for a witch. While they had magic at their disposal, they were physically human and lacked all the extra benefits the archdemons had been blessed with.

We'd never been confined to a human form the way the witches were.

Our immortality was pervasive, sinking into every fiber of our being in a way that couldn't be denied. We were stronger and faster. We possessed better senses than the witches. That didn't even begin to touch on the elements of magic we had that I'd never encountered in any of the witches who had died, given that they all came to Hell to pay for their sins against God.

But Margot ran at the tree line, pushing her frail human body to the limits. I watched her for a moment, the familiarity of a vice sinking into my skin. It made my magic tingle, my addiction to her so potent in the air as she ran that I groaned long and low as I fed from it.

I inhaled as I swallowed it down, taking a moment to savor the thickness of it. Her magic tasted like she smelled, something sweet and light like vanilla, with a hint of rosy florals as I drank her down. Only when I'd fed fully did I step closer to her, her shoulders squaring even as she ran. She spun in an impressively smooth maneuver, stopping her sprint and sliding over the wet grass at the edge of the woods.

She never once slipped or fumbled, placing her feet shoulder-width apart as she faced me and her elbows bent at her sides. I recognized the stance all too well, a fighter's stance if I'd ever seen one. The tension in her body didn't ease when her eyes found me, when she realized it was me who had sought her out in this secluded place where no one could see her, where no one would hear her scream.

Smart little witch.

Where so many others might have started to fall into complacency, soothed by the comfort I'd provided in her time of need and the multiple interactions she'd successfully walked away from without any harm coming to her, my songbird wasn't convinced.

She watched me like the predator I was, seeing the violence that had been inked into my skin as Lucifer's second-in-command. For every battle I'd won, for every war I'd prevented within the hierarchy of Hell on His behalf, He'd granted me an Enochian tattoo that lent me more and more access to the Source by my own right instead of drawing magic through Him.

Her chest heaved with the force of her breathing, her skin slick with sweat in spite of the chilly autumn air. She wore a baggy red T-shirt that hung down to her knees, her white leggings fitted to her like a second skin. She'd pulled her short hair back into two little braids that went down the sides of her head, her face bare of all traces of makeup. She looked so young without all the adornments that were expected of the Red witches, her natural beauty something she should have been able to embrace freely if she'd desired to. It served as a stark reminder that she'd only had twenty years to come into her own, most of those spent in childhood.

What had I been like twenty years after my creation? I'd been made into adulthood, never having been a child like the rest of the demons. Even those I'd created who served me within the Third Circle I called home had been made as fully grown beings.

I had no idea what it was to be a child, what it was to grow and suffer an ever-changing body.

"What do you want?" she asked, breaking the silence as I studied her, trying to make sense of the feelings stirring within me. I thought it was almost sadness, a longing for something I'd never even considered missing before.

I shifted uncomfortably, not wanting to provide the truth in my answer. But something in the fragility of her face without the mask she donned to interact with her own kind made me do it anyway, feeling like the least I could do was match the vulnerability she'd exposed twice now in two days.

This was the real Margot, beneath the expectations of her Coven, and yesterday had been the Margot she could become if given the chance. The one who rose above the society that wanted to hold her down and keep her obedient, speaking out against those who wronged her without heeding the fear that made her tremble.

"I was worried about you. Haven't seen you around the school today," I said, neglecting to inform her that I had, in fact, gone to each of the classrooms I realized she frequented in my borderline obsessive stalking of her over the course of the last few days since she'd sung for me. We didn't always speak, didn't always converse, but I knew she saw me lurking.

Her eyes widened in surprise for the briefest moment before she caught herself, schooling her features back into that impassive expression that drove me crazy. I wanted to see the emotions on her face, wanted to watch them play out like my favorite movie. "I'm fine. No need to worry about me," she said, reaching down to grasp her leg behind her. She stood on the remaining foot with more balance than many managed on two, going about the motions of a post-workout stretch before she started walking.

I followed after her, hating that she had the nerve to walk away from me. "We both know that's bullshit," I said, moving more quickly than she could with my longer stride and catching up to her. I took up pace beside her, allowing her to continue on her evening walk even though my presence clearly made her uncomfortable. "A woman who is fine doesn't run like that."

She snapped her head to the side, glaring at me derisively. "Did it ever occur to you that maybe I just like to fucking run?"

The curse in her husky tone sounded more forbidden than it should have. "Running is one thing, running yourself to the breaking point is another. That's a coping mechanism if I ever saw one."

She scoffed, her mouth twisting into a smile as the sound burst free. It coated my skin in warmth, wrapping itself around me like a spell all its own. "What are you, my therapist now? Somehow I think I'll pass on taking any advice from the likes of your kind. Thanks but no thanks," she said.

"More like the demon on your shoulder," I offered, smiling wryly at her. "But I know a thing or two about vices and addictions. It's a dangerous path."

"How fortunate that my habit is a healthy one," she returned with a sardonic smile, the fake sweetness angering me. I hated the mask, hated the false pretense she constantly donned in an effort to appear okay.

"Songbird," I said, my voice dropping into a low whisper as I tried to convey the seriousness of this conversation. I wanted the real her, not the show pony they'd turned her into. "In all honesty, what happened yesterday—"

"Don't," she snapped, her feet stopping immediately. She turned to face me, her brows deep slashes of frustration as she issued the order. Despite the strength and determination written into the lines of her face, her legs were far less sturdy than they'd been only a moment prior.

She'd run herself too hard, her energy depleting and muscles aching already now that the adrenaline was wearing off and she could feel her true exhaustion.

"It would be perfectly understandable if you weren't feeling fine," I said, continuing on in spite of the warning in those burning mahogany eyes. They were like tiny pinpricks of flame when she was angry, hinting at the depth of the rage she kept carefully tucked away.

"I said don't," she said again, holding up a hand as if the words weren't enough to communicate her desire not to have this conversation. "I said I'm fine and I meant it. I will be fine just like I always am. The last thing I need or want is an archdemon nagging at me because he's too stupid to know the difference between actually liking someone and being trapped under their fucking spell."

The words were harsh, but the way she sank her teeth into her bottom lip contradicted them, hinting at her uncertainty in speaking them. My songbird wasn't used to standing up for herself, attempting to turn a new leaf since the day before.

It said something about *my* addiction to *her* that I would gladly give her a safe place to explore that, letting her hurl whatever insults were necessary at me and taking them in stride without returning them.

Hell, maybe I even liked them.

"Everybody needs somebody to turn to," I said, shrugging my shoulders and trying not to consider the fact that it had been a long time since I'd felt that. My brother was the closest I had to that sort of bond, and I didn't see anyone else stepping in to fill the role.

She leaned in, coming closer without ever touching me. The scent of her filled my lungs, those deep eyes glaring up at me. "That doesn't mean I'd ever choose you," she said, the quiet words lacking all emotion. That made it strike harder, an honest truth that wasn't buried in rage and anger she couldn't control.

It should have pissed me off to be so easily dismissed when I was genuinely trying; instead, I found my mouth spreading into a wide smile as she faltered.

She shook her head as she retreated, making her way up to the school and leaving me to linger at the edge of the woods. Her hips swayed as she went, not in a way that she forced, but with the natural sex appeal of a woman who just radiated lust even when she was so determined not to.

The meek Margot of a few days prior seemed like a thing of the past when it was just the two of us, her sass driving the conversations and dominating space. She might claim not to rely upon me as a safe space or person to turn to, but the change in her demeanor said more than her words could argue.

I shoved my hands into my pockets as I made my way back up to the school, abandoning my patrols for the night in favor of stalking my favorite witch and making sure she made it back to her room safely.

This goddamned spell would be the end of me.

If I found her sudden burst of confidence so attractive, there was no doubt that others would, too.

And the witch was *mine*.

7

MARGOT

I left class quickly, ducking my head in an effort to avoid the archdemon who seemed to follow me everywhere I went. He kept his distance, never coming too close in the moments between classes but making it appear as though he was there more for my protection than anything.

When something similar to this happened in the past, I'd felt intimidated by the presence. It had felt like a violation to my personal boundaries, like something to fear.

But when Beelzebub followed me, there was a quality to him that felt like a bodyguard, keeping people from bothering me. It meant that I moved through the halls more peacefully than I might have otherwise, the recent events making me a subject of interest to all those who wanted to know the details I wasn't willing to share.

He didn't bother me, but his presence made certain no one else did, either.

I hated feeling appreciative for anything he did, but the quiet accord we'd reached was one I didn't want to think about going away.

"Margot!" Keane yelled, catching my attention from the stairs above me as I made my way down toward my next class. "Hold up!"

I paused on the stairs, debating whether or not I could pretend

I hadn't heard him, but my hesitation gave me away. I forced a polite smile to my face as Keane made his way down the stairs, joining me on the landing where I'd paused to wait for him.

"Hey," I said, my voice a quiet murmur when he finally approached. He reached out, tucking a strand of blond hair behind my ear in an affectionate move that I hated every time he did it. I twisted away, making sure he wasn't able to touch my skin.

"I've been trying to catch up with you for two days. Where have you been hiding?" he asked, his low voice serious.

"Wherever I can," I said, offering the truth that I didn't think anyone should be surprised by. I hated being the center of attention, hated the feeling of eyes on me for any reason. Having everyone stare at me for *that* reason was even worse.

Keane's face twisted, morphing into shock, as if he hadn't expected me to be so blunt with my truth. I supposed it wasn't something I typically did, preferring to hide behind pretty lies to make everyone around me feel better.

But by choosing to protect their peace, I found myself constantly sacrificing my own.

The walls around my heart built a little higher with every day that passed as I became something that existed solely for the purpose of pleasing others and making them feel good about themselves even when they actively chose to disrespect boundaries I set for my own peace.

I was done with that shit. My truth, my peace came first now.

"Oh," he said, laughing it off like I hadn't surprised him. "Well, you don't need to hide from me."

"I don't?" I asked, tilting my head to the side. Keane had made his intentions for our marriage very clear from the time we both came of age, finding our match to be a pleasing one when I didn't. While he was kind and sweet and handsome, I'd done everything in my power to dissuade him from wanting to move forward with our betrothal.

"I'm going to be your husband, Margot. You can come to me

when you need a shoulder to lean on. I wish you'd told me that this had happened. It makes so much sense now when I look back at the way you kept yourself distanced from the rest of us," Keane said, his statement getting worse with every word.

"Who said I need someone to lean on?" I asked, the bitter smile I offered surprising even me. "I've been navigating this on my own for longer than you can *imagine*. I don't need you to help me. You don't even know me, Keane."

"Margot," he said, stepping toward me and reaching out to take my hand. "I've known you since we were kids."

"Please don't touch me," I snapped as I pulled back, not allowing his touch when I normally might have just suffered it in silence. "Being in my vicinity does not mean you know me. The Covenant deciding that we would be married one day doesn't mean you have some right to know about my life. Even if it did, they're fucking gone now, and I have no intention of following through on their edicts for my life."

Keane's face fell, his expression dropping into one of horror. "What are you saying?"

"I'm saying that you deserve to marry someone who is capable of loving you. Who wants to be with you and looks forward to seeing you when they come home every day. That isn't me, and it isn't ever going to be me. I am never going to love you, because I don't have that in me. I don't intend to marry."

"Margot," Keane whispered, the hushed tone of his voice urgent. "Your mother is going to be the new Erotes Tribunal member with your aunt gone. You're her eldest daughter."

"My sisters can continue the line when they're older. My aunt never had children—"

"Not for lack of trying! Do you realize how many decades she spent trying for an heir? Fertility is already dwindling within the Coven—"

"Because of what the Covenant and the Tribunal did to make it that way. I refuse to be beholden to this Coven to fix the wrongs they committed. If our ability to procreate is going away, then maybe it should! Maybe we've committed so many fucking wrongs under their leadership that we deserve to be a dying breed!" I snapped, the volume of my voice carrying through the cavernous stairwell. I was all too aware of the eyes on us as I shouted the condemnation at Keane, hearing the promise of Willow's voice in my ear.

Screw them. This was their natural consequence, and I'd be damned if they forced me to right their wrongs even after they were gone.

Keane reached for me again, his face gentling. But his hand never made contact with my skin, even when I forced myself not to retreat. Beelzebub's presence appeared at my side immediately after he crossed the traffic in the stairwell to reach me. He grasped Keane by the wrist, his hand looking enormous on the smaller man's forearm as he stopped him from making contact. "I believe she asked you not to fucking touch her," he growled, the menace in those words reserved solely for Keane.

Keane swallowed as he stared up at the archdemon, his gaze traveling to mine. "Am I missing something here?" he asked, the words meant for me. I had no doubt he was putting the pieces together, having seen us together in the Tribunal room and probably having heard the rumors about our conversation in the library.

"It's not what you think," I said, forcing through my disdain for touch to reach forward and grasp Beelzebub by the fingers, slowly unwrapping them from Keane's arm and patting Beelzebub reassuringly as he let that arm drop to his side.

"So you're not fucking the archdemon?" Keane asked, immediately reverting to the misogynistic bullshit I'd come to expect from everyone but him.

"Not that it's any of your business, but no, I'm not. I've never had any interest in sex. You know that," I said, offering the stern reminder of all the times he'd offered himself up as an outlet for my magic, as a source for me to feed from in turn. I hadn't ever taken him up on it.

Keane glanced toward Beelzebub out the side of his eye. "Are you sure he got that memo?"

"He heard me sing," I offered in the way of explanation, watching as understanding dawned on Keane's face. He nodded, as if it all suddenly made sense.

Beelzebub snorted, crossing his arms over his chest as a single brow rose. "I'm fairly certain I'm not the only one. I'm just man enough to admit it."

Keane bristled. "I didn't need to hear her sing to love her, asshole."

I rolled my eyes, stepping away and leaving them to bicker amongst themselves. They called after me, but I couldn't have cared less to continue in that way of conversation. Keane was lost in his foolish claims to love me, so absorbed in the *idea* of me that he couldn't even understand you couldn't love what you did not know, and Beelzebub was just . . .

Sigh.

It seemed men of all species were obnoxious as Hell.

I didn't turn back to see if either tried to follow, continuing on my way down the stairs and taking care to appear unbothered to everyone I passed. Gone were the days I prioritized what they thought of me, but old habits were hard to break and the mask that I wore was harder to shed than I wanted to admit.

I rounded the landing two stories down from where I'd left Keane and Beelzebub, a harsh whisper inside my mother's classroom making me slow on instinct. I didn't want to face her after I'd fled the Tribunal room; the blood and death around me had been too much for me to bear in my moment of vulnerability.

The rage the Coven had shown to its elders, however justified, had resulted in the kind of gruesome death that horrified me. My aunt had been practically torn apart, her skin bruised and left in shreds as witches took out the wrath of all they'd almost lost under her and the rest of the Tribunal's guidance.

It didn't stop me from worrying for my mother, who had held as much affection and admiration for her sister as I thought her capable of. "And how long do you think it will take before Willow interferes in our customs further? She's already supplanted the Covenant and placed herself upon their throne. It's only a matter of time before she manipulates the Tribunal to serve her purposes," a familiar voice said.

I recognized the voice of Keane's uncle, Uriah Peabody, as I pressed myself into the wall beside the door they'd left cracked open. It seemed a foolish conversation to have in the open, but I realized that he likely didn't care what Willow thought of him. Those who opposed her and her way of life had always been vocal about doing so, so certain in their beliefs and the actions they took in defense of them that they never stopped to wonder if they were the villain of their own story.

They never stopped to question whether or not Willow may have been right.

"Likely not long at all," my mom said, but her voice lacked all the panic that Uriah's had possessed. There was no urgency in the knowledge that she wouldn't retain the Tribunal seat she'd gained with my aunt's death, her matter-of-fact tone shocking me.

She'd worked all her life for that seat, endeavoring to earn her title as her sister's heir every day of her life. She'd drilled that notion into me, wanting to see the same dedication from me even though I had no desire to serve as her heir. That title could go to one of my sisters when they were older or to my cousin for all I cared.

"Then how are you so calm? She'll undo everything we have worked for," Uriah said, his voice remaining low and quiet even as his anger grew.

"Relax, Uriah." My mother sighed, the familiar sound of her

heel tapping against the floor in her impatience. "Who is it that you think Willow will choose to represent the Erotes line on the Tribunal?"

I paused, understanding dawning as I realized what my mother believed would come to pass. Should the day arrive where Willow disagreed with who the legacies chose as their representatives on the Tribunal, it would stand to reason that she would plant the friend she could trust to drive the Reds of this Coven back toward balance.

She would choose me.

A rough breath left me as I shrank farther against the wall, pulling a book out of my book bag to pretend to read when other students passed me by and studied me curiously. I'd be late for my next class, but I couldn't be bothered to care as I waited out the conversation.

What did Uriah mean when he spoke of what they'd been working for? Had they as heirs been *aware* of what the previous Tribunal had attempted?

"Margot is no better than Willow. Did you not see her display at Willow's side?" Uriah asked with a scoff. "We lost Itan because of her."

My heart sank into my stomach, the condemnation in those words all the assurance I needed of what people thought of me. Whether they thought I'd lied or just did not care that it had happened in the first place mattered little.

All that mattered was that I didn't matter to them at all.

"She is misguided in her allegiance to Willow, but we cannot fault her for seeking vengeance against Itan. The man raped her repeatedly for years," my mother said, and I fought for breath as everything within me froze.

Had she put the pieces together after the Tribunal and realized I must have been telling the truth all that time?

"That may be, but Itan was *useful* to us, Fritha. Without him, we don't have the ability to do the binding ritual—"

"I have done my part. I have sacrificed my daughter to the cause as the Covenant asked of me, even knowing the cost. Itan may be gone and unable to do it again in the future, but Margot has already been bound. Take comfort in the fact that Margot will be physically unable to do what Willow wants from her should she supplant me."

A binding ritual?

I shoved my book into my bag, my entire body primed to run. I warred with myself, trying to decide if I should demand answers to the questions swimming in my mind or if I should seek out Willow and share what I'd learned.

"And what of the other houses? Our heirs are not friends with the new Covenant, and there's no guarantee that they'll be chosen to take our place. She could choose someone who has not been bound and destroy everything—"

"Then I suppose it is time to convince your heirs to befriend the little necromancer, isn't it? Really, Uriah, not all wars are fought in bloodshed. Some of the most important battles are won in quiet manipulations. Think like the Red you are. *Charm her,*" my mother snapped, her heels clicking as she walked deeper into the room. I tucked myself against the wall, hugging the doorway in the hopes that Uriah wouldn't see me when he yanked the door open, stomping his way across the landing.

He didn't look back, leaving me to slip into the open door before I lost the nerve.

My steps were slow, cautious as I approached where my mother leaned over her desk, her eyes on the stack of papers before her as she scrawled a note. "Mom?" I asked, my voice wavering with the word. I didn't want to consider that it could be true, that she could have known what Itan did prior to the day before.

She couldn't have believed me when I was a child, couldn't have known that I spoke the truth. To lie to my face and tell me it was just a nightmare would have been unforgivable. It would have been inconceivably cruel, and while she was far from perfect,

I refused to believe she was that fucking empty inside that she would leave her own daughter to suffer that way.

She dropped her pen in surprise, turning wide eyes up to me for a moment before she recovered. That carefully crafted mask she'd handed down to me covered her face, a smooth smile tipping her lips up at the corners.

She was the personification of beauty and grace, of hiding everything she wanted to remain unseen in the darkest corners of herself. I'd never known just how deep her shadows ran, never expected the truth that I'd just overheard.

"Margot," she said, standing to full height and coming to step around the desk. "I wasn't expecting you."

There.

The slightest hitch in her breath, the tiniest falter in that facade as her smile twitched. Tears filled my eyes as I stared at her, my horror growing with each passing moment as I worked to connect the pieces.

"Did you know?" I asked, choosing to dive right in rather than play this game where we danced around our truths and hid who we really were.

"Know what, Margot?" she asked, the tiniest roll of her eyes. It was an attempt at the usual disdain she showed for my directness, for my inability to play the game she was so gifted at. The fact that she could pretend she didn't know what I was talking about was all the confirmation I needed, my fingers beginning to shake in the rising anger I felt toward the woman staring back at me. I pressed on, clenching my fingers into fists to attempt to control outward signs of it, knowing her well enough to know that I could only push too far if I wanted to have this conversation.

And while I already knew the truth, some distant part of me, the tiny girl that existed in my past, still dared to hope that I was wrong.

"Did. You. Know?" I asked again, enunciating every word to convey my seriousness. This was not a conversation that I would allow her to derail. This was not something she could distract me from.

"Darling, are you alright? I know yesterday must have been traumatic for you, but to come in here with accusations like that isn't fair to me," she said, the gaslighting words making me scoff in disbelief. My skin flushed with heat, bypassing the warmth of irritation immediately. I felt as if I might melt, a thin sheen of sweat clinging to my skin like humidity in the air in spite of the autumn weather and the flames crackling in the fireplace at the corner of the classroom.

"What's the binding ritual?" I asked, pressing forward as I took more steps toward her. I tilted my head to the side as I studied her, my gut churning and sloshing like a violent sea with every step.

Her smile dropped off her face, that careful veneer abandoned as realization dawned. "It's impolite to eavesdrop on conversations that do not concern you."

"If I am the subject of all your secret conversations, then I think I should be privy to them, and if you don't want me to be, then maybe consider closing the Goddess-damned door!" I snapped, the warmth of magic filling my eyes.

I knew what I would see if I looked into the mirror, had seen it too many times on the faces of others when they tapped into their magic. Even when not touching the lust that drove my magic, I could not ignore the surge of anger that rose up to defend me, making my eyes glow red like molten lava.

That rage didn't stop the clogging of my throat or the need to cry, to weep for the relationship I'd never really had. For the secrets she'd kept all my life. It was a torrent of emotion within me, the two sides of my grief clashing together like storm clouds over the sea.

"What did you hear?" she asked, making me shake my head as I strode toward her. Anger made my arms tingle with magic, creeping up my skin like bugs crawling over me. Even now, knowing

I'd heard her, she couldn't just own up to the truth of what she'd known, of what she'd *done*.

I rounded the corner of her desk, striding up to her in my anger. My fingers wrapped around her throat, shoving her back to the stone wall with a force I shouldn't have possessed. She clawed at my hands, snarling when I pinned her there and watched her.

"Tell me about the binding ritual," I said, my words steady in spite of everything that threatened to tear me in two. She looked down at my hands and my forearms, a slow smile spreading as she laughed lightly, the sound filled with glee in spite of her predicament. I followed her gaze, stilling when I saw what she saw.

My nails had grown into long, pointed black talons. The faint glimmer of scales covered the back of my hand with the slightest blue and purple tint to them as the light played along the surface of my skin.

"It worked. It actually worked," she said, her breath coming in an easy exhale of wonder.

"What did you do to me?" I asked, releasing her suddenly and stepping back. The scales on my arms began to fade as I put distance between us, my anger abating in the face of my fear over something that should have been impossible.

She took the opportunity to step up to me, cradling my face in her hands. Her perfectly manicured fingers ran over what had to be scales on my temples before they faded entirely, the scratching sound unlike anything I'd ever heard before.

Those scales faded, too, her warmth sinking into my too-cold skin when they left me.

"I made you powerful beyond your wildest dreams," she said, smiling at me as if I would appreciate the monster she'd turned me into. I shook my head as I stepped back, the faintest indentations at my wrists making me wince. It reminded me of being bound the first time he came to my room . . .

My thoughts trailed off as I drew the conclusions in my mind. Binding rituals used the act of tying knots to connect two people together or to bind something to itself. It was something that few witches knew how to do, the intricacy of the knots needing to be specific to the cause, but they sometimes used them to make a person unable to enjoy a certain bad habit any longer.

"You let Itan *bind* me?" I asked, but I didn't need her answer, already connecting the pieces.

But what had he bound me to?

"He bound the piece of the Source within you," she said, her tone chipper as she returned to her desk, pulling out a notepad and taking down notes of all that she'd seen. "You cannot pull new magic directly from the Source and you cannot return her magic to her, either. It is merely trapped within you, an endless loop of power that twists and turns within you until it becomes something else entirely. It enables you to access the darkest parts of Red magic by starving you from the light. You cannot feed the Source and can only take from those around you endlessly."

They'd used me to starve the Source, intending for me to sit on the Tribunal and twist the magic of my house from my seat of power. The Tribunal members were meant to serve as representatives, but also the key channelers of the Source on earth. What we had first passed through them before being distributed.

If I could only channel darker magic . . .

Goddess.

Itan had said they'd fix it after the Vessels were gone. There had to be a way to undo it. I just had to hope that someone else knew how. I took comfort in that knowledge, as I pushed forward to understand the implications on the rest of my childhood.

"Was my rape part of it?" I asked.

"No," my mother said, her face horrified, as if expecting that of her was beyond the realm of possibility at this point. "Itan is the only one who understands the nuance of these knots. They have been passed down through the Brays for centuries, from heir to heir as an ancient knowledge. No one before has ever thought to attempt such a thing, so when he went to the Tribunal and said he knew how to do it, there was no one else who could. He offered to do us the favor of binding the next generation of heirs, but there was a price."

A price.

"We all knew he had certain inclinations, but we didn't know how deep they ran until it was already done. The price of his magic was our silence and willingness to turn a blind eye to it. We swore a blood oath, Margot. We could not intervene," she said, sighing as if it relieved her to finally have the truth out in the open. I crossed my arms over my chest, nostrils flaring at her audacity to be relieved in this moment that was so catastrophically horrific for me.

No matter what she claimed, she didn't fucking care what the cost of this power had been. She'd have paid it one hundred times over, because in her mind the ends would always justify the means.

"You all sold your eldest daughters to him," I said, realizing that there had been *others*. More than I'd thought. I'd never heard a whisper of it from them, never seen the signs, and I wondered if they thought of me the same way.

"He gave you a tea that was supposed to help you sleep through the binding," she said. I'd always suspected my memory of that first time was hazy because of my age, because of the years that had passed since then. "The others never woke until morning."

"But I did," I said, turning and making my way toward the door. I couldn't bear to look at her any longer, couldn't stand the knowledge of what she'd allowed to happen to me and to all those other girls. I needed to bring them together, to tell them what their own parents and elders had knowingly subjected them to.

Did they even know? Did they even remember?

"Your magic was always strong, even before you came of age. You were able to resist the pull of sleep," she said, the words the most twisted version of an apology that I would ever receive from her. "I regret that it hurt you so deeply, but what he was able to do is nothing short of miraculous. You have a siren form, something that has been lost to the Reds for centuries!" she said, her voice turning desperate as I moved to leave, smart enough to realize that my knowledge of this would be the end for her.

Willow would not stand for this. I would not stand for this.

"Fuck you," I spat, the harsh words making her eyes widen as I turned to level her with a glare. I'd never dared to speak to her that way, never dared to challenge her so directly out of fear of repercussions. Obedience was pivotal to the Red houses, something so deeply ingrained within us that I didn't have a single memory of one of my peers cursing at their parents. "I hope you get everything you deserve for what you and the rest of them did to this Coven."

I retreated from the room, immediately moving to seek out Willow and share the information that she *needed* to know.

Hoping like Hell that she knew how to untie the knots of a binding spell, so that she could free me from this twisted reality of what my magic could have been, what it *should* have been. Hoping she'd be able to help me help the others, because I didn't know how to give them clarity if they didn't even remember their assaults.

Did I let them live in peace to save them from this pain that throbbed within me, or did I tell them the truth that had been kept from them for years?

I made my way through the halls that were largely empty as the rest of the school had already settled into their next period, leaving me alone in my reflections. Even as I tried to rationalize it in my mind, clinging to the possibility that it wasn't true, I knew it was. The reality of what she'd done, what she'd knowingly subjected me to, felt like thorns shredding my heart open.

I hadn't thought much of my relationship with my mother,

knowing it was strained at best, but I'd thought it was better than *this*.

What she had agreed to was unforgivable, and I found myself gazing down at my hands as I trailed them over the dark, solid wood railing on the stairs. My nails were back to the flawless red manicure that was expected of my kind, my skin soft and supple in the way that only care and dedication could maintain.

There was no trace remaining of the monstrous form that had shown itself in my anger toward my mother, and if it hadn't been for her reaction to it, I might have thought it to be a figment of my own imagination. The sirens were something that only existed in legends and myths, so far removed from the witches of this Coven and how I knew them to be.

Lucifer had gifted the siren form to others throughout history, to women who had been wronged by men who were all too willing to abuse their power. He'd gifted it to the original Erotes and Peabody witches, but that form had simply ceased to exist within the Reds by the second generation.

The last Erotes witch to have the form I now held within me was Amelia, the same witch who had asked Lucifer to gift her a magic that would allow her to take her power in the same form men had tried to use against her. They wanted to condemn her for her actions out of wedlock? She'd make that in itself her power and use it against them instead.

If Itan had unlocked my siren form by performing a binding ritual and cutting me off from the Source, he had to have utilized very dark magic to do it. It went against everything the witches were supposed to be.

The Source existed in two halves, polar opposites mirrored back at each other: the light and the dark, the Earth and the underworld. But for all those differences, we were the same at our core.

As above, so below.

We were meant to be the light to the demons' darkness. We

were supposed to be the life to their death. Monstrous forms were part of their magic, not ours. So how had he been able to twist my magic into the darkness?

I was so focused on my own thoughts as I made my way down the stairs, so fixated on the color and shape of my fingernails and trying to get to Willow as quickly as possible all while dreading it, that I never noticed the shadow that appeared on the landing below me.

I rounded the corner, descending the last step before the landing just above the main level. The grand entryway below was oddly quiet as I glanced over the stairs, keeping my head down to move past the male figure I thought nothing of.

The shadow of wings played in the light streaming through the stained-glass window, casting an enormous figure on the stone below me. "I'm not in the mood, Beelzebub." I sighed, striding forward to walk past him.

He didn't respond, and I hoped the absolute exhaustion in my voice was enough to dissuade him from fucking with me. I didn't have the energy to deal with his persistence or bizarre combination of contempt and fascination.

He stretched out a hand, grasping me by the elbow and forcibly pulling me to a stop. My book bag slid off my shoulders, crashing to the ground at my side as I spun to glare at him. The face that stared down at me wasn't Beelzebub's, the leaner frame clothed in a suit that the archdemon would have refused to wear with his seeming aversion to shirts.

The angel's face was so like Lucifer's that I did a double take in confusion; the only indication that there was something different about him was the sprawling white feathered wings that fanned out behind him dramatically. His face was carefully blank, an expressionless mask as he studied me for the briefest of moments.

My mouth opened, my lips parting in a shrill scream as realization dawned. He lunged forward, wrapping his wings around me and trapping the sound in the cocoon he made. My own voice was too loud in my ears, the grimace on his face the only confirmation that he was even remotely affected by the magic that I poured into that sound. Time seemed to slow as he moved, his body primed and functioning in a single smooth movement as it caught up with his wingspan.

His fist connected with my temple, the blow knocking me sideways and into his wings. I felt myself fall, felt the moment he flinched back from the contact when I touched him and he let me fall to the floor, carelessly forgotten.

Then there was only black.

8

MARGOT

I woke slowly, the pounding in my head making me groan. The sound came out muffled, and the pressure on my tongue was unrelenting as my eyes peeled open. Panic came instantly as the gag tied around my mouth made me call out uselessly.

The room surrounding me was unfamiliar, an ornate and opulent space nearly unrivaled throughout the rest of the school. The walls were lined with ebony shelves, the ceiling framed into squares to match. An enormous chandelier had been crafted from selenite, the crystals hanging down in the center of the room as I fought to maneuver onto my stomach. My hands were bound in front of me with a coarse rope that chafed at my skin every time I moved. Once I managed to turn over in spite of the pounding in my head, I fought to get from there up to my knees, leaning my weight onto my forearms to do it.

As I knelt on the purple-and-gold woven rug beneath me, I reached up to try to shift the rope and ball of fabric out of my mouth. It was too tight, tied behind my head in a spot that I couldn't seem to grasp as I fought to untie it.

As much as I cursed the power that came with my voice and my song, having it stripped from me in my time of need made me realize how much comfort the promise of it gave me in my daily life. I was practically defenseless without it.

Practically human.

I wanted to know how long I'd slept, but there was no clock lining the walls. Only books upon books and vintage portraits in golden frames. A deep purple sofa sat at the edge of the rug, and a low wooden coffee table was in the center as I scanned the space for weapons I might be able to use in my current state. Outside of bashing an archangel's head in with a heavy tome, my options were limited.

Voices came from a door to the right of me, which I recognized as a match for the door in the Tribunal room that led to the Covenant's private quarters. I tried to shout through the gag in my mouth, the sounds muffled and useless as I forced my way to my feet.

I stumbled over the edge of the rug, stepping onto the smooth stone surface and banging my hands on the door. The knob refused to turn as I fiddled with it, desperately trying to alert someone to my presence within that room.

"Hmmmmm!" I called out, making my voice as loud as I possibly could. The door opened suddenly, the archangel's tall form filling the gap as he glared down at me. I knew he had to be Michael given his likeness to Lucifer, as the two of them were identical twins according to our histories.

Grabbing hold of my rope-bound hands, he yanked me out of the Tribunal's private quarters and tucked me into his side, keeping his wings distant and taking care not to touch me with them. I made a mental note of his aversion to having them touched, prepared to use that to my advantage if I needed.

Tears streamed down my face as I took in the sight of Willow bent over the open gate to Hell, her stomach pumping blood from the wound where a dagger protruded from her. Her eyes finally connected with mine, and I saw for myself just how weakened she was. Just how much the injury and the opening of the portal had taken from her.

She couldn't find the energy to fight against Iban, against a boy who was human for all purposes thanks to the sacrifice he'd made.

"You're going to be a good girl and stay put for me, Willow, or so help me, I will slit her throat and make you watch her die," Michael said, the warning washing over my skin. My purpose in this became obvious in that moment, understanding dawning on me.

It was never about me.

Willow had shown she cared for me, that she wanted to protect me against those who would do me wrong. Michael and Iban had decided to use that against her, and it killed me that the knowledge had to have come from the boy I'd considered a friend for years. That I'd grown up with and lived alongside Iban all my life, only for him to hand me over as a pawn in whatever game he was playing.

I shook my head, my nostrils flaring with anger as I struggled in Michael's grasp. I hoped I could convey what I needed to her, even in silence, to tell her not to give up and give in. Some things were more important than me, more important than she or I could ever dream to be. Restoring the balance to our home was one of them, and while I understood very little about her relationship with Lucifer, I knew in my bones that they were meant to do this together.

She nodded as if she understood—the movement so minute that the men didn't see it. They so rarely saw the intricacies of female interaction, so often dismissing them as unintentional and unimportant.

But we knew it for what it was—a relic ingrained in our DNA from the centuries women spent under the thumb of male oppressors. A way for us to look out for one another without being noticed.

Willow released her hold on the knife, sinking into the touch and violence Iban showed her. Letting him believe he'd won, I realized, playing into the arrogance he possessed about his own unimportant place in this world. I did the same, letting Michael hold me to his side with the threat of his blade in his free hand to keep me compliant. Let him think my fear was enough to turn me to a sniveling mess.

Let him fucking underestimate me.

"She shouldn't be breathing," Michael said, warning Iban as Willow's eyes drifted closed.

The boy who had once been my friend brushed Willow's hair back from her face and turned her to look at him. There was a softness in his expression that had no business being there while he held a knife in her belly. "Sweetheart, it's not too late for you to repent," he said, his voice gentle. The words were so unlike anything I'd ever heard from him, as if he was nothing more than a manipulated mouthpiece for the angel in the room.

"You're even dumber than I thought if you believe that . . ." Willow snarked back, but the words trailed off. I couldn't decide how much of the weakness was an act and how much of it was genuine, and the very thought of this world without her in it was horrific to me.

Just as I was about to lunge for Michael's wings, determined to tear the feathers from his flesh, the Tribunal doors burst open as a male form flew through the air. Beelzebub landed in the room, staring at Willow and her precarious position. He took a single step forward, pausing as his gaze swept around the mostly empty room to assess the threats he may need to fight.

His gaze collided with mine, his eyes widening as his body went solid. Caught between the spell I'd placed on him unintentionally and his very carefully curated, intentional loyalty to Lucifer, he froze in place and didn't know what to do.

He didn't know who to save, the conflicting needs making his stern brow furrow.

I shook my head, silently pleading with him to go for Willow. She was injured and in need of help. She was important to Crystal Hollow and worth saving for that reason alone.

I was just me.

He looked to Willow, the two of them exchanging a glance before he turned back toward me and lunged toward Michael. "No," I gasped, realizing he'd made the wrong choice. The archangel tossed me to the side violently, sending me careening off-balance. I flipped head over feet, unable to stop my forward momentum as I rolled.

"Margot!" Willow screamed, trying desperately to tear her hands off the seal. "She's your friend!" she shouted to Iban, her voice the only solid thing in the world as it spun. I caught myself as I fell into the seal, throwing my legs wide with all thoughts of modesty forgotten. Willow's blood covered the edges of the seal, pouring out as she thrashed against Iban's hold and tried to reach me.

I grumbled against the gag, feeling the panic in my own voice as my feet slipped slowly over the stone. I wasn't going to be able to hold on for long, wasn't going to stand a chance of supporting my own weight this way.

My only shining light in the darkness of those moments while I waited to fall was the reality that with me gone, Beelzebub wouldn't be torn. He wouldn't hesitate to save Willow, and I had to take a little comfort in that.

My right leg slipped, making my entire support collapse beneath me. I fell through the doorway, tumbling out of reach as Willow screamed, "MARGOT!"

My own scream was muffled, but it mirrored Willow's as air rushed up to greet me. I fell through the air, my legs kicking and lashing out but there was nothing around me. I was weightless for a few moments, unable to see the ground beneath me to know what might wait for me.

I whimpered as I closed my eyes slowly, ready for the end that would surely come on impact. This was the moment I died, the moment that I could never come back from.

Beelzebub dove through the doorway just before my eyes closed, his wings tucked in tight to his sides so he could fit through the hole with ease and gain speed. His arms were outstretched, reaching for me as he fought to get to me in time.

He wasn't going to make it.

I let my eyes drift closed finally, not wanting to see the devastation on his face in the moment I hit the ground. I didn't want to see his agony and have that be the last thing I saw before I died, especially not with the bittersweet knowledge that he would be freed shortly after.

The grief he felt would fade with my death, freeing him from my spell and leaving him with only the hatred he felt for the way I'd made him betray his own loyalties.

The leather of his wings surrounded me as I drew in a shocked breath, wrapping me up in a tight embrace. He twisted us in midair, placing his massive body beneath mine only a second before we struck the ground. Taking the brunt of the fall, he did everything he could to shield me from the impact.

Dirt flew around us, pelting into his wings with distinct thuds of rock and sediment. The sound of our crash echoed in our ears, making them ring with the sound of bells, and for a moment I wondered if it was even possible for Beelzebub to have survived that.

"Hmmm," I groaned, wiggling my hands where they'd been pinned beneath our bodies. Beelzebub didn't move for a moment, making me fear the worst. I would never forgive myself if he had died to protect me while under my spell, if the price of my magic was to take a life.

His eyes flew open finally, staring up at me intently as if he needed to see that I was okay. His gaze traveled over me, searching for injury as I shook my head to tell him I had none. Forceful impacts of something new slamming against his wings made him grunt, but he never let whatever it was touch me as he kept me tucked safely between his body and his wings, forming a shelter that I feared stepping out of.

"We might have to fight our way out, songbird," he said, his voice gentle in spite of the way his entire body flinched in pain in time with a tearing sound from outside my shelter. "Can you do that for me?"

I nodded, even as my entire body filled with apprehension. We were going to have to fight *what?*

Beelzebub nodded back, unfolding his great leathery wings as he sat up. He took me with him, moving quickly to untie the knot that bound my hands and tearing free the rope that gagged me. I spit out the fabric that had been balled up on my tongue, my relief immediate as Beelzebub touched my face, cupping it so sweetly for a moment of intimacy I couldn't ignore.

I kept my eyes on him, attempting to tune out the fighting that surrounded us. Movement was everywhere, and I shuddered to think of what exactly existed around me. "Arms around my neck," Beelzebub ordered, and I hesitated for only a moment before I did as he told me and tried to ignore the warmth of his skin on mine. He looked up, maneuvering to his feet with me in his arms.

He twisted and turned, holding me tight as he took the scratches and strikes meant for me. He tried to unfurl his wings only for them to be cut and torn by the demons surrounding us. There were too many of them to count, so many that Beelzebub couldn't fight alone.

He wasn't, I realized as I dared to peek out the side of my eye. Jonathan fought alongside him, protecting my back with vicious snarls for the demons who threw themselves at him.

All this was for me, I realized with a stark reality. All this was the hunger for the living.

Beelzebub yanked me to the side as he fought to get free just as a rush of air came funneling down through the doorway above. Two of the archdemons plummeted down, crashing into the ground beside us. They got up within seconds, joining the fight and working to protect me.

"Get her out of here, Beelzebub!" one of them shouted, but he couldn't spread his wings wide enough to take flight. Every time he tried, a demon jumped onto them and used them against him.

Another demon slipped through the gateway, coming to

Beelzebub's aid the moment he landed. They fought together in a way that communicated they'd done so countless times before, moving as one.

There was a commotion up above us as Michael and Lucifer grappled at the doorway, and I saw the moment Willow thrust her head back into Iban, using the last of her strength to break his nose. She tore her hands free from the magic of the portal with a scream of agony, blood gushing from her hands as she tore the knife from her stomach. Spinning on her knees, she swept her arm out in a single sweep and cut Iban across the throat.

Michael fell into the pit, losing the fight with Lucifer at the moment Willow shoved Iban into his path, the human's body landing atop Michael's as he grabbed the edge of the pit in desperation. Lucifer did not hesitate to step on His brother's fingers, sending both of them careening through the doorway into Hell.

Michael fell through, but Iban exploded into a mess of blood and gore, serving as the needed sacrifice to save Willow's life. Beelzebub fought desperately to get his wings spread, to take off, only for the demons to drag him back down to the sand as Michael landed beside us.

Beelzebub roared out in pain as his gaze connected with mine, an apology in it that told me everything I needed to know.

I wasn't going home.

I looked back to the doorway to Crystal Hollow, at Willow's panicked face staring down at me as we both shared a moment of understanding.

She knew as well as I did that none of us were going to make it out in time. Glass covered the doorway slowly, creeping across the gap and cutting me off from the only home I'd ever known. With all the chaos surrounding me, I felt only guilt that Willow would blame herself. I could see that guilt already etched into the tense lines of her face, her mouth open as she called for me, but I couldn't hear her through the glass.

Jonathan whimpered as a demon landed a blow against his

chest, leaving three bleeding wounds behind. He leapt into my arms for safety, transforming into his feline form in the moment before I released Beelzebub, caught Jonathan, and curled him to my chest between the archdemon and me.

Willow's eyes were wide and panicked as the glass filled the boundary between planes, her hands frantically smacking against the surface as if she could break through. I watched her nails claw at the window, her blood staining the glass.

The stone that slowly spread to cover the seal was tan where it rested over the bloody smears she'd left behind. I couldn't tear my eyes off that seal, couldn't focus on the fighting happening around me.

It covered the gateway to Crystal Hollow as it closed.

And Willow was gone.

PART II

9
MARGOT

The Present

With both arms wrapped around an archdemon's neck and not a weapon to my name, I had little hope of surviving the onslaught of demons and souls calling for my blood. The sound of them around us was like nothing I'd ever heard before, vicious and growling creatures that were desperate for the kind of blood that only I could provide. Archdemons were neither living nor dead, a gray area that didn't call to the hunger of lost souls and lesser demons.

I couldn't make myself move. Couldn't make myself tear my gaze away from that now-closed doorway above my head as if it would simply reopen to allow us to escape.

I knew Willow didn't have that kind of strength left, but it didn't stop me from waiting to see her try.

Beelzebub groaned, crying out as his wing jerked against me. The sound of pain was enough to pull my attention away from the doorway, and I stared at the gold of his Enochian tattoos where they glowed beneath my arms.

The faint glimpses of the demons and souls around us were enough to make me flinch in fear, some of them entirely humanoid but for the blank look in their eyes. Others were distorted blurs of motion, muscle, and sinew bending in ways that were unnatural to living things. Their bones cracked and joints popped around us, the sounds like something from one of the horror movies I'd studiously avoided watching.

Sometimes, fiction was far too close to reality.

I couldn't see the landscape beyond the writhing flesh of demons moving and attempting to reach us, the archdemons who had fallen in with us doing their best to form a wall between us and the coming threat.

"Get her out of here!" one of them shouted, swinging his hand and cutting through one of the demons who fought to get closer to us. Blood sprayed onto my cheek, the proximity of the demon too close for comfort as I gasped at the unfamiliar warmth the violence brought.

Beelzebub's hands cupped my cheeks, cradling my face in his grip with a gentleness so at odds with the warpath of the demons around us. "I need you to snap out of it, songbird," he said, that name striking me in the chest. It forced me to shake off the trauma, wincing when his wings tugged me in close and more of my body lined up with his. Skin touched skin, the feeling too warm for comfort in this place where the heat was so dry and stifling. Sweat slicked my body, a mix of adrenaline and the heat making me feel sticky as I nodded up at the archdemon who was doing his best to keep me safe.

"Get me a fucking opening then!" Beelzebub shouted back to the archdemon who had yelled at him. His tone was entirely different from the one I had come to know in the limited time I'd spent with him. This was the commander of Lucifer's armies. This was His second-in-command, who must have led Hell through the centuries when Lucifer's soul had been trapped within a Vessel in Crystal Hollow.

The archdemon with fiery red skin grappled with Michael, the archangel struggling without fingers that he must have lost at some point in his fight with Lucifer. If the archangel was anything like what I'd come to know of the devil and His demons, it would take time for his magic to heal him in this place that was so far removed from the father who had provided him with magic in the first place. His feathered wings flapped and smacked against the archdemon, and it seemed to cause more frustration than hurt, leaving the red one sputtering with rage.

Two of the other demons moved with Beelzebub, taking up his rear as he tried to step back from the worst of the fray. I felt Beelzebub shudder as something scraped down his wing, tearing through the fibrous tissue as I nodded up at him. He used his injured wing to throw whatever had hurt him off, nodding back to me as he settled his hands at my waist.

I flinched away from the touch on instinct, nodding through the reaction to encourage him to continue. I could deal with the consequences of being touched later, if I survived, but for this moment I needed to focus on allowing Beelzebub to do what was necessary to save us both without fear of repercussions from me.

He gripped me tightly, tugging me tighter into his enormous frame. Heat pulsed off those golden symbols scrawled into his chest, the light held within them glowing brighter as my hands brushed over them.

I forced myself to tighten my arm around his neck, sandwiching Jonathan between us as I struggled to cradle him with one arm. The cat's blood leaked out onto me slowly, his wounds deep but not life-threatening, and I knew he would be alright with medical attention.

If we managed to escape.

Beelzebub crushed me to his chest, bending his knees as I clung to him. He jumped into the air, the massive expanse of those bat-like wings spreading wide. They caught the wind as demons reached for us—for me, I knew beyond a shadow of a doubt. They had no interest in Beelzebub, only trying to go through him to get to me.

His wings flapped, sending a burst of air toward the ground. The demons closest to where we had been fell to the ground as we went airborne. Beelzebub flew even as blood dripped down from his wing to land on the ground below us, the tear in his wing forcing us to fly a crooked path. He grimaced through the pain but never stopped, taking us past endless rolling hills of deep red earth. Lost souls moved along the surface of the dirt in writhing piles. They looked like bodies, though I knew they wouldn't have come to Hell with a physical form the way I had; they still managed to hurt and maim one another.

Lava poured down from the mountaintops, spilling out of craters at the highest peaks as chunks of volcanic rock flew through the air before falling down to the ground and crushing souls beneath it.

Fire and brimstone dominated this place, the scent of burning and charred flesh potent in the air as Beelzebub flew.

Only when we put distance between ourselves and the gate to the realm of the living did the landscape below us begin to change. Demons became less frequent, their red flesh fading into memory. The souls who remained this far from the gate wandered aimlessly, with space to move freely without the violence of another interfering.

"The First Circle," Beelzebub said, his voice loud enough to drown out the sound of the traveling air. He stopped beating his wings, settling into a smooth glide that hitched every time he needed to move his injured wing as the silence and peace of flight overcame him.

Some of the tension left his features, replaced by a calm I'd never seen on the tense male, making him look so much less harsh. His square jaw softened as if he lived in a constant state of gritting his teeth, his red eyes roaming the ground below.

"Limbo," I said, nodding my understanding. I hadn't known what part of Hell the seal opened into, but it made sense that it would be the outermost boundary. While it was the circle for those awaiting judgment and sorting into the circles that claimed their sins, it was also home to those who had not sworn themselves to God but lived otherwise virtuous lives. Limbo was the least severe of the Nine Circles.

It was a circle I would not be permitted to stay in when I died because the sin of my magic would condemn me elsewhere, like all witches. We each had our home within Hell, where our magic resided like a mirror.

The ground below us became more hilly than mountainous, the ebb and flow of the land feeling more natural than the even, flat plains of red earth beneath the seal itself and the harsh volcanic peaks that surrounded the plain. A building loomed in the distance, onyx stone jutting out of the hillside. The tops of the palace were pointed like spires, reminding me of the gothic architecture of churches like Notre-Dame.

The windows at the front shimmered with the light of stained glass, reflecting off the red earth in the front. Beelzebub veered to his left in a sharp turn, gliding toward the palace. We descended slowly, crossing over the gate that lingered in the front of the building. Beelzebub shifted me, drawing a startled gasp from me as he quickly moved a hand behind my knees and cradled me in his arms.

He landed smoothly, not even pausing as he shifted into an even gait and strode toward the doors of the palace. A male demon thrust them open, his skin a darker shade of brown than Beelzebub's medium olive.

"Beelzebub," the demon said, stepping aside to hold the door as the archdemon carried me in. Jonathan jumped down from my hold immediately once we were through the threshold, shaking off the dust that had settled on him during our flight. He twisted his body immediately, licking at the three slash marks on his chest.

"Stop that," I scolded him as Beelzebub set me on my feet. Squatting down, I bopped him on the nose. "Bad kitty."

He glared up at me with his eerie purple eyes, a look of pure disbelief as he swatted at my finger defiantly.

"The cat might need stitches," I said, interrupting Beelzebub where he spoke to the demon. Reaching out with a cautious hand, I waited until he turned to look at me. "May I?" I asked, gesturing with my chin to his injured wing. When he nodded and turned to give me his back, I wrapped my fingers around the edge, pulling it out so that I could examine the tear in the membrane. I swallowed, thinking of the cost of all the physical touch we'd both had no choice but to allow in the urgency of survival. "As might you," I added, stroking a tender finger over the tear to brush dirt away from the wound.

Beelzebub made a sound that was half groan and half growl—anything but menacing—and turned his head to look at me slowly over his shoulder. I swallowed, pursing my lips together as I held his intense dark stare.

The other demon cleared his throat. "Should I try to send for a healer? It could take some time to track one down," he mused, eyeing the place where I still held Beelzebub's wing in my fingers.

I released it, taking a step back and averting my eyes. The way he eyed that touch made it feel like something intimate.

"The cat will only need a couple of stitches. You're capable of tending to him, and do it quickly before he licks himself raw," Beelzebub said to the demon, but his stare never left my face. I felt it from the corner of my eye, but couldn't bear to meet it. Not when I had the distinct feeling I'd just committed some sort of fucking foreplay.

In front of another man.

"What about you, sire?" the demon asked, reaching down to scoop Jonathan into his arms. The cat hissed, sinking his claws into the male's flesh, but the demon didn't so much as flinch.

"I'll manage on my own. Waiting for a healer will take too long, and the wing will heal wrong if it isn't stitched together quickly," Beelzebub said, shrugging his shoulders.

"There is truly no healer in Purgatory?" I asked with a sigh. I hated the very notion that we would be delayed by waiting for one, but also didn't see a way for Beelzebub to twist his body in the right way to do it himself.

"People don't come here hurt. They come here dead," the demon said, answering my question with a raised eyebrow.

"How do you expect to be able to stitch your own wing? Can you even see what you're doing?" I asked, pinching my nose between two fingers.

"Not particularly well, no, but unless you would like to volunteer to do it for me, I haven't got much choice," he said, the casual ease with which he dismissed help from any others taking my breath away.

"I'm no healer," I argued, raising my gaze to glare at him finally. He smirked at the ire in my face, that weird response I always got when he finally pushed me past my limits. "Is there no one else who can do it?"

Beelzebub pursed his lips, seeming to think over the question before he finally answered. "No one I trust not to fuck it up intentionally. I don't care to have to tear it open all over again, and you'll quickly learn that asking favors of demons comes at a price that is often far worse than the initial problem," he explained, pausing as if choosing to give me a moment to allow that information to sink in. "Satanus and Asmodeus will be here shortly!" he called to the demon who'd greeted us. He turned his back, gesturing for me to follow him as he made his way to the stairs.

"I don't know how to do stitches," I admitted, following after him. In Hollow's Grove, his presence had felt dangerous, but here, it was a comfort. He was the one familiar thing I had to cling to when my entire world had been torn away.

"You could always heal me in other ways, songbird," he teased, both of us knowing that most Reds would merely offer him pleasure and use that energy to heal him. He also knew that I wouldn't, and his words lacked the punch that I would have felt from anyone else.

There was a certain comfort in him already knowing where my limits were.

"Stop calling me that," I argued instead of responding to the empty taunt. He guided me to the top of the stairs, stopping in front of a door. He tested the knob, guiding me into the privacy of a beautiful bedroom.

I tried to ignore how pretty everything was in spite of the darker color palette, feeling completely at ease with the red that surrounded me. "Why? So you don't have to admit how much you like it?" he asked, closing the door behind him.

He moved for the dresser, tugging open a drawer and pulling out a needle and something that looked like a cross between fishing wire and thread.

I swallowed, not knowing how to find the words to admit why I hated that fucking nickname so much.

The day he gave it to me, the first time I laid eyes on Beelzebub, he'd caught me singing to myself. It had only been the faintest hum; I thought I was alone in the courtyard Willow loved so much. I loved the way her flowers had strayed toward me as if they, too, couldn't resist the magic of my song.

I couldn't have imagined there was a demon watching, listening to me sing, and falling prey to my spell.

Every time he called me that, every time he referenced the magic in my veins, it was only another reminder.

He was caught under my spell, whether I liked it or not, and no matter what I did, one thing remained true.

I couldn't free him, and I'd stripped away his free will as harshly as Itan had taken mine.

Beelzebub might not have felt any outright suffering from my violation, and he likely never would. But if I could only *not* sing to him and not touch him, then one day, the spell would wear off on its own and he could move on with his life.

Leaving me in fucking peace, finally.

10

MARGOT

The demon seemed to realize there was something trapped in the weight of my gaze, his own features softening as much as I thought him capable of. I glanced back at the entrance behind us, taking in the open door. It was a modicum of comfort, the knowledge that anyone could walk by at any moment. That we were not well and truly alone in the confines of a bedroom.

I hadn't allowed myself to be caught with a man behind closed doors since Itan had taken everything from me for the last time, since I'd gotten too old for him to desire and been saved from his attentions. I swallowed, letting my eyes drift closed as I considered my options.

I knew the situation I'd somehow maneuvered myself into was dangerous, that bedrooms were where men used the excuse of desire to mask their violence, which could be far more damaging than the threat of death.

"Songbird," Beelzebub said, his gentle voice making my heart leap into my throat. It came from the other side of the room, making it clear that he hadn't taken my moment of weakness with my eyes closed to take advantage and intrude on my space. His respect for my needs was somehow almost worse, like I spent my time around him waiting for him to reveal his true nature and tear away the illusion that he might have cared.

The demons outside the manor might have destroyed my body

and torn my flesh, but at least the worst they would do was kill me. Beelzebub was caught under my spell, drawn to me in a way that wasn't entirely his fault. I didn't know what the consequence of that would be for the male who seemed to be carefully controlled in all other facets of his life, and that unpredictability felt impossible for me to navigate.

Somehow the hope that maybe he would be *better* than the others I'd known felt so much more dangerous to my soul than if I knew him to be untrustworthy like all the rest.

"Margot," Beelzebub repeated, the sound of my name snapping me out of my frozen trance. I couldn't decide whether to fight or flee, whether to wait it out or run before I lost the chance.

I opened my eyes, finding Beelzebub in the exact place he'd been when I closed them. He dropped his hands to his sides as I met his shocking red stare. He dropped the needle and thread on the bed unceremoniously, his own healing cast aside as he studied me. "I—I can't," I said, shaking my head and taking a step back toward that open door.

When I'd come to this room with him, I'd fully intended to do what I could to help with his stitches. I knew how impractical it would have been for him to do it himself, and something in that warning about asking demons for help had struck me.

He was alone.

He might have been surrounded by siblings and demons who could have and should have, for all purposes, been family to him, but there was no one here he trusted enough not to harm him. I related to that more than I wanted to admit, because even though I had spent my entire life surrounded by witches and a Coven that was my home, there wasn't anyone I'd felt comfortable turning to when I needed help. Much like me, there was no one he could ask to help with something that was so critical to his well-being.

But he'd asked me, and I wanted so badly to be that person for someone else.

His face softened, the harsh lines going gentle in a way that shouldn't have been possible. He *saw* me far too clearly for my comfort, as if he could read me like one of the books I'd laid out in the library to study while he watched me. I didn't know that anyone had taken the time to observe me so fully that they could interpret the signals in my body. "I can't control what happens to us out there. This is Hell, songbird. They use and abuse and manipulate however they can to get what they want, and I will do whatever I must to keep you safe from them. That means that sometimes, I may need to act quickly without stopping to consider the choice you might have made for yourself," he said, nodding his head toward the open door. I turned to follow his stare, toward the safety of avoiding this situation that was laced with danger. I felt trapped between two bad situations, a certain death out there and the unknown within these walls. "But in this room with me, you're in control," he said, keeping his body very still. I both appreciated and hated him for his patience, for the fact that he seemed to see straight into the dilemma coursing through my veins. I wanted nothing more than to remain oblivious, to know that I was safe inside my head. But something about Beelzebub saw straight into me, read every motion of my body for what it was and knew how to turn me inside out.

"How am I in control in here?" I asked, studying the room intently. "What is it about these walls that will protect me?"

His chuckle was completely inappropriate, as if he found my question amusing. "It's not the room that will protect you, Margot. It is my presence within it and my interest in allowing you to control at least this. I am fully aware of just how stripped of control you will feel throughout the Nine Circles. The least I can do is give you a safe space to lay your head," he answered.

"A safe space? Why would I ever think of a room you occupy as a safe space? You could do whatever you wanted to me and no one would intervene to save me!" I asked with a bitter smile. I think my outburst shocked me more than him, and that gentle curving smile only widened, as if it pleased him greatly that I had the gall to yell at him.

He leaned his ass into the edge of the dresser, gripping the edge with both hands. I definitely didn't notice the way his forearms flexed with the motion, something that should have served as a reiteration of the power imbalance between us.

He was twice the size of me, tall and broad and covered with muscle that should have been fucking illegal. It was like walking around with a loaded gun, a weapon constantly at his disposal, except where a man with a gun could be disarmed, this was just part of him.

Innate and unnerving, he and Leviathan were the biggest creatures I'd ever seen. Monstrously beautiful and terrifying all at once.

"Why would you need anyone to save you from me?" he asked, tilting his head to the side as he tried to figure me out. I felt that gaze poking at me, trying to learn every secret that was mine to keep. It was bad enough he knew that Itan had harmed me because of the way Willow had executed him, because of the way I'd supported that decision and stood up when she'd put him on trial unexpectedly. I didn't regret it. *Nothing* could make me regret knowing his life had ended with my name fresh in his mind, but I hated the vulnerability it brought.

The wounds it had opened for all to see.

"Because you're dangerous," I said, spitting the words at him.

He flinched, his head kicking back as if I'd struck him. He took a single, slow step toward me, pausing when I tensed. "When have I ever harmed you?" he asked, his brow tense. His mouth had turned down ever so slightly into a frown, as if it wasn't just me who needed that reminder.

I didn't have an answer to that, and I hated it. He might have frightened me and made it clear that he held disdain for my kind, but he'd never harmed me so much as just . . . watched me.

"You're right about one thing," he said, daring to take another step toward me. "I am dangerous, but not to you, songbird," he said, staring at me as if he could press the intention of those words into me and make me believe them. "You're important to Willow and she is important to Lucifer. For that reason alone, I will never harm you. But even if that weren't true, you are not some helpless damsel who cannot protect herself. All you'd have to do is sing."

It was my turn to flinch, turning my stare away at the prospect of using my magic against someone intentionally. After the consequences it held for me even when I hadn't meant to do it, I could never bring myself to purposefully put someone under my spell. It would take away their will, and that would make me just as evil as Itan.

"I won't do that," I said, dismissing the notion immediately. Perhaps it would have been better to lead him to believe that I would enthrall him entirely if it meant my survival, that I would control him to keep him from harming me.

But even if he'd tried to hurt me, I didn't think I could bring myself to do it. I didn't think I could bring myself to become a monster like Itan, to strip away someone's consent in such a way . . .

Even if he was hurting me, I didn't want to make anyone become a slave to my will.

"Why not?" Beelzebub asked, his curiosity practically burning a hole in the side of my face. "Hell isn't safe for the living, and I can only do so much to protect you. I need to know that you'll protect yourself if it comes to it. I learned enough about the Reds while I was in Hollow's Grove to know that enthralling your enemies is how your kind defend yourselves, so why wouldn't you—"

"It's none of your fucking business," I snapped, shocking him with the venom in my voice. I drew in a deep breath, forcing my feet to move forward and picking up the needle and thread from the bed. "Now sit down and put your hands in your lap before I change my mind."

Beelzebub narrowed his gaze on my face, constantly evaluating and trying to understand the change in my mood. I glared up at him, the dimming light in the room making the bright, shining gold of his Enochian tattoos seem all the more vibrant. The light from them played off his features, making him look far more angelic than he had any right to be. Whereas Lucifer had once been an angel, Beelzebub had been created from the pits of Hell itself, as had each of the archdemons. Each one had been gifted a circle to claim as his own, and each archdemon possessed the qualities of the circle he'd been created from.

They were the darker reflections of our own magic.

"I can do it myself if it makes you uncomfortable," he said, tilting his head to the side. His wing twitched as if it wanted to argue that he could, in fact, not do this himself. He rolled his eyes. "Or I can ask Raum."

"You said asking a demon will come with consequences," I said, challenging the offer. Had his warning been an exaggeration and a lie?

"It will undoubtedly, but it should be my price to pay. Not yours," he said, glancing down at where my hands trembled with unease.

I sighed, unable to allow him to come to further harm because of this injury. He'd protected me, whether because of Willow or because of my song. "You were injured protecting me. This is the least I can do."

Beelzebub finally moved toward the bed, sitting on the edge and making himself smaller. He was still imposing, his height still greater than mine even as he sat. His legs were spread to the perfect width, and I knew I would have been able to fit between them perfectly. To nestle myself between his thighs and touch his golden brown skin for myself. I swallowed as he smirked at me, winking as if he knew the path my thoughts had taken and it amused him that I wasn't impervious to his effect. Turning his body to the side, he lifted one leg to rest it atop the mattress so his other foot that remained on the floor ran parallel to the bed itself.

I studied his profile for a moment. The slight angle of his upturned eyes was breathtakingly beautiful, but the strong curve of his brow above them was too harsh to be pretty. A contradiction that continued down to the sharp angles of his jaw, which looked as if it'd been carved from the rock of Hell itself. The Enochian runes danced over his skin as I forced my feet to move past him, perching on the edge of the mattress behind him. One of his leathery wings fanned itself over the mattress, laying out as if it, too, needed a rest.

His injured one extended down to the floor, a deep tear in the fibrous flesh. I studied the part where the wings connected to his spine, unable to resist laying a finger atop the connective tissue there. Warmth spread to my finger at the contact, a shiver running up Beelzebub's spine as his head curled forward. He turned his neck to glance at me over his shoulder, a smirk on his face that was more than just a tease.

It was a carnal promise, his deep red eyes boring into mine as he ran his tongue over the top of his bottom teeth.

"Careful, songbird. They're sensitive," he said, earning a swallow and a nod from me. I tore my finger away from his skin, the part where the black of his wings blended into the brown of his skin. It was like watching muscle move, parts of the flesh that were normally on the inside so obvious from the outside. "Another reason I don't want anyone but you to touch them."

I threaded the needle with deep breaths, tying the end and using my teeth to tear it off the spindle. "Doesn't that mean they'll hurt more?" I asked, wishing we had a numbing agent to ease the pain.

As well as other sensations.

"It does," he admitted, smirking at me as he smiled over his shoulder. "You worried about me?"

I flushed, my face warming with the heat of my embarrassment as I avoided his gaze and reached out to grasp his wing. He shuddered, a deep growl rumbling in his chest that forced me to drop it. "I'm sorry. I didn't mean to hurt you," I said, my face twisting with sympathy.

"Didn't hurt," he grunted, his fist grasping the blanket on top of the bed and squeezing. It bunched in his grip, making something unfamiliar tingle along the surface of my skin.

I swallowed, wetting my suddenly dry lips as I forced myself to gently grab his wing once more. He didn't growl a second time, his entire body tense as I tried to touch him as little as possible.

Wiping the excess blood away with my fingertips, I slid the needle into his skin. I shoved down my nausea at the feeling of his flesh parting for the needle, focusing in on the wound and sealing it closed. The alternative was using sex to heal him, using my body to offer him pleasure and feeding on his, offering him pure, uninterrupted energy in exchange. I didn't have that in me, couldn't allow that to happen.

So I stabbed my way through his flesh, reaching around his wing to pull the needle back through to the other side, over and over again. I knitted his flesh, brought him pain, all the while knowing I could have made him feel *good* instead. If only I were braver. If only I were less of a selfish coward.

But I wasn't. I was just me.

11

MARGOT

My magic pulsed in time with the warmth of arousal that covered Beelzebub's body, his skin pulsing with a tingle of awareness. I couldn't *not* feel it with my fingers touching the surface of his wings, even as delicately as I could manage. I forced my way through my nerves, though, choosing to focus on the fact that he had yet to act on the desire I knew he felt. Choosing to focus on the hope that his self-control gave me.

All this physical contact would have deepened the call of my song and the pull he felt to me, but he still sat without harming me regardless of the fact that he'd fallen prey to the music others had used for evil. Centuries ago, Lucifer had given the same magic to a group of women who'd been thrown overboard in the sea just outside Greece. The legends of the sirens had prevailed, leaving behind myths that most convinced themselves came down to nothing more than a representation of the danger of the ocean, of the treacherous waves that would claim the lives of men who were brave enough to sail.

It was not lost on me that men explained away the circumstances where women took back the power that had been stripped from them. Used and abused and cast aside over the course of centuries, my Coven had become a refuge for women and formed a matriarchy where men were so often seen as less. Where they had to make the choice between procreation and the continuation of their family line, and the power that came along with keeping their magic.

We forced them to make the choice that so many of our sisters were forced to make in the world outside Crystal Hollow.

Children or a successful life outside the home. They could not have both.

Just as women so often found themselves at a disadvantage in their careers if they had children.

And if the men as a whole decided to simply stop having children, then we would have made our bed. We would have ended our own bloodlines, and we would have no one to blame but ourselves, no matter the reasoning behind the choice.

No matter if it had been for the very purpose of preventing Willow's existence.

A pang of longing struck me in the chest, wondering if the choice would continue on now that her reality had come to pass. She'd already freed Lucifer from Hell, done what the Covenant had been so desperate to prevent. I couldn't imagine my friend would be so willing to allow men to suffer in the same way she was intimately familiar with women being treated in the outside world.

She knew the reality of the human world far better than most of our Coven.

"You're awfully quiet back there, songbird," Beelzebub said, the soft murmur of his voice pulling me from my thoughts as I slid the needle through his flesh again. The tear in his wing had ripped through the fibrous center, but the part that felt more solid and ran through the top was undamaged, thankfully. I imagined he wouldn't have been able to fly us out of harm's way if that had been damaged, the structure oddly muscular.

"Do you think I'll ever make it back home?" I asked, voicing the thought that I hadn't dared to breathe. The thought of being unable to warn Willow of what Itan and the Tribunal had done was entirely unforgivable. The very notion that she might play right into their plans and I would remain helpless to prevent it was enough to make me rage.

After all they'd done, after all they'd sacrificed that wasn't theirs to give . . .

They didn't get to fucking win.

Beelzebub's voice was tired as I finished the last stitch, tying off the strange thread that felt more like gel than actual string. "I'll make sure of it," he said. His voice held all the conviction I expected to hear, but there was a note of tiredness in his voice as he said it.

I didn't fault him for it, not knowing what he'd given in order to get me to safety—the pain he must have endured flying with that injured wing. Whether it was a consequence of his hearing my song or his loyalty to Lucifer, and Willow by extension, I didn't care to know. Either way, I knew not to let the gesture touch *me* too intimately, because when it all came down to it, the reality was it had nothing to do with me.

I was just a by-product of his actual goal.

Beelzebub lifted his wings, shifting his weight up the bed until he rested in the center. Laying his head atop the pillow, he watched me with an ease that spoke of how little he feared me. My song had made him feel safe, when I could just as easily gut him while he slept and be rid of him.

I didn't. Wouldn't.

"You should rest. It will help you heal faster," I said, watching the gel of the thread shimmer within him. The gold light that radiated off the tattoos pulsed with magic, and I couldn't bring myself to ask how they'd come to exist. In this place, all magic came from one source.

Lucifer.

"Stay close. You're safe here with me. The lord of Purgatory is better than most, but I still can't promise the same of him if you wander in his home," Beelzebub said, his eyes drifting closed as exhaustion claimed him. I considered humming to help him pass into the realm of sleep more smoothly when he grunted in pain as he shifted his wing, but decided against it. I didn't want to risk extending the amount of time he would spend drawn to me, not until I knew how long I would need him to keep me safe. I didn't think I could use it intentionally even if I'd wanted to, even if it meant he would leave me there to rot when he no longer desired me.

I made my way to the door, glancing out at the dangers that waited beyond the small gateway to our private space. My eyes landed on the demon who had welcomed us to Purgatory where he remained at the base of the stairs, staring up at me with a raised brow. Beelzebub's reminder that even he did not trust the other male made me swallow, my anxiety rising as I realized just how closely he was watching us.

I forced myself to give a small, unassuming smile before I retreated back into the room I had no intention of leaving without Beelzebub now. Closing the door quietly, I sealed myself into the room I would have thought I couldn't stand to be in, my heart rate rising with the soft click of the latch. Not with the male slumbering on the bed, his deep, even breathing broken up by the occasional snore.

I stepped around the cabinet of drawers that sat beside the door, leaning my weight into it. The floor groaned as the furniture slid over the surface, scraping the wood beneath it. I didn't stop until the full weight of the cabinet rested against the inside of the door, creating a barricade. I wasn't foolish enough to believe it would do much to stop a demon, but perhaps it would buy us enough time to react.

I eyed the chair at the bedside with a sigh, my muscles already tensing with the realization that it would be where I spent the night. If I stayed awake, there was nothing a sleeping demon could do.

Right?

He looked uncomfortable, splayed atop the berry-toned comforter. The throw pillows weren't as soft as the ones beneath them, the fabric textured and indenting the side of Beelzebub's face where he lay there. With a disgruntled groan, I grasped the comforter where it was folded over beneath him and carefully tugged it down, fighting to shift it beneath his massive body without hurting his wing.

"How much do you fucking weigh, you giant oaf?" I asked, moving from one side of the bed to the other to shimmy it until it reached the bottom of his ass. I grasped his legs one at a time, yanking the blanket down before dropping his legs to the bed so they fell to the sheets with a thump. He didn't stir, the depth of his sleep bringing a sweat to my brow. I couldn't bring myself to tuck him in with his boots still on, so I worked to unknot the laces and drew them off his feet. I heaved a sigh as I stared down at his prone form, something immensely more intimate about him being nearly barefoot. He was *always* shirtless; an ego the size of his was unable to be contained by a top that would cover the rippling muscles of his abs and the runes that covered him and made him feel distinctly *other*.

I chewed my bottom lip, shaking my head to shove the sight of him out of my mind. I grasped the blanket in my hands, tugging it up to his armpits to tuck all the tempting sight of him away. It was not lost on me that while I had to sing to him to enrapture him in my spell, he was an archdemon. His very creation had been to aid in tempting the souls of humans to sin, in stealing them further and further from the reach of God until they became Hell's property when they died.

At least, that's what God would have us believe.

While I knew my soul was condemned to this place upon my death as a witch with a connection to the Source, I couldn't help but question everything I knew. The Covenant had led us to believe that Lucifer walking the earth would have been the greatest of evils, that He would have created a literal Hell on earth and enslaved the Coven to suit His purposes.

But all I'd witnessed Him do in His time on Earth was worship

His wife and allow her to step into the power she so clearly possessed as the first of her kind.

If that was evil, I didn't think I wanted to know what was *good*.

I sighed as I curled up in the armchair next to the bed, fidgeting until I found the most comfortable way to lie. I ended up curling onto my side, facing the headboard of the bed and tucking my legs into my chest.

I didn't dare take my eyes off him while he slept, wanting to know the moment he woke.

Others of my kind would have probably taken the opportunity to feed from the demon, claiming the last of the strength he possessed in an effort to fortify themself against the coming dangers. I wouldn't fault them for it, because even I knew it would have been the smart, logical thing to do. If it hadn't been for my own aversion to *taking* what wasn't mine, I might have genuinely considered it.

The wall opposite me was covered in the greenery of vines I knew Willow would love, a sign of life in a desert that seemed so barren. She would reach out and grasp those leaves, drawing strength from the fact that *something* could survive in this place.

If that plant could do it, then so could I.

Lust was my power. Lust was my magic.

So why couldn't I get past my own fucking issues and trauma and take that power for myself the way Willow would have?

I sighed, letting my eyes drift closed and shutting out the symbol that reminded me so vividly of my home. Beelzebub groaned on the bed, stretching in his sleep. Everything in my body went tight as he turned onto his side to face me with an ease that seemed impossible given I knew exactly how much he weighed. If I hadn't known he was asleep, I might have thought he was seeking me out even in his rest.

He reached out across the bed, his brow furrowing when it met the cool mattress beside him. His hand roamed over the surface as if looking for something.

For me?

I swallowed, flinching back from the bed even though he couldn't reach me. He grabbed the spare pillow, pulling it to his chest and snuggling it in a way that almost made me wonder what it would be like to be held so gently.

He nuzzled into it, a soft sound coming from his throat. I froze, fearing the implication of the threat that may come in his sleep when he was less in control of his own actions. The sound bared the slightest hint of teeth, a reveal of the curve of his fangs triggering memories better left forgotten. I didn't know if demons fed in the same way the Vessels did, but the distinct fangs hinted at the possibility.

I'd been forced to endure Reaping after Reaping, countless Vessels taking from me what I wouldn't have given. Some were more gentle, easing me through it because they could sense my fear. Not all the demons had been abhorrent; some had shown me kindness in my darkest moments. But there had also been those who had reveled in my fear, taken pleasure in my pain and the loss of my will.

But Beelzebub didn't move to close the gap and bite me. Instead he curled the pillow into his chest, and breathed it in as if his life depended on it. His body relaxed in his sleep, his injured wing coming down to cover himself like a blanket and wrap him in a cocoon.

If I'd had any doubts that I'd done the right thing by choosing the armchair instead of risking the bed alongside Beelzebub, that wing served as my proof. I could only imagine the darkness surrounding him in there, my eyes focusing on the light streaming in through the window to my left.

I settled deeper into the chair, readying myself for a long and sleepless night as the deep, even sound of Beelzebub's breathing filled the room around me.

12

BEELZEBUB

The soft sound of a whimper broke through the silence surrounding me, drawing me from sleep slowly. I groaned as I fought to go back to sleep, curling my wings in closer around me like a cocoon. When the noise repeated, I slowly peeled open my eyes to stare at the leather of my wings blocking my view. Everything in me stilled, keeping surprise as my ally as I waited to assess the situation now that my attempt to sleep was forgotten.

The next whimper was higher pitched, the distinct sound of pain making me throw back my wings.

Margot sat with her knees curled into her chest in the chair. Her stunning face was pinched with fear or pain or both, whatever nightmare consumed her making its way into the waking world. She whimpered again, the sound sinking beneath my skin in a way that felt like an unwanted intrusion.

I groaned, rolling onto my back even though it was awkward with my wings beneath me, and rubbed my hands over my face.

The witch was having a nightmare, probably because she'd been too stubborn to just sleep in the bed where she might have gotten a better night's sleep than sitting in a chair that was too small for how long her limbs were.

Turning my back to her, I resolved to let her sleep and hoped that she'd find her own way through the nightmare.

What the fuck did I care that one witch had a bad dream? They'd been the cause of so much suffering and abandonment of those of us Lucifer had left behind, maybe she deserved to know a hint of that pain and loneliness.

"Stop," she pleaded, her soft, breathy voice torn apart by a sob that caught in her throat. I felt it within me, striking against me like the bang of a drum. The goddamn spell she placed on me had put me in her thrall, made it impossible to ignore her pain.

That only made me all the more determined to fight the pull to help her, to let her suffer alone since she'd made me care in a way I wouldn't have on my own. I would never hurt her for Lucifer. I would protect her and see her reunited with her Coven for Him.

But I would not let her pull my strings with delicate cries that should have meant *nothing* to me.

She groaned again, the sound so full of pain that I couldn't help but remember her concern that she might have hurt me when she stitched my wing the night before.

"Source be fucking damned!" I hissed, throwing my wings wide and moving to her side of the bed. I twisted my body and placed my feet on the floor, moving to stand and crossing the short distance between Margot and the bed. I tapped her shoulder where her shirt covered her skin, carefully avoiding touching her physically. The contact we'd had the day before had been necessary for survival, but this wasn't. "Wake up," I said, poking her gently at first and then with increasing pressure.

Her body swayed but her eyes did not open, her head thrashing from side to side as if she could fight off the images of whatever was attempting to harm her in her dreams.

"Wake up," I said, my voice getting louder. I wrapped two fingers around the top of her shoulder, shaking her slightly in an attempt to wake her. To do it, I leaned into her space, hating the way her sweet scent filled my lungs.

I hated it.

I hated everything about her. The way she made me want to understand every thought inside her pretty head, the way her reactions and the intensity of her emotions fascinated me. I hated the way her scent and the feel of her skin on mine sank deep into the numbness I'd felt for centuries, making me feel *interested* for the first time in as long as I could remember.

Everything before her had been a bland activity to pass the time, a duty and a job that needed to be achieved or an itch that needed to be scratched through one sin or another.

I hated that she felt different, and that I couldn't even believe any of it was real because it was all just a consequence of her magic. I had possessed countless humans to wander the earth over my centuries of life, had tormented them with obsessions that were horrible for their health to speed their journey to Hell simply because it amused me.

But never had I understood the inability to control one's own body and escape those vices . . . until Margot.

She made me feel weaker than I would ever admit I was.

She made me feel human.

She whimpered, and watching a single tear streak down her cheek was the final straw for me. My grip on her shoulder softened, my voice dropping to a low whisper. "Wake up for me, songbird," I said, forcing my own magic into the words. The compulsion slithered over her skin where my breath touched her temple, dancing along the surface of her face before it sank into her.

Her eyes snapped open suddenly, a startled scream tearing up her throat. I jolted at the horrific sound, covering her mouth with my hand more harshly than I'd intended when it burrowed into my ears and made my brain feel like it was being stabbed.

Margot planted her hands against my chest, the contact immediately sending a surge of warmth through me as her magic reached out to dance with mine. Her perfectly manicured nails grew and shifted into something black and gleaming as they elongated. I stared down at them in surprise, quirking a brow as

Margot dug them into my skin and attempted to push me away. She had practically bent herself backward over the chair in her effort to get away, making me release her mouth finally as those fingernails dug deeper into my skin and drew blood.

"Let go of me," she said, her voice breathless with fear. She struggled in the chair even though I barely touched her, nearly catapulting herself over the edge of the chair. I caught her, feeling like I held a feral animal in my arms.

"You'll hurt yourself," I said, covering her hands with one of my own. I shifted my other hand back from her shoulder to cup them gently, running my thumbs over those claws as her eyes bled to black before my eyes. Blood welled in the marks she'd left in my arm, and her nostrils flared as if she could scent it in the air.

"Let go!" she shrieked, shoving me back hard enough that I stumbled. My wings bumped against the bed, a tiny twinge of pain accompanying the collision. Margot launched herself from the chair, standing on shaky feet as she curled over herself and gripped her stomach. Her mouth curled into a grimace as if she was in pain, and I moved slowly to help her.

I didn't know everything about the Red witches, but I knew that her reaction to this was strange. This wasn't something that happened to her every day.

She held out a hand, making me freeze in place as she peered up at me from beneath her lashes. Her mahogany eyes were devoid of all warmth, in them a cool-toned darkness that had me nodding my agreement. I would give her the space she needed to get her magic under control, to rein it back within herself. There was a flash of something moving over her skin at her temples as she closed her eyes with the struggle, drawing in deep breaths as she attempted to calm herself.

Her nails retracted, her eyes filled with the life I'd grown used to all over again.

What kind of magic had Lucifer given the Red witches, exactly?

I suddenly wished that I'd shown more interest in the workings of Margot's Coven, beyond a particular disdain for Lucifer's wife and the ways she'd altered all our best-laid plans. Perhaps I'd stand a better chance of understanding the way her mind worked, of getting into all the nooks and crannies that made her who she was, if I understood how she'd been raised. "It's okay, songbird," I said, attempting to reassure her in the only way I knew. I couldn't touch her, couldn't cross the distance between us and help her lose herself in the physical way I would usually distract a struggling female. I *knew* Margot had been hurt, but I hadn't known the extent of the trauma it had left her with to this day.

I hated that I wanted to touch her. Loathed the fact that I wanted to do it to bring her comfort. There was a depth to her call that was so far beyond the physical that I struggled to wrap my mind around it. But the worst part was having the desire to soothe her, and not being allowed to.

So what did that leave me with?

"How is any of this okay?" she asked, her face twisting as she glared at me. Her voice dropped lower, the husky note that seemed ever present fading into something dark and menacing. "We are in *Hell,* Beelzebub! The seal is closed and I'm fucking stuck here with you!"

Her words were said with the utmost disdain, as if she couldn't bear the thought of me being near her. And yet all I could do was think of the way my name sounded on her lips, of how pretty her mouth looked as it formed the syllables. I stared transfixed at the plump flesh at the perfect bow at the top of her mouth and only looked away when her nostrils flared with anger.

Ugh.

"Neither of us want to be stuck here together, that I can promise you. I waited centuries to escape this place only to plummet down into the depths to try to save a fucking witch of all people," I growled.

"I didn't ask you to do that," she said back, her voice soft and sad and melancholy in a way that pulled at the space where my heart would have been if I'd been human.

I wanted to cheer her up, and for that, I knew I had to make it so much worse. We both needed the reminder of exactly what this was, for both our sakes. "Didn't you?" I asked, flinching in time with her. "We both know I wouldn't have been so willing to jump through that gate if it hadn't been for your song."

Margot flinched, the words striking my intended target. I regretted them immediately, felt the urge to heal the hurt I'd caused.

Maybe the reminder was more for me than it was for her.

She nodded her head in understanding, her pretty face pinched in pain as moisture welled in her eyes. "I'm sorry," she said, her voice soft and broken.

"Don't be sorry, songbird," I said, some of the bitterness leaving my voice. I couldn't keep up my facade of anger when faced with her sorrow, couldn't stay mad at our situation when she was so melancholy before me. "I know you didn't do it on purpose, but that doesn't change the reality of what this is."

She swallowed, her throat moving with the motion as she turned to look away from me. "You're right. It doesn't," she said in answer.

"I know you have your demons. But I'm not like the human men who have wronged you, because I'm not human. I'm not like him, and I am not going to touch you unless you *want* me to. If you never want me to, then I'll accept that. Because that is the bare minimum of what you are owed," I said, watching her head snap back to meet my stare.

Her mahogany eyes were wide with shock. "Beelzebub," she murmured.

I flinched.

There was power in names.

"I need you not to say my name again, songbird," I said, willing her to understand how much I meant that statement. My name in her voice did something to me, unraveled layers of my control that neither of us could afford to lose.

"What?" she asked.

"I like it, more than I want to admit, and I can't like it. Do you understand what I'm saying?"

Margot held her hands out in front of her, twisting them with subdued energy that seemed to attempt to mask her need to move. I knew from the time I'd spent watching her that this was a moment she would have gone for a run, when the emotional contradictions within her made her compelled to move and push herself until she was so tired there was nothing left.

"I don't know," she admitted, a question in her voice. She didn't dare to theorize as to what I actually meant, didn't dare to hope that I was just as disinterested in being attracted to her as she was in *having* me attracted to her.

"You and I are never going to fit. I am a demon, and you are a witch. We are everything that each other has grown to hate. It doesn't make sense, and it can't make sense. If I am going to keep you safe in this place, then I can't get caught up in you and your spell. I can't like the way you say my name. I can't like the way you look at me when you think I'm not looking. I can't do anything but protect you for Lucifer and bring you home. And when I do, it doesn't matter how interesting I think you are, I'll leave you with Willow and never look back. Because this cannot happen," I said, leaving no doubt as to the meaning of my words. I'd hoped that the assertion would ease some of her tension, allow her to rest easy in the knowledge that I had no interest in being further enslaved to her will.

"Do you think I don't know that?" she asked, her voice so hollow it shocked me. I'd thought it would reassure her that her body was safe with me; instead it seemed to make things worse. She picked at the skin on the side of her nail, anxious energy thrumming through her. "I know exactly what I did to you, as unintentional as it might have been. I warned you to stay away from me, but you didn't."

"I know," I acquiesced. I'd made our situation worse by giving in to the call, because in Hollow's Grove there had been so little at stake. I couldn't rid myself of the witches without pissing Lucifer off, and to convince Him to do so would take time.

There hadn't seemed to be any harm in finding a witch to entertain myself with in the meantime. None of it would have mattered after I grew bored with her.

She left me, making her way to the window and staring out over the red earth of Purgatory.

"What do we have to do to get me back home?" she asked, turning to face me finally. All traces of discomfort and sadness were gone from her face, the brief moment she'd allowed herself over and done with. The Margot standing before the window was all business, to the point and direct in a way I hadn't seen her.

Desperate to be free of Hell, or desperate to be free of *me*?

The thought stung far more than it should have, considering I'd said pretty much the same to her face.

"We need to make our way to the Ninth Circle. The manor there holds the only form of communication we will have with Lucifer, and from there we can make a plan for Willow to open the portal again. Assuming she's still alive, anyway," I said, noting the way Margot winced at the mention of the fate she didn't know. Her friends were lost to her for the time being, and while the main threat had plunged into Hell with us, there was no telling what other threats might have made themselves known in the hours since we'd fallen.

"It sounds like you'd best be on your way, then," Margot said, dropping down into the window seat and planting herself as if she refused to be moved.

I grinned, the confidence in her voice with that dismissal calling to the part of me that enjoyed the challenge.

Stubborn, difficult little witch.

13

MARGOT

On anyone else, that grin would have been deeply unsettling. It would have been a warning of something to come, something that I would take no pleasure in. But when Beelzebub's mouth spread into a wide smile, the fangs at the corners of his mouth flashing for the briefest of moments, I felt transfixed to the spot. As if my feet had sprouted roots, trapping me in place so that all I could do was stare up at the way the smile transformed the brutal sort of beauty that shouldn't have been possible. How was it a man could be so large, so imposing, with features that seemed carved from stone and sin itself, and still look so playful and young when he smiled like that?

His red eyes blazed like a pool of lava as he tipped his chin down, staring straight into my eyes as if they were the window to my soul. The color was as familiar to me as looking in a mirror, the same shade adorning my skin on a daily basis as one of the Red legacies of the Coven that waited for me on the surface. "Would you care to change your clothes before we leave? Or are you comfortable in your uniform?" he asked, and I felt the slow pass of his gaze as it dropped from my eyes to take in the flush that warmed my cheeks and spread over the freckles dotting the bridge of my nose.

I expected him to shift that gaze lower, to drop it down over the curve of my mouth and throat and then linger on the line of cleavage that the low V-neck of my uniform always revealed. My lungs expanded with a breath while I waited for it, so accustomed to the unabashed lust and perusal that few bothered to temper.

Reds were made to be appreciated, and many drew power from the simple act of inspiring lust in others.

But Beelzebub's stare remained transfixed on my face, echoing the words he'd given me only a few moments prior. We would never happen, could never happen, and there was a certain comfort to be found in the knowledge that even under the spell of my song, he was determined to resist and keep our interactions simple.

Straightforward. Without the complications of lust or emotions or any form of entanglement. There was some safety in that, one that I hadn't felt in the presence of a man for as long as I could remember.

Even if he wanted me, he didn't *want* to want me, and that counted for something.

Right?

I tried not to let the thought take root inside of me, tried not to allow the admission to be anything more than it was meant to be.

This could be the truce between us.

I swallowed, turning my gaze away from him and taking a moment to solidify myself in the knowledge that we could work together moving forward. Perhaps it had been foolish of me to think something as simple as a song could manipulate a male like Beelzebub into giving in to baser desires. He probably wasn't used to hearing the word *no* and didn't need to struggle with the girl who had no interest in sex. He probably had countless conquests who simply lay at his feet and waited for him to touch them with his strong, muscled hands. I wondered if his partners ever danced the line between wondering if he would fuck them or kill them, if those hands would be gentle or wrap around their throat and watch the light leave their eyes.

I wondered if they feared him as much as I had. The thought was startling as I realized it was in the past tense, because I didn't fear him the way I had when he first came to me in the courtyard. I may not have trusted him, because I still knew what he was capable of, but I no longer thought him the uncontrolled brute who had snapped Willow's neck for the Hell of it.

"How long will it take you to get to the Ninth Circle?" I asked, crossing my arms over my chest.

"Just me? It would take a matter of hours. I could simply fly there, but it is not so simple with you. You'll need to visit each of the circles and earn the right to pass through them individually. You'll need to show that you are in control of each of the sins to be able to move freely through Hell," he answered, quirking up his brow when my body went taut.

"And if I'm not in control of them?" I asked, swallowing down my nerves. The ominous phrasing struck me straight to the chest, leaving me with the feeling that my return to Hollow's Grove was anything but guaranteed.

"Then the circle where you fail will claim you and you won't be able to leave until you are in control," he said, shrugging as if it were inconsequential. As if we didn't speak of damning me to the very place he'd spent centuries trying to escape.

I was a Red witch. This would be my resting place one day as it was, and I had absolutely no desire to see that day come sooner than necessary.

"I am not going to Lust," I snapped, my fingers trembling with the thought. The Second Circle was the one that would claim me when I died, my magic condemning me to it immediately. The scales of judgment would make that choice easily, with little to be weighed that could outdo the magic I'd been born to. Just as a Green witch would be condemned to Gluttony, and a Yellow to Wrath, that was the natural order of the balance between the witches and the demons.

I wouldn't have any chance of proving to be in control of the very sin and magic that I'd avoided using altogether.

I didn't know how to control it, only to avoid it.

The idea of the Second Circle being so close to me made me feel suddenly naked in my uniform, and I turned to the dresser at the side of the room. I pulled open the top drawer, finding it filled with men's shirts and closing it with a disgruntled sigh to move on to the next one.

"You don't want to communicate with Lucifer to arrange a time for Willow to open the doorway?" Beelzebub asked. He knew as well as I did that remaining in Hell was not an option for me, that I deserved to have my life free from the torments of this afterlife before being confined to the torture waiting for me after my death.

"I see no need for my presence for you to do just that. You've lived an eternity as a fully functioning person without me to supervise you. I assume you are capable of managing this task on your own," I snapped, shoving another drawer closed when I found it filled with only men's clothes. They ranged in size, making it clear that this room didn't belong to any one person. There were clothes that *almost* looked like they would have fit me if not for being too long, and I knew for a fact that Beelzebub would never get his legs in *those*.

He moved to the dresser, grabbing a pair of the larger black pants from one of the drawers. He tossed them onto the bed, leaving them there and making his way to the closet at the side of the room. The pants on the bed reminded me almost of sweatpants, but the fabric more closely resembled leather by the looks of it.

"I am capable of communicating with Lucifer without you, but I will not be leaving you behind, songbird," he said, tugging open the closet door. "I already explained that I need to keep you safe. There is no one in Purgatory that I would trust to look after you while I am gone."

More feminine clothes hung in the closet, smaller in size with the shape that would fit my body more appropriately and not strain at my curves in the way a man's straight clothing would. I moved to the closet and shuffled through the hanging garments, looking for something that would offer me more coverage.

I gravitated toward one of the few red items, the color calling to me like a symbol of home. The red pants looked to be crafted from the same material as the ones Beelzebub had set out for himself, and I ran my fingers over the surface. I'd been both right and wrong to describe the fabric as being close to leather. The surface was smooth and cool to the touch, but there was a give that leather would never be able to achieve, a stretch to the material that I hadn't expected and reminded me of leggings.

"There's absolutely no one that you could leave me with who would keep me safe? No one who is loyal to Lucifer? I find that very hard to believe," I argued with a scoff. I couldn't keep moving through Hell, not when the Second Circle waited for me. I couldn't continue to remain at Beelzebub's side, not when his tirade this morning had penetrated the numbness around my heart.

I needed that fear of him to remain in place, because that was what kept me safe. My awareness of the intentions of the people around me hadn't failed me yet, and believing him when he said he wouldn't hurt me was more dangerous to me than anything else.

"Loyalty is fickle. Lucifer hasn't been here in centuries, songbird. It is difficult to remain loyal to someone who abandoned you, and many are just as likely to hurt you out of spite because of what you are. Hell is no place for a living and breathing witch. There's only one demon I would trust with you, but he isn't powerful enough to protect you if others were to find out you're here. We cannot simply wait for Willow to open the gateway, either. You saw what the demons and souls were like there. It's too dangerous. I don't have another choice but to bring you with me, as much as we would both like to avoid that," he said, dismissing any suggestions I might have made.

"How is me dying any worse than getting trapped in the Second Circle?" I asked, hating this with every fiber of my being. No matter what choice I made, I was never going to leave this place.

"I'm not going to let you get trapped in Lust, but you're going to have to trust me a little. We'll get you through, and I'll do whatever I must to make that happen," he said, that gentle look in his eyes communicating exactly why this was a terrible idea.

Trust.

"I don't know if I can. I don't know if I'm capable of trusting someone like that," I said, hanging my head forward. I reached out and grabbed the matching shirt, tearing it off the hanger and tossing it to the bed to wait for the opportunity to change.

He sighed, moving to the bed and gathering the pants he'd set aside. He tucked them under his arm, and for a moment I thought he might change then and there, but he didn't and moved toward the door to the hallway outside.

"You have a choice to make. There is no way for me to travel through the Nine Circles fast enough to guarantee your safety if I leave you here. It will take half a second for a demon to decide to make a meal out of you, though admittedly, decidedly longer for them to actually ingest your corpse. That is the fate that will befall you if you choose to remain here rather than trusting me to give you a *chance* at survival. Yes, you will have to be weighed by each circle. It isn't often that living bodies arrive in Hell. Most of its inhabitants are mere souls who are condemned to this place, but a living being cannot step foot upon Raum's scales and be assigned to a circle. You'll have to pay your respects to the lords who would otherwise see you in chains," he explained, listing out my options, if you could call them that.

Neither was a picnic.

"You make it sound like such a lovely vacation. Is it any wonder I don't want to go?" I asked, scoffing as he kept his face carefully blank.

"Let me finish," he said, the stern note to his voice making me pause.

"If there were a way around it, I would not subject you to the torments of Hell. But if I do not bring you through the circles, the lords will feel your presence here regardless, if they haven't already. Some even fell through the gateway with you and know you're here, and it is only a matter of time before they all make the journey and come to judge you at once. You can either face each of the sins one-on-one or be buried in the onslaught of them all without me here to help you through it. I would not leave you to face that alone, songbird," he said, and even I had to admit, facing all the sins at once felt like something that would tear me in two.

What would that even look like?

"So either you come with me, or we both wait for the lords to come before we even begin our journey. One will save time and be more likely to result in your freedom, but the choice is yours in the end. I won't make it for you when it is your life to live," he added, making my breath stall in my lungs.

The choice was mine.

It may have only been the ability to choose how I died, but it was mine to make regardless.

"Beel—" I started to say his name, cutting off when I realized what I'd nearly done.

His mouth parted, as if he might say something but decided better of it. "I'll give you some time to get changed and think about your options. I'll be close enough to keep you safe, but lock and barricade the door after I leave," he said with a smirk, shoving the dresser to the side with a single hand so he could open the door wide enough to pass through.

Then he was gone, and I closed the door and did what I could to make the room safe.

Like he'd needed to tell me to.

I finally bent down, unknotting the laces of my shoes and toeing them off my feet. It didn't seem as though he planned to return too quickly, but I didn't dare risk nudity for any longer than necessary. I shoved my foot into a pant leg forcefully, determined to change quickly. My other leg followed, and I shimmied the pants up my legs. They tucked up beneath my skirt, which I only raised when I was confident the pants were in place and covered the tops of my thighs and the lacy underwear that barely covered the most intimate part of me. Reaching behind me, I unzipped the back of my uniformed skirt and let it fall to my feet, kicking it to the side. I tore the coordinating top off the hanger, the black of it nearly translucent in places.

I tugged it over my head over the camisole that had been part of my uniform, letting it settle into place. Only when the wide bandeau part of the shirt settled over my breasts, the underwire within keeping them in place, did I work the straps of the camisole down my arms and pull the garment down over my hips to discard it as well. The translucent part covered my chest up to the neck but for a plunge at the center that revealed the smallest line of cleavage, a crisscross of straps working over my collarbone and shoulders.

The top was short, just barely brushing the top of the pants but leaving me covered enough to feel comfortable. I felt better with more fabric to cover my body, looking toward the door where Beelzebub had left me to change in privacy in an almost gentlemanly fashion.

What he didn't understand was that I'd seen what a gentleman did in the dead of night, that I knew good manners often hid the cruelest of beasts, and I greatly preferred the honesty the demon offered. He may not have been a good man, but he had never claimed to be. He never claimed that his demented actions would be for the greater good, never hid behind that excuse in an attempt to seek absolution from his victims.

There was something beautiful in the way the archdemon knew he was a monster and owned the part of himself that so many others would have been ashamed of.

14

BEELZEBUB

I left Margot alone for several hours, giving her the time she needed to process the information I'd given her. It seemed like an easy choice to me, but I didn't dare pretend to understand the nuance of human emotion. Archdemons and demons didn't experience them, and though I had spent my entire existence surrounded by human souls, the complexities of what drove them in life hardly mattered once they'd been condemned to eternal torture in Hell.

I didn't dare go far from her, not with the knowledge of the other demons roaming the halls of Raum's home. I might have been able to keep the lord of Purgatory appeased and entertained with my presence, but that wouldn't stop any of his underlings from wandering too close.

For that reason, I stayed with Raum in his office at the foot of the stairs, forcing him to keep the door open so I could monitor the door to the room where I'd left her. It was intended to house what Raum referred to as *forcible guests*, demons who weren't quite prisoners but that he didn't want roaming freely through his home either. It might have been locked from the inside instead of the outside on this day, but that didn't change its purpose in the end.

Margot was not free to wander, and doing so would only lead to her getting hurt. I hoped the room had served as the temporary haven she needed and provided her with the solitude I knew she preferred from the time I'd spent watching her in Hollow's Grove, but I wouldn't always be able to offer her this moment of peace on our journey. The sooner she realized there was no true safety in Hell, the better off she would be. The only constant she could rely on, the only thing that would protect her from the dangers of this realm, was me.

But she wasn't ready to talk about *that,* and I didn't have any inclination to force the conversation. We were both trapped in a purgatory of our own, waiting for the day that her enchantment wore off and I stopped feeling drawn to the witch I should have hated. Her kind had taken Lucifer from me for centuries, had destroyed the illusion I'd held that it would always be Him and me facing the world together.

But He'd abandoned me without hesitation, all too willing to spend centuries apart rather than take me with Him. There'd been a time when the knowledge that He trusted only me to see to His affairs in Hell in His absence had soothed some of my bruised ego, but that time had long since passed.

I groaned, dropping into the seat opposite Raum where he sat on the other side of the desk he occupied. The vantage point allowed me to watch Margot's door still, but I didn't miss the way the closest soul startled at my sudden proximity. There was no paperwork atop the surface of the desk, nothing to indicate that this was a place of work aside from the furniture itself. The walls were covered in black painted bookshelves that were immaculately taken care of despite the piles of books he'd loaded them with. Raum was the lord of Limbo, in charge of Purgatory, where all souls entered when they first died. Under normal circumstances, when the person died before plummeting into the afterlife, he was responsible for weighing the soul and determining what sin claimed ownership of them. There was an enormous eight-pointed scale atop a dais at the corner of the room, the metal and mechanisms creating a sort of star shape if one were to ever look down upon it from above. The very center held golden coins, and as a soul stood before it, one rolled down into a bowl.

A coin for an act of sin.

Each of the soul's life choices were tallied, weighed as the soul whimpered for absolution. Praying to a God that would not hear him from this place, if he ever would have from the earthen plane.

The soul that waited before the scale eyed the mound of gold coins that had gathered in the point dedicated to Fraud, swallowing nervously as Raum waved his hand passively. The coins retreated into the center as a blast of wind tore through the room, catching the soul and dragging him out the open door beside the dais.

Carrying him to Fraud itself.

"Next," Raum said, drawing my attention away from the scale to look over at the woman who would face judgment next. Some souls were quick to be judged; others took hours on end. The very thought of sitting at this desk and presiding over judgments day in and day out made me fidget.

The mirror of the sun above the surface had begun to set, and as much as I wanted to allow Margot to continue to have peace, there was little choice but to pull her from her haven and feed her. She had to be starving. I toyed with the cup on the desk before tossing back a sip of the amber liquid. The strength of the liquor burned a path down my throat, so much stronger than the alcohol had been in Hollow's Grove. I'd missed it, I realized. Missed the strength that could knock me on my ass if I wanted to sink into oblivion. Obsession and avarice weren't my sins, but gluttony could apply to far more than just the desire to lose oneself in food and drink.

I'd rather have sunk into Margot than the bottle, for once in my miserable existence, and I despised that for myself. She'd sung herself right into the depths of my sin, twisting my favored vices and making this growing obsession with her more powerful than any of them.

"Djall? Could you go ask our guest to join us, please?" Raum asked, and I knew the demon was having the same thoughts. But even more than that, he was a creature of habit. He ate at the same time every day, keeping a predictable, mind-numbing schedule he clung to with a desperation that I would never understand.

The female demon appeared in the open doorway to the office, nodding her assent before she disappeared up the stairs. "I'll do it," I called, pushing my chair back to stand. The thought of her seeking Margot out in the room she'd claimed as a sanctuary made me tense. If anyone was going to wander into her space, it would be me. I also didn't think Margot would be inclined to leave the room for anyone but me after my warnings earlier, and the last thing I needed was her revealing how much I'd shared of the nature of demons and the relationship I did not have with my brothers.

"Don't be silly," Raum said, flashing me a smile that was all teeth. I moved anyway, following Djall on her way up the stairs. She beat me to the door, rapping her fist against it three times.

"Lord Raum would like to request your presence for dinner," she said simply, but there was no sound on the other side of the door.

"It's alright, Margot," I said, sidestepping Djall and nudging her out of the way. I placed my hand on the door, dismissing the demon with a wave of my hand. I heaved a sigh of relief when the demon relented and vacated the landing, returning downstairs where Raum waited.

I didn't need to worry that Margot would ever pick a fight she couldn't win by any means, but I did need to worry that she wouldn't even try to defend herself. She might have magic at her disposal, but she refused to use it due to her own loathing for the way it manifested, and that meant, in a place that was teeming with the energy of the Source, she was at a great disadvantage.

"Songbird?" I asked, knocking on the door softly. "You've got to be hungry." The sound of the dresser being pushed back from the door made me smile, the knowledge that my songbird had done as I'd told her warming something within me.

She tugged open the door slowly, peeking out until she saw me staring down at her. Then she opened the door fully, her body encased in a red shirt that skimmed over her curves and the red pants I'd seen her pull from the closet. She looked so much younger bathed in all that fabric, her features somehow more cautious, as if she didn't quite know what to do with herself.

I held out a hand for her to take, nodding when she ignored it and stepped around it into the hallway. I wanted to be proud of her for not letting her fear keep her grounded to that tiny room, but there would be some circles in Hell where getting her to sit still would be what was best. We were safer in Purgatory than we would be in some of the other circles. Raum and I had a better relationship than I shared with most of the other lords, very little tension lingering between us. Perhaps that was due to the fact that he was a noble demon who had risen in the ranks by his own merit, but was not an archdemon with the same level of power and proximity to the Source and Lucifer. We would never be equals, purely for the fact that we'd been created in very different situations and with different purposes.

We could not be rivals striving for our creator's attention, not when Lucifer barely paid Raum any mind Himself.

That didn't mean Raum wouldn't try to manipulate me or any situation I found myself in to his benefit.

The other archdemons and I, however, butted heads like siblings competing for our father's affection, even in His absence. I had better relationships with some of them than others, but all of us were prone to bickering and jealousy at times. My own twin brother, the demon who had been created on the same day and from the same earth as me, was the only one I even remotely trusted. Belphegor had not become an archdemon, my form taking too much of the Source as Lucifer created us simultaneously, and that had made my brother bitter as a child.

He'd grown out of that in the centuries since our childhoods, thankfully, and we had a deeply connected relationship now, but that didn't mean we hadn't come to blows plenty of times.

I made my way down the stairs, feeling Margot following quickly at my back. She'd changed from her heels into a pair of sturdy boots, and I was grateful for it. She'd need them in the burning sands of Purgatory as we made our way to the Second Circle.

Raum emerged from his office as we made our way down the stairs, looking at Margot with unabashed lust even though she'd done everything she could to safely hide her appeal beneath fabric. His mouth spread into a broad smile as he looked her over, her shoulder-length blond layers framing that heartrending face that was like a painting of an angel.

She stepped off the last stair at my side, raising her chin as we made our way toward Raum. Her body was tense at my side, framed in what I assumed she wanted to look like confidence, like she was at ease with the male gaze on her.

I knew better, knew how uncomfortable his staring would make her feel. Even still, I couldn't entirely blame him. I knew all too well that I was drawn to her like a moth to a flame.

"Well then," Raum said, snagging my attention. His stare was on me now, his nod certain as he turned to guide us toward the dining room. I followed far less smoothly than the grace Margot displayed, stumbling over myself as Margot's eyes found mine. The brightness of her shirt reflected on her face, adding color to her cheeks and brightening her eyes until they looked like molten lava. Raum rounded the edge of the doorway, pausing just within the dining room and holding out a hand for Margot. She took it cautiously, sliding her palm against his in a way that felt far more intimate than just a casual brush of skin. Everything in me tightened as I stood, closing the distance as Raum raised her hand to his mouth and pressed a kiss to the back of it.

Margot flushed, tugging back her hand in an attempt to keep

the contact as brief as possible without offending the other demon by rejecting him.

I growled.

Raum smiled, turning to me with a lightness and humor on his face that said he knew *exactly* what he was doing, driving me to the point of insanity that I couldn't seem to control.

"I do so hate to abandon you so quickly," Raum said, ducking his head forward. "But duty calls me elsewhere."

It was bullshit and we both knew it. He *never* missed his precisely timed meals for anything.

He nodded to me, making sure I knew exactly what he was up to. Giving Margot his approval to move through to the next circle when I could convince her to make the journey alongside me, but also leaving us alone so that I had a chance of convincing her to do just that. Her fear would keep her stationary if I allowed it, and I didn't trust leaving her with Raum for one second.

Especially not after the way he'd looked at her.

I moved forward, holding out my arm as Raum left the room. Margot sighed but came up beside me, refusing to take my proffered arm. The fact that she'd allowed Raum to touch her might have irritated me greatly if I didn't understand the reasoning behind it. She and Raum didn't have this infernal pull between them. The risk of her magic bleeding into him through touch was great, though it would have been less potent without the initial influence of her song to drag him under her spell.

I pulled out her chair, watching as she lowered herself into it with the kind of elegance that couldn't be learned. She was all smooth movements and rhythm, aware of her body in a way that made every action feel like a dance.

Every movement felt like seduction.

She turned to me as I took my own seat far less gracefully, mimicking her motions as she lowered the cloth napkin to her lap. "You must be starving," I noted, taking the first platter and serving her a small portion. Food in Hell was different from the food on the surface; even though many of the plants we managed to grow and animals we kept as protein were *mirrors* of what existed on the surface, I didn't profess to know Margot's tastes well enough to know how they would translate to what she could find here.

She stared down at the fruit I'd placed on her plate, the slices nearly a match for her dress. "What is it?" she asked, watching as I scooped a larger serving onto my own plate.

I took the next platter, serving the edible flower onto her plate as she watched and tilted her head in curiosity. "A fruit that blooms on a prickly cactus tree that grows in the desert of this circle," I explained, waiting for her to taste either that or the blossom on her plate. But she waited for me to continue serving her roasted meats and root vegetables to accompany what I'd already served.

When she finally raised her fork, she paused to look at me. "Will eating this do anything to me?" she asked, the hesitation in that question far too nervous for my taste.

"Do something how?" I asked, stabbing a piece of root vegetable with my own fork and guiding it to my mouth. I chewed thoughtfully, swallowing so she could see that it wasn't poisoned.

Margot flushed. "In Greek mythology, Hades trapped Persephone by offering her pomegranate seeds. If I eat this, will I still be able to return home?" she asked, drawing a smirk from me.

"Are you comparing me to Hades?" I asked, keeping my tone light and playful.

"Most mythology was grounded in some version of the truth," she said with pinkened cheeks. "I just don't want to reduce my chances of making it above the surface again."

"No, eating our food will not trap you in Hell, songbird," I said softly, nodding to her plate. She poked the fruit with her fork, guiding it to her mouth and sniffing it. Her pink tongue stuck out slowly, licking the surface of the fruit as she tested the flavor before sliding it into her mouth and eating it with relish.

I bit back my groan, adjusting my seat as discreetly as I could.

"I hardly think it matters at any rate. Whether you've decided we'll make our way to the Ninth Circle and back after speaking with Lucifer or wait for the lords here, your body would not last that long if you did not eat, and then you would be trapped here in death anyway," I said, watching as her face went blank. She continued to eat, her own hunger forcing her to ignore the discomfort those words gave her. She couldn't afford to let her strength flag, not if she wanted to stand a chance of passing through the circles.

"It doesn't really feel like I have much of a choice," she said, the numbness of the statement making it clear that she had spent her time in solitude trying to find a workaround. She dreaded the journey we would have to make, but she wasn't foolish enough to choose certain death over it either.

"Not all choices are good ones," I said with a shrug as I placed another forkful of food on my tongue and chewed. Swallowing before I continued, I said, "Sometimes it's just the lesser of two evils."

"Spoken like a true demon," she said, her voice bitter and hollow. It lacked any and all of the hope I'd grown used to hearing from her. "I need to get home as soon as possible, so I will do whatever it takes to make that happen. Is me coming with you going to be the fastest way?"

"Would you like more to eat?" I asked, reaching forward to serve her once again.

"I would like an answer!" she asked, slapping my hand away from the serving spoon. She stared at where she'd touched me as if she couldn't believe she'd done so, and I resisted the urge to smile at her.

Telling her she was adorable when she was angry would get me nowhere.

"No, the fastest way would be for me to fly ahead and leave you behind. But this is the way that is most likely to result in your returning home at all. Facing the lords on your own will not go well for you, and whatever it is that has you so antsy to return to Hollow's Grove won't matter much when you're condemned to Hell permanently, or dead," I answered, placing my fork on the table beside my plate and steepling my hands over it.

"I don't understand why they wouldn't be loyal to Lucifer. Surely they know that He could return at any moment now that Willow knows the ways of her magic," she argued.

"They are demons," I said, wishing that she understood how brittle loyalty could be between our kind. Allegiances were constantly shifting and evolving, reshaping and creating something new. With Lucifer gone, I trusted no one fully in this place.

It was literally new territory, a kingdom without its king, because I had stepped in to fill the power vacuum and now with me gone . . .

There was no one.

"So are you," she spat, the venom in her words accompanying the motion of her pushing out her chair. She stood, staring at me with the faint sheen of tears in her eyes.

"Exactly," I growled, pushing to my own feet. My hands curled around the edge of the table, leaning into it and closer to her as I spat the word. "I know what they are all capable of, far better than you ever will. It is the very same thing that *I* am capable of, and you would do well to remember that the next time you think to doubt that I know what is best for you here. My only goal is to keep you safe, so the last thing I need is you making that difficult at every turn."

Margot stared at me for a brief moment, huffing out a breath.

And then she turned on her heel, fleeing the dining room and making her way back to the false haven she'd created. I stared after her for a moment, wondering if I'd pushed too far.

God be damned.

15

MARGOT

I retreated to the bedroom Beelzebub had taken me to initially, not having the words left to fight with him. Even his outburst was one of frustration and not true anger, and that left me reeling more than it should have. I *knew* I was being difficult in my need to return to the surface as quickly as possible, and I would suck it up and do what was necessary to make that happen.

But that didn't mean I had to be thrilled that I would do it with Beelzebub at my side. I wanted a lonely, empty room where I could lock myself away and wait until it was time for Willow to open the door to Hell; instead I'd have to travel with the one male I found insufferable.

Would he keep me safe? Yes.

Would he also be so hot and cold that I didn't know what to expect or even what I wanted to be true? Also yes.

I hauled open the door, slipping through the passage into the red bedroom. My hands slid into my hair, tugging at the roots as my mouth opened on a silent scream.

I just wanted to go home.

I wanted the comfort of my own bed, of the chair I placed in front of my door every night and the bells that hung from my doorknob to alert me if anyone even attempted to open it. I'd done everything I could to create a place that felt safe to rest my eyes and sleep, and I didn't know how I would function without it in this place filled with demon lords who wanted to test me and would trap me here forever if I failed.

I turned to close the door behind me, barely glancing up from the floor as I grasped the doorknob and used it to swing the door closed. The sound of flesh slapping against it drew my stare up to meet Beelzebub's fiery stare. He glared down at me, the tension in his jaw hard enough to chisel stone as he held the door aloft. His fingers were splayed wide, revealing just how massive his hand was with knuckles slightly bent and fingertips that dug into the wood to reveal the anger that corded his every muscle.

"I am doing my best to remain patient with you," he said, holding the door still. He didn't move to step into the room, but kept himself planted in the doorway, pausing on the threshold as if he didn't want to invade the room I'd claimed as my own.

"This is patient?" I asked, crossing my arms over my chest as I backed away from him.

"Yes, it is. You're being difficult strictly for the sake of it at this point. I have explained why you need to come with me," he said, continuing on with whatever reprimand he thought to give me like I was an errant child having a tantrum and not a woman filled with fear over what was to come. "But it is beyond difficult to reason with you when you fight me every step of the way," he added, and I moved farther into the room to put distance between us.

I sighed, dropping my chin to my chest. My cheeks burned with warmth, a feeling that was distinctly reminiscent of shame flooding through me. "I'm sorry," I said, shaking my head as I moved toward the window to look out.

Beelzebub took my words as an invitation, stepping over the threshold and entering the bedroom when he felt my anger slip away. "I just want to help, songbird, but you've got to let me. We can't keep going around in the same circles. We're wasting time," he said, crossing his arms over his bare chest.

Not for the first time, I wished the bastard would wear a fucking shirt. His comfort in his own body was disarming at best, distracting at worst.

A distraction I neither wanted nor could afford, to be exact. Of all the people in the world for me to feel that frisson of awareness for, that tingle of attraction and the *what if*, he was the last one I would have chosen.

What if I was normal? What if I could stand the thought of being touched?

"Then let's go," I said, raising my chin with a faux confidence I didn't feel. I was absolutely terrified by the prospect of leaving the room that had started to feel relatively safe and wandering out into Hell. I very vividly remembered the way the demons and souls had fought to get to me, and that alone would have been enough to send me spiraling into a corner to hide under any normal circumstances. The threat of the lords was another thing entirely.

But Willow needed me. She needed the information that only I seemed capable of sharing, and when I needed her, she'd do whatever it took to be there.

I owed her the same.

Beelzebub studied me for a moment, trying to peer into the sudden determination on my face. I felt the way he read me like an open book, pausing briefly before he gave a stern nod and turned to the open bedroom door. He glided down the stairs at a smooth pace that I had to hurry to follow, accepting two canteens from the demon who waited at the bottom of the stairs.

He stopped suddenly as the doors opened, revealing the reddened, sandy earth of Purgatory. I crashed into his back, my cheek slamming into the center of his wings. My hand swung forward with the sudden loss of momentum, tapping against the back of his thigh as my forearm brushed the smooth fabric of his pants where they covered his ass.

I stared up at him, rooted to the spot as he twisted to look over his shoulder at me. I could barely meet his eye with the way

I felt my cheeks flush with embarrassment, scrambling back to put distance between us as he held out a canteen for me to take. I slid the strap around my waist, tying it into a tight knot in an attempt to ignore the satisfied grin on his face. Raum emerged from the room at the foot of the stairs, leaning into the doorway as he watched us.

"At least buy me dinner first, songbird. What kind of man do you take me for?" Beelzebub teased, the lightness in his voice so at odds with the nerves I felt. Beelzebub grabbed me by the hand, tugging me out the open door before I could change my mind.

I glanced back to find Raum waving a cheerful goodbye, his other arm crossed over his chest as he laughed.

The door closed behind us, and we were lost to the sands of Purgatory.

At least two hours passed before we so much as paused, and I was left to struggle to keep up with the pace Beelzebub had set with his legs that were much longer than mine. He didn't seem to be aware of my struggles, and I didn't care to voice them. If I was going to do this, if I was going to make this journey through Hell itself, then I knew I couldn't allow anyone to see the barest hint of weakness.

I had learned enough, surrounded by the manipulations and politics of a corrupt Coven as I had been, to know that anything would be used against me.

The heat of the desert pressing down on us didn't help matters, my entire body warming and growing slick with the distinct sheen of sweat. Sand clung to me when random bursts of wind tore through the desert, making my skin feel gritty. Beelzebub didn't break a sweat as he trudged through the deep sands, and I found myself hating him for how little he was affected by something that exhausted me.

The sand beneath my feet was uneven, mounds of it having formed into little hills in the wind that we had to make our way over or through. Sharp, jagged rocks protruded from the ground in the distance, but there was nothing else around us.

I took another sip of water from my canteen, relishing in the moisture it provided to my dry throat and mouth that had begun to feel like sandpaper.

The only saving grace was the distinct lack of heat coming off what I supposed passed for a sun, so that I at the very least didn't need to fear a sunburn on top of it all. I'd been born and raised in a tiny secret village in Massachusetts, descended from the English settlers who had claimed Salem centuries prior; the sun and I did *not* get along well.

"How is there daylight?" I asked finally, peering up at the mass of dim light overhead. It wasn't as bright as the sun, and wasn't as solid. Whereas the sun was something very visible to pinpoint in the sky, this felt like looking up at it from underwater. It was blurry and not quite tangible.

The "sky" seemed to fade into nothing, to have both an end that came too soon and to be endless, a feat I knew was impossible. We had fallen through the portal into Hell below us, landing deep within the chasm of the earth, or at least it had felt like it. I had no knowledge of whether or not Hell was actually within the earth, or if the gateway had brought us to another realm entirely. I didn't pretend to be the most dutiful student when it came to the legends of Heaven and Hell.

"Heaven and Hell are direct mirrors of the earthen plane," Beelzebub answered. My ankle twisted suddenly, nearly collapsing as sand slid down the hill and nearly took me with it. Beelzebub moved to stabilize me but hesitated to touch me, and I nodded him off to communicate that I was fine. "Lucifer may not be able to make a sun the way His father could, but He can certainly mimic one here, in a place drowning in the Source," Beelzebub continued, turning to keep walking. I scrambled to follow after him, hating that out here I was entirely dependent on him. Any objection I may have staged would have been an impossibility, a threat with no intention of following through. I wanted him to know that when I threatened him, I would make good on such promises, that they weren't hollow and to be ignored.

We both knew I had no choice but to stick with him.

I followed him, finding the sandy ground beneath us increasingly difficult to walk on. I'd never been allowed to leave Crystal Hollow, only knowing the beach at the bottom of the cliff. So few people bothered to make their way down there, outside of the White witches who favored the crystals that grew from the cliffside, that I could probably count on one hand the number of times I'd touched sand before.

But this sand was different from the sand of the beach I knew; it was deeper and softer, allowing my feet to sink in up to my ankles like it could swallow me whole. It made it even more exhausting to trudge through.

My boots could only do so much to stop me from feeling the scorching heat of the red earth, acting as a barrier to prevent me from being burned, but the suffocating warmth drenched my socks in sweat as we walked.

"Is every circle like this?" I asked, wiping the sweat from my forehead.

"Not at all," Beelzebub said, placing a hand on his forehead to block out the setting light in the sky as he looked toward the horizon. I followed his gaze, feeling like I'd suffered through the sight of a mirage intended to torment thirsty souls.

There.

Barely visible in the distance, an oasis of a garden existed. It was lush, with trees that hung over and shielded a pool of water tucked in between sand dunes. Flowers bloomed all around it, making the land seem fertile and teeming with life, such a stark contrast to the otherwise completely devoid First Circle that would haunt my dreams.

I raised my canteen to my lips once again, my mouth dry in spite of Beelzebub's constant reminders for me to drink. He didn't seem to need as much water as I did, but he took great care to make sure I didn't dehydrate in the unfamiliar heat.

His deep chuckle was his only response as he took the canteen from me, strapping it around my waist once again. "You aren't seeing things, songbird. The garden is really there."

"How?" I asked, allowing him to slide his hand into mine in my rapt fascination with the oasis. The calluses of his fingers grated against my sensitive skin, touching every nerve ending and lighting me on fire where he touched me. I resisted the temptation to pull away, not wanting to allow him to know I was so bothered by his proximity. It didn't make sense to be so affected by something so simple.

I was the Red witch, and yet sometimes it seemed like it was me who was trapped under his spell.

We approached the haven, trudging through the deep sand. I stumbled to the side in my hurry to reach the place of sanctuary, drawn to the shaded seclusion like a moth to a flame. Beelzebub seemed to decide he'd had enough of waiting for me to make my way through the deep sand, moving so quickly I didn't even realize he'd swept me off my feet until I hung suspended. His chest pressed against the side of my face, his Enochian runes glowing as I stared up at him with wide eyes. He kept his hands placed respectfully, gripping my bicep as one arm supported my mid-back, and the other was tucked into the back of my knees.

"You really hate the heat," he observed, barely glancing down at me as he navigated the sand without trouble.

"We don't get many overwhelmingly hot days in Crystal Hollow," I said, staring at the haven as he approached. When it was only a few feet away, I patted at his chest without a word, pleased when he obeyed the silent command and placed me on my feet. I took the few steps toward the haven, sighing in contentment when my booted feet touched the distinct sponginess of grass. There was something beautiful in the softness beneath me, in the way the green blades didn't shift to the side and knock me off-balance. I took a few steps toward the pool, determined to bathe myself in the cool, relaxing waters until Beelzebub grabbed my forearm gently, shaking his head at me wordlessly as he guided me into the trees.

He looked around, as if searching the desert surrounding us before he approached one tree in particular.

"The water's a trap meant to lure you here. It's no mirage, this one really exists, but there are creatures who call it home and are very, very hungry for flesh. It isn't often that a living being somehow wanders into Hell, so they have to survive off pure energy for survival. Eating you would be decadent, like eating a chocolate cake after a lifetime of kale," he explained, smirking when I grimaced up at him. I wasn't sure I liked that analogy, and I couldn't even pinpoint why.

Perhaps it was just the disgusting nature of talking about *eating* me.

"Then why bring me here at all?" I asked, crossing my arms over my stomach.

"This is the entrance to the Second Circle," he said, smirking as he studied me. He pried one of my arms away from my belly, covering the back of my hand with his and threading his fingers through the gaps between mine. The words had no sooner left his mouth than I felt the distinct proximity of lust, of the magic that called to what flowed through my veins.

"So soon?" I asked, my voice trembling. The statement was almost laughable, because a few moments prior, I would have given anything to escape the heat. But the nearness of the very circle that frightened me more than any other erased any relief I'd felt.

"Look at me," Beelzebub said soothingly, reaching out with a hand to catch me under my chin. He shifted my stare up to his, and he seemed as shocked by the gentle touch as I did, as if the inclination to comfort me was as strange to him as it was to me.

He hated me, I reminded myself. Hated my kind, and the feeling was mutual.

So why did some of the tension leave my body, dropping my shoulders from where they'd risen into my neck as I looked at the red eyes that reminded me of home?

"I can't do this," I whispered, despising the vulnerability the words revealed. I felt close to tears as his face softened from surprise to empathy. I'd have thought him incapable of such a thing, with emotions that were so distant compared to the ones I wore openly on my sleeve.

"Yes, you can. You're a survivor, and you're stronger than you give yourself credit for," he said, moving half a step closer to me. He leaned down over me, his chest only a breath away from mine. I lingered, staying trapped in that moment as his lips parted ever so slightly.

His head lowered as he curled his back further, pressing his forehead to mine. My intake of breath was sharp, his scent filling my lungs as I stumbled back and put distance between us again for both our sakes.

He cleared his throat, shaking his head as if he could shake off my spell. "When we arrive in Lust, I am going to do everything I can to convince Asmodeus to permit you to pass. I've got a plan. Just trust me, and follow my lead," he said, brushing his hand against mine.

The slow glide of his pinky finger against my own raised carnal images that flashed through my head, the distinct feeling of bodies pressing against me flooding my system. I knew it was the proximity to the entrance to the Second Circle playing games with my body, and the knowledge that we would soon pass through was daunting.

Self-control was already difficult. How would it be once we entered?

I glanced toward the pool once more, and I could have sworn I saw the distinct ghosts of bodies writhing together around the gardens surrounding us. I shook my head, forcing the imagery out of my mind. "How do we pass into Lust?" I asked, steadying my voice.

"Pick an apple, songbird," he said, pointing upward. I allowed my gaze to follow and saw the apples hanging from the branches just above my head. I wouldn't be able to reach them on my own, so I searched for any that hung just low enough.

There were none, but I paused in my perusal when a single yellow apple stared back at me. It almost shimmered like gold, the color so breathtaking and metallic as it glittered in the fading light that my words came without thought. "That one," I said, studying it intently.

Beelzebub moved quickly, bending so he could grasp me around the backs of my thighs. He lifted me up with the press of his arms wrapped around just above my knees, keeping my legs pinned together. I had a moment of appreciation, knowing he'd acted in the way that would be more comfortable for me—less intimate.

I reached up to take the apple, pausing as he shifted his grip on me, supporting me with one arm so he could take my hand in his.

As one, we wrapped my fingers around the apple and pulled, tugging it free from the branch with a snap.

And we were plunged into a swirl of red and black, tossing and turning through it as if suspended in darkness.

16

MARGOT

The gardens on the other side of the portal opened. An apple tree that mimicked the one from the desert sanctuary spread wide, forming a doorway, as we were thrown out through the gap. The subtle fairy lights twinkled as Beelzebub wrapped me in his embrace when I stumbled off-balance and careened forward. He steadied me, his broad chest pressed against my spine as his massive wings curled around me, caging me into a net of safety as he pulled us to a slow stop. He held me suspended in his grip, my own toes dangling less than a foot off the ground until he eased me down and his wings spread wide to allow me my first unhindered glimpse of the Second Circle.

I swallowed, glancing at the stairs that ascended out of the garden area we'd emerged into. They led to a huge balcony overlooking the cliff, the railings ornately carved from mahogany. A few stragglers remained on that balcony, their attention drawn to us as the tree shifted behind us and closed the pathway back to Limbo, cutting me off from my escape as my stress climbed ever higher. I knew this place, felt its call in the depths of my soul.

This was the circle that would claim me when I succumbed to my mortality, the place that would become my home for an eternity once I joined the damned. This was where my aunt's soul had come to rest after the Coven tore her apart for her corruption.

Lust.

I swallowed as the bystanders turned away from us, seeming to find us uninteresting in comparison to whatever they were watching at the bottom of the cliffs below. They leaned over the railing, their attention fixated in a way that made my skin crawl. I didn't even know what it was they watched yet, but something in the flush of their cheeks and the intimate positioning they took with their partners was confirmation enough that I did not want to be here.

Beelzebub gave me a moment to acclimate as he straightened and stepped up beside me, turning his head to stare down at me as I watched the bystanders on the patio. "What are they looking at?" I asked, hating that I needed the answer. I needed to prepare myself for what I was about to see, for the suffering I would witness that had somehow become entertainment. The legends of what occurred in the Nine Circles constantly circulated in Hollow's Grove; they were a message to enjoy our time and live to the fullest of our ability with little regard for piety. What difference did it make when you were already damned simply for possessing magic from the Source in the first place?

"They're watching the souls who are not currently in Asmodeus's favor," he explained, taking the first step forward. It was slow, giving me time to ease into the motion and grasp the words before we reached the steps that would lead us up to what I had to assume was a viewing platform. "They remain nude for an eternity, and they're dragged over the cliffs so that their flesh that so defined their sins is torn and shredded on the rock. The Second Circle strips them of their worldly beauty, turning them into nothing but meat and bone."

"And these people watching? Are they the demons native to the Second Circle?" I asked. The horror that filled me knowing that this was like foreplay, that this sign of violence had somehow become twisted into something arousing in this house of horrors, came with a sudden gasp that I suppressed with a choked sound. I couldn't even be surprised, not when I'd personally witnessed what humanity was capable of. We were the ones who were supposed to have a conscience, who were supposed to care what happened to our own kind.

Demons had always been known to be cruel, to enjoy and thrive on the suffering of others. Of course they would get off on the torment here, reveling in the tearing and rending of flesh.

"Some, but not most. Most of Asmodeus's demons are too busy with the festivities inside to occupy their time out here," he said, shocking me as I studied the collection of maybe ten pairs lingering along the boardwalk-type patio.

"These are souls condemned to Lust? Why are they not condemned to the same fate as the ones on the cliffs?" I asked, hesitantly taking the elbow he offered as we reached the bottom of the steps. He guided me up them slowly, and I felt completely out of place as I took in the attire of those lingering on the patio. The dresses and tuxedos were formal, but they were far more indecent than I would have expected of any event above the surface. The men who wore tuxedos had long since lost their coats, their dress shirts unbuttoned and sleeves rolled up. Some men wore their ties tied around their throat in a tight knot that was held in an iron grip by their partner; others had already unfastened their belts.

I clenched my teeth at the sight, shifting my attention to the woman closest to me. Her deep ruby gown skimmed the floor, but the fabric was mostly sheer. A single panel that was not see-through hid her intimate places from view. The top was lace and dipped low in the front, the back bare in a way that seemed to be a cross between lingerie and an evening gown. In spite of the revealed flesh, she moved in a way that was all confidence, comfortable in her nudity in a way that I could never hope to achieve. So many of the Reds were similar above the surface, seeing their bodies as something to be embraced and wielding their sexuality like a weapon. There'd been days when I'd dreamt of feeling that way about my skin, days when I'd wondered what it would feel like not to wish I could hide every inch of myself, to disguise the evidence of my abuse that came in the scars that lingered both on my skin and in my mind.

She was beautiful, tossing her head back lightly with the quiet murmur of a chuckle as her painted red lips spread into a blinding smile, her dark hair cascading down over her bare back and brushing against the curve of her ass.

Asmodeus approached the couple, trailing the backs of his fingers over the woman's cheek in a moment that felt like a betrayal of everything I knew about genuine affection. It was far more intimate than I'd have expected given her proximity to another man, hinting at a relationship that extended back further than this night.

"Amelia Erotes has been with Asmodeus since her death," Beelzebub said, answering the unvoiced question.

Erotes.

Asmodeus glanced toward us, a sly smile spreading over his handsome face when he took in Beelzebub's presence. That gaze dropped to me, the outer ring of his eye so black it was like a night without any light. The center of it was a deep red, bleeding out into the black circle and blending seamlessly. I wanted nothing more than to turn away from that knowing stare, feeling it sink inside me as he held out an arm for the woman at his side without looking away. She took it, following the direction of his attention.

Her brow rose, and I wondered if she knew what I was. If she had seen enough of her descendants end up in the Second Circle that she knew how to tell us apart from all the rest. From the humans who were guilty of the very sin that so defined our lives. I tore my gaze away, looking at Beelzebub where he stood beside me. The building towered behind him, extending seemingly into the stratosphere, but the ground level consisted of a wall of windows with no interruption to the sightlines of the cliffs where the rest of the souls confined here suffered.

Inside, the light was dim and red, making it difficult to see what was happening within.

The only thing I could make out was movement, writhing masses of motion that made me turn away as my chest and cheeks heated with embarrassment. I should have been expecting something of that nature, given where we were, but to be confronted with it so publicly was another thing entirely. Beelzebub covered my hand with his where it rested over his arm, the soft touch doing nothing to still the racing of my heart.

I felt the magic of the Second Circle dancing over my skin, tormenting me as it brought all the things back to the surface that I was determined to shove down into the well of power within me. But I could do this. I could witness the acts that had scarred me and walk out the other side.

So long as no one touched me, I would survive.

"Margot," Asmodeus said with a familiarity he hadn't earned. He and Amelia stopped in front of us, her head tilting to the side as if she could see exactly what I was. "I can't imagine you've yet had the opportunity to meet your ancestor. This is Amelia, the original Erotes witch."

Amelia took my hand in hers, cradling it gently as she touched her thumb to my wrist and waited. "Your heart still beats," she said, her voice low and soft, more disbelief than anything. Her own thumb did not echo with the steady rhythm of a heartbeat. It couldn't, I realized.

Because Amelia was long since dead.

I nodded, pulling my hand back. I forced it to happen slowly, escaping her touch as if it didn't bother me horribly to feel her skin against mine.

"What is she doing here?" Amelia asked, rounding on Asmodeus. I expected the archdemon to reprimand her tone, to remind her of her place in the circle he ruled over. Instead he chuckled, the sound potent in the air. It touched me, raising the hair on my arms as it tried to sink inside, a seduction in itself and laced with the very magic Lucifer had given to the Red witches.

"Relax, pet," Asmodeus said affectionately, running his fingers through Amelia's hair. "She fell through the gates in the battle with Michael, just the same as the rest of us."

Appeased, Amelia leaned in with a soft smile, pressing her mouth to my cheek demurely. I returned the favor even as my skin crawled with nerves at the very notion of being touched here, like tiny insects crawling over me in a warning of what was to come.

I'd have preferred the bugs.

"Why don't you take her to change into something more appropriate for tonight's festivities?" Asmodeus asked, his gaze narrowing sharply on the place where I gripped Beelzebub's arm tightly.

"That's not necessary. We're just passing through," Beelzebub answered, offering another pat of reassurance.

"Oh no, I *insist*," Asmodeus returned, his teeth gleaming as he stressed the word. Something passed between him and Beelzebub, some kind of silent communication that felt far more political than brotherly. "Amelia has thrown me such a lovely party to celebrate my return, I would be remiss if Margot was not given ample opportunity to get to know Amelia and the future that awaits her."

Something in Amelia seemed to settle, and she dropped her hands to her side as she studied me curiously. "Yes, you simply *must* stay for the festivities now. Come with me and I'll help you get ready," she said, forcing me to look toward Beelzebub. I'd been so desperate for him to leave me in Purgatory, wanting to avoid this entirely in favor of the limbo that would not harm me, but now that we were here, I was terrified to leave his side.

He was the only constant I had, the only person whom I felt remotely confident wouldn't take from me.

"You'll be safe with Amelia, songbird," Beelzebub said, leaning toward me to stare into my eyes as I willed my bottom lip not to shake. "She will see that you are taken care of, and she won't leave you until she has returned you to my side." He turned all that attention to Amelia, to the woman's face that was far softer than I could comprehend. "You should go and spend some time with your ancestor away from all of this, and I'll speak to Asmodeus on your behalf."

I forced myself to separate from Beelzebub, taking the arm Amelia held out for me and letting her intertwine us together as she led me to the doors leading into the building.

"Amelia?" Beelzebub called out as she pulled the door open. "If any harm comes to her against her will, not even Asmodeus will be able to protect you. Am I understood?" The warning raised the hair on my arms, the threat of violence on my behalf warming my chest.

Men had been violent *to* me, but none had ever been violent *for* me.

That distinction pleased me more than I cared to admit.

Amelia giggled in a low tone, but nodded her agreement. "She is safe with me, Lord of Flies," she said, patting my arm gently and guiding me through the now open doors.

I immediately wished we hadn't gone inside. The writhing I'd seen was so much worse without the glass to separate us, my eyes adjusting as Amelia made her way through the path at the center of the room. She headed for the stairwell at the rear of the building, completely unbothered by the sexual acts occurring all around us. To the left, someone moaned: a woman laid out on her side at the edge of an ottoman while a man fucked her. Just beyond that pairing, a man knelt before another man with his throat spread wide. People everywhere had split into pairs or sometimes groups, seeming to find enjoyment in the acts they committed if the pleasure and sounds in the room were any indication.

Pleasure I'd never even begun to feel.

I swallowed as we rounded the bottom corner of the staircase, making our way up the first few steps and putting some distance between us and the sex below. I looked back toward the doorway, feeling the weight of eyes on me. Asmodeus stood, talking to Beelzebub animatedly, but Beelzebub's eyes were locked on me, his head tipped in thought as he watched me for my reaction to all that surrounded us.

He didn't so much as glance at any of the men or women lingering in various stages of undress, nor spare a thought for any of those who walked by him like they might entice him to join them in such things.

His eyes were only for me, his gaze tracking me until we rounded the top of the stairs and moved out of his sight. It shocked me to realize how much of my comfort had slipped away, fading into anxiety the moment I lost sight of him.

Hiding beneath his concern for my well-being, his red eyes burned with a hint of restrained lust that sparked something low in my belly, that stoked the flames I hated to feel building within me.

It was just the magic, I reminded myself.

17

MARGOT

Amelia's bedroom had dark textured wallpaper, golden filigree adorning it with antique furniture and accents along the walls. The built-in bookshelves were painted the same black, covered by books of all shapes and sizes and genres. Her bed was covered with pillows, a mix of red silken sheets and velvet throws making it look like an inviting haven of mixed colors and textures. There was a book tossed over the foot of the bed, the weathered cover and spine hinting that it had been read more than once. It felt like the kind of room that had been built to remind her of Crystal Hollow, of the gothic luxury I'd grown up in, but whereas most rooms designated to Red witches were overwhelming in the presence of the color of our magic, this had been done moderately with balance at the forefront.

"You have excellent taste," I said as she guided me to the chair in front of her vanity. My face stared back at me in the mirror as I lowered myself to sit, the comfortable cushion absorbing my weight and taking some of the pressure off my feet and my ankle that had begun to ache since I'd twisted it in the sand. The mirror on the wall matched the vanity itself, hand-carved designs scrawled into the black surface and painted with a deep antique gold that had lost the shimmer that might have made it too gaudy to be pretty. I turned my gaze away from my reflection to run my hands over the art of the vanity, greatly preferring the beauty of craftsmanship to the face that would stare back at me.

A face that hadn't brought me anything but pain.

"You are perhaps the first Red witch I have encountered who did not obsess over their reflection the moment I sat them in this chair," Amelia said, toying with the ends of my hair where it met my shoulders. She fluffed the layers, and I felt the weight of her stare on the side of my face. It left me little choice but to meet her gaze in the mirror, to carefully skate over my own reflection to give her a small smile and a shrug before my attention shifted to the intricacy of the mirror itself. The border reminded me of the gate that had separated Hollow's Grove from Hell, and I couldn't help the tremble that came to my hands.

I held them tightly in my lap, hoping to disguise the moment of weakness so that Amelia wouldn't see it.

"It is most ironic, considering you have one of the most objectively breathtaking faces of all the Red witches that have come to the Second Circle," she said, raising a hand to wrap around me. She moved slowly, as if she were already aware of my skittishness. Her thumb and finger caught my chin, tipping them up so I couldn't *not* look at my own face without drawing further attention to my reluctance to do so.

Upturned mahogany eyes stared back at me, burning like embers on the edge of being smothered. My cheekbones were high, my lips soft and plump without overwhelming the more delicate features of my face. My skin was ivory, the slight bronze of a tan gracing my skin that never seemed to go away. "I've heard that a lot," I forced myself to say, nodding through the pain of that reality. When I'd been only a girl, the Council had identified me as the beauty of my generation, and for the Red witches who prided themselves on things like sex and beauty and attraction, it had been a victory.

A championship of excellent breeding. Someone to be paired off with a handsome man in the future so we could continue to grace the Erotes line with beautiful children.

It was the same proclamation and attention that had brought Itan to my door at night, seeking to own something that was never his to touch. A proclamation that had confirmed me to be my aunt's eventual heir, and what I now knew had condemned me to the fate the Council chose.

The ends justified the means. My assault was simply an unfortunate consequence that they brushed off.

Amelia smiled, returning her hands to my hair. She sprayed it with water and applied product to it, beginning the process of braiding it into small sections to let the wave set and refresh after my journey through Purgatory. "When I was young, the minister noticed me. I believe it began as an attempt to arrange for me to marry his son, but he eventually fell in love with another woman and married her against his father's wishes. I thought it would be done and maybe I would have a chance of choosing a husband for myself, as best we were allowed at the time anyway. I had no shortage of suitors knocking on my parents' door, but the minister refused them all in favor of taking me as his second wife. My parents were thrilled," Amelia said with a chuckle, but there was no humor in it. I found myself looking into the mirror of my own volition now, watching her face as she worked on my hair and the emotions that played over her features so plainly. It was such a stark contrast to the way the witches of the Coven worked to disguise any and all emotions as a sign of weakness.

"Did you have to marry him?" I found myself asking, thinking of how old he must have been to have had a son her age. The parallel between the minister and Itan, who had a nephew my age, wasn't lost on me, and I found myself waiting for the moment she would give me a happy ending to the story that hadn't ended well for me.

"No," she said, giving me a rueful twist of her lips. "I'd gone to the church to pray one day, and he caught me there alone after most of the others had left for the night. He didn't appreciate that I refused him that day, so he accused me of being a witch and they put me in jail. I was there for two weeks while he waited for me to repent under threat of death before Charlotte made her deal with Lucifer. His children went on to accuse countless others after she rescued me and brought me to Crystal Hollow, and I'm sure they were all killed for similar reasons as me. Petty reasons. All those people who died during the witch trials, none of them were actually witches. My favorite fact of our history is had it not been for their petty jealousy and accusations, our kind would have never come to be . . ." She trailed off, allowing those words to sink in.

"You all chose to become the very thing they'd accused you of," I said, but there was no judgment in the words. I understood the choice they'd made, because how could I not? To be condemned for something everyone involved knew wasn't true was a frustration that none deserved, false allegations that would change the course of history forever.

"We were dying either way. What difference did it make? So when Lucifer asked me what kind of magic I would like to possess, I knew I wanted nothing more than to take all the jealousy and desire that had condemned me to my cell and make it my power. I wanted to take what they had made into a weakness, what they'd turned into something abhorrent, my beauty, and make them *kneel* before it. That is what the darkest part of being a Red witch is all about. Finding power in desire."

Everything in me stilled, her words loosening something in my mind. They were an echo of my mother's—of what the binding ritual had done to my magic when it separated me from the Source. "The darkest part?" I asked, trying to feign casualness. I didn't want to raise any flags about what she might reveal out of fear that she would stop sharing her story, that she would stop teaching me the lore that I'd never be able to get from history books and a corrupt lineage.

"Yes," she said, her smile twisting in a way that came off self-deprecating. "It was not my finest moment, though I like to believe it was understandable under the circumstances."

She didn't offer any further information, and my curiosity got the best of me as I pivoted my body in the chair suddenly, spinning to meet her stare head-on and foregoing the mirror entirely. "But what you're talking about is *lust*," I argued, surprising even myself as I reached out and took her hand in mine. Touching another Red always brought a small measure of comfort, because I could not easily manipulate them to my will.

Touching another Red didn't come with the same consequences as touching all others.

"What else would I be talking about?" she asked, her smile faltering as she stared down at me with such confusion. I couldn't ignore the missing pieces, the implications in her story and her statement about our magic.

"But lust is the *only* magic we have. You said it is the darkest part of it, and that implies that there is something light in us," I said, my desperation clear. Her brow furrowed as she studied me, stroking her thumb over the back of my hand.

"Magic is neither good nor evil. It simply exists within all of us, but it is balanced. Every darkness has a light," she said, using her hold on my hand to tug me toward the window overlooking the gardens. Couples lingered in the shadow of the trees and flowers, stealing moments of intimacy. She pointed to one couple in particular, a brunette woman leaning against a tree while a blond woman cupped her cheek, leaning in close enough to touch their foreheads together. The moment was so reminiscent of the one I'd shared with Beelzebub in the sanctuary before entering the Second Circle that my breath caught. "When you look at them, what do you see?" she asked, turning her attention from the couple to watch me as I studied them.

"I see lust," I said, my eyes falling to the place where the blonde trailed her fingers up the slit in the thigh of the brunette's dress.

"That is no mere lust," Amelia said with a soft chuckle. "Look deeper. Feel what they feel."

I raised my hand to the glass of the window, pressing my

palm against it. I reached out with trembling fingers, sending my magic coursing through the pane and into the gardens so that I could feel their connection. It was different than what I'd come to know of lust, warmer somehow.

Like the comfort of a fire in the hearth during winter. It was not the hot, balmy passion of sweat-slicked bodies, but something stronger that tickled at my senses.

"What is it?" I asked, flinching back from Amelia's shocked gasp.

"It is *love*, Margot. That is our light. That is the true purpose of the magic of the Reds, not the lust we use against our enemies, but the love we can use to make the world a better place. Happy people who are in love with both themselves and their life partner do not feel the need to harm others. Love can inspire great change," Amelia answered, and my gaze dropped to where she ran her fingers over my wrists. The skin shifted as she pressed her magic into it, the indentations of rope revealing themselves to her.

My binding.

"Do all in the Coven bear these marks?" she asked, her jaw clenching as she guided me back to the chair and set me in front of the mirror once again.

"I don't think so. Only the Tribunal heirs," I said, considering what my mother had revealed in our brief conversation before everything went to shit.

"I am not familiar with the magic of bindings, but I do know that only the person who bound you can unknot your magic—"

"And if he's dead?" I asked, suddenly horrified by the implication of what that binding meant. I'd never been in love, never felt an inkling of that heavy emotion or even recognized it in others. Had Itan taken that from me, too?

"Then it would take something very powerful to snap those bonds," she said sadly, hanging her head forward for a moment as she fiddled with my hair once again.

I swallowed, picking at my fingernails as my gaze dropped to them. I felt my face twist, trying to find the words to communicate how her story and revelations had left me feeling. "Why are you telling me this?" I asked.

"Because I see a little of myself in you, Margot. You're afraid of what you are, and until the day comes when you learn to love yourself, you'll never be able to come into the power that those bonds took from you. I can feel your magic simmering away inside of you. It's trapped there and it is going to overwhelm you. You're a ticking time bomb, and it will eventually explode if you don't embrace it and release it regularly," she said, stepping around the chair. "I understand that it is more complicated than it should be with you cut off from the Source, and the lighter side of the magic that would have offered some balance to all that darkness, but that understanding will not change your fate." She set to doing my makeup, continuing on through the process of preparing me to join the festivities downstairs even though I wanted nothing more than to stay locked within this room.

"You don't understand. I can't stand being touched—"

"There are ways around that. Your own pleasure is a release, and it does not matter if it comes at your own hand if that is what you choose." I protested, and she held up a hand to silence me before she continued on. Pleasure was not something I had any interest in for myself, refraining from it entirely for fear of what would happen to me once I opened that door. "You can plant visions of pleasure into the minds of others while barely touching them if that is easier for you. If you feed their release, it will release some magic for you as well. But be mindful here, Asmodeus's magic has a numbing effect on us. It can strip away our inhibitions and make us far more susceptible to the pull of lust. For what it's worth, it may be worth taking advantage of that numbness for a night."

"Okay," I murmured, stilling when she returned with a red gloss to paint my lips.

"Either way, Asmodeus will not allow you to pass through to the Third Circle without giving *something* to the magic. I suspect Beelzebub is attempting to convince him as we speak, but Asmodeus will not be swayed to go against the rules. He never is," she said, taking my hands and guiding me to stand.

I nodded my understanding, trying to think of what I could do that wouldn't require what I could not give. What I could give of *lust* without spiraling into a tunnel of grief and trauma.

"Now," Amelia said, stepping back to grab a deep red dress off a hanger in the closet. She carried it over, and I quirked a brow. "Let's get you dressed."

I nodded, stepping behind the privacy partition in the corner of the room before I stripped off the clothes that Beelzebub had given me in Purgatory. "I don't have any other undergarments," I said, shucking everything into a pile I stacked neatly at the side of the partition.

"That's alright. They aren't allowed downstairs," Amelia said, making me twist my lips in annoyance.

Fucking rules.

She handed the dress around the edge of the partition, leaving me to pull it over my head. The straps were so thin they dug into the tops of my shoulders, the square neck dipped low. It hugged me through the stomach and hips, falling in an asymmetrical hem that skimmed the tops of my thighs. From there the fabric shifted to lace and fell to my knees, leaving far more revealed than I would have liked, but the necessities were covered. It wasn't lost on me that it was far more modest than the rest of the dresses I'd seen and what Amelia herself wore, and I couldn't help but feel gratitude for that at least.

I stepped out from behind the partition, watching as Amelia's mouth spread into a wide grin. "He doesn't stand a chance against you," she said, her face lighting with the delight of a challenge.

"Who?" I asked, allowing her to take my arm and guide me to the door of her bedroom.

She laughed, the sound full and hearty without a hint of the seductiveness I'd found watching her earlier. "Oh, this is going to be *fun*."

18

BEELZEBUB

"Come on, Asmodeus," I groaned, glancing around the communal area where his favored pets waited to entertain him. Some of them had already engaged with partners, seeking pleasure from one another while they waited for him to make his choice of who he might favor that night. Like he was some kind of a blessing and not a pain in the ass, as if it was an honor to engage in sexual games with a man who got off on suffering as much as he did pleasure. His favor was easily gained, but just as easily lost, and each of these poor souls who existed in the luxury of his home believed they would be different. That he would favor them for an eternity the way he did Amelia, keeping them here and allowing them to avoid the pain of the fate that awaited them on those cliffs. But in all our time here, in the centuries since Amelia had arrived and filled the void, nobody had even been aware how Asmodeus felt, no one had piqued his interest in such a way. No one had earned the right to remain, and all had returned to their eternity when he tired of them. It shouldn't have been possible for the witch to ensnare him as the lord of Lust, yet his infatuation with her company never faded.

"You know I cannot just allow her to pass. She has to earn the right like any of the other souls who think they can just stroll through my circle," he said, keeping his voice low. It wasn't common knowledge among the souls that they could avoid their eternity of suffering by earning the approval of each of the circles, by passing through each one and offering up their sins for judgment. While some knew, I was sure, few ever made it past their own circle. Few could conquer the sin that had claimed them, keeping them trapped endlessly.

"She's not even fucking dead! Why should she need to pay the circles with her own sins when she still breathes? She's hardly looking to become one of us," I said with a scoff. The idea of my sweet Margot desiring to become a demon was an impossibility, her fear and terror of this place founded in a lifetime of lessons about the evils at play here. I couldn't blame her, because I'd seen them for myself over my eternity of life, but I had to admit, I'd seen less pure goodness on the surface than I'd expected.

Her Coven had been misguided at best, cruel and deserving of their eventual fate if we focused on reality.

"The rules are the rules, Beelzebub. If I waived them for her, it would open my circle up to the possibility of needing to do so in the future. I cannot allow souls that *belong to me* to have a free pass just because you want to fuck one of them," Asmodeus said, the tone of his voice hardening. He wasn't known for his anger because the lifestyle he led was one of casual, late-night comforts and sleepy mornings in bed. He was flirtatious and at ease, relaxed where I had to be structured. For him to be the stickler for rules was a flip in our relationship I had never seen coming. Usually I was the one who had to harp on the other lords to keep to our natural order.

"She isn't yours," I said, watching as his brow rose at the growl in my voice. At the way the Enochian runes covering my body seemed to shimmer with their agreement. I grasped my necklace between my fingers to calm my violent energy, fingering the scythe that was my weapon of choice. With a flick of my wrist, I would have it in hand, able to defend Margot should it come to that.

But no matter how hard I fought, no matter who I killed,

I wouldn't be able to drag her through the boundary between the Second and Third Circles if the lust here didn't will it to be possible.

Asmodeus readied his stance, having known me long enough to recognize when I was ready to fight. Our impulses ran hot, but where mine ran to fighting for the ability to consume my possessions thanks to the gluttony that was mine to command, his ran to fucking them. He glanced over my shoulder, his eyes straying to the top of the stairs as his brows rose. "Tell that to her magic," he said, leaning closer to speak the words softly.

He was right, I knew. Because even though Margot so rarely dared to touch the magic that hummed within her, it was impossible to miss. It radiated off of her like waves of light, making her skin appear to shimmer faintly like a goddess. "She is more than her magic," I said in dismissal, despising the order of things for the first time in my long existence. The need to protect her was so at odds with the way I was meant to feel.

I was supposed to revel in the fact that another witch would suffer.

I sighed, hating that I'd had to resort to the second part of my plan to get Margot through the Second Circle without any cost to her. "If you won't let her pass out of loyalty to Lucifer and what He would want, then do it as a favor to me."

Asmodeus stilled, his face turning thoughtful. Favors were not something the archdemons handed out often, a commodity we rarely dared to deal in with one another. The ways that the receiving party could demand they be paid back were often far more terrible than just facing the initial problem.

Yet here I was, offering myself up on behalf of a witch that had wormed her way beneath my skin and sung a song I couldn't unhear.

"Tempting," Asmodeus drawled, lifting a hand and tapping his fingers against his bottom lip thoughtfully. "I never thought

I'd see the day that the great and mighty Beelzebub would need a favor from me."

"Don't expect it to happen again, so I suggest you take me up on this offer while it lasts," I grunted, crossing my arms over my chest as I waited for the inevitable.

Only a fool wouldn't take the offer of a favor from me.

"No," he said, drawing the word out far too slowly for my liking. "She matters to you if you're willing to make me an offer like that. Now I am very interested in finding out why. I can only do that if I have some more time with her, you see?" he asked, a twisted chuckle escaping his mouth. It was gleeful, almost childlike, as if he enjoyed the prospect of keeping my favorite toy trapped in a cage to which only he held the key.

"You fucking asshole—"

"There is a way for you to avoid all of this, you know," Asmodeus said, his grin spreading as he turned to make eye contact with one of the women who trailed her hand over the back of his shoulders as she passed. "Invoke Dominion and she's all yours. None of us would be able to attempt to lay claim to her if you do," he said, and I pursed my lips in frustration.

I hadn't shared that option with Margot, because I'd known beyond a shadow of a doubt that it was not an option. She would never forgive me if I tried to do it, would be repulsed by the very notion that I would lay claim to her and tie her to me and me alone. It would make me no better than Itan, acting without thought or care for what she wanted. "I can't do that to her," I said, and the words seemed to surprise Asmodeus as much as they did me.

I couldn't do that to *her*. No mention of what being bound to one woman for eternity would do to *me*.

Fucking witches.

He smirked, catching his bottom lip between his teeth as he shifted his attention to the space behind me. It left me no choice but to drop my grip on my scythe, turning to find Amelia and

Margot arm in arm at the top of the stairs. Amelia had paused there, a smile across her face as she spoke to Margot. I saw it from the periphery of my vision as my stare narrowed in on Margot, my gaze sweeping from head to toe and back again.

Her hair was freshly styled, free from sweat and sand from our journey. Whatever Amelia had done to it, the loose curls framed her stunning face perfectly, accentuating the natural brown hues of the makeup she wore. She wore less than Amelia, and yet what was there brought out her natural beauty.

Amelia pulled her arm out from Margot's after patting the other woman reassuringly, descending the staircase with the grace she'd learned after centuries of life in this twisted court. I let my gaze drift from Margot for a brief moment, for the first time noticing the similarities between their faces. While Amelia had dark hair and light eyes, she was Margot's opposite in most ways but the angles of their faces, the softness of their features and delicate femininity to the curve of their jaws and the shape of their noses were all the same. Nearly identical, even.

That was where the similarities ended. Amelia was taller, more willowy, where Margot was an hourglass. She was much taller than Willow and most of her other friends, but curves were packed onto her frame, making her look like walking sin. The dress Amelia had given her, fitted in her waist and hugging her hips, brought out each of those curves as she started a slow, meticulous descent down the stairs when Amelia reached the bottom and turned to hold out a hand for her.

I was horrifically aware of the silence in the room, of the moans that had stopped and the breathing that had quieted to watch her. I couldn't separate my own desire from the need pulsing in the room, the power of lust coating my skin and strengthening the natural attraction that pulsed between Margot and I like a tangible, breathing thing. As much as it pained me to admit, even without having heard her song and feeling the call to her, I would have known Margot was breathtaking and wanted her.

Her eyes came to me, her chest rising with her nerves. I forced myself to still, to try to give her a safe place to land as I approached the bottom of the stairs to wait for her.

But attraction didn't explain the way my breathing hitched. It didn't explain the very way my heart beat for her. That part was just the call of her song.

It had to be.

I couldn't stop my gaze from leaving hers, from taking in the lines of her body, the swells of her breasts as they spilled out the top of her low-cut dress. The red fabric hugged them, the faintest hint of her nipples visible through the fabric. Everything in me went solid at the sight, my cock thickening in spite of my best intentions as I took in the clear sign of the very last thing I'd expected to find on my songbird's body. On either side of her nipple was another, smaller mark.

She was *pierced*.

I swallowed, my mouth suddenly dry as my gaze rose back to hers. Her lips pressed together, understanding lighting her eyes as she wet her mouth with her tongue. She moved with more sway than I was used to, her hips moving from side to side as she came down those stairs. As if her usual control had already been shed, her body lost to the magic of the circle and releasing her from her inhibitions. As a Red witch, she was more susceptible to the magic here than most, her body complying with the sin that owned her without regard for what her mind wanted.

If that was the case, this night would test every bit of my control. I wouldn't allow her to make choices that would not be entirely her own, wouldn't allow her to give me parts of her I hadn't yet earned, and it shocked me just how fervently I *wanted* to earn them. No matter how much I may have wanted to take them, to take them and claim them and use them as a reminder when she tried to change her mind when we left the next morning. Her body already belonged to me. It was her mind I needed to possess, her mind I needed to convince to give in to whatever this fucking pulsating attraction came down to.

It was more than lust, making my blood simmer with unfamiliar warmth.

She reached the bottom of the stairs, pausing on the final one to glance between Amelia and me. If she went with Amelia, I had little doubt the Red witch would guide her to engage in the festivities, to give herself into her lust wholeheartedly. It wouldn't even be done maliciously; I knew Amelia well enough to know that. She seemed to believe nearly everything could be solved through sex, that it could be the ultimate outlet for all the pain that Margot held within, and would do it out of a desire to help Margot.

It certainly had been an outlet for Amelia personally, and while I was beyond grateful the witch had found that way to deal with her own trauma when she'd needed it, I hoped she could see that she and Margot were not the same in spite of their relation.

Margot turned to me with a deep sigh that deflated her chest, raising her hand cautiously to place within my waiting palm. I smiled down at her, tucking her into my arm and raising a wing to shield her from view. I didn't obstruct her vision of what was in front of her, but used it to offer her privacy from prying eyes that might be behind us.

"Thank you," Margot said, her voice soft enough that only I could hear as she peered up at me from beneath her lashes. She didn't so much as tip her head up to meet the full weight of my attention, but she reached out and ran a single finger down the edge of my wing. The light, teasing touch shot straight to my groin, and I fought back the strangled sound that clawed up my throat from my shock. She *knew* they were sensitive, and still she'd chosen to touch them.

Her inhibitions were already lowered, her walls dropping bit by bit, and the night had only just begun.

I was damned.

19

MARGOT

Beelzebub and I made our rounds, circulating the room and mingling with those who were not otherwise occupied. If it hadn't been for the sex happening all around us, it might have felt like a formal event.

Like a ball, rather than the free-for-all it was.

"Is it like this every night?" I asked, turning to look up at Beelzebub's face more fully. I hadn't wanted to allow myself to look at him, hadn't wanted to see his rough, handsome features in the dim lighting. The red lights did something to his eyes, turning them molten as I met his gaze.

"I can't say that I've spent a great amount of time here. From what I've seen, this is a bit grander than is typical," he answered, surprising me into a moment of thought. I knew enough to know that the circles all existed within Hell, but outside of Lucifer's influence over them all, they largely functioned independently in the same way the Covenant ruled over the Coven, but each head of family was responsible for their own line. In this place, that knowledge seemed to matter so much less. It seemed natural to have Asmodeus in charge of all this, while Beelzebub somehow didn't belong here. It was like handing a Red witch a crystal; sure, it was pretty, but their connection to its magic wasn't the same.

He watched some of the couples with rapt fixation, but there wasn't the same hunger in him that I saw in others around us. There wasn't the same hunger in him that I *felt* in me.

We strolled in a moment of silence, and I wondered how much longer we would need to remain downstairs before I could retreat to the privacy of a bedroom. Before I could separate from Beelzebub and the danger he presented to me under *normal* circumstances, let alone with Asmodeus's magic coating my skin and making mine rise to the surface. I felt like I might come out of my skin, like the heat pooling between my thighs would drive me to make a mistake I would very much regret come morning.

"Come with me," Beelzebub said, guiding me toward the double doors that led to that patio that overlooked the cliffs. In the distance, the hillside was stained with blood, the imagery sobering some of my desire. It felt wrong to say it was a welcome sight, but it was the one I'd needed in that moment—a stark reminder of what waited for me if I failed to move past the Second Circle.

Beelzebub pulled his wing back, leaving me feeling suddenly cold as he leaned forward onto the railing and crossed his arms over each other. His head hung forward, his chest moving with slow, deep breaths.

"Are you alright?" I asked, mimicking his stance. I didn't lean as much as he did, worried about the length of my dress and what it might lay bare. Particularly given that there was no underwear to shield me from view.

"He's trying to decide how to tell you that you will be required to partake in the festivities if you wish to leave," Asmodeus said, emerging through the doorway behind us.

"Impeccable timing as ever," Beelzebub groaned, raising a hand to pinch the bridge of his nose. "And also untrue at that. She doesn't have to partake in the festivities."

Asmodeus rolled his eyes as I turned to face him. "You must give something to the magic of lust to show you are in control of your sin if you wish to leave. He is correct in his assertion that it needn't happen at the party. It could also happen behind closed doors if you wish it."

"But surely abstaining from my so-called sin is all the evidence needed to show I am in control. What greater control can there be?" I asked, crossing my arms over my chest as Asmodeus's attention dropped to my breasts.

"Abstaining implies you are afraid of it. It implies you do not trust your self-control to put it to the test, and that means that you belong here. With me and mine," he said, sweeping a hand behind him to the party still going inside. "Amelia is fond of you and has requested I make space for you within the manor. So long as she remains so, you will be allowed to reside here with us. You need not fear the cliffs. It is a far better life than most can hope for here."

I swallowed, turning a venomous glare back at Beelzebub. "You knew about this? You knew what I would have to do to pass through?" The hurt that built in me shoved all arousal out of my system. He knew enough of my history to know why this was *impossible*. He'd said to trust him, that he had a plan.

I'd been dumb enough to believe him.

"I thought an exception could be made given that you are still alive, songbird. I didn't know he would hold you to this ridiculous fucking notion, and I thought he may allow me to pay your debt," he said, reaching for me. I sidestepped the grasp, shaking my head as I retreated back into the party. Amelia waited just within the doors, staring at me as if she knew exactly where the reality would push me. She was the only other familiar face, the only one I could even hope would be honest with me.

"What do you need?" she asked, her voice soft.

"Distract him," I said, whispering the words as I retreated from him. I knew enough of lust, and from my time with the friend who would take this as a challenge, the beginning of a plan had started to form in my mind. It couldn't only be *my* lust that would satisfy the requirement, couldn't only be my body that would satiate it. When Beelzebub stormed through the doors after me, I glared at him, clearing my throat so he would hear it as a low hum building. I let it loose for a moment, watching him go still as his eyes widened. The magic clawed its way up my throat with sharpened talons, feeling as if it would tear me open from the inside in its desperation to be free. I pushed through it, sinking into the spell that I laced around the hum in my throat.

But this song wasn't meant for him. It wasn't an outpouring of emotion that would call to anyone nearby, but a specific, directed call I hummed to attract women alone. It was higher pitched than the song I would have used for men, more sweet than seductive, but it was pleasing all the same as the four women closest to me closed ranks and approached.

"Songbird," Beelzebub said, watching as I turned my attention to Amelia, touching a gentle finger to the closest woman's cheek.

"Not me, darling." The woman's brow furrowed as she followed my gaze to Beelzebub, tracking up over his muscular frame like he was something to be devoured. My guilt was immediate, knowing that I would have never turned my magic on anyone and used it to trap them under any normal circumstances. But the hurt that pulsed through me felt more potent than normal, rage simmering alongside my own lust and the lust of those around me. The woman I'd bespelled wanted him, desired him as her eyes trailed over his form. I could feel that hint of attraction within her, feel it pulsing under the spell. "*Him*," I said, ushering the command that made Beelzebub's mouth drop open in shock. The woman left my side to do as my magic demanded, making her way to Beelzebub with swaying hips.

This magic, this power that danced at my fingertips, was exactly why I didn't allow myself to use it. No one should be able to command free will and the sexuality of others like this. It was monstrous.

I didn't allow myself to read into him, to look for signs that he may or may not find her attractive. I didn't want to unpack why the notion that he might desire her left me feeling devastated and numb, making a hollow form in my gut.

"*Margot,*" Beelzebub muttered, holding out an arm to keep the first woman away from him. She stroked a finger up his chest, a teasing touch that made that hollowness fully settle in my belly. It stung like hurt, which made no sense given it was my own doing.

"See that the Lord of Flies finds an outlet to satisfy himself for the evening," I said to Amelia, glancing down at the bulge that had long since formed in his pants. He'd been aroused since the moment I descended the stairs, doing his best to control it for my benefit and doing everything he could to shield it from my view. He'd taken the effort to make me comfortable with him, even though he had to be uncomfortable himself. It wasn't fair to expect him to abstain, too, given there were plenty of partners who would be willing to help him alleviate the pressure in ways I couldn't do.

I *wouldn't* do. Not with him.

I turned my back on him, making my way through the crowd that had formed to watch as he tried to keep the woman's hands off him. Without casting a glance for who I grabbed, I snagged the closest hand on my path away from him. A man laughed at my side, closing his fingers around mine as I guided him to Amelia's room. I had to hope she wouldn't mind what I was about to do, but I somehow suspected that her room had seen far more illicit acts than what I would be capable of doing. We hurried up the stairs, and I guided him into the room. Closing the door behind me, I turned for the first time to face the man I'd grabbed. He was handsome enough, blond and nearly shirtless, with gleaming muscles like the surfers from California. His was a much leaner build than Beelzebub's and I shook off the impending comparisons of things I couldn't want.

"Do you want me?" I asked, watching as his head jerked back.

He reached out, attempting to touch my cheek as I flinched away. "What's your name, pretty?"

"Margot. Now, do you fucking want me?" I asked, my patience reaching its limit. I needed consent before I did this, needed to know I wasn't taking from this poor soul in a way that would be a violation. I needed to finish here, to go witness the end of Beelzebub's . . .

I couldn't even think the words without vomit rising in my throat, and I hated that I cared. Hated that he'd gotten under my skin when he'd never consented to this attraction. I'd stripped the most valuable thing he had from him, forcing him to want me when otherwise he might have just allowed me to rot in Hell.

I needed to see him with the woman he chose. Needed to watch him fuck her so I could erase this irrational need from my mind and remind myself that attraction was just lust. That any person could fill the void, and that whatever Beelzebub felt for me wasn't special.

It was just a spell, and he was surrounded by the spell of lust while we lingered in the Second Circle.

"Yes, I want you," the man said with a chuckle. "But that will be hard to act on if you don't let me touch you."

"Do you consent to me getting you off?" I asked, strategizing my way around having to let him touch me. I planned to simply plant a vision in his mind, to utilize the magic of dreams that was so difficult to access. It would cost me a great deal of energy, but the alternative of touching him wasn't something I was prepared to give.

"Sure," the man said with a chuckle as I pointed to the same chair I'd occupied when Amelia readied me for the night. There'd been a reason she encouraged me to sink into my magic, to let myself feel arousal and pleasure. I dragged it away from the vanity, placing it in the center of the room.

She'd known damn well I wouldn't be able to leave here if I couldn't find a way to tolerate using my magic, but she'd given me ways to do that. Willow would never have allowed herself to be trapped in a situation where she was powerless, not without fighting back and doing everything she could to outsmart the system. To use brute magic to fight her way through it if she needed to.

My magic didn't work in the same way, but that didn't mean I couldn't use it to my advantage. The man I intended to use to do just that sat on the chair I'd gestured to, spreading his legs as if he intended for me to kneel between them. I scowled, swallowing as my tongue felt thick with disgust. "Take off your shirt," I ordered, turning to the curtains hanging from the windows. This room had an unobstructed view of the cliffs, the very threat that hung over my head waiting to claim me when I eventually died. I tore the golden rope from where it tied the curtains back, rending the fabric as I spun back to tie my chosen participant to the chair, putting myself in the position of power I needed to make this work.

I needed to know he couldn't touch me, couldn't hurt me for me to be willing to lose my magic, to drive his need higher and higher until he became a plaything for the Second Circle, feeding the offering it required of me.

The door slammed open, Beelzebub's stormy face filling the doorway. His chest was covered in shallow scratches, his eyes murderous as he took a few steps into the room and surveyed the situation. The rope held in my hand felt suddenly heavy under the weight of that gaze, but it turned away from me just as quickly. His steps took him to the center of the room quickly, not even giving me time to shout a warning as he grasped either side of the man's head in his hands. He'd turned to look at Beelzebub over his shoulder, staring his death in the face as the archdemon twisted his head sharply to the side, the resounding crack filling the room as I dropped the rope to the floor and scrambled forward.

The corpse swayed to the side, toppling off the chair and falling with blank, unseeing eyes as it stared up at me, twisted at the neck to face the wrong direction entirely as I swallowed the vomit threatening to rise up my throat.

"What is *wrong* with you?" I asked, the shrill sound of my voice bringing Amelia to the door.

She stared at the body on her bedroom floor, a grin of absolute glee spreading over her face. She leaned into the doorway, crossing her arms over her chest as she surveyed us. "This is about to get very entertaining," she said, earning a glare from Beelzebub as he spun to stalk to the door. He gave Amelia a gentle push, swinging the door closed in her face as I gaped at him. When he turned back to look at me over his shoulder, I couldn't breathe.

"Tell me, songbird," he said, twisting his body to stroll toward me, feigning a casual ease we both knew was fake. I backed away, wincing when he took the other man's place on the chair, kicking the body to the side with a disgruntled sneer. "What exactly were you planning to give him?"

20

BEELZEBUB

Margot fled up the stairs with the man she'd chosen, leaving me to stand in the center of a circle of women she'd used her magic against.

It shouldn't have bothered me so much that she was capable of turning them on me and walking away. It shouldn't have haunted me to know that I could never have done the same, because the very idea of her being behind closed doors with another man made everything in me tighten into an ache. My jaw clenched as I grabbed one of the women by the wrist, pushing her back without preamble in my rejection as she dragged her nails over my chest.

Her touch was wrong. It left me feeling cold and callous, holding none of the traces of warmth that filled me the moment Margot's skin touched mine. I snarled at the next woman who moved to touch me, her face twisting with shock at my revulsion.

Burying my hands in my hair, I tugged at the edges where it was pulled into a messy bun at the back of my head.

This had been her choice, and I had to respect it. I had to honor the fact that she'd been so willing to choose *anyone* but me, that she'd done it to save me from what her touch would have done to the enchantment she'd placed on me.

"You're just going to let her go?" Amelia asked, waving a hand to dismiss the women who lingered too close. Who were too determined to put their hands on me and use touch to convince me to play with them. Any other time, I might have taken them up on it.

"She made her choice," I said, my voice as dejected as I felt. The anger was nearly all-consuming, taking the lust dancing over my skin that Margot had stoked into roaring flames and twisting it into the other side of passion.

Wrath.

Wrath that couldn't be explained outside of accepting that it was just another consequence of her song.

"You disappoint me," Amelia said, her voice quiet as she studied me. "I thought you cared too much to allow her to do something that she'll regret." She sighed, pursing her lips as if she was so exhausted with the way demons constantly disappointed her.

"I don't *care,*" I snapped, baring my teeth at the witch who was so like the one I wanted to be with in that moment. "It's just her spell. I heard her sing and I've been trapped in this fucking hell ever since."

Amelia froze, taking a step closer to me with a scoff of disbelief. "You fucking idiot," she said, sinking her teeth into her lower lip. "You are an archdemon. Your soul is already owned by Gluttony so fully that there is no room for any other sin. You cannot be controlled by the magic of lust. If you could, you would not have been able to resist the call of Asmodeus's magic in this place. You would have already found a partner and joined the festivities."

"You're wrong," I said. The magic of the witches had to be different from that of the demons. I could be immune to the darkness of Asmodeus's magic but still be pulled in by the lightness of Margot's.

Right?

"By all means, demon. Continue to tell me how my magic works. It's not like I have spent centuries here, or tried to pull you and the other archdemons under my spell for my own entertainment when I'm bored. What would I know?" Amelia asked, her face twisted in anger at my dismissal.

"But that's not possible. I heard her sing, and I haven't been able to leave her alone since. I've been obsessed. I stalked her when we were still in Hollow's Grove! I have done everything I can to keep her safe since we fell through the portal to Hell. Why would I do that if I am not under her spell?" I asked, my frustration growing as I tried to wrap my head around her claim.

Amelia grinned up at me, reaching out with a single hand to touch her palm to the center of my chest. She pulled it back, drawing a swirl of thin red tangles out from my skin. They danced in her hand, twisting and writhing in a round mass. "Margot may not be capable of recognizing the magic of love when she sees it, but I am," she said, her words making me snap my stare away from the red tangle to her eyes.

No.

That was impossible.

"Obsession is a form of lack of self-control and the desire to overindulge in something, or in this case, someone. That is *your* sin, Beelzebub. Not hers or any spell she has placed you under. You are obsessed with her because your magic recognizes what you have yet to admit to yourself. You love her," Amelia said, keeping her words low enough that Asmodeus would not hear them. Protecting Margot and what my feelings for her could mean if any of the other archdemons knew. They would see her as my weakness, use her against me at every turn.

"I can't be," I said, arguing the point even though the truth of it had already settled into me. Amelia had touched me, the *original* Erotes witch, and I'd felt absolutely nothing. No call to act on the magic of lust that surrounded us all in the Second Circle.

There was only Margot for me.

"The witch is yours, Beelzebub. So what are you going to fucking do about it?" she asked finally, smirking when I pushed past her and made my way to the stairs.

Minutes had passed since I'd lost sight of Margot, for the entirety of my world to be turned upside down. The black mass

I'd thought existed where a heart should have been didn't seem to care that she was a witch and I was a demon, that I'd gone to Hollow's Grove fully intent on condemning all the witches to the Hell I'd lived in.

I blacked out, seeing red as I took the steps two at a time in my haste to get to her. To stop her from doing something she would regret and that would hurt me now that I understood what this feeling was lurking beneath my anger.

It was pain. The kind of pain I'd only heard of in stories from people who were foolish enough to fall in love. I'd never thought to join their numbers, never thought I could be dumb enough to tie myself to another being in such a way when I knew all too well how disappointing people could be.

I made my way to Amelia's room, because even though I couldn't see the doorway to know that's where Margot had gone, I knew her well enough to anticipate that she would go somewhere that was familiar to her. In a place that was entirely new, she would go where she'd already begun to feel comfortable over walking into an unknown.

I slapped my hands on the door, shoving forward with a force I would have taken back if I could. The door burst open before me, revealing Margot standing behind the chair where the man she'd grabbed sat. He gripped the side of the chair as he turned to look at me, his mouth popping open in shock as I took a few steps into the room and surveyed the situation.

Margot held a piece of rope within her grip, her intentions clear. It should have eased some of my tension that she felt the need to restrain her chosen partner, when I'd been allowed to touch her on and off, however casually, since we'd come to Hell.

Instead, it only filled me with anger that she hadn't simply chosen me in the first place. That she'd been so anxious to avoid me that she'd been willing to subject herself to *this*.

I didn't give either of them time to react as my anger dictated my actions, driving me to the center of the room. Grasping the man's head in my hands, I stared him in the eye as I twisted his head sharply to the side. The resounding crack filled the room as Margot dropped the rope to the floor and scrambled forward in an attempt to intervene.

The man's body swayed to the side, toppling off the side of the chair and falling to the floor, forgotten by me. I turned my stare to where Margot swallowed and stared at me with wide eyes.

"What is *wrong* with you?" she asked, her voice rising in pitch. It drew Amelia to the door to her bedroom, having followed after me.

She stared down at the body, a grin of glee spreading across her face as she leaned against the doorway with her arms crossed over her chest. "This is about to get very entertaining," she said. I glared at her as I spun and stalked to the door, giving her a gentle nudge into the hall. I swung the door closed in her face, completely uncaring that it was her room Margot had chosen to hide away in.

"Tell me, songbird," I said, twisting my body and strolling toward Margot. I kept my body languid and casual, working to shove down my anger as I worked through the revelations that had rocked my world. I stepped around the edge of the chair and lowered myself into the space the other man had occupied, facing Margot where she stood behind it as I kicked the body out of the way with a sneer. "What exactly were you planning to give him?"

Margot couldn't seem to tear her eyes off the unconscious male on the floor, her eyes wide with shock. "What have you done?" she asked, floundering for words as I looked at her over my shoulder.

"Were you fond of him?" I asked, studying her response. She turned those wide mahogany eyes to me, watching as I kicked him again. It didn't matter to me that he couldn't feel it in that moment, if she kept looking at him, I would desecrate his body and leave nothing more than ashes.

"You killed him!"

I scoffed, leaning forward to pick up the rope from the floor where Margot had dropped it in her haste to scramble back. "You can't kill what is already dead, songbird. Give him a few hours, he'll wake up eventually. Though he will stay away from you when he does so unless he wants me to do far worse the next time I catch him looking at you."

She gaped at me, those pretty lips spread wide as she sputtered for a response. "There was no reason for that."

I shrugged, keeping my seat even though I wanted nothing more than to close the distance between us, pin Margot to the wall, and kiss her until she couldn't breathe. Knowing that what I felt was genuine had changed everything for me. There was no denying our inevitability now.

"I disagree," I said, quirking my head to the side as I ran my tongue over my bottom teeth.

"Fuck you," she said, gathering the steel in her veins. She shook her head once, striding past me in an effort to reach the door. I reached out with my wing, blocking her path and then grasping her forearm, yanking her to a halt at my side. "Let go of me," she snarled.

Placing the rope in her hand, I kept my wing in her way as I raised my arms over the back of the chair, leaning into it and putting them in place so that she could tie me to the legs. Her eyes bounced over my form, lingering on my chest as I arched back into the seatback, making my intentions clear. If she wanted her partner bound and unable to participate, if she needed that to find her pleasure, then I would gladly allow her to tie me up for an eternity if it meant I got to feel her skin against mine. The desperation she'd filled me with knew no bounds, sinking deeper within me with every minute that passed. I wondered how I hadn't seen it.

I had somehow fallen head over heels for this woman I'd thought I hated.

"No," she said, shaking her head.

"What's wrong, songbird? You were so ready to take what you wanted from *him*. I am here, and I'm perfectly willing to let you have your way with me," I said, smirking as I peered up at her. She fumbled for a response, her eyes darting around the room as if she couldn't bear to meet my gaze. I knew she was confused, but I also knew it was too soon for me to explain the shift in my behavior.

Margot wasn't ready for me to tell her how I felt.

"He isn't you," she said finally, shaking her head again.

The notion that she would prefer anyone else to me was laughable, and I grinned at her as I spat the words that weren't fair, that would push her too far, too quickly. I knew it, but I found myself saying them anyway. I wanted to make her come undone; I wanted to tear her apart until all she could see was me in the same way she'd infiltrated my mind, embedding herself in my skin like a blessing and a disease that I would never be rid of.

"Careful. That sounds dangerously close to an admission that I scare you, Margot," I said in challenge, grinning when she twisted the rope in her hands and finally stepped up behind me. Her fingers brushed against my wings as she worked quickly, tying my arms to the legs of the chair with quick, deft movements that made me wonder how many times she'd done this. How often she'd had to do this to survive her upbringing in that fucking Coven that would have made her face her greatest fears all in the name of magic and power.

"How do you carry your head so easily? It must be fucking heavy with the size of your goddamn ego," she said, stepping around to stand in front of me. I tested the bindings, tugging at the ropes gently with small enough motions that she didn't notice them.

"It's only a big head if it's inaccurate, so why don't you let me show you the truth in my arrogance?" I asked, dropping the words lower. Margot shifted on her feet, and I knew it was due to the fact that she was far from unaffected by the magic of the

Second Circle. Beyond that, she was far from unaffected by *me*. Put the two together, and the little siren didn't stand a chance of controlling herself no matter what her intentions may be.

"I don't want to avoid using you for this because I'm attracted to you," she said, her nostrils flaring with her anger as she took a step closer. When I sat, she was only a few inches taller than me, putting us impossibly close as I spread my thighs to allow her to step into the trap of them. "I was using him because he gave me *consent*. I understand that may not matter to you, but it does to me."

I grinned at her, finding the fault in her argument. Whatever this was, she'd twisted it up in her head so fully that she couldn't find a way out anymore. "I fail to see where I am unwilling to let you do whatever you want with me, little siren," I murmured, watching as her face dropped.

"You're already under my spell. You cannot give consent anymore," she argued.

Her eyes probed my face as my smile dropped, studying me for the horror she seemed to think was sure to come. "Don't," I said, finding it increasingly difficult to navigate the nuances of this conversation without revealing the truth of what Amelia had told me. "If this was all a spell, you would not feel the effects of it, too, but I think we both know you do. I think we both know that whatever this is between us is mutual now, and that means it is more than just me hearing your song." I wished I hadn't allowed her to tie me up after all. I wanted to reach for her, to draw her into an embrace that was far more about comfort than anything sexual. That fucking bastard had made her think she was a monster, without ever sharing the truth of it with her.

Even if I hadn't been immune to her song, you could not create something from nothing. Magic didn't work that way. There had to be a kernel of attraction for her magic to sink into me, putting its hooks into me so fully that I would never be able to get free.

If I had been able to fall under her spell, she would have had my consent with that alone. It likely wouldn't have been the case for everyone, but it would have been enough for me.

She didn't answer, choosing to ignore my words and the implication of them. She wasn't ready to own up to her own attraction. The only thing I could do was to convince Amelia to teach her the nature of Red magic, to teach her the limitations and rules around desire that made what she believed *impossible* in actuality.

Instead of arguing, I leaned into her narrative, letting her maintain her control over it. She needed it, and I'd let her keep it for now if it meant she stayed within my reach. "If this is all a spell," I said, trailing off until Margot raised her eyes to mine fully. She squared her shoulders, waiting for the judgment she felt certain would come. "Then it is no wonder I'm held captive. There is no one breathing who could look at you, who could know you, and not willingly fall prey to you. If this is a spell, then all I can do is hope that you never release me from it, my songbird."

21
MARGOT

He stared up at me, those red eyes full of understanding he hadn't earned. I hadn't done anything to give him more than basic knowledge about what I'd done to him, yet he stared at me as if I were the victim in this situation. As if I were the one caught within a misconception, trapped in my own spell.

He'd already known he was under my spell. He hadn't been operating under some delusion that this was genuine and had never even bothered to insinuate it was anything more.

So what changed?

Feather-light wings fluttered within my chest, the faintest stirring of emotions I'd long since buried as deep as I could. The well I'd shoved them into threatened to bubble over, heated by the intensity of his statement. The implications were unfathomable, and even if I logically knew it was only the spell talking, I couldn't shake the questions they raised within me.

He doesn't want to be free.

My knees locked as I stood before him, forcing myself to remain still as I searched for another path. I didn't dare touch the man before me, knowing that it would do far more harm than good. Even *if* he'd been capable of giving his consent, I wasn't able to keep this simple. I wasn't able to touch him without feeling, wasn't able to simply make this a means to an end in the way I needed. I wouldn't have said that what I felt was the same as what

Amelia had seemed to sense in that couple embracing outside. But I felt *something*, a warmth that trailed off into the coldness of a void before I could grasp it.

Like it was constantly just out of my reach, but I wasn't certain I wanted to take that final step to follow after it.

I shook my head, swallowing as I forced my knees to bend. I nearly stumbled as they buckled beneath me, but disguised it as I moved to make my way past Beelzebub once more. He didn't reach out to stop me this time even though we both knew that no common rope could hold him tight if he did not allow it. Instead, he waited until the moment I reached the door, my hand wrapping around the knob and preparing to escape into the potent air of Hell's Second Circle, a place that would give any sex club a run for its money, to look for another willing victim. "The way I see it, you have three options," he said, his voice low. He didn't shout it to command my attention, but the steel in his tone was enough to make my spine go rigid. Warning pulsed inside my head, the danger in his voice making my eyes close as I waited for him to finish. "The smart choice is to get your ass back here and use me, however you need, to fulfill your obligation to Lust so that we can be done and move on from this place."

"I think we have very different definitions of what *smart* entails in this situation. For me, staying as far away from you as possible is the wise choice. So I will pass on whatever it is you think is happening here," I snapped, turning the knob in my hand. I pulled it open, the door creaking on its hinges as I glanced back at Beelzebub. His wings were held high, only the bottom tips scraping against the floor, and spread out around him. The lines of sinew and muscle within them were somehow artistic, and I imagined many women had enjoyed trailing their fingers over them, tracing the map they created. I moved to step through the door, shaking off my hesitation as he continued on with no regard for the need I'd expressed in my rejection.

"The second option is we remain here indefinitely. This is not the home I would have chosen for either of us, but I guess we will at least have the promise of eternity together to look forward to, and you can wait until the spell of your song has undoubtedly worn off and gain my consent then," he said, his shoulders and wings rising with the motion of a shrug as I watched. The statement lacked the sarcasm I would have expected to hear, all the hatred and anger he'd harbored for my witch heritage gone and leaving the words feeling too genuine. "But you did say you were in a hurry to get home, didn't you?"

"And the third?" I dared to ask, crossing my arms over my chest.

"You can choose the very futile path and walk out that door intending to choose another partner to fulfill your needs. If you do that, you should do so knowing that I will simply keep killing anyone you touch," he said. There was no anger on his face that should have accompanied the threat of violence, just a blank look that made his promise feel matter-of-fact. "You're mine, songbird. I am asking you not to make me feel the agony of knowing you've chosen someone else. I can't do it. Don't ask me to watch another man touch you knowing it should be me."

My hackles rose even as my skin tingled with awareness that felt less like anger and more like heat.

Where did he get the nerve?

"I don't belong to anyone," I said, walking away from the door to stand next to him. I wanted him to get the full force of my glare, the full weight of my independence as I stared him in the face.

"Is that so?" he asked, sinking his teeth into his bottom lip. My eyes tracked the movement, the stirring within me far too fixated on the bite that should have been mine. I shook off the thought as soon as it came, knowing it was just the magic coating my skin, bringing all my worst impulses to the surface, stripping away my will in a way that felt volatile. "Then prove it, songbird. You have a willing victim right here. You walk out that door and we both know it's to protect yourself from feeling something—not to protect me."

"You yourself said that we needed to keep this simple for the sake of your ability to protect me. I'd rather not die just so you can play with me," I argued. Touching him, using him would only make the spell worse, but I needed to move on before the magic of the Second Circle made me do something I would truly regret. Before it stripped away my inhibitions entirely and left me a mass of needy flesh that had little control over my own body. That was the promise of Lust, of the presence of the lord who presided over it.

Beelzebub shrugged. "I changed my mind. I have more than enough motivation to keep you safe regardless of whether or not you allow me to touch you. I am done making excuses for why this isn't right. I know what I feel," he said.

I glanced toward the open doorway, warring between my two options. Staying here until my song wore off wasn't one. I needed to get back to warn Willow before she allowed the heirs to take their Tribunal seats. I didn't fully understand the consequences of what the binding ritual had done to us and our magic, but if what Amelia had said was true and I was cut off entirely from the magic that had been intended for me, did that mean that any witches who lived under me on the Council would suffer the same fate?

The Tribunal members were meant to be the conduits for their houses, for all magic to channel from the Source and through them. How could that happen if the connection had been tied into a knot?

I didn't want to be the person who put my need to keep Beelzebub at arm's length before the needs of my people. The thought of playing games with him and watching him kill anyone I tried to touch didn't horrify me as much as it should have after learning they'd recover, but it would be a waste of time. I understood the resolution written into the lines of his face. He was determined to make that not an option for me, and I wasn't even certain it was something he could control.

Heaving a deep, aggravated sigh, I swung my leg over his, lowering my body slowly until I straddled his thighs. The feel of him between my legs made me pause, but I reminded myself I was in control of this situation. This was a choice, and while my options hadn't been great, this was the one I'd chosen. I could walk away. I could wait out the spell and then he would no longer desire me.

But I wanted to move on. I wanted to get the fuck out of Lust and away from the heat that swirled in my belly, only getting stronger as I stared down at Beelzebub.

I chose this, and there was no denying the familiarity and warm comfort that came from trusting Beelzebub to let me guide us through it. I wouldn't have been able to say the same for a stranger I grabbed from downstairs.

His eyes met mine, his brow cocked to show that of all the plans I could have executed, this was the one he hadn't been expecting. "Your hands stay bound," I said, my voice quiet as I raised my hands to his chest. I touched him, fighting back the tremble in my hands as I glided them lightly over his skin. His runes glowed brighter as I touched them, his eyes falling lidded as I finally tucked my face into his neck. My lips touched his jawline, a teasing glide as I made my way to his ear. Each heave of my lungs seemed to happen in time with his, putting our chests together. The thin silk of my dress did nothing to shield me from the feeling of his heat against me, from the brush of his body touching my sensitive, pierced flesh.

He surrounded me with his warmth, his wings coming around us. They didn't seal me in, leaving an opening behind me where I could escape, but it felt like a shield.

Like the comfort of a blanket on a winter day spent staring at the falling snow through the windows.

I let my eyes fall closed, sinking into the deep well of power that I kept tucked away. It was fuller than I remembered from the last time I'd touched it, the last time I'd attempted to allow a shallow release to ease it free. My own magic coated my skin too easily here, chasing away Asmodeus's and warming my skin beneath the slick of desire as it catapulted to the surface. It mingled with the magic of the Second Circle that permeated the air, seeming to settle into this place as if it recognized it intuitively.

The song rose in my throat, a deep, throaty hum that would have come even if I had not willed it. The moment I let that magic loose, I was lost. The moment I drew it to the surface in this place, it overwhelmed me.

"*Fuck,*" Beelzebub groaned beneath me, his hips bucking into me as my own moved of their own accord. I'd barely needed to touch him, simply offering teasing touches as my magic did the work for me. I sat a little deeper, giving him the full extent of my weight as I reached a hand to the back of his neck, tangling it in the hair at the base of his neck. He groaned as my mouth pressed into his neck, my tongue darting out to taste his flesh as a strangled gasp interrupted my song.

In the distant haze of my memory, I knew this wasn't right. I knew I hadn't intended for it to spiral like this as I ground against him, feeling the ridge of his length through his pants. The absence of any underwear meant there was only the thin, smooth surface between us to stop him from sliding inside me, to stop me from giving him the one thing I could not.

My body responded to his touch, even when he could not physically do anything to me. My body recognized him and my need for him, pulling back from his neck to stare down at him. My lips moved with softly murmured words, with a song I hadn't thought I'd known. His stare tracked the movement, studying my lips intently.

I grasped his face between my hands, lifting his stare to mine as I lowered my mouth to his slowly. My mouth lingered just a breath away from his, so close to touching but unable to close that final distance. I clung to reality, trying desperately to ease the magic out of my own body and into his. "Songbird," he groaned, the words a breath I inhaled. They filled my lungs with my intake of breath, the warmth spreading through me as I fought to come back to reality.

In all my time as an Erotes witch, I'd never lost control of my own lust. I'd done only what was required of me and moved on, but this was different.

This called to a part of me I wanted to know.

"Fuck it," Beelzebub gasped, lifting his chin and closing the distance between us. His chest heaved as his mouth touched mine, his breathing stopping immediately as I sighed into him. His kiss was gentle, restrained, as if he was asking me for the permission to continue.

I deepened it immediately, tugging on the back of his neck to bring him closer. He raised his body to press into me more tightly, his posture going straight as I sank into his lap. He struggled against his binds but didn't attempt to break free. I gripped his face more firmly, molding my mouth to his as his tongue danced with mine. The taste of him inside me was like a war on my senses, something so distinctly *him* that somehow matched his scent. He erased the floral of my perfume and filled it with the freshness of mint. He replaced the vanilla and cinnamon spices that accompanied the florals with the roughness of his leather and cedar.

My song sounded weaker, but the cords of magic in the air pulsed stronger than ever as we lost ourselves in each other. My hands glided down his chest and over his abs, sliding between our bodies, and my pinky finger brushed against the hard length of him. He groaned into me as I gasped, breaking our kiss to stare up at me.

He was hard and heavy, practically begging for release as I slid my pinky over the tip of him. A spot formed on his leathers, warm and wet as our arousal drove higher.

In my haze of magic, I reached for the waistband of his pants, determined to tug them down and free him from the confines. To feel his skin against mine in that intimate area, to touch him to my core and feel his heat like a brand inside me. He tore his mouth from mine, shaking his head with a smile. "Easy, songbird. Just like this," he said, the words soft in spite of the way my song grew louder. My magic attempted to get him to consent to what it wanted. His answering smile was soft, as if he saw right through to what was driving me and knew what I needed even though I was lost. "I don't need to fuck you to come for you, songbird."

He shifted in the chair, curving his lower back to give me a better seat. I adjusted in his lap, settling down on top of him as I crushed my mouth to his again. My hips ground back and forth, desperation for release driving me. Beelzebub participated as he could, letting me take what I needed from him until he finally groaned long and deep, his body going taut as release stole the breath from his lungs. I stilled in his lap, watching his face as the pleasure played over his masculine features. His eyes closed slowly, his mouth dropping open slightly as he smiled through it.

I leaned forward, all too aware of the way the position put my breasts in his face, and untied him from the chair. I scrambled off his lap, reality crashing back in as the magic I'd summoned faded. Fed, satisfied by his release, it swirled around on my skin and left a glittering trail of beauty in its wake, feeding me better than any food could have hoped to. I felt stronger than I had in years as I adjusted my dress, but the feeling was fleeting as my belly cramped with the effort to shove the fresh wave of magic away.

It wanted the one thing it had been deprived of, the thing it had never been gifted in all my years of life. The release that would send my magic spiraling out through the world, freeing it from the confines of my body.

There was just too much kept locked within me.

I bent over slightly, curling my arms around my stomach as I tried to find the lid to the well, to shove it back over the top and contain the magic that now roamed free. The Second Circle entwined with it, dancing in a circle around me to try to strip away my will once more. I clung to it with every fiber of my being, willing my hands to stay still.

"Margot," Beelzebub said, and I looked up to find him standing. He walked toward me slowly, treating me like the caged animal I felt like in that moment. I whimpered as a fresh wave of pain hit me in the chest, trying to claw its way out of my body. "Let me help you," he said, and we both knew what he meant by *help*.

Let him touch me. Let him bring me to the same release I'd given him.

But I didn't deserve it, not after what I'd done. Not with the monster I was. I was no better than Itan, taking from those who would not have given if it weren't for what I was.

I didn't get to feel pleasure in what I'd chosen.

"No," I said, denying him as I took another step back from him. "I'll be fine. It's just this fucking place."

"I don't think that's true," Beelzebub said, gesturing to my hold on my abdomen, on the center of my being where my magic waited. "When was the last time you had an orgasm, songbird?"

I didn't answer, turning my gaze away as if he might see the answer in my eyes. As if he might somehow be able to read me and understand that I hadn't ever experienced that pleasure. I didn't want to become a slave to my desires, didn't want to let my sins rule me. The best way to keep my sin at bay was to never allow myself to feel it, to never allow it to corrupt me in the way it had so many others.

Beelzebub came closer suddenly, grasping my face and turning me so I met his stare. His eyes were wide and shocked, bouncing over the lines of my face as he searched for a contradiction to what he'd already seen. "*Margot,*" he said, the worry in that tone sinking inside of me. The elders had warned me of the dangers of denying myself, of keeping it contained.

Eventually, the magic would take control. Eventually, it would erase my will and unleash itself on the closest target.

It had already tried, and only Beelzebub's restraint had kept me from making a terrible mistake.

His restraint that shouldn't have been possible under my spell. If it hadn't been for the pain in my stomach, I might have spent more time trying to process what that meant, but I stored it away for another time.

But I would never let those warnings come to pass. I would never allow myself to become that monster. When we reached the day that I could no longer control it, that would be the day when I gave up altogether.

"I'm fine," I said, straightening and standing tall, finally, as I shoved the pain down deep. As I tried to lock it away where he couldn't see the agony I lived in every day. At some point, I'd gotten used to the deep throbbing pain, but every time I released it, every time I put it back into the cage of my body, it was like breaking the bone all over again.

Somehow worse than ever.

"Get on the fucking bed, Margot," Beelzebub snapped, his eyes flaring with anger.

"You can't fucking fix me, Beel," I said, hating the sting of tears in my throat. I wanted nothing more than to be strong enough to shove them away, to not give in to the angry torrent coming my way.

"You aren't broken, songbird," he said, the gentle tone of his voice making my bottom lip tremble. "You just . . . need a little help taking that power back. Let me help you."

"No," I said, squaring my shoulders in spite of the tears falling down my cheeks.

"Then do it yourself at least," he said, closing the distance between us. He took my hand in his, guiding it toward my center as I jolted back from the prospect.

"No," I repeated.

"For fuck's sake! I can't just stand here and watch you suffer!"

"Then leave," I said, already turning away from him. There was a shower in the bathroom, and I fully intended to set the temperature to freezing and plunge myself under the cascade. To chill my heated skin in an attempt to quell the desire and mingling pain.

Beelzebub's mouth opened as if he might argue, his eyes darting over the determination on my face. He grimaced, his face twisting before I disappeared into the bathroom and locked myself in.

A few minutes passed before the door closed in the bedroom as Beelzebub left me to suffer alone.

Just the way I liked it.

22

BEELZEBUB

I snagged the bottle of Brimstone off the bar counter, ignoring the demon who glared at me for the theft. He backed down quickly enough, his ranking in Hell far too low to go toe-to-toe with an archdemon on Asmodeus's behalf. I had no doubt he would report my infraction to my brother in arms, but I couldn't have cared less.

I already felt the need to make sure I was with Margot at all times, a deep pulsing obsession that rivaled even the greatest of my gluttonous urges. I couldn't believe I hadn't recognized the symptoms of my newest obsession, but I'd never had a *person* occupy that space within me. Knowing that she was one second away from snapping? From losing every tendril of control that kept her from giving in to the darkest parts of magic that would make her a mindless, careless creature of nothing but impulse and urge?

She would never forgive herself for it, and yet she couldn't seem to be convinced of the advantages of taking her own releases. Of giving herself the pleasure that would satiate at least the most violent of urges and enable her to maintain that careful balance of control without risking herself.

I picked an empty corner of the room, dropping down onto the love seat. It stunk of sex, and I had little doubt that whoever had occupied it before me hadn't been gone for long. I fidgeted uncomfortably, avoiding touching the cushion with my bare hands.

Gross.

Amelia approached, a sly smile on her face as her stare dropped from my face and the bottle in my hands to the wet stain on my pants. I'd been in such a hurry to get away from Margot, to not have to witness her self-inflicted pain, that I hadn't stopped to think about what had happened.

She'd made me come in my pants like a schoolboy, and now I wore the signs of that in the middle of a fucking orgy. Even worse, I'd been happy to do it, knowing that it was a step in the right direction. I hoped my restraint would help convince her that I was not only not under her spell, but also that she could trust me to protect her consent even when her magic tried to convince her to act outside of it.

"Did you and our little Red witch enjoy yourselves?" she asked, her nose lifting as she scented the air—no doubt smelling Margot on me. Amelia had always been a little more . . . animalistic than the other original witches, her magic so steeped in primal reactions and base urges that it seemed to pull her a little more toward the wildness in her blood.

"Didn't even get my damn pants off," I mumbled, tossing back a swig of the fire whiskey. It burned the entire way down my throat, warming the parts of me that had chilled as Margot's magic wore off. While I wasn't immune to the other sins around me, they couldn't strike as deep as they would have with someone who belonged to them and the effects didn't last outside the moment.

"I hope Margot enjoyed herself thoroughly. That poor girl needed the release desperately," Amelia said, her soft smile telling me that she saw straight into whatever power Margot held contained inside her. "With her magic bound within her as it is, she cannot give the excess back to the Source. She just keeps absorbing over and over again, making her need for orgasm all the more important to her control over her power and her form."

I winced, hating that I needed to be the one to give her the bad news, to share that I hadn't been able to convince Margot to let out her power. "She wouldn't let me . . ." I trailed off.

Amelia stilled, that soft smile falling from her face as she jerked her head back. "Surely you're kidding. Please tell me you did not leave her unsatisfied!"

"If I'd forced it, I would have been no better than *him*. She said no, repeatedly. What was I supposed to do, Amelia? I won't force myself on her when she isn't ready," I said, standing from the love seat. I set the bottle of whiskey on the side table, pulling at the ends of my hair. "She made her wishes clear."

"I don't accept that," Amelia said, spinning on her heel. She turned back for her bedroom, leaving me with no choice but to follow after her. I had to hope I could mitigate the violence swirling around her, keep her from doing something that would hurt Margot in the end. Racing up the stairs, I followed after her with slower steps thanks to my longer stride. She paused at the top of the stairs suddenly, a complete contradiction to the urgency with which she'd been determined to reach Margot. "There is something you should know about her, before you get in too deep."

I went cold, all the warmth leaching from my body at the severity of those words. She'd told me to go after Margot only an hour prior, was the catalyst that made me realize exactly what this was.

Now I was in too deep?

"What?" I asked, allowing her to grab me by the arm and pull me away from the people lingering nearby.

"At some point in her life, Margot's magic was bound through a ritual by another witch. She is cut off from the Source, and that means all that magic stays trapped within her. It twists and writhes and becomes dark when that happens. That means that she cannot connect to the lightness of the Reds. She can't *feel* love, Beelzebub. Until her bonds are broken, she won't be able to love you back. She can be drawn to you and feel a certain tug and comfort in your presence, but she isn't capable of recognizing that emotion. She didn't even know what it was when she was staring at a couple who were very much in love. That emotion—romantic love—is lost to her for the time being," she explained. I nodded, because even though it was a revelation and Amelia meant it to be, it also wasn't.

I understood Margot better for it now. It wasn't so much that my songbird wanted to deny her feelings for me, she just simply didn't know how to put them to words. She didn't know how to recognize them for what they were. She couldn't choose to love me until we released her from her binding. Loving her would come with pain until then; it would come with rejection and a lack of understanding, but she'd be worth it. "I understand," I said.

"There's more. Because Margot has so much magic stored up within her, we both know that she is barreling toward an explosion. When her body takes over, that darkness will claim her form. I haven't felt power like Margot possesses since the first generations of Reds," Amelia explained, but I knew as well as she did that she was dancing around the real admission. The implication of what all that power might mean for Margot.

"What are you saying?"

"If Margot were to lose control of her magic completely, I believe she'll shift into her siren form," she said finally. "And I don't know that she'd ever be able to come back from it."

"A witch with a siren form hasn't existed for centuries," I said, my voice trailing off. The thought that Margot might become so mindlessly lost to the magic of lust that she fed on those around her until they died would be a fate worse than death for her.

Fuck.

"The bloodlines have been diluted over time. The magic spread too thin as the population grew, but Margot takes it in and keeps it forever. She has this well of power that is unlike anything I've ever seen. It's unnatural, and it is going to destroy the woman you know. There is not a doubt in my mind that she cannot remember a day where she wasn't in pain because of it. You have to convince her to help herself, to find a way to release it slowly," she said, turning from me finally and shoving the door to her bedroom open.

Amelia turned for the bathroom, the sound of running water reaching through the closed door. It was unlocked when I turned the knob, stepping into the room to find Margot huddled in the corner of the shower, her legs curled into her chest.

I swung open the door, stepping into the shower without care for the icy water plunging down my back. Touching a hand to Margot's forehead, I gasped as I pulled back. "She's burning up," I said, looking to Amelia for help.

"Bring her to the bedroom," she said, and I did as I was told. Margot's dress was plastered to her body as I lifted her from the shower floor, the shivers that racked her frame sinking into mine. She was so hot to the touch, as if the magic inside her were burning her from the inside out. I lowered her to the mattress, barely having time to straighten before Amelia pressed the tip of a blade to Margot's chest. She carved a line down the center, stopping when I reached out to take the knife at Margot's pained whimper.

"What the fuck are you doing?" I asked, ignoring Amelia's glare as Margot turned eyes to me that had bled to black. The hint of scales at the edge of her face made me swallow, coming face-to-face with the siren that lurked within her—confirmation of Amelia's suspicions. Her cheeks had gone gaunt, her features narrowing as the scent of blood drew her more monstrous form to the surface of her body.

Margot's own fingers curled, the edges of black talons protruding from her nail beds as Amelia continued cutting through her chest, drawing a perfectly straight line. Blood slid over her skin, permeating the air with something heady and smelling of sin. "There is magic in blood," Amelia said, dipping a finger into the blood. She held it out to me as Margot's eyes rolled back, sleep claiming her and saving her from the agony I'd left her in. She rubbed it on my arm, the heat of arousal spreading over me immediately. It drew a groan from me, my body immediately hardening with the need to fuck.

Was this what Margot lived with daily?

Fuck.

"That should ease some of her pain for now, but it's a bandage for a situation that has no resolution if she doesn't help herself. She's going to lose control, Beelzebub, and it's going to happen soon," Amelia said, heading for the door with a sad look back at Margot.

"How much time does she have before . . . ?"

"I really couldn't say. It could be days, could be a week. You have to get through to her, and you have to do it fast. For tonight, do yourself a favor and go find something to fuck that out of your system. I know I'm going to," she said, nodding to the blood on my arm and leaving the room. I took the seat beside the bed where Margot slept, not daring to touch her body with the magic now coating my skin and making me feel hornier than I could ever remember being. She was so peaceful, so quiet. I didn't want to fill the air with anything that might disturb that.

So I sat there in silence and bore the weight of her magic in her place.

23

MARGOT

My body ached with a deep pulsing feeling that thrummed through my center. Rubbing at the lingering scar that curved down my chest between my breasts, I studiously avoided Beelzebub's watchful gaze as we made our way down to the dining room for breakfast. I shuddered to think of what might await us when we arrived. I had the distinct feeling the early hour would mean nothing in this place where the souls so deeply embraced the sin that confined them here. Perhaps it was the knowledge that an eternity spent doing the very act that had brought them joy while they'd been living was far preferable to the fate that awaited them on the cliffs.

Maybe it was just the freedom that came from acceptance once it could no longer be avoided. I couldn't help but think of the parallels that could be drawn between the souls trapped here and the choice Charlotte Hecate had made. If she was going to be condemned for witchcraft, she might as well do everything in her power to be guilty of the crime.

I envied the freedom in that choice, the ability to simply accept oneself for what they were and thrive within the confines of their own expectations. I wished I could sink into that familiarity, to find the place where my magic and I became one instead of it simply feeling like a passenger intruding within my own body, taking root where there should have only been me.

"Are you sure you're feeling up to this? We could rest today, leave tomorrow if you need more time," Beelzebub said, and I shook my head at his constant need to pester me. Even the suspicion that his intentions were in the right place wasn't enough to stave off the annoyance I felt every time he inserted himself into my business. I hated the feeling of being a burden—despised the sensation that he was obligated to care for me between the song that held him captive and the allegiance he felt toward Lucifer. He'd only grown more attentive after the night before and what had happened after we'd . . .

I didn't even want to think of what we'd almost done.

"I'm fine. I just need to get the fuck out of this Goddess-damned circle," I grunted, not caring enough to restrain my tone. The snappiness of the words was evident enough to make most turn away, but he kept that soft gaze on the side of my face. He was an immovable force, a tempest waiting to erupt into chaos and wind at the sign of trouble, and it didn't bring me comfort to know that was at my beck and call.

I didn't trust myself enough not to use it.

I strode forward through the entry to the dining room, my eyes darting around and searching for the carnal acts I felt so certain would surround me. If I could take them in all at once, maybe the repeated shocks would ease and the tension of the magic couldn't build.

But there was no sex in the room, nothing even to remotely indicate the sordid acts that had occurred in the manor only the night before. The participants sat around a long, rectangular table at the center of the room, sipping juice and coffee and holding their heads in their hands. It reminded me of the hangovers I'd seen being nursed after the students of Hollow's Grove got into a few too many bottles in the woods after they snuck out, but I hadn't been left with the impression that these people had been drinking enough to justify *this*.

I stared at them in confusion, my attention turning to Asmodeus as he stood from the head of the table in a smooth, elegant glide. His lithe body moved toward me slowly, his swagger so close to a prowl that I took an involuntary step back and ran into Beelzebub's chest. He settled a single hand on top of my shoulder, a silent support that I hadn't wanted only a moment before. But it made me still, made me swallow down my own apprehension as the archdemon before me spread his mouth into a feral grin, revealing the glint of teeth that he ran his tongue over.

He stopped before me, risking Beelzebub's wrath to touch a fingertip to the scabbed-over flesh on my chest where my top had left it revealed. "There's our little firecracker," he said, grinning as Beelzebub's hand slid off my shoulder. He curved his arm around my waist, wrapping me in a harsh embrace. Asmodeus's attention left me, going to the Lord of Flies where he stood behind me. I didn't need to turn to feel the rage in Beelzebub's glare, to watch the battle arc between them like sparks of lightning. Asmodeus removed his hand smoothly, raising his finger and drawing it into his mouth as if to taste me. "Please, come sit, Margot. It would be so rude of me not to offer you nourishment in exchange for what you gave us last night."

"What I gave?" I asked, following after him as I studied the people at the table. Amelia sat beside the chair Asmodeus had vacated, her cheeks full of color whereas the others' were pale and slick with the sheen of sweat.

"The magic Amelia carved from your chest," Asmodeus answered as he pulled out the chair to his opposite side. I settled into it as Beelzebub growled beneath his breath, scaring the person who sat on my opposite side until he toppled out of his chair. His movement was sluggish as he got to his feet, moving to an open chair farther down the table as I watched in complete bewilderment. "It was more than enough to feed this circle for the next week, and she only kept half of it. I cannot imagine what you have kept locked away inside of you. Magic that we will make great use of here instead of letting it go to waste!"

"If she only took half, where did the other half go?" I asked as Asmodeus took his seat at the head of the table. I watched in horror as his gaze slid to my side, glancing over to Beelzebub with an arrogant smirk.

"He didn't tell you that he absorbed the other half? His control is remarkable really. Amelia came downstairs and immediately shared that magic with the others, casting a wide net so that everyone had the privilege of feeling such unrestrained lust. But our precious Beelzebub never emerged from that bedroom, sitting vigil at your side all night. I do wonder if that is to account for his surly disposition this morning. Any normal demon would have fucked the first woman he laid eyes on with that much lust riding his body. He must be very smitten with you to abstain from such a release, little Red witch. He always was the softest of all of us. The most *loyal* to his cause."

"That's enough," Beelzebub snapped, standing from the dining room table. He held out a hand for me, and I narrowed my gaze at it. Opening myself up to the magic surrounding us, letting the tiniest inkling of it seep inside, I felt the magic swirling about him, the aura of desire that he hadn't bothered to rid himself of.

It shouldn't have pleased me that he'd rejected the opportunity to find pleasure in the body of another. I should have been horrified to know the deep, tumultuous storm that waited inside him, begging for release, and the knowledge should have set heavy on me that he bore that pain because of me.

Because he'd taken it from me, so that I wouldn't hurt anymore.

Instead, something within me practically purred with satisfaction—content in the knowledge that if I'd been willing, he would have chosen me. He would have picked me out of this entire room filled with the greatest beauties I'd ever seen—all genders and bodies to choose from.

He would have picked me.

It warmed me for only a moment before it fizzled out, leaving me to grasp at the remains of something that had soothed my insides and coming up empty-handed. Beelzebub didn't miss the momentary softening, his head tipping ever so slightly to the side. He mistook it for concern, the harsh line of his mouth going soft as he murmured to me, "I'm alright, songbird."

I shook off my care that something had been taken from me, shoved down the dreams of being able to care and to love so fully. They were not meant for me, and caring for a person in a way that was anything close to romantic would be a mistake under the best circumstances, never knowing if that person was with me for their love of me or for my magic. Falling for someone who had already been exposed to my song twice was the stupidest move a Red witch could make if she wanted something genuine.

I wanted someone who wanted me. Not the Red witch or the siren. Not the pretty girl whom the Council was so sure would grow into a great and terrible beauty.

Me.

Beelzebub knew the moment had passed, sighing as he turned his attention back to the lord of Lust. "We're leaving," he said as I placed my hand in his, helping me rise from my seat. The breakfast on my plate sat uneaten, and though hunger made my stomach churn, I couldn't bring myself to grab a morsel off that plate, not knowing we were already on the edge of something violent when Asmodeus's brow rose in response. He stood from his seat as Beelzebub guided me out of the dining room, hurrying me through the manor. I had to run to keep up with his fast pace, and he quickly matched me in stride as we darted out the front doors and onto the patio. We turned right instead of left, moving away from the garden where we'd entered the Second Circle.

Asmodeus threw the doors open behind us, walking out of the manor as if he didn't have a care in the world. "She belongs here, Beelzebub!" he shouted, Red magic swirling about his arms as we raced off the other side of the patio and hurried into the lush greenery of the surrounding landscape.

"Lucifer would argue otherwise!" Beelzebub snapped, shouting the words back. I saw them for what they were, an attempt to remind Asmodeus that there may be consequences for his attempt to keep me here against my will. While the devil Himself may not have given one moment of His time to care about what happened to me, He *did* care about keeping His wife happy.

And Willow would stop at nothing to help me be free. I might have only known her for a short time, but in that time she had advocated for me and my rights more than anyone I'd known in my entire life. She didn't murder Itan only to watch me be trapped in the same Hell as him so soon. I glanced back at the cliffs with a shudder, hoping he had never entertained Asmodeus enough to be freed from that torment. Of all the souls who resided here, he deserved the most suffering out of any I'd personally known.

"Do you trust me?" Beelzebub asked, skidding to a stop suddenly. Something hazy lingered in front of us, some sort of barrier that I could see through if I focused. While this side contained lush gardens teeming with life, they were nothing compared to the overabundance on the other side. There was no trace of civilization to be found, no sign of people anywhere, and yet the trees rocketed toward the sky and arched over the gardens, the flowers and vegetables within larger than anything I'd ever seen. "Margot, do you fucking trust me?" Beelzebub repeated, snapping my attention back to him.

"I don't understand," I said, confusion lacing my tone as I met his gaze.

I was vaguely aware of Asmodeus approaching at my back, of the polarizing Red magic to either side of me. The boundary before me seemed to exist as if it had been crafted from the magic of the circle itself, but Asmodeus radiated with it as he came to a stop behind me. He held out his hand, palm facing up in invitation. "Margot," he said, his voice dropping low. It was the faintest murmur, but I felt it strike me in the chest, sinking into my belly. Heat churned there, swirling within me as if Amelia hadn't taken any the night before. He rekindled that magic anew, my lungs heaving as I tried to push it back. I took a step toward him, my body moving even as my mind screamed in protest.

"No!" I yelled, voicing the pain as I reached out for Beelzebub at my side. He took my arm, restraining me so that I couldn't go to the man who stood before me. Asmodeus's beauty was undeniable, it always had been, but there was something more potent about it when he fixated his magic on me. His eyes seemed to glow brighter, and the angles of his face were like the most perfectly carved sculpture from antiquity. "I won't."

"You belong here with us, Margot," Asmodeus said, his voice like a song. I felt my own voice rise to my throat, practically choking on it to keep myself from answering that call. I knew to do so would condemn me, felt it in my bones like someone was trying to warn me. "Stay with me."

Beelzebub left my side, rushing across the gap between him and the other archdemon. Shoving Asmodeus into a tree, he pinned him there with a hand at his throat as he pummeled his fist into his face. Asmodeus grinned through a mouthful of blood, and the scent of it on the air only made the need building within me stronger. I took another step toward the two, drawn to the magic in the air even if I hated it.

"No!" Beelzebub shouted, holding out his free hand. I stilled, staring at his palm as he fought for breath.

"Step through the boundary. Gluttony is on the other side, songbird. I'll follow as soon as you're through," he said, shoving harder at Asmodeus's throat as the other archdemon struggled against Beelzebub's hold. He was no match for Beel's strength, sputtering and gasping as he drew a finger down Beelzebub's bare chest. The motion was so sensual it made something within me clench, but Beelzebub ignored him as if he was used to his antics and his undermining way of fighting against Beel's brute force.

Fighting off the paragon of lust himself.

I stilled, horror running through me.

Beelzebub was *immune*.

"She can't. I forbid it," Asmodeus said, grinning at me. The seduction of the smile was ruined by the blood staining his teeth, but it was more than just the dampening effect it gave that made me take a step back, gritting my teeth against the call to go toward him.

No man tells me what to fucking do. Not anymore.

Beelzebub smiled as if he knew just how thoroughly Asmodeus had fucked himself, his deep chuckle of amusement forming a different heat within me. Instead of feeling compelled to go near him against my will, the warmth within me felt like approval, like comfort and acceptance and the warmth of a fire on a winter day. I kept my glare on Asmodeus as I took another step back, raising a hand to stroke the thin boundary between the two circles. Red magic rose up to greet me, twining itself around my fingers as I hesitated in fear.

What if it didn't allow me to pass? What if it rejected me?

"Look at me, songbird," Beelzebub said, the soft tone making me obey in spite of myself. His red stare was soft, his mouth curved into a smile that I felt in the depths of my soul. "You can do this. Don't you dare shrink yourself to fit into the box he wants to put you in. You are more than he would have you be."

I felt the weight of those words in my heart, the implication striking deep as I turned my stare to Asmodeus. He was so like the others I'd known who wanted me to conform, to behave as a Red witch should.

To embrace the magic that had never felt like mine.

Fuck that.

I severed the bond between Asmodeus and me, cutting the cords of red tendrils he'd extended out to me. They swayed in the wind as I turned away from him fully, looking at Beelzebub from the corner of my eye.

"That's impossible," Asmodeus muttered behind me, but I didn't give his words time to give me pause.

I plunged myself into the boundary, into the Red magic that would consume me if I allowed it.

And I trusted that Beelzebub would find me on the other side.

24

MARGOT

I landed on the other side, sprawled out on the grass with a laugh bubbling in my throat. Magic still rode my body, making my skin feel warm and flushed when it had no place being so any longer. I took the moment alone to center myself against its influence, to ground myself as I pushed to sit up. Shoving all that power back into the well within me, I allowed it to resettle without the constant prodding energy of the Second Circle. I felt it resting on the other side of that boundary, waiting like it would welcome me with open arms, but it had allowed me to pass regardless.

Beelzebub burst through the boundary, his gaze finding mine immediately. He grinned as he saw me sitting on the ground, holding out a hand to help me up. I allowed it, rising to face Asmodeus's rage-filled features on the other side of the boundary. He didn't motion to pass through to the Third Circle, not with Beelzebub standing guard beside me.

We were surrounded by Gluttony, a kingdom crafted from excess as I looked around and took everything in. "How did we manage to pass through here without Asmodeus's approval?" I asked, allowing Beelzebub to guide me with a hand at my waist, turning me in the direction he wanted us to go. I walked beside him, immensely grateful for how easy it was to navigate the springy grass of Gluttony compared to the deep sands of Purgatory that had been literal Hell to walk on. The boots on my feet were far more comfortable without the scalding heat attempting to penetrate the soles, and I felt my body flag as it enjoyed the ease of our stroll.

"We would have needed his approval to pass through using the portal, but Asmodeus greatly overestimates his own importance. His sin may not be pride, but that doesn't mean his vanity over his own sex appeal hasn't done damage to his overinflated ego in all facets of his life," Beelzebub said, smirking down at me as I stared up at him from the side of my eye. "It is our job to make sure the circle we are responsible for is fed, not the other way around. We serve the magic. Somewhere along the line some of us have forgotten that and act like it exists to help us."

"Careful, you are in grave danger of sounding like Willow," I said, grinning through the warning.

Beel grunted, the smile drifting from his face as his expression turned hesitantly thoughtful. "I will admit my first assessment of your friend may not have been fair or true to the nature she has shown in the time that has passed since. I believe she simply does what she believes is right at every turn, and while that may sometimes lead her astray in certain aspects, she does it with the best intentions."

"That sounded perilously close to a compliment," I said, unable to hold back my laughter.

He smiled down at me, turning to face me more fully as we walked as if he couldn't bear not to look at me at that moment. I sank my teeth into my bottom lip, turning my gaze away with a flush. I studied my surroundings more thoroughly, from the massive lilies to the biggest oranges I'd ever seen growing on a tree that stretched toward the sky.

"I'll deny every word if you ever share it," he said, earning a chuckle from me.

"I would expect nothing less, demon," I snarked, letting us lapse into silence.

I was brimming with questions about Gluttony, about how

far we would need to travel and what would be required of me in this place. I didn't think it would be much, given that Beelzebub was the lord of this circle and would easily grant me permission to pass.

We walked in silence for only a few moments, Beelzebub's body close to mine even though he made no move to touch me as we traveled. I felt him at my side, brimming with energy that was my fault, and guilt plagued me knowing he hadn't been able to release it since. Acknowledging that energy pulsing between us felt dangerous, like acknowledging something better left unspoken if I wanted to remain in my safe little haven of denial.

What had happened between us the night before had been a mistake, a necessity if we wanted to escape the Second Circle. Even still, it lingered between us, neither of us knowing how to broach the conversation I wasn't ready for. I wasn't ready to tell Beelzebub that if it hadn't been for the excess magic, I never would have lost control the way I had. I didn't know how to tell him that I respected him for putting a stop to things when I hadn't been able to, for exercising restraint on my behalf. It went a long way to earning my trust, to me understanding that my body was safe with him.

Sometime in the night, the lines between us had shifted. He was no longer the one who couldn't be trusted.

I was.

The realization of his immunity to my magic was a complex one, leaving me relieved that I had not, in fact, stripped him of his consent and will after all. If Asmodeus himself couldn't do it, I didn't stand a chance. But that left me with one thrilling yet horrifying reality I needed to face.

Beelzebub wanted me, and that desire was genuine. It wasn't the consequence of my magic, or a pull he couldn't control. How long had I spent wondering what it would feel like to be desired and to know beyond a shadow of a doubt that it was real and not a ploy of magic?

I cleared my throat, not willing to dive into that conversation just yet. "Thank you for believing in me. For encouraging me when I needed it most. Without you there, I never would have been able to evade Asmodeus and step through that boundary," I said, swallowing thickly as I glanced up toward the sky. "And thank you for last night. For staying in control when I lost it. I don't know what I would have done if—"

"You don't need to worry about that," he said, and for a moment my heart fell into my stomach. I wondered if the night before had changed his opinion of me, if he no longer desired me in the same way he had. Maybe my behavior had shattered whatever illusion of higher standards he'd seen in me, and just as I was realizing the truth of his attraction, it had passed—a fleeting thing in the wind.

The thought wasn't as welcome as it should have been.

I swallowed, my tongue feeling thick in my mouth as I fought to find casual words. He couldn't know the contradictions within me, the mess that I'd become, thanks to him. "I don't?"

He smirked, gripping me by the hand as he pulled me to a stop. I paused, turning to him and keeping my face carefully blank so he wouldn't see the nerves within me. He leaned forward, touching his forehead to mine and waiting. The gesture was so like what Amelia and I had observed through the window that I swallowed thickly, my throat closing as my gut swirled.

His eyes remained on mine, searching for any hint of rejection or objection as one of those callous hands rose slowly. He toyed with the ends of my hair before sliding his hand beneath the curtain of my hair to cup my jaw, holding me captive in a gentle embrace that was so much more than lust. This was the danger that lingered beyond sex, the true damage that waited for me on the other side of the pleasure I could not have.

It was the possibility of love. Lingering just out of reach. My wrists throbbed where the marks of my magical binding lingered just out of sight, spreading an ache through me for what I would never truly feel.

This.

My eyes drifted closed, lashes fluttering as I sighed into him, tension bleeding out from my body as he cupped my cheek with his other hand. The warmth of his palms sank into me as we shared breath, the intimacy of the act—of simply breathing the same air and existing as one—rending my nerves from me.

His mouth touched mine gently, the faintest brush of his lips pulling a sigh from me. He swallowed it, pulling me tighter into his chest when I didn't pull away.

I couldn't find the will or the strength to do so, sinking into him more fully as I raised my hands to rest on his chest. Our kisses the night before had been full of intensity, of lust and longing and all the headier aspects of this strange, pulsating attraction I couldn't deny any longer. This was the other side of the coin, everything soft and emotional and intimate as my nails dug into his flesh, drawing a groan from him. He deepened the kiss, his tongue slipping inside to taste me.

Nobody had ever kissed me this way, like I mattered beyond an itch that needed to be scratched.

Beelzebub held me like I mattered, like he believed I was more than the box life had put me in. I tasted his sin on his tongue, the obsession that drove him to possess things. It crashed into me, tangling with my own sin and becoming something different altogether before he finally pulled back and stared down at me. His stare was heavy and meaningful when I opened my eyes, and I realized again that it hadn't been me who had pulled away and ended the embrace.

"I don't want to be something you regret, songbird," he said, releasing my face and taking a step back. He watched me as if he saw just how deeply affected I was, as if he wanted me to sit with that and consider what it meant for me and for us. "I want to be your everything."

He turned, resuming his earlier pace and leaving me no choice but to get my shit together and follow after him. He stayed close, capturing my hand in his, though he didn't push any further contact.

"You're a menace," I said, huffing a laugh in an attempt to hide just how deeply he'd affected me with that kiss.

He turned to look at me over his shoulder, the curve of his mouth a hint that I wasn't fooling anyone. "Only for you, Margot."

I resisted the urge to touch my tingling lips, to rub the numbness from them as I realized a very real, simple truth.

I was so far out of my element, fighting a battle I didn't stand a chance of winning.

What kind of monster did it make me that I had never been so happy to lose?

25

BEELZEBUB

The landscape changed as we walked, the hours behind us seeing the land shift from the fervent lands filled with the largest delicacies and plant life of any of the circles of Hell. Though the path we walked was still teeming with life, the area surrounding it had begun to fade into the mud pits that kept the gluttonous trapped in the sludge they'd filled themselves with in life. Worms crawled through the muck that I knew from experience was as cold as ice. Margot was largely silent at my side as we headed in the direction of the manor, and I couldn't help the smug satisfaction that churned through my gut.

I'd silenced her protests with a kiss, stolen all objections from her mouth.

Something had shifted in her when we escaped the Second Circle, and I couldn't put my finger on exactly what it had been, but it had definitely been for the better when it came to letting me inside those walls she'd built to the sky.

Dealing with Margot felt like walking a tightrope. If I pushed too hard in any direction, she would topple right off the side and plummet to the ground. It was a careful balancing game, a give-and-take to make her see the value in allowing me to get close to her. She had to want me enough to go against her own staunch morals and fear that she might take something that wasn't freely given. She had to be willing to challenge the worldview she'd sharpened into a pointed weapon to keep the world out.

It would take time for my songbird to realize that she was not sensitive like glass, only a moment from cracking. She was sensitive like a bomb, ready to explode with power at any given moment.

She tripped as I watched, reaching out to grasp her as she stared down in horror at what had appeared in her path. A hand emerged from the mud, reaching even though there was no body visible beneath the thick, viscous mud at our side. Only the shoulder to the hand protruded, stretching toward the sky with grasping fingers as the fucking thing reached for Margot again. Pulling back my leg, I prepared to kick it back into the pit that had become its resting place.

"There are *people* in there?" Margot asked, her voice incredulous. She distracted me with her words, reaching down as if she might grab the soul and pull it out of its eternity of suffering.

"Margot, no!" I yelled, grasping her around the waist and pulling her back. The Source didn't take kindly to those who took from her, who stole the souls that had comprised the powers of the circles for so long. The Source may not have approved of her confinement in this place, but that didn't mean she could just allow her power to slip away, either. We dealt within the confines of the fate we'd been given, even those of us who had been wronged.

Margot looked up at the tree beside her when the branches rustled, and we watched as a small black blur leapt from a branch to land on the hand where it reached for her. Jonathan sank his teeth into the fleshy part between the thumb and forefinger, shaking his head as he tore through the skin. The hand flinched back, diving back into the mud as Jonathan leapt for the shoreline, landing just beside Margot and me. He shook his head from side to side, flinging mud from his mouth before he finally stilled, rubbing his tongue on the grass to get the rest off.

He heaved, his mouth opening on a gag as he mewled, turning a judgmental stare toward the mud pit and backing away a step. "Jonathan!" Margot said, leaping out of my hold to wrap the fucking cat in her embrace. He nuzzled into the side of her face, purring as she cradled him like he was some kind of baby and not a cursed creature who had once been a murderous, misogynistic bastard.

But all was forgiven because now he had fur.

Women.

"You were supposed to stay in Purgatory," I said, raising my brow at the little shit. He pressed his face more tightly into Margot's, his paws kneading at the flesh of her arm in contentment. He didn't seem to care what I thought, and I knew it was because he'd gotten his orders from Willow, the *consort* that was his master. "Let's keep moving."

"You could at least pretend to be happy to see him! Look, no more boo-boo," Margot said, her voice rising into that sweet baby voice women insisted on using with children and animals.

"Boo-boo? He's older than you are," I said, rolling my eyes as I strolled forward. It wasn't much farther before we would reach the safety of my manor, giving us a place where Margot could finally get a good night's sleep and some food to satisfy the hunger I knew had to be tempting her with everything around us. Whether it was a healthy caution that made her hesitate to touch any of the food we passed or some knowledge she already had, she hadn't made any attempt to eat.

Smart girl, either way. The food around us was a trap meant to ensnare those who were too gluttonous to resist temptation into the mud pits, our way of testing whether or not a soul was meant to remain here. Her lack of instinct to touch the food would be her test that would allow her to pass through—the magic of the Third Circle in agreement with me.

She didn't belong here.

A giant figure loomed at the gates that beckoned in the distance, stretched across the single bridge that would allow us to reach the safety of my home within Hell. Jonathan hissed as we came closer, walking the narrow path to lead up to the gate. The mud curved around the path, cutting us off so there was no going off the road to get around the enormous dog.

Cerberus bowed her head, chuffing as she scented the air. Her tail wagged as she recognized my scent, turning so her good eye faced me. She'd been blinded sometime in the years before I'd found her in the wilds, her left eye opaque and white. "Hey, sweet girl," I said, stepping forward to rub her nose with an open hand. She pressed into the touch, turning to Margot as Jonathan jumped down from her hold and backed away while hissing.

Margot crossed her arms over her chest as Cerberus smelled her, quirking a brow as she glared over at me. "Sweet girl?" she asked, clearly finding some kind of amusement in the term of endearment.

I shrugged as Cerberus drooled onto the ground, the saliva coming dangerously close to landing on Jonathan where he stood gaping up at the dog that was easily ten times his size. Cerberus nuzzled into Margot, making the woman's expression soften as she petted the top of her head gently. Only when she'd gotten the pats she thought she'd earned did Cerberus turn her attention down to the cat mingling at Margot's legs, moving to sniff him.

The cat swatted her across the face when she came too close, claws bared as if they would do anything against the massive dog. Cerberus blinked, staring after Jonathan as he twirled around Margot's legs with his tail raised high and swirling about like he was proud of himself. I nodded to Margot, wrapping an arm around her waist as she scooped the insufferable cat into her arms and I guided her through the gates as they swung open to beckon me home.

It pleased me greatly that Margot didn't flinch or move away from my casual touch.

The manor before us was a sprawling estate of opulence. Plants of all kinds filled the surrounding property. People ate peacefully on blankets across the yard, tucked into shaded alcoves provided by the ample trees as they looked out over the mud pits to the gardens beyond. The building itself was tall, with spindles and spires and dormers protruding from flat walls. Windows covered every inch of the property, a golden light shining from within as I guided Margot up to the first step that would take us to the foyer.

"It's like something from a fairy tale," Margot said, her eyes widening as she took in the size of the home. The wings split off in each direction, the gothic architecture standing out against the brightness of the landscape. "And nothing like Lust."

"We all have our personal tastes," I said, shrugging as I shoved open the doors. They parted with an easy push, spreading as Margot stepped over the threshold and entered the only place I'd ever been able to call home. "This is mine," I added, as I followed after her, taking in the sight of her bathed in the light from the chandelier overhead. It seemed to dance over her skin, making her glow with a pulse of light in a place that reeked of death.

"It's perfect," she said, offering the thoughts I hadn't even asked for. I didn't need to, not with the knowledge that Hollow's Grove had felt like home, too, its style so similar to the one I'd chosen for myself all those years ago.

"I'm glad you think so," I said, closing the door behind me. If we couldn't find a way to return to the surface, if Willow couldn't open the portal in time to bring Margot home, *this* would be her new home.

Right where she belonged in spite of her lack of affinity for the magic, with me at her side.

26

MARGOT

The light within was almost blinding as the chandelier spun in a circle, casting a pattern on the stone entryway surrounding me. The effect was stunning, a remarkable display of craftsmanship that made the room feel like a piece of art. "Lord Beelzebub?" a male voice asked, and I spun to look at the demon who stood atop the stairs. He hurried down them, throwing his weight into Beelzebub's in a friendly hug as the two men patted each other on the back.

"Moloch, shouldn't you be convening with the Order?" Beelzebub asked, glancing toward the clock hanging on the wall in the formal dining room through one of the arched doorways. The ceilings were high within, curtains pulled half-closed over the angled windows that stretched from floor to ceiling and covered the front and opposite side wall. A subtly patterned wallpaper adorned the walls behind the built-in shelves of dark redwood, the color a deep midnight blue that would have been too dark if not for the size of the room and the natural light filtering in, as well as the candles that hung from the chandelier over the massive table designed to seat at least ten. Voices drifted out from the room, even though I could not see anyone from the angle I had peering through the doorway.

"On my way there now. They'll be thrilled, but confused, to see you back here so soon," the other demon said, gesturing Beelzebub forward. He finally turned his eyes to me as Beelzebub reached out and took my hand in his, entwining his warm fingers with mine as the demon's stare fell to the statement in that touch.

"We ran into some trouble with Michael above the surface. Satanus hasn't sent word that he was bringing him to the prison?" Beelzebub asked, concern lacing his voice. I had to watch the exchange, my attention shifting back and forth between the two men as they had a silent conversation. The other demon's stare was full of suspicion as he looked at me, his mistrust of me and the news I was undoubtedly privy to evident in the twist of his lips.

"Must have slipped his mind. Typical Satanus," the demon said with a roll of his eyes. "Should I have one of the staff show the woman to a room while we convene? Perhaps she would like a bath and some time to rest? This is no place for a witch, let alone a Red."

"The woman's name is Margot," Beelzebub said, his voice laced with a bite of aggravation. "She stays with me. I have no secrets from her."

I swallowed, the intensity of that statement filling me with warmth. The very notion that someone would be honest with me willingly, that I wouldn't have to pry the truth out of them, was so unknown to me. Beelzebub trusted me with his secrets. Could I trust him with mine?

"Very well," Moloch said, nodding his head thoughtfully. His disapproval was clear in the bitter smile he plastered onto his face, accompanied by a frustrated shake of his head as Beelzebub spun away to lead me into the dining room behind us.

The table was ornate as we passed by it, and I couldn't resist the urge to run my hand over the carefully crafted lines of wood and the chairs that mimicked the circular pattern etched into the table. "You like it?" Beelzebub asked, his attention fixated on where my hands explored the grooves and lines in the wood.

"It's beautiful," I said, pulling my hand back. A flush warmed my cheek, the moment feeling far more carnal than it should have with Beel's intense red stare on me.

Moloch strode around us, but I couldn't pull my stare away from Beelzebub as he shifted closer to me. "Beelzebub!" a feminine voice said, breaking the moment as I turned to face the woman making her way toward us. She glided forward on heeled feet, a terracotta-colored dress swirling about her legs. It hung loosely off her shoulders, draping over her body like it had been cut to fit her and made of the finest fabric. It molded to her flawlessly. Her lips spread into a familiar smile as she closed the distance between her and Beelzebub. Her arms spread like she intended to touch him, and the sly glance she gave me was full of questions.

I tried to pull my hand back from his, wincing when he tightened his grip in a refusal to release me. "Proserpina," Beelzebub said, his voice devoid of all warmth. The woman's smile faltered, her brow furrowing as she wrapped her arms around him and hugged him far too tightly. Her body pressed into his with the contact, marking what she believed to be her territory. Jealousy bloomed behind my eyes, my teeth clenching as I fought back the urge to tear her arms from his body. I had no right to feel that way, even as she pulled back and ran her hands over his chest affectionately.

Beelzebub for his part took a step back, leaving her hands to fall away as he shifted closer to me, putting my body between him and the demoness. Proserpina's gaze shifted down to me fully, taking in the sight of me as Beelzebub twisted our arms, raising our clasped hands so that his arm rested across my chest, joined with mine at my hip. His breath fanned over my temple as he leaned closer, and I felt like I'd found myself caught in the middle of a war of wills.

She wanted him, that much was clear, and the gluttonous were not accustomed to being deprived of the things they wanted.

The question that I had yet to figure out was about the nature of their relationship prior to this moment. Proserpina certainly behaved as if she knew Beelzebub intimately, but that didn't mean she did. Maybe it was just my wishful thinking, but I hoped it was more an instance of a woman who *wanted* to be intimate with him rather than one who already had been.

I wasn't stupid enough to think that Beelzebub was a virgin, but that didn't mean I wanted to see everything I would never be staring back at me, or compare myself to the confident, experienced women of his past.

"Everything alright?" a man asked as he stepped up, his blond hair shaggy as he shoved his hands into the pockets of the same soft leather pants all the men seemed to wear.

"We're fine," Proserpina murmured, recovering quickly with a breathtaking smile that had a malicious edge. "I simply didn't realize Beelzebub was going through a blond phase again."

"Don't," Beelzebub warned, his arm tightening across my chest. The growl that came from him was for her, not for me, but I knew at that moment exactly the nature of their relationship. My muscles tightened with anger, my own cruel smile rising to meet hers as hunger made my stomach cramp.

If I hadn't already come to the conclusion, her next words would have confirmed it. "He'll come back to me again when he's done. He prefers brunettes," she said, turning away to smile at the man who had come up to support her. He smiled as if she were an unruly child, and even though the words hadn't been directed at me, there was no doubting the intended target of her cruelty.

"Margot . . ." Beelzebub said, and though he continued speaking, I stopped hearing him over the ringing in my ears. I didn't want his excuses, especially not when he didn't owe me anything, but that didn't stop me from craving blood from the woman who had so callously tried to wound me when she knew nothing about me. I'd lived enough of my life surrounded by women who might have torn one another down at the first opportunity. It had taken the development of my closest friendships for me to realize just how toxic those relationships were.

And how much more they said about the person wielding their own cruelty than about the victims.

I was so tired of being someone's punching bag, of being the recipient of unnecessary cruelty. I was done lying down so that others could kick me more easily.

I tore myself away from Beelzebub so suddenly that he stumbled forward, unraveling myself from his grip as I stormed toward the demoness. She turned as I approached, a condescending smile falling from her face as she took in the sight of me. The hand I raised to her throat was covered in the faint sheen of scales, iridescent in the light streaming in the windows as I wrapped them around her throat. My gums ached as I rolled my neck, lifting the demon from the ground so her feet kicked aimlessly as she stared down at me in horror. I strode forward, slamming her into the wall so harshly that it shook beneath the force. Books thumped against one another on the shelves closest to us.

"What *are* you?" she asked, her hands grasping at her throat. She dug her nails into my skin, drawing my blood to the surface. The scent of it mixed with the hunger erupting through me, the need to tear her limb from limb and gorge myself on her so unlike me that I blinked.

The anger rocketing through me was unlike me. It didn't feel like mine, and yet I couldn't deny my fury that she thought she could own something that I wanted.

The admission, even to myself, didn't sober me as much as it should have. Instead, it spurred me on, letting me sink into that gluttonous feeling and the need to keep Beelzebub for myself.

The need for him, and all his attention, to be *mine*.

"Holy shit," the blond demon said, stepping forward to stare at the side of my face. "It's been centuries . . ."

"Enough," Beelzebub said behind me as he moved to stand beside me so I could see him from the corner of my eye. "I have no problem with you playing with her, songbird. Just try not to give in to that desire to eat her, at the very least. That taste is hard to get rid of, and I'll be very upset if I have to taste her when I kiss you later."

I snarled, turning toward him as I bared my teeth. Teeth that shouldn't have been as long as they were. I stared down at the scales on my arms, confusion dawning through the jealous rage that consumed me. It was there for a fleeting moment and then gone, just long enough to notice the faint blue tint to my skin. Like I was already dead and rotting, like I'd been trapped beneath the surface of the water and drowned.

The siren form my mother had given so much for me to have.

"Aren't you going to do something?" Proserpina said, her voice going shrill as tears filled her eyes.

"Looks like Margot has it handled to me," Beelzebub said with a shrug, leaning his shoulder into the wall as he stared at me. "It's about time someone put you in your place when you show your whole fucking ass."

"Beelzebub, you've got to be fucking kidding me. Control your girl or I will," the blond said, earning a snarl from me. It was obvious there was a certain level of comfort between the group and Beelzebub, and that only drove my anger higher.

The sound was echoed by Beelzebub's smile dropping off his face, pushing off the wall with his shoulder as he closed the distance between us. "Remember your place, and no one *controls* her," he said, the words laced with malice. Proserpina reached out for him, touching a hand to his arm like it might entice him to offer her aid, but his attention didn't so much as flick toward her or away from the blond. He twisted his arm, catching Proserpina and pulling her arm back at a bad angle while the man watched. "You lay a hand on my woman, and it will be the last time you have hands to put on her," he warned, the threat sending a ripple up my spine.

The man huffed, looking back and forth between Beelzebub and me as if trying to make sense of our bond. I leaned into Proserpina's space, nearly touching my forehead to hers in something akin to affection. Trailing a single black nail over her cheek, I watched the blood well beneath the line I drew. I leaned closer, dragging my tongue over the droplet of blood where it slid from the wound. I pulled back more slowly than I wanted to, revulsion making my stomach churn as the sweetness of her blood danced over my tastebuds. "You no longer have the right to touch him," I growled, waiting for her responding nod. She didn't seem particularly inclined to Beelzebub anymore since he'd allowed me to put my hands on her anyway, but I followed it with a threat that could have probably remained unspoken. "The next time you do, I won't only take a sampling."

"I thought sirens only ate men?" the blond man asked as I pulled back, dropping Proserpina to the floor. Beelzebub was at my side immediately, wrapping his arms around me and guiding me toward the mirror on the wall. The gaunt face staring back at me was anything but beautiful with hollowed-out cheeks and bluish skin. I looked like I belonged in the depths of the ocean, not trapped in the confines of Hell. My eyes had bled to black, filling the whites and the irises, but was slowly receding as I stared at myself. The iridescent scales that played at my temples fading back into smooth skin, my cheeks filling and life returning to my features.

"I don't discriminate," I said, turning to face the group that I had to assume comprised the Order of the Fly in Beelzebub's absence.

"I think it's best we got some rest," Beelzebub said, guiding me back out of the dining room. He didn't waste any time on those we left behind, instead guiding me to the stairs.

He led me into what I had to presume was his bedroom, closing the door behind him. It horrified me to realize that there was none of the telltale fear that usually came when I was locked behind a closed door with a man, only a sigh of comfort at the thought of finally not having to deal with external threats.

Moving from the hardwood floor to the soft shag rug that covered the center of the room, I took in the space around me. His ceiling was arched, a massive bay window offering him a view of the mud pits out the back. With an ornate black headboard and dark walls, the room was devoid of almost any hint of color. A seating area in front of the bay windows called to me, and I dropped into the first chair with a ragged sigh.

"You should lie down for a bit. Get some rest," Beelzebub said, gesturing toward the bed.

I wrinkled my nose, shaking my head. "I don't want to think about who's been in that," I snapped, fighting back the urge to vomit.

Beelzebub chuckled as he knelt at my feet, sinking back onto his haunches as he raised one booted foot and untied the laces. "You didn't seem to mind when it was Amelia's bed, and I think we both know she has had far more partners than I have," he said, finally tugging the boot off. My sock followed, and he gripped my foot in both hands, massaging the tight arch of muscle on the underside with deft fingers that were *definitely* meant to distract me from the matter at hand. "Unless it's not so much about the potential of bodily fluids, and more that they were in there with me."

There was a teasing lilt to his voice, and I ground my teeth together to keep from cursing him out and showing my hand. "I thought we were in Gluttony? Why am I being so affected by completely illogical envy here?" I asked finally, wincing at the confirmation of my feelings. While I was certain there was a magical explanation for it, at least one I could lean into, I hated that there was no way to disguise what I'd been feeling after my antics downstairs.

Beelzebub pressed his thumb into the center of my foot, gliding it down to my heel in a move that drew a moan from me. I covered my mouth immediately when he smirked, his gaze turning heated. "If those are the sounds you make when I rub your feet, then I shudder to think what you'll sound like when I make you come," he said, making me tug back my foot. The words served as the sharp reminder I needed, grounding me in the knowledge that this would never work.

"Beel—" I started.

"The reason you were so jealous about Proserpina touching me," he said, changing the conversation as he stripped off my other boot, "is because you are a Red. Gluttony is about overindulgence of vices, drugs and alcohol, but also food, and you, my love, feed your magic through sex."

I swallowed, fumbling for a response because that couldn't be true in these circumstances. "If that's the case, wouldn't I be jealous of anyone being touched? Wouldn't I want to eat them all?" I said with a scoff.

"We all have our favorite foods, Margot. If presented with a buffet of options, are you going to gravitate toward the carrot . . . or the chocolate?" he asked, rubbing his hands over my foot for a moment more before he stood fluidly, catching my chin between his thumb and forefinger.

I stared up at him in shock, my face aching with the effort of restraining my smile. "Did you just compare yourself to a piece of chocolate?"

He shrugged with a smirk. "It's your favorite food, isn't it?" I stared up at him, the grin fading from my face at the knowledge. It wasn't like it was a well-kept secret, but it did mean he'd been paying even closer attention than I'd thought before we fell through the gate to Hell. He leaned down, touching his mouth to the corner of mine in a quick brush before he pulled back just far enough for me to see his broad, playful smile. "I'm going to go hop in the shower. Let me know if you get hungry."

He stepped around me, and I turned to watch him go as he shucked his pants off before he turned the corner into the bathroom, baring the full length of his body to my view. His wings blocked his midsection, but there was absolutely nothing standing in my way of a view of his ass as he stepped out of his pants with grace. I turned back to face the bed before he could turn the corner and give me a full show.

Nope.

No.

I sat on my hands, refusing to admit that I was even the mildest bit curious.

Nope.

27

MARGOT

Having passed the simple test of not being tempted by the food that lined the walkway of Gluttony, Beelzebub gave me his permission to continue on our journey as the lord of Gluttony. After an awkward night spent with Beelzebub vacating his own bed to sleep in one of the chairs, his broad body sprawled out with his feet propped up on the chair opposite him, we made our way out of the manor he called home. The portal to the next circle was marked by two green hatches that led into the cellar outside, and Beelzebub twisted the key in the lock to pull the chain through and open them for me.

 I took the first step down into the depths of the cellar, plunging myself into darkness. Torches lit along the wall as I walked, illuminating the path so I could see my way through the tunnel I found at the bottom of the stairs. Beelzebub moved behind me, his steps oddly quiet for a man of his size. I could almost believe I was alone, plunging into the depths of Hell, but I was already there, and the monsters had no reason to hide in cellars in this place.

 I reached back for Beelzebub as we moved through the tunnel, drawing him forward to my side so I could see his broad form out of the corner of my eye. He had the grace not to look smug about it, instead just squeezing my hand in his as we moved toward the open doorway at the end of the hall. The glimmer of gold shone in the dim lights within, making my steps quicken as I approached.

The pile of gold coins was taller than me, stretching toward the ceiling in the center of the room. Gemstones and other wealth glittered at the edges, spread into corners amidst silver and jewelry. If I hadn't already known the order of the circles from my lessons at Hollow's Grove, the presence of a literal dragon hoard of treasure would have been a dead giveaway as to what came next.

Greed.

"Pick a coin, songbird," Beelzebub said, keeping his hand clasped in mine so we could travel through the portal together.

I bent forward, my fingers lingering just above the pile of coins. "Does it matter which one? Will it change anything?" I asked, my thoughts giving me pause. I didn't want to make the wrong choice, especially because I hadn't bothered to ask questions that might have given me the answers I needed.

"The coin determines where we end up in Greed. Each coin represents a room in the secure wing of Mammon's manor. In those rooms will be staff members waiting to prepare you for your entry to life at Mammon's court," Beelzebub said, making it sound far too formal for my taste.

My lips twisted into a scowl, my nostrils flaring as I considered the words and the hidden implication behind them. "Are you sure we can't skip it?" I asked, pursing my lips as Beelzebub released my hand, leaving me to make my choice as he reached down to stroke a finger down the coin that seemed to call to him. It didn't seem like this would be a journey we would take together, and I tried not to let my apprehension of being separated show as I looked through the coins, searching for the one that might call to me personally.

Each had subtle differences behind the glaring face of Mammon that stared back at me. Though the lord of Greed still remained in Crystal Hollow with Lucifer, it seemed there hadn't been any great pains taken to remove his likeness from this aspect of his territory. One coin had the image of weighted scales embedded in the space behind his head, the next a butterfly fluttering through the air, but the coin that caught my eye had the etching of burning wings swooping through the air. The feathers of those wings were incredibly detailed, so much so that I wondered if they would be soft when I finally wrapped my fingers around the coin, or if I would instead feel the heat of the flames.

I caught Beelzebub's eye as he nodded me on, and I plucked the coin out of the pile with delicate fingers. My stomach twisted with the sensation of falling, of the floor giving out beneath us as the coins before me were suddenly airborne. They plummeted toward the ground, a ground that I could no longer see; the space where it had been was now nothing but a deep, dark pit. My hair billowed out at my temples, gravity forcing it upward as I fell amidst the torrent of coins. I couldn't see Beelzebub through the chaos, couldn't find him through the gleaming gold that surrounded me.

Still, I held fast to the coin clenched in my hand, squeezing it so tightly I felt the phoenix where it transferred to my palm.

When I landed, it was with a bounce as I sprung up from a net sewn from golden thread. I squealed as I landed again, my body thrashing about as my legs collided with each other as if I were a newborn calf. Three women descended on me the moment I settled into the nets, reaching in to grab me by the ankles. The two who'd gotten their hands on me tugged me over the net, uncaring for the way it rubbed at my skin. I spun around, searching for Beelzebub in the netting only to find myself well and truly alone with the three strangers standing over me as they pulled me onto the tile floor.

They assessed me, heads tipped to the sides in thought.

Bright green eyes stared out of each face, a perfect match for one another. Their faces were equally identical, and the green dresses draped over their forms were one and the same. I'd seen plenty of twins in my life, but this was different. This was as if they were the same person split into three, their movements a perfect mirror of one another. "Your coin," the first said, shocking me that she'd been able to speak without the others doing the same. I'd been so certain I was imagining the multiples, that they'd duplicate every act, but they split off in different directions as I fumbled to hand the first my coin.

She stared at it, quirking a brow as she tossed it to her sister who had moved to the armoire at the edge of the room. The one who'd taken the coin from me held out a hand, tugging me to my feet with force that immediately lifted me to standing. There was no awkward transition; I was simply lying down one moment and standing the next. It was clearly an enormous dressing room, with little furniture outside the vanity and stool that was surrounded by makeup. I winced, wishing we could skip the pomp and circumstance. I'd been trussed up like an object only two circles ago and had no desire to have a repeat experience. I spent a great deal of time trying to ignore beauty in general, to function through my life while putting in as little effort as I could possibly manage.

I'd cut my hair short originally because my mother had forbidden it, condemning it as something that would reduce my femininity. I rejected those ridiculously old-fashioned standards, trimming it more often than I probably needed so that it never passed my shoulders. I had nothing against the women who found absolute joy in perfecting their appearance, glad they'd found something that made them happy.

I was far happier clad in leggings and running the path around the edges of the woods surrounding Hollow's Grove, working my body to the point of exhaustion so that I had a chance of quelling the rising tide of lust I had to subdue at all times. I was happier finding a moment of seclusion to sing without witnesses, without anyone to hear the power in that song.

I didn't do well in the spotlight, and as the first of the women shoved me onto the stool, I flinched back from her prodding fingers poking at my face before she grabbed a facial cloth and dipped it into the bowl of water on the vanity. Scrubbing it over my face harshly, she used her other hand to keep my head still so she could stare down at me in irritation. "No makeup?" she asked, pursing her lips in thought as she looked at the unblemished cloth.

"You don't need to do this. I'm fine just like this," I said, motioning to stand.

One of the other women came up behind me, and it was only in the reflection that I saw what lingered beneath her skin. Her face was gaunt, her eyes dark and soulless. Her mouth gaped open like a maw, her jaw unhinged as if she would devour me. I flinched back, my fight-or-flight instinct kicking in as she leaned toward me. "All women want to be beautiful," she said, gathering my hair in her hands. She pinned it to the top of my head with a long stick, twisting the hair around it expertly in that way I'd never been able to achieve on my own. The updo left my neck visible, and the feeling struck me with vulnerability. My throat looked so unprotected this way, with her razor-sharp teeth far too close for my comfort.

"Not this one. I don't feel the need to make myself beautiful for myself, and I certainly don't care what others think," I snapped as I shook off her touch. "Especially not when all men desire is a pretty possession to put on the shelf." The words didn't feel true to me anymore, not after seeing the way Beelzebub had treated me so differently from my would-be husband that the Covenant had tried to force on me for breeding.

One of the other women leaned in, a makeup brush in hand as she set to work applying it to my face. I tried not to grimace, knowing too well the only thing that would achieve would be creases within the makeup. "Beauty is a man's greatest weakness and your greatest strength if you should choose to embrace it," she said, leaning forward so that her reflection flashed in the mirror. The other remained at the armoire, searching through the gowns held within and deep in thought. "We know something of being a monster, but beauty allows us to sheathe our claws until we need them."

"I'm not a monster," I said, but the words came out weak. They tasted like a lie, especially in light of what I'd done in Gluttony, the way I'd nearly *eaten* someone just for implying she'd slept with a man that wasn't even fucking mine. It only confirmed everything I'd already known about my magic and the way the Coven had used it.

"You cannot change the way they see you," the woman touching my hair said as the other stepped away with her makeup brush, swapping it out for another as she applied a rosy blush to my cheeks. The other lined my eyes as she worked, making me feel overwhelmed and surrounded as they worked on me. "All you can do is change the way you feel about it. You can be ashamed of it and all of them to make their weakness your own, or you can craft it into your strength and make sure it is the sword that impales them in the end. Adorn yourself in pretty fabrics and soft smiles and sharpen your teeth in secret so they never see the bite coming."

The last of them finally emerged from the wardrobe with a gown draped over her arm that took my breath away.

The delicacy of the fabric, the gem-tone color, all of it was a thing of beauty.

But it felt like armor all the same.

28

BEELZEBUB

The mask covering my face did absolutely nothing to hide my identity, not with the characteristic wings that adorned my back. The staff who'd attempted to prepare me for the masquerade had been disgruntled to realize they had no clothing they could dress me in, nothing outside of a change to more formal pants. They'd needed to hurry to cut the back of the dress shirt they were determined to force me into, hand-sewing it once it was over my wings and settled against my skin. The feeling of fabric drove me crazy, the pinching and pulling and restrictiveness that I was so unused to.

The fabric tugged at my wings when I raised them higher, shifting them back and forth so I could attempt to free myself from the tightness of it. "Lord Beelzebub," a man's voice said at my side as I watched the dance floor, looking desperately for Margot. I had to believe they'd finished preparing her, given the complications in finding me something suitable to wear. How long could it possibly take to ready an already beautiful woman for a ball?

"Mephistopheles," I said, acknowledging the demon who had taken Mammon's place. He was his closest friend and he trusted him, but I found that very few who stepped in to fill the power vacuum when we left Hell had good intentions. They saw the opportunity to ingratiate themselves to Lucifer, hoping He would expel the magic needed to make them into archdemons.

"Is Lord Mammon with you?" Mephistopheles asked, his eyes searching the crowd much like mine.

"No," I grunted as the room went silent and still. Those who had been dancing stopped mid-step, freezing in place as I watched them turn. Margot's siren call rang in my head, the memory of her song and the purity of that husky, melodic voice resounding as if I were hearing it for the first time again. Turning slowly, I found her approaching from behind me, drawn to me in the same way I had been to her. They'd dressed her in a gown of deep purple, the fabric shimmering with tiny sparks that looked like embers of a flame. It was sheer where it played at the bottom of her legs, the delicate layering there shaped into individual feathers that cascaded down to the floor.

The dress was strapless, the center dipping lower to show a delicate line of cleavage. Feathered white wings seemed to spring from her back, peeking over her shoulders as the edges burned away into the color of flames. Like a phoenix rising from the ashes, a songbird caught unaware, she moved as if her body were fluid. The grace in those movements was so much more than she'd ever allowed before, the full force of her allure striking me straight in the chest as her mahogany eyes glowed like the embers on her gown. Whatever staff had prepared her had drawn the same iridescent scales on the side of her face, an illusion of makeup hinting at the power no one else here knew she possessed.

There'd been a time when the legends said the sirens were women who were half bird rather than half fish, and looking at Margot in this moment, I knew it could have easily been either, or both. They'd pinned her hair back, trailing the scaled makeup down the sides of her delicate neck and onto her collarbones and the tops of her breasts. Everyone else in the room wore a mask, their face adorned with delicate filigree and fabric meant to conceal for an evening.

But Margot stood in a mask of her own making that kept the vulnerable parts of herself hidden from view.

She was the most beautiful woman in the room, and in this moment, I had no doubt that Margot knew it. For once, instead of fearing the power in that beauty, she leaned into it. I took the last few steps toward her, closing the distance between us. Though her lips didn't move, I still heard the delicacy of that song in my head, still felt the pull of compulsion to close the distance between us once and for all, but knew it was driven by my own obsession with her.

Activity resumed through the room as I thought about how much I wanted to hear that song in real time again, the dancers stumbling as they struggled to pick up their dances mid-song.

"Dance with me," I said, and Margot's brow rose at the non-question as I took her hand and guided her into the center of the floor.

She surprised me when she nodded, raising a delicate hand to my shoulder. She stared at the fabric covering my chest as if she didn't know what to make of it, as if she hated having the shirt between our skin as much as I did. Her hands were adorned with gleaming golden rings, my runes pulsing through the white of the dress shirt as I took her waist with my free hand. I raised our joined hands to her shoulder level, holding them out as I stared down at her meaningfully, waiting for the song that was ending to come to a stop. When it did, Margot took a deep breath, readying herself for something that was probably as close to singing as she could get in such a public place.

The next song began, and Margot followed my lead as I guided her through the steps. Her movements were smooth and elegant, the definition of well-practiced beauty. Where others went through the motions, Margot wore a wide smile, her joy at moving along the dance floor evident in every extension and line of her body when I spun her out and pulled her back in quickly. I dipped her low, dragging my hand from her chin and down over the front of her throat, through the center of her breast, and to her stomach as I pulled her back up to stand.

Her eyes glowed like embers of a flame, burning away in that breathtaking face that had absolutely no right to be so fucking perfect. Her lips parted to reveal the tiny gap between her two front teeth, her tongue peeking out to torment me as she laughed. She was blissfully unaware of the audience that had formed, of those who stood at the periphery of the dance floor and watched her with greedy gazes, seeing her as something to be possessed, a treasure to be locked in the vault, when all I saw was a woman who was meant to fly.

Her skin pulsed with light, glowing from within like the iridescent scales painted on her skin as she fed, the sensuality of the dance and those watching her with lust and greed mixed into one twisted, tangled knot of sin offering her a feeding that she wouldn't have taken willingly. Still, she didn't stop dancing, and I couldn't bring myself to speak the warning. To tell her that the risk of taking more magic into her system was another bloodletting, another release that she would forbid herself from having. I could still hear the faint whisper of her song that she didn't dare to voice, as if it lingered just beneath the surface, begging to be set free.

Her fear limited her, kept her locked within a cage of her own making. No matter what I did, I couldn't be the one to turn the key.

Margot needed to be the one to free herself, to step outside that cage willingly and embrace all that she was and all that she could be. If I tried to tear her out of that little haven she'd crafted, I'd be no better than those who had abused her in the past.

So I spun her again, twirling her and watching the joy light the features of her face with the soft light that emanated from her like moonlight, longing for the day when she could be this free all the time.

Hoping more than anything that she would allow me to stand at her side when she did.

29

MARGOT

I woke the next morning, the bed beside me cold and empty when I rolled over. My memory of the night before was hazy as I pushed to sit up, and the camisole I'd changed into before bed was cool against my skin. Wrapping my arms around my chest, I threw the blanket back and went to the bathroom, searching for where Beelzebub might have wandered. I might not have remembered much, but I knew he'd danced with me as we sipped wine, laughing and spinning when I was far too inebriated to remain graceful as I did so.

The bathroom door was open, the space empty as I stepped inside. My face was bare of makeup as I took in my reflection, my porcelain skin glowing brighter than I could remember it being. I knew, in a distant sort of mind, that I'd fed while we danced, drawing energy from those around me. It should have left me feeling like I might burst, the strain of keeping the excess locked within me making me feel ill. Instead, I couldn't find a trace of sickness in my body, feeling rejuvenated rather than condemned.

Turning away from the mirror, I went in search of Beelzebub, making my way to the door that would lead to the hall outside the bedroom we'd claimed as ours the night before. When I'd gotten too tired to continue, he'd guided me up the stairs, keeping me from rubbing my hand over every opulence we passed. He'd given me privacy to change, only stepping in when I slumped forward, and helped me brush my teeth and wash the makeup from my face so I wouldn't look like a disaster come morning. I greatly appreciated it today, but I thought I might have called him an overbearing control freak at that moment.

All I'd wanted was a bed and the warmth of him snuggled against me, and he'd granted me that after telling me he didn't want to hear me complain in the morning. I intended to keep my word, because I'd made it rather difficult for him to escape when I clung to him as he tucked me in beneath the covers, dragging him down to the mattress with me. When he could have taken advantage of the situation, he'd only held me until I fell asleep.

It had been a deep sleep, the kind that I did not wake from once in the middle of the night.

I stopped with my hand only inches from the door, the sound of voices on the other side giving me pause. One was distinctly Beelzebub's, but I didn't recognize the other one. I did, however, recognize when I was the subject, laughter in his voice that felt mocking and cruel.

"What's up with you and the Red witch? You two looked awfully cozy last night," the man said. I swallowed, piecing it together as Beelzebub chuckled in response.

"Margot? It's nothing like that," Beelzebub said, making my heart plummet into my stomach. I took a step away from the door, uncertain if I wanted to continue listening to the truth of how he saw me. He'd done such a good job convincing me he was interested in me, genuinely making me wonder if I'd been wrong to dismiss him as the same as all the rest. "Just having some fun since I'm stuck with her until I get her back to Lucifer."

"Ah, just another conquest then. I wondered how you thought that would work when . . ." the other man said, but I was already retreating fully from the door, climbing back into the bed and sliding beneath the covers. I wanted nothing more than to find clothes, to dress myself before he could return so I wasn't half naked in sleep clothes and vulnerable. But I couldn't seem to move through the anguish tearing me in two, my hand rising to touch my chest where my heart felt detached and numb, as if it had simply stopped pumping blood through my body.

The door opened as I looked out the windows on the opposite end of the bedroom, staring at the mountains where the condemned rolled a boulder crafted from gold up the side, doomed to repeat that fate every day, never truly possessing the treasure they sought so desperately. I related to that more than ever as I avoided looking at Beelzebub, knowing that I would have to continue through the circles of Hell with him at my side, stuck in this new knowledge that changed everything.

How could I look at him again, knowing it had all been a lie? And one he hadn't *needed* to tell me at all. We were stuck together regardless, so a game like this felt impossibly cruel.

"Good morning, songbird. How did you sleep?" he asked, coming to the bed and sitting on the edge. I curled my knees into my chest as he reached out to touch the top of my thigh through the blanket, putting a stop to the contact that he no longer had any rights to.

"Fine enough, I guess. When are we leaving?" I asked, pursing my lips as I studied those souls, hopelessness seeping in. The odds that I would ever be free of this place seemed to dwindle with every day, because I had no way of knowing if Beelzebub even intended to keep to his word about returning me home. He could just as easily claim something horrible had happened to me here and abandon me.

Lucifer would never know the difference.

The urge to confront him about what I'd heard and keep it to myself warred within me as he studied me intently, his body tensing as he took in the clear change in my demeanor. "We can leave as soon as you've eaten something. Are you feeling alright?" he asked, and it was that gentle tone that I'd gotten so used to hearing all over again, the cruelty and mocking gone like they had been a mirage.

"I'm good," I said, shoving the blanket back. It hit Beelzebub as it went, making him jerk back in surprise as I swung my legs over the side of the bed and stood. Making my way to the closet, I searched the clothes that had been left there for souls passing through, scanning for a pair of pants and a top that would suffice. I missed my own closet; even if it wasn't filled with things I would have chosen for myself, at least they were mine.

I missed the safety of my bedroom, missed being alone, where I was far safer than I could ever be out in the open like this, with a demon as my companion—however unwilling and burdened he might be by my presence.

I took the first outfit that looked like it would fit, uncaring that it was black and not my house colors. I stripped the camisole over my head with my back to Beelzebub, attempting to ignore his sharp intake of breath as I did so. My sleep shorts followed, falling to the floor so I stood there in nothing but a pair of panties that cut high on my hips and ass. I knew I'd shocked him, my nudity never something I chose to actively engage in.

The harsh truth was that the numbness surrounding me felt far too much like the place I retreated to when I was hurt and just wanted to get my suffering over with. When my mom and aunt put me through a particularly difficult training session to attempt to lure my magic out, or when I had to tolerate being fed from for the Reapings, I sank into the deepest part of myself, where nothing in the physical mattered anymore.

That was where I'd gone to escape the sting of Beelzebub's betrayal. His opinion no longer mattered to me at all. He was just another man looking to use me, and I knew what to do with that. It was the *more* that had made me nervous, the idea that he would stick around for longer than it took for him to realize I would not end up in his bed.

The bed squeaked as he stood, and I shoved one of my legs into the first hole of the pants. The other followed and I jumped to raise the pants into place, hurrying as I felt him approach.

I readied myself for the altercation that was doomed to follow, for him to attempt to touch me in ways I didn't want. Instead, his fingers barely ghosted over the small of my back, tracing the lines of the faint white scars that were only visible in certain lighting.

I waited, the moment hanging between us as he took in the sight of what none had ever bothered to notice before him. The shirt was gathered around my elbows as I prepared to tug it on, but I couldn't seem to move with the knowledge that he *saw* me. It seemed so wrong for him to be the one to know the secrets I kept, when he didn't bother to actually care about what they meant for me. "Sometimes I dream that he isn't already dead," he said, his voice soft and tormented. I pulled away, finally yanking the shirt over my head. It settled into place as I adjusted my breasts, lifting them into place within the tight fabric before tugging on my socks and shoes.

"How nice for you," I said, stepping away. Beelzebub reached out, grasping me at the elbow to prevent me from escaping. His brow furrowed as he stared down at me, probing me for answers that I wouldn't give him. He'd only lie and make excuses if I confronted him, so I decided to use the knowledge to guard myself against his vicious attacks on my heart.

"I dream I have the opportunity to make sure he suffers the way he deserves," Beelzebub said, acting as if that would do anything to change my behavior.

"Look around you," I snapped, tearing my elbow from his grip. I gestured to the windows with the view of the horrific punishments that happened on display, that the demons who resided in Hell found pleasure in witnessing for their own entertainment. "When will it ever be enough? Don't you think there is enough cruelty in this world as it is?" I asked, watching as horror played over his features. I blinked, surprised by the moisture of tears that clung to my lashes. I couldn't remember the last time I'd cried for anything other than what Itan had done. The last time something had penetrated the misty haze around my heart so thoroughly to affect me this deeply, and I hated him all the more for it.

The first tear fell, trailing down my cheek as I shook my head harshly, turning away from him and making my way to the door. "No. I won't be the reason you use to justify this on your conscience. You want to punish him because you're a fucking demon, and that's what you do. You're cruel and you hurt and—"

"What did I do?" He closed the distance, reaching down to cup my cheeks in his hands as I shoved him away, forcing him to take a step back. He was such a good liar, his words sounding so heartfelt that my mouth twisted in pain, my throat threatening to close.

"Don't touch me," I snapped, holding out a hand to keep him at bay.

"Songbird, I can't fix it if you don't talk to me," he pleaded.

I forced steel into my voice, raising my chin and glaring at him through lidded eyes as I turned for the door. "Some things can't be fixed, Beelzebub. This is one of them," I said as I passed, ignoring his sharp intake of breath. It threatened to sink inside of me, to rattle around in my lungs as if it were my own.

But it didn't. Instead there was only that gaping emptiness and rage within me. So much rage that it threatened to light me aflame.

"Alright, let's just get you something to eat and then we'll go," he said, hurrying to take up pace beside me as I made my way through the disgustingly opulent hall. People were suffering, all while these assholes lived like treasure hoarders.

"I'm not hungry," I mumbled, hurrying down the stairs to the front door.

"You need to eat something," he said, moving to stand in my path before I could walk out and leave Greed in my rearview. "At least—"

"I said I'm not hungry! Get out of my fucking way," I shouted, watching as Beelzebub looked at the crowd that had started to gather to watch my display. I wanted to embarrass him, wanted him to feel only a moment of the humiliation I felt knowing that he'd played me like a fiddle and I'd been stupid enough to fall in love with the sound it made.

His gaze snapped back to me, his eyes hardening as he stood taller. "Fine," he grunted, sweeping his arm out as he stepped to the side. "You're so fucking determined to be alone? Then be my guest, Margot. The portal to Wrath is half a mile south of the manor."

I studied him for a moment, taking a deep breath. Was I really about to venture out into Hell on my own?

Anything was better than this.

I tore my attention away from him, stepping past him with my head raised high, and I left him behind as I continued on my journey to speak to Lucifer and get home.

30

BEELZEBUB

I watched her go, rubbing my hand against my mouth as I took a step back and put more distance between us. She disappeared from my view, heading south as instructed. She was so careless, so oblivious to the danger that waited for her out there without me to guard her. She'd been lulled into a false sense of security by the distinct lack of serious trouble we'd run into so far, but she hadn't stopped to think that it might have been my presence that kept the demons at bay.

The new souls in Purgatory hadn't yet learned the truth of what I could do to them if they got in my way, but the souls through the rest of Hell were familiar enough with at least one of the archdemons that they avoided all of us studiously.

She was in danger, walking alone this way. I blinked as I tried to decide what to do.

Did I respect her wishes and allow her to be alone? She'd made her intentions clear, condemned me for fuck only knew what, and been willing to brave the very circles that had terrified her only days ago in order to get away from me.

I shook my head, rubbing at my forehead as I tried to make a decision. That tug in the black hole at my center where my heart should have been led me in one direction, my mind in another. The logical part of me knew that I should let her go, explain to Lucifer that I'd done what I could but I couldn't protect the witchling from her own recklessness. I could make my way to the Ninth Circle more quickly without Margot in tow, wait for her in the comfort of Lucifer's lavish palace.

I lost track of how long I stood there, aware of the eyes that watched me stare after Margot. I turned to find Mephistopheles studying me as if he could see right through the lies I'd fed him that morning in my desperation to keep Margot safe from his collection. She'd already put on enough of a show the night before by simply existing, attracting the demon's attention when she would have been far better off hiding in the shadows and remaining unnoticed.

He couldn't want to own what he did not see.

But he'd seen her, and worse than that, he'd seen that she'd meant something to me. He'd seen that she was valuable to me, and the sin of greed was stronger in him than most. He was a slave to it, entrapped by the compulsions that drove him to collect the people and things he viewed as treasure, hoarding them here in the mansion in Mammon's absence.

I'd told him she didn't matter to me in the hopes it would reduce her value in his eyes, and judging by the tight press of his lips, the demon knew it now. The muscles on his forearm flexed as he raised his arm, signaling a demon forward with two curled fingers.

He'd follow after her now that he knew the truth, and Margot's only hope of escaping capture was reaching the portal before Mephistopheles and his men. I considered my choices, waiting as he watched me to see if I would follow after Margot—to see if I cared enough to go with her even after she'd eviscerated me publicly. I held his gaze, the crystalline white of his stare boring a hole in me as we remained trapped in this moment.

Him waiting for me to follow. Me wondering if Margot would hate me for following after her, for offering her the protection she claimed she didn't need or want.

The harshness of my words from earlier that morning played

in my head as I snapped to look after Margot, realization dawning with an anguish that made my toes curl in my boots.

She'd heard me.

It was the only explanation. I'd been so certain that she was just pushing me away, putting distance between us as a way to protect herself because I was getting too close to breaking through her walls completely. It had blinded me from the truth that was *right* in front of me.

I took the first step, hurrying into a run as I followed the path Margot had taken to the portal to the Fifth Circle. I was vaguely aware of the shuffling of feet behind me as Mephistopheles moved to follow, but I couldn't waste time to look back at him. Not when Margot's safety required me to reach her first and hustle her through that portal before they could get to her. If he forbade her from using it, we'd have to fight our way out of the situation and get to the boundary, where she would need to prove she could overcome her own greed to the magic of the circle itself if she hadn't already.

But I suspected she had the moment she left me; that she'd been willing to leave me here when she clearly viewed me as hers meant that she was willing to sacrifice her own greed for the well-being of another. If she'd heard me, she'd thought she was nothing more than an obligation to me when I had come to mean something genuine to her. She could have tried to ensnare me with her song since she didn't realize it wouldn't have the same effect on me, could have done whatever it took to keep me. Someone who was compelled by greed would have done just that.

Greed was not one of Margot's greatest sins, and as such the magic hadn't been able to touch her as deeply. It hadn't been able to stoke the flames of emotions already lingering within her, and she could free herself from it easily.

To plunge straight into the circle of wrath, with anger in her heart from my cruel words.

"*Fuck*," I hissed as I ran, sprinting past the hillside where souls worked to push that gold boulder up the incline before them. Sweat slicked their bodies, hands slipping along the surface of the gold repeatedly. It rolled back each time they lost control, often crushing bodies beneath it in its descent.

I scoured the souls at the base of the hill, looking for Margot in the crowd as I sprinted past. I didn't see her blond hair in the masses, despite knowing that she would have been tempted to try to intervene. She *hated* the constant barrage of pain and suffering that surrounded her here, unable to compare the reality of it to everything that happened on Earth.

It wasn't all that much worse here, simply more consistent and it lasted for an eternity, but life came with the highs that made the lows feel all that much worse. The contrast between the two, the moments of hope that things might improve, was almost as bad as the suffering itself.

The portal ahead came into view, an armory building with the cross of two swords etched into the wooden door. Margot was nowhere to be found as I scrambled to a stop at the door, shoving it open with my shoulder and bursting into the armory.

It was empty, Margot's gleaming head of golden hair nowhere to be found. The sound of Mephistopheles and his men came through the trees behind me, and I swung the door shut and turned the lock, looking through the weapons hanging from the wall. It was impossible to know what, if anything, had been taken, since the magic in this place of violence rejuvenated itself as soon as it was needed, but I found myself looking for an empty place regardless. I needed the confirmation that she'd come this way, that she'd passed through here, before I continued into Wrath and risked leaving her behind.

A spot on the wall glimmered with a faint yellow glow, a trident sparkling with the hint of magic as it replenished. I grinned, imagining Margot picking up the weapon of the legendary sea god out of pure spite, unknowing that it would likely be one of the most useful weapons to have at her disposal as she faced the circle of Wrath.

I grasped a small dagger off the wall with one hand, my other already grasping the scythe necklace from my throat. Tugging on it, I pulled it free as the clasp unsnapped. I swung it down from my chest as I plummeted into the portal, the world around me suddenly consumed by flames. The armory disappeared, burning before my eyes as the weapons on the wall melted with the extreme heat that was but a kiss of warmth on my skin. My scythe extended to full length as I moved, snapping my arm down to extend my elbow as the floor dropped out from beneath me, caving in the flames as the structure burned. Becoming a massive weapon that only the archdemons could wield, it swung out at my side, the blade curving behind me as I landed on my feet and dropped to one knee to absorb the shock of my landing.

Wrath was on fire, an eternal flame burning in the pits where the bodies of souls battled one another endlessly. I stood at the edge, gazing into the pit as I swung my scythe in a warning. The soul who had dared to reach for me retreated, eyes wide as I turned to the narrow path that Margot would need to take to reach the manor. The flames glowed yellow, but the waters of the canal that ran through the pit of souls ran red with the stain of blood.

The path was winding as I searched along it, hoping Margot had gone in the right direction. Given the state of the trident rejuvenating, she couldn't have gotten far. I scanned the banks of the pit, my heart dropping into my throat when I didn't immediately see her. I raced forward, heading in the direction of the manor in hopes of finding her safe on the path. Maybe she'd run, fearful of the creatures reaching for her. I couldn't blame her. Their bodies were forever altered by the battles they fought. Faces were so swollen that eyes sealed shut, limbs hung limply at the sides of others. The symptoms of their violence were evident in every inch of their scarred skin, from the burns to the seeping wounds.

"Margot!" I called, stopping as I looked for her. I searched all over again, my breaths shaky. I licked my lips, slapping my hand over my mouth as I looked.

I couldn't be too late. She couldn't have succumbed to her anger so quickly, not because of me and what I'd said to *protect* her. My own anger rose, drawn from me like poison in this place that fed from it. If she'd only fucking stopped to talk to me, I could have explained. I could have made her understand and we would have continued on together.

A scream tore through the air, the sharp and shrill sound of it making everything within me tighten as I raced forward. The sound was alive, the absolute terror in it the kind of fear that could only come from the living.

The dead had nothing left to fear, for the worst had already happened to them.

They'd already died and gone to Hell.

There.

I found her, a single arm swinging the trident for all she was worth. She'd managed to keep herself from being pulled into the pit, severing the arms of the first soul who'd grabbed her. His hand remained clutched around her ankle as she scrambled back, kicking at the hand with her other foot in an attempt to get the extremity to release her.

Her victim shoved his chest into the muddy bank, inching his way up to go for her a second time. Another soul climbed on all fours at its side, her head twisted backward as if someone had snapped her neck and she couldn't find peace in another death. Margot screamed again as the woman reached for her, wrapping sharp nails around Margot's thigh as she swung her trident.

It embedded in the side of the woman's face, the resulting spray of blood soaking Margot as she sputtered and stilled in shock. Her horror gave the third soul time to reach her before me, grabbing her around the throat. She released her trident immediately, her hands flying to try to shove the creature that had once been human off her. He was too strong, yanking her onto her back on the path and dragging her toward the pit on the other side.

"Fucking sing, Margot!" I yelled, her head snapping to the side as her eyes met mine. I was closing the distance, but not moving quickly enough even as my wings pumped at my back, propelling me forward. She gasped, a strangled sound coming out as the soul pressed against the front of her throat, silencing the song she might have used to protect herself.

Her head dropped to the side as the woman at her legs yanked her in the other direction, Margot's mouth opening with a silent scream as sharpened nails sliced through her pants and tore the flesh within. She was going to be torn in two before my very eyes, and I pushed my body to the limit as I launched over a gap in the path and swung my scythe down, cutting across the man's throat and cleaving his head from his body.

Margot sucked back a huge lungful of air, her chest expanding with it as she clutched at her throat. There was no time to stop and consider the deep red marks already forming where he'd held her, nor the guilt that would plague me later for this being my fault.

All that existed in this moment was the rage coursing through me, boiling my blood like the lava churning in the pits. I spun my scythe around my back, my hands dancing over the shaft as I struck out with my foot, kicking the woman in the back of her head. It spun around on her neck with a quick snap, righting itself on her spine. She gave only a moment to look dazed before she withdrew her talons from Margot's leg, launching herself at me. I swung my scythe again, cutting her across the chest as I stepped over Margot carefully, driving the souls back into the pit where they'd been trying to drag her.

The scythe was a torrent as I swung it over my head, dipping low in the next step to take out the first surge of souls at the knee.

They pounced as one, jumping onto me in numbers too great even for me to fight off.

My wings spread behind my back, preparing to launch me into the sky to avoid the dangers of the souls who had been driven into a frenzy by the scent of Margot's blood. Weight on my back pressed at my spine, a claw ripping down the very center of my wings where they joined to my back. I flinched, a roar on my lips as I spun to tell Margot to run, to get her to flee before it was too late.

Her eyes widened as if she knew exactly what I was about to tell her, her head shaking as her mouth opened into a scream. No sound came, and her hand reached to touch her abused throat.

I sank back into the fight, spinning with the force of a hurricane and tearing through flesh with my scythe at my side. Arms clamped down on it as they grabbed me, dragging me down the muddy bank and into the pit of flames. Fire burned my legs, the heat of the lava threatening to burn me alive if I didn't get free. But the weight of those souls on top of me was too much, forcing me to sink deeper against my will. Claws tore at my flesh, rending the scythe from my grip and tossing it out of reach.

A hand was at my throat, talons digging deep as they sliced across the flesh, and I knew the end was near. Blood poured from the wound, spurting out into the pit and the hard press of bodies that surrounded me as the sound of Margot's scream finally broke free.

My body went limp, the fight draining out of me with each fresh torrent of blood. In my last moments, I saw her face. Saw the smile transform her from a rare beauty to a goddess, heard the vibrancy of her song when she'd sung freely in the courtyard that night. I'd been doomed from the moment I laid eyes on her, seen the freedom in her face as the plants themselves swayed toward her, offering her the sanctuary she needed to be herself.

If I had to die for her to live, all I could do was hope she'd run.

If she made it to safety, it would be worth the eternity plaguing me in the circle that wasn't my own.

The song in my mind grew louder, the chords deeper and more meaningful the closer I came to death. It wasn't until the weight lifted from my shoulders that I rose up to the surface of the bodies. Instead of forcing me beneath the surface, they raised me up to it. Warm skin touched my throat, Margot's hand covering the wound as I stared up into her shockingly beautiful face. She glowed from within, her magic making her radiate as her lips moved in time with the song playing in my head.

Reality crashed back in with a sear of blinding pain, my legs burning and throat an open wound. Her voice was deep and husky, a commanding presence as her mahogany eyes pulsed with red light.

Consciousness faded away; her face was the last thing I saw as my eyes finally drifted closed.

The world went silent, her song fading as my world went black.

31

MARGOT

I froze, the song dying on my lips as I stared down at his too-still face. His chest rose with a haggard breath, the faintest bits of life clinging to him. I picked up my song again, desperate to bring him back. To break his immunity and tangle him up in my magic so deeply that he could not leave me, not even in death. His face didn't change, life fading out from him as I watched his blood pump over the hands I held tight to his throat, trying to keep it within his body and applying pressure the best I could.

"I'm afraid that won't do him much good, love," a man's voice said, his footsteps loud as he made his way along the path. He waved a hand at the souls waiting at the edges for me to stop singing, to stop commanding them away. Reaching into the pit, Satanus grasped Beelzebub's scythe and plucked it from the carnage. The blade was covered in blood, a mess of death and destruction that Beelzebub had left in his wake. He'd fought against the undying, struggled to keep me safe even though he had claimed not to care for me.

I refused to take my hands from Beelzebub's throat, staring up at Satanus's red-tinted skin. His horns, sharp and deadly weapons, curved up to the sky, and he tested the weight of Beelzebub's scythe.

"You have to help him. Please," I begged, staring up at the

other archdemon who had been propelled into Hell with us in the battle with Michael.

The most monstrous-looking of all the archdemons tilted his head to the side as he studied me, that lingering yellow gaze lowering to Beelzebub. It trailed over the blood covering him without emotion, seemingly uncaring for the state of the man who should have been like a brother to him. Beelzebub's warning about the relationship the archdemons shared was loud in my mind, Satanus's body language all the confirmation I needed.

They didn't care about one another at all.

I clenched my teeth tightly, feeling Beelzebub's pulse slip away. His skin was too slick with blood, making it nearly impossible to hold my hand on his throat steady.

"*Please,*" I begged again, a strangled sob catching in my throat. I couldn't lose him, couldn't allow him to be torn away from me. Not like this.

My hands throbbed with the pressure I used to try to keep his lifeblood from spilling out, the tension spreading to my wrists. My forearms throbbed with the force of it, a tightening happening at the joint where my hand and forearm connected.

I thought the bones might snap if I pushed any harder, if my desperation reached any higher. I couldn't imagine making my way through Hell without Beelzebub at my side any longer, but even worse than that, I couldn't imagine returning home without him.

And now I was going to lose him at the same moment I realized there was nothing this strange, new feeling could be except a single truth.

I was falling in love with the archdemon.

"What will you give me if I help him, little witch?" Satanus asked, stepping closer. He closed the distance between us, catching me under the chin and forcing my attention away from Beelzebub's prone form. I swallowed, my face twisting with pain and disgust.

I knew where this would go, knew what favor he would ask. I'd lived this reality one hundred times over, seen the way that the cruel twisted situations to get what they wanted from the women who revealed their weaknesses. I hadn't wanted to have one, hadn't wanted to acknowledge what the butterflies in my stomach meant every time I looked at him.

Hadn't wanted the world to know there was a way to hurt me. A way to make me a willing victim.

I nodded, tears streaming down my face as I looked back down at Beelzebub. He was so peaceful beneath the blood, so quiet, like he merely slept. I should have just let him go, shouldn't have forced him to stay here with me against his will.

But I couldn't.

"Anything," I croaked, my hands trembling on Beelzebub's throat. I looked back up at Satanus, determination making me raise my chin. "I'll give you anything if you help him."

Satanus reached out, dipping a single finger into the wound on my thigh. I groaned as he pressed it deep, swirling it around in the laceration, and then raised it to his mouth. He tasted me, watching me intently before he placed his free hand on my shoulder. His other hand curled, his thumb and middle finger pressing together.

I cried out as my wrists twisted. The ropes that had become an invisible part of me for so long winked into view, coated in Beelzebub's blood. They'd tightened on my skin to the point that my hands had turned purple, the flesh starved of blood flow. "Please," I repeated, my voice a hoarse whisper. This plea was not spoken for Satanus where he watched, but for me. For relief from the tightness in my hands and my chest, the pain arching through me as Beelzebub's pulse weakened with each breath.

The ropes around my wrist frayed as moisture wet my eyes, the sob unable to claw its way up my throat. It shifted into a cry, into a scream of pure agony as those ropes snapped in two.

A torrent of magic slid through me as they fell to the ground around Beelzebub's neck. It slammed into me so sharply it chased away the numbness I'd clung to for so many years. My hollow filled with warmth, with all the emotions that came with the lighter side of the Source as she rocketed through my veins. She did not hesitate to fill each and every cavern within me, sucking the overflow of dark magic and lust from me and offering me something different.

Giving me something *more*.

Understanding was immediate, coming with a rush of pure agony. Emotion made my tears fall freely, the loss and grief of all that I stood to lose in those moments the most cruel torture.

I hadn't known how I felt, hadn't been able to grasp the depth of this connection until the bonds were released.

The snap resounded through the clearing, my body going weightless as I felt like I'd been turned inside out. It lasted only a moment as my organs rearranged within my body, everything cramping, and just when I thought I couldn't take it anymore . . .

I landed on a soft surface, a bed beneath me as a woman pried my hands from Beelzebub's throat. I blinked past my disorientation, watching as she tied a bandage around his throat to replace my hand. She stepped away when it was done, vacating the room and leaving me with the two archdemons. Beelzebub's eyes remained closed, his body lying flat on the surface of the bed as I rounded to look at Satanus.

"You said you'd help him!" I shouted, rising to my feet. I left the bed, approaching the bastard who showed not a hint of emotion. He wasn't pleased by Beelzebub's condition or the fact that he'd trapped me into a deal I wouldn't have made under any other circumstances, he was merely . . . empty.

There was something lacking within him as he curled a brow at me, shrugging—a piece of him that should have been there and wasn't. "And help him I did," he said, nodding toward the bed. "I brought him to a safe place where he can heal. The rest is up to him."

"He can't heal from this! No one can," I snapped, throwing out an arm to show where the bandage was already turning red with blood. The pressure wasn't enough, and every moment wasted was another moment closer to death. If he'd been mortal, he'd have been dead almost instantly.

"If you want him healed so badly, little Red witch, then do it yourself. It makes no difference to me either way," he said, turning and striding out the open door. He pulled it closed behind him, leaving me to spin and look at Beelzebub. My hands were soaked in his blood, covered in the sign of his impending death.

It wasn't exactly a good way to set the mood, but I screamed my frustration. At war with myself, I tore my pants down my legs, shucking them off and pacing back and forth along the floor at his bedside.

I'd said I'd do anything. I hadn't planned on *this*.

The bed was still beneath me as I sat down on the edge, placing one hand on top of his thigh. His pants had been torn open in various places, his wounds visible through the gaps. I slid my hand into one of them, touching the bare skin above one of his wounds. He was cold beneath my touch, too fucking cold to walk away from this if I didn't do the one thing I'd forbidden myself to do all my life.

There wasn't much that could make me do this, that could make me desperate enough to brave the one thing that terrified me more than anything else. To risk the high of an orgasm, to feel that crush of pleasure that consumed so many, felt like condemning myself to the addiction I'd been born into. Like dancing with temptation, even knowing I would walk off the floor with scars that ran deeper than any wound could reach.

I shook my head as I slid my free hand into my underwear, willing to risk that if it meant Beelzebub would walk away from this. If it meant his death wouldn't hang on my shoulders, the memory of him racing across the burning plains to reach me, of the way he swung his scythe through the air like an avenging God.

He'd come for me, been there when I needed him the most, and the least I could do was return the favor.

There wasn't a hint of arousal to be found, but I spread my legs wider and leaned my ass against the footboard of the bed, rubbing my fingers over the flesh at the apex of my thighs. I whimpered when nothing happened, when I couldn't get his bloody form off my mind. I closed my eyes, shutting out the visual of his suffering, and focused on the memory of the night we'd spent in Lust. I focused on the feeling of him between my legs as I straddled him, on what I'd felt when I ground against him. Sliding my fingers lower, I let one glide inside to mimic the motions I imagined he would have made if he hadn't stopped me.

The respect he'd shown, the restraint, had only made him more beautiful, and I added a second finger with that thought in mind. My body answered, responding with a slickness that coated my fingers. I moaned, the sound soft and foreign to my ears.

I'd never made that sound before Beel. Never felt even a hint of what so many had been desperate for.

My body warmed with the tingle of magic as my body tightened, the warmth spreading through my belly and sinking in deep. Another whimper as the heel of my palm ground against my clit, the pressure adding to the pleasure as it built within me.

A masculine groan came from the other side of the bed, making me fling my eyes open in shock.

Beelzebub stared back.

32

BEELZEBUB

Margot's hand stilled, her eyes wide as she moved to take her hand from her own underwear. I struggled to wrap my mind around what I saw, around what she'd been willing to do to bring me back.

"Don't stop," I grunted, sitting up slowly. My body ached, every inch of me throbbing with the massive number of injuries covering my body. My throat was sore, the flesh torn and unforgiving. Even though the bleeding had stopped, Margot's magic serving to accomplish that much so far, it would take time to heal the wounds that would have killed me otherwise.

But none of that pain changed the fact that I was already harder than a rock in my pants, staring at Margot's delicate fingers as she moved them slowly and gently once again.

I swallowed thickly, desperate to replace them with mine but not willing to break this moment. It mattered to me, knowing what I did now, that Margot's first orgasm came at her own hand. That it wasn't something I'd given to her, but something she took for herself. A pleasure she should have never deprived herself of, hers to claim anew.

"Beel," she said, her voice breaking off with the barest hint of a sob. I knew the emotions clogging her throat were at risk of chasing away the desire I felt in the air, the scent of it sweet and thick as it tangled with her magic, touching my wounds and working to heal them slowly.

"I'm right here, songbird," I said, attempting to chase away the thoughts of just how close I'd been to death. The thought of her making her way through Hell alone nearly killed me, especially when she'd been so close to death herself before I found her. She moved her hand, shifting it higher as two fingers moved beneath the fabric of her underwear. She circled her clit, her head dropping back ever so slightly as her mouth fell open. "I want to see you," I said, keeping my voice gentle.

I didn't dare move as her eyes widened, her stare searching my eyes, and I knew she was weighing her options. Deciding if this was something she wanted to allow the man who'd just claimed she meant nothing only an hour prior. I waited for her signal, my heart in my throat as she nodded slowly, standing from the bed with a slow, cautious ease that made me want to whisper in her ear, to tell her everything would be alright.

She hooked her fingers into the waistband of her panties, hesitating to slide them down for me. I moved to the edge of the bed, covering her hands with mine and helping her guide them down slowly. Her breath hitched when my seated position put my mouth so close to her, so near where I wanted to kiss more than anything I could ever remember wanting before.

Instead, I forced myself back to the bed with a groan, watching as she settled herself back against the footboard. With my legs out of her way, she spread her own farther, dropping them open so I could see all of her. She arched her back over the footboard ever so slightly, putting her pussy on display for me as she touched herself again. The sight of her delicate fingers dancing over her flesh nearly brought me to my knees. A moan dragged its way up my throat as the wound on my neck pulsed with fresh warmth.

"You're so fucking beautiful," I rasped, watching her as she ran her tongue over her dry lips. She reached lower between her legs, pumping two fingers into her pussy with slow glides. My hand rose slowly, touching myself through my pants. I couldn't *not* adjust myself with how perfect she was spread out for me, her long legs crossing the bed and creamy flesh so soft as she moaned.

"I want to see you," she said, her voice tentative. Uncertain, but her gaze dropped to my groin, to the hand that had taken to stroking myself through the fabric.

I froze, everything in me stilling as I tried to understand the best path forward from this moment. Did I trust that she knew what she wanted, or did I try to hold her back so she wouldn't regret this?

"Are you sure?" I asked, taking in the quick and sharp nod. There was no hesitation in the affirmation as her hips thrust forward, pressing more firmly into her own hand as she worked herself slowly, tenderly. She was learning her body, taking the time to understand what she liked as I watched, and the knowledge would be something I planned to use to my advantage very fucking soon.

I paid attention to each quickening of her breath, to each gasp and moan, to the movements of her hand that had earned them. As I tugged my pants down over my ass, I learned her body as she did. It might not have been my hands on her, my fingers buried in her pussy, but I memorized everything she liked all the same. Margot whimpered as my cock sprang free, sinking her teeth into her bottom lip. I knew what the angle would reveal, the piercing on the underside of my cock where it met my balls. I wrapped a hand around my length where it curved up toward my stomach, stroking it gently as Margot's attention remained fixed on the touch.

She blinked, shaking her head as her attention shifted back to my face. I grinned at her, watching as a hesitant smile came to her mouth in response.

"I don't think—"

"Don't worry about that right now, songbird. All you need to worry about today is letting me watch you come," I said, shoving her worries away for tomorrow. Whatever it was that had started to take her out of the moment was a concern for another time. "I want to watch you soak your fingers. Nothing is evil, Margot. Lust can create something beautiful, too."

"I—" She broke off, her fingers hesitating as I reached between us.

I held her, refusing to allow her to stop when she was so close. I didn't touch her tender, swollen flesh, but looked her in the eyes as I smirked. "Without lust, none of humanity would exist. Without it, I wouldn't have you," I said, earning a strangled gasp from her mouth. She huffed a laugh, but her hand resumed its playing, working her clit with me so close. I leaned my forehead against hers, holding her gaze as I stroked my cock. Her breath hitched, her fingers working faster. She was going to orgasm before I was ready, her body already primed, but I knew enough about Red witches to know that her orgasm would pull me over the edge with her.

"With me," I said, holding her gaze as she gasped. She curled her body forward as she tightened, her eyes blazing like the brightest flames I'd ever seen.

And then she came, her magic bursting out of her like a storm. Her body shook with the force of it. My cum soaked my hand as she stole my pleasure from me and absorbed it, a give-and-take balance that brought her body into harmony more than I'd ever seen from her. The tense lines of her face smoothed out as I released myself, staring into the fires of her eyes. The glow she always carried seemed brighter, making her look like a goddess as she reached forward. Her hand smelled like her pussy as she peeled the bandage away from my neck, staring down at the freshly healed pink flesh in shock.

Her gaze roamed over the rest of my injuries, shifting to the side to look at my wounds and the burns on my legs as I laughed. Bringing her hand to my mouth, I pressed her fingers against my tongue to get my first taste of Heaven.

"Everything you do is beautiful, Margot," I said, shrugging as she sagged forward, her mind trying to understand the intensity of the magic she kept inside her. "Why would this be any different?"

She laughed, launching herself at me. She tackled me to the bed, hugging me so tightly that I didn't dare to move. Even though she seemed to have forgotten, we were both nude from the waist down. Her pussy was so close to my cock, but I shoved down the desire building anew.

This witch would be the death of me if she didn't fuck me first.

33

MARGOT

My skin felt too sensitive after the hot shower that had washed all of Beelzebub's blood away. He'd insisted we get changed and move on from the Fifth Circle, wanting to arrive in the next before we rested for the night. I didn't dare to ask what his hesitation was with staying here, but I had the sinking suspicion I already knew.

The memory of Satanus's lack of emotion as Beelzebub died was fresh on my mind, and I wondered what the story was there. He helped me slip into a change of clothes, gliding the pants over my legs. I'd been tempted to resist, but it seemed foolish now that he'd seen *everything* there. I flushed as he stood, smirking as his unblemished body moved toward the door.

He didn't have a single scar, his form completely free from wounds or any indication that he'd been so gravely injured. Mine wasn't so free of marks, the skin around my wrists raw and irritated from where the ropes had snapped free.

Beelzebub's eyes strayed to them, a question in that gaze that I refused to answer. The memory of Amelia telling him that I'd been bound was hazy in my memory, but his gaze was warm and understanding.

"How?" he asked, voicing the question I'd hoped he would allow me to avoid. Admitting to my feelings, admitting I was no longer trapped in my unfeeling cycle was not something I was ready to do.

"It happened when you were dying," I admitted, wincing because even that felt too close to an admission. I didn't know what to do with the new feelings swirling inside of me, with the warmth I felt every time he looked at me.

I didn't know how to do any of this.

Beelzebub nodded, an understanding smile crossing his face. "I'll be here, whenever you're ready to let me in, songbird," he said, stepping closer and touching his mouth to my forehead sweetly. It warmed me more than normal, sinking into my gut and making my skin tingle with goose bumps.

How had I gone through my life without ever feeling *this*?

"Where's my scythe?" he asked, stepping back and looking around the room as if trying to connect the pieces. "How did you get me here? The last I remember, we were still in the path between the pit of souls."

I swallowed, wringing my hands as I studied him intently. I didn't know how this news would be taken, and it made me nervous to be honest. "Satanus took your scythe when he rescued you from the pit," I said, wincing when his muscles seemed to freeze solid.

"Satanus pulled me out?" he asked, his voice low. His frame was tense, his shoulders raised high as he closed the distance between us. He cupped my cheeks in his hands, staring down at me intently. "Did he also bring me here?"

I swallowed, nodding my agreement.

His eyes shuddered closed. "Tell me you didn't," he said, his voice pleading. His forehead touched mine, the pleading in his eyes striking me in the heart. In the same place he'd torn in two. I couldn't bear to be the reason for that expression on his face, no matter what he thought of me.

"Didn't what?" I asked, smiling up at him as I tried to play it off.

But I knew enough about demons, and Beelzebub had warned me enough to know what he meant. I'd made a bargain, and I would one day be beholden to whatever terms Satanus set forth. One day, I'd have to give him whatever he wanted in exchange for saving Beelzebub's life, and even though it made anxiety churn in my gut, I couldn't regret it.

He stood before me, whole and unharmed, and for that it was a price I would willingly pay.

"Tell me you didn't make a deal with him," he said, his voice raising in tenor. His anger was palpable, but he couldn't understand that I wouldn't rise to that occasion. Not for this, but I could direct it elsewhere. Distract him so I didn't need to continue lying.

"Of course not," I scoffed, shrugging out of his hold. "What do you think I am? Stupid? Why would I make a deal with a demon for a man who just sees me as another conquest?"

His face fell, and I knew then he realized what I must have overheard before he came after me. There was no indication of surprise on his face, only a resignation that he'd known this moment was coming. "It wasn't what you think," he said, the gentle tone of his voice serving to reignite my anger. I was still immensely happy that he'd survived, but that didn't mean I could just erase the pain he'd caused me.

The hurt I'd never meant to feel.

It was so much worse now that the bindings were gone from my wrists. My emotions moved through me in a torrent, threatening to sweep me away on stormy seas.

"I fail to see what else it could have been. It's better this way. I'd rather hear the ugly truth than listen to your pretty lies for another second," I snapped, making my way toward the door to dismiss him. He'd said we needed to move on to the next circle, and I fully intended to keep moving. I might not have known what the story was between him and Satanus, but that didn't mean I wanted to linger with the archdemon who made me uncomfortable at best.

"Mephistopheles likes to collect things that matter to others. His favorite possessions are the ones he steals from other people and locks away so they can never be found again. What do you think he would have done if he had found out I cared for you?" he asked. My shoulders dropped forward as I turned to face him slowly, forcing a casual smile to my face to hide the hurt he'd caused.

He didn't get to know. Didn't get to see.

"Who the fuck is Mephistopheles? It sounds like a Goddess-damned disease," I spat, my harsh laughter sounding strange even to me. It wasn't mine, that bitter, cruel sound that came from my throat.

"He might as well be as far as I'm concerned. He rules in Mammon's absence. He wanted to *collect* you, Margot. I told him you were nothing to hide the truth, because if he knew . . ." He trailed off, leveling me with the full force of his stare. "If he knew I was in love with you, he would make sure I never saw you again."

I stilled, gaping up at him, at the words I'd never *wanted* to hear. "Take it back," I said, shaking my head.

"I'm trying!" Beelzebub snapped. "I'm trying to tell you I was lying to him. If I'd known you had overheard us, I never would have let you leave like that," he said, taking a step toward me that I matched backward.

"The other part! Take it back!" I screamed, wrapping my arm around my stomach protectively. The butterflies that fluttered there were a complete betrayal to myself, an unreasonable notion that I could have *this*. "Take it back."

"Songbird," he said, his voice breaking as he closed the distance between us quickly. He pulled my arms away from my stomach, threading his fingers through mine as he brought them to his chest. He squeezed my hands, the grip reassuring even as he looked at me and swallowed. "I couldn't take back the way I feel even if I wanted to. You have burrowed your way into my soul and branded me with your mark."

My lip trembled, the reality of the situation making my heart crack in my chest. It felt like it was a bleeding, gaping wound, like it had struck me right down to my bones. I wished that his words could be real, that there could be truth in them instead of just the manipulation of my magic making him believe them, but this made me question the realization I'd had about his immunity.

It wasn't possible without magic.

"I sang. In the pits. I sang to try to save you," I said, curling my fingers into his chest as I spoke the words. "This isn't you. You don't mean it and one day you're going to wake up and hate me for taking your will from you."

He sighed, smiling down at me. "I'm an archdemon, Margot. Your song doesn't work on me, not the way you think, anyway. It can emphasize attraction that already exists, but there is a great difference between thinking you're breathtaking and loving you all the way to your bones. Lust is not my sin. I am so filled with gluttony that there is no room for your song to take root."

"I don't understand why you wouldn't have said something before the Second Circle. You *hated* my kind, just as much as I was afraid of yours," I said, facing him as I spoke. I raised my chin, puffed out my chest, so confident in the knowledge that this, too, was another deception.

"You weren't ready to hear it. You weren't ready to accept the fact that maybe, just maybe, someone out there saw through those mile-high walls and was willing to scale them to end up on the other side with you. I know that to be true, because I wasn't ready either. I missed the signs of my own immunity, and it wasn't until Amelia pointed out my stupidity that I realized the truth. I will wait however long it takes for you to see I am not only here because of your song. I'm not going to leave you," he said, making the smug expression fall right off my face.

I wanted to deny it—wanted to tell him that blaming me was a cop-out.

But was he wrong?

A few days ago, I'd have laughed him out of town if he'd claimed to want to be with me because of who I was and not for the magic in my song. But now . . .

Now I stared at him, considering his words carefully. Accepting them as truth still wasn't something I was ready for, because what happened if it was true? What happened if he loved me?

Was I capable of loving him back now that my bindings had been broken?

The flutter in my stomach said yes, and I wished I could clip that fucking thing's wings and tell it to shut up.

"I don't expect you to say it back, songbird, but you needed to know why I was willing to lie to Mephistopheles. You needed to know the truth before we continued down this road together. Now let's go get my fucking scythe and get the Hell out of this place," he said, taking my hand in his on our way out the door. We made our way through the manor of Wrath like he'd spent a great deal of time here.

I knew so little and so much about him all at once, with centuries of history to catch up on if I wanted to understand him fully.

It seemed insurmountable, and yet I couldn't shake the feeling that *none* of those details mattered. That no matter what they revealed, he'd still be Beelzebub.

And I'd still be standing here, falling in love with him.

34

BEELZEBUB

Margot had paid her price to Wrath and passed her test when she defended herself and me against the souls who'd tried to kill us, and Satanus was all too happy to give her permission to leave his circle when we collected my scythe from him.

The portal from Wrath to Heresy was thankfully close to the manor at Wrath, and the way Margot continued to look over her shoulder as we left the manor in our rearview set me on edge.

"Everything okay?" I asked, keeping my hand at the small of her back. I'd kept my scythe in my hand since retrieving it from Satanus, unwilling to lose the time it would take to release it if danger struck. We'd both come so close to death, and it grated on me that Satanus was the only reason either of us was alive.

Margot hadn't run, hadn't left me after I'd fallen. While I wanted to be furious with her for not putting her own safety above everything else, for not respecting my wishes and getting somewhere safe, I couldn't help the way my chest warmed with the reality of it.

She would have rather died than leave me. In the face of that, I didn't need her to speak the words to know exactly how she felt. Margot was mine just as much as I was hers.

"Of course," she said, smiling at me as she leaned into my side. I'd expected her to seek distance between us, but instead she seemed content to remain as close to me as possible. She'd barely looked at Satanus when we asked for his blessing to pass through, and I couldn't help the sinking suspicion that there had been more to their interaction than Margot wanted me to know. Whatever he'd said to her had wounded her, but Margot's self-hatred meant that there were so many sore spots he could have poked to achieve that effect.

The cemetery appeared out of the plains just beyond the fires. The massive statue at the front served as a force of impending doom. The scythe that was the twin to mine curved over the archway at the front, threatening to cleave the unworthy in half. Margot hesitated as we approached, mystified by the granite stonework that somehow looked soft and fluid. The demon holding the scythe had leathery wings like mine, their broad width spread out behind him. His third eye, resting in the center of his forehead and larger than his other two, stared down at those who approached his arch. His blue eyes were the color of the ocean, his face so similar to mine that Margot looked between us in confusion.

Guiding her through the archway, she winced as she stepped through the boundary that the portal had brought closer than the actual fringes of Wrath were. The cemetery expanded out before us, surrounding us as the portal back vanished from view. The ground we walked on was soft, absorbing us so slowly that we sank bit by bit as we stood. I pushed Margot forward, keeping her moving through the watery graves of Heresy, where those who violated the balance came to rest. The cemetery had been filled far more quickly recently, thanks to the Covenant's twisted edicts. Any who were not buried properly, whose magic could not be returned to the part of the Source that had gifted them with it, came here.

Those who had been shut in a box, the burials that horrified Willow so deeply, had all come to rest in this place.

While there was suffering in the other circles, there was also kinship. There was a sense of belonging and rightness, whereas the souls doomed to this place had been separated from the very thing that had defined their lives. Over time they lost all sense of identity, all memory of who they had once been. So many blamed the devil for the punishments of Hell, for the structure and the simple fact that it was where the souls who were condemned came to suffer, not stopping to think about the fact that He was just as much a victim of this place as they were. That we'd all been put here to enact His will, with absolutely no say in how it all came to be. The circles had been formed, the demons and archdemons who ruled them drawn from the very earth and magic that God had put here out of spite against the Source.

Hell was a cage, but it wasn't made for the souls he sent here to suffer.

It was made for *Her*.

Margot's hand stretched up to cover her mouth, seeing the freshly laid dirt covering each of the graves where a witch resided. Where someone had been led astray and suffered an eternity for it. She moved to the freshest grave, the dirt still loose and not yet packed by the waters that stretched over this land during the night hours, drowning the souls within their graves. She leaned forward, her feet sinking into the earth beneath her as she struggled to read the name on the grave.

"We should keep moving," I said, calling to her from the safest part of the path between the tombstones.

She nodded, but her eyes widened as she reached forward, wiping the dirt from the name on the granite. She took the first step away, putting distance between herself and the tombstone. She screamed as a skeletal hand burst out of the dirt, grasping her ankle and yanking her down into the mud. The dirt in the grave shifted as I took a step toward her, but Margot held up a hand and shook her head, turning over on the earth and getting to her feet.

Susannah Madizza's skeleton climbed out of the grave, her

bony fingers digging into the earth as she rasped for breath. Dirt fell free from her jaw, dripping down through her bones to land at her feet. She'd turned yellow with age since her true death, since the moment Lucifer had decided *this* would be her final resting place. After what she'd done to Willow and all that she would have done if He hadn't interfered, she would never know peace.

"Margot," I said, my voice a warning as Susannah stretched across the distance, reaching for her.

"Margot," Susannah repeated, tapping her finger bones together as she fidgeted with her hand. Her voice was rough and raspy, but she took a step toward Margot as if she might drag her into the grave with her.

My songbird took a step back, moving away from Susannah's grave with an instinctive knowing that took my breath away. She could feel the magic surrounding the grave, the boundary that Susannah would not be able to pass, I realized. I stepped up beside her, wrapping my arms around her and leaning forward to rest my chin on top of her head.

"They're here because of you," Margot said to Susannah, emotion clogging her throat. She'd been one of the witches who had been so misguided, so led astray by the witch they'd trusted to teach them the ways of balance and lead them down the path to the Source.

Susannah's head shifted up to me, her blank eye sockets seeming to peer through me. "You revolted against the matches I chose, but let this creature touch you willingly? Your womb is worth more than a demon, girl."

"Yet you agreed to let him touch me," Margot said, and that statement sank into me. Rage churned in my gut. The implication that there had been greater knowledge about what Itan had done was new information for me. Margot raised her chin, stepping up to the magical boundary. She placed her hand against it, grinning at Susannah ferally when she did the same. Their hands all but touched, separated only by the magic that kept Susannah trapped. "You made me a prisoner in my own life. It gives me peace to know that you will finally know that fate," she said, stepping away from the grave.

She reached for me.

"Margot!" Susannah screamed after her as we walked away, continuing on our journey to the manor of Heresy.

And the brother that waited for me there.

35

MARGOT

The manor in the Sixth Circle, Heresy, looked far more like the gothic churches of Europe than a home. The building was tall and narrow in width, with towers that jutted toward a sun-filled blue sky. A rose window sat in the front of the building, perfectly centered among the natural-colored stone columns and gables. Gargoyles sat atop the roof, staring down at us as we approached. Their eyes glowed red within their still faces, guardians watching all who chose to enter. There was a lightness in Beelzebub's step that I hadn't expected after all that had transpired in the past day, and he shoved the front doors open without care for formalities.

"Lord Beelzebub!" the butler said, a jovial smile lighting his face as he stepped forward. He clapped the archdemon on the back, the motion so familiar and less restrained than I'd seen in most of the other circles. The inner foyer around us was a sprawling hall with a domed ceiling at the back where light shone in the skyward-facing windows. The rose window at my rear cast a pattern of light on the floor, an illusion of shapes and shadows.

"Good to see you, Vrasarth. Is my brother around?" Beelzebub asked, and I spun to look away from the shapes on the floor so I could look at him fully. He grinned, showing a complete lack of shame for the secret he'd kept.

"I'll fetch him for you," Vrasarth said, nodding to me politely before he darted away.

"Brother?" I asked, genuinely curious as to how that had even happened. Demons were not born, they were created. Beelzebub hadn't had a childhood. He hadn't been raised in the same sense that I had.

He'd simply been nothing one moment, and then existed the next—a fully formed adult archdemon with thoughts of his own. "If you want to analyze it deep enough, all the archdemons are like brothers to me. Lucifer is the closest thing we have to a father, so that would make us half-siblings or close enough. But Belphegor and I were made on the same day. My magic had taken root long before his, waiting for the Source to free it from the earth and put it into the body Lucifer had crafted for me, and yet she saw fit to create both of us on the same day. It took years for the others to come to be, so I have to assume there was a reason for her decision. We've been close ever since."

"We were taught that Belphegor wasn't an archdemon, though," I said, attempting to keep the words light even through my confusion. I might have said it had been a lie, but all the archdemons had come through the gate with Lucifer.

Belphegor had not.

"He was meant to be," Beelzebub said, nodding thoughtfully. He looked toward the stairs at the corner of the foyer, as if keeping vigil for his brother and carefully crafting his words in case they were overheard. "Lucifer assumes it has something to do with forming two of us on one day, but He can't be certain what went wrong. The Source has never told Him why she didn't give Belphegor enough magic of his own to claim archdemon status. He still rules over Heresy, but he's more susceptible to the magic in other circles than the rest of us, so he rarely leaves. When we came to the surface, he carried Lucifer's cot to do his duty and actively chose to return to Hell before the portal closed. He will never leave this place."

"That must be difficult for him," I said, looking around the manor that now felt like maybe he was compensating for something. All the manors had been grand in their own way, but this was something different entirely. This rivaled the opulence of greed, with no reason as to why that might be the case. The statues at the corner of the room depicted nude figures, carved into white marble that was reminiscent of Greek antiquity instead of the gothic architecture surrounding them. Many of them were in an intimate embrace, hinting at the sin of lust as I looked around for signs of the other circles. Vines twined around a column, the leaves large like I remembered from Gluttony. The flames of Wrath climbed at the base of the rose window as I spun, protruding from the wall to look more realistic in the relief above the door.

Confusion made my brow furrow as the demon hurried down the stairs. It was the same one who had been etched into stone at the portal, the reaper waiting to cleave intruders in two. His face was so similar to Beelzebub's, a distinct combination of beauty and roughness, but his frame was smaller than the one at my side. He was leaner and a bit shorter, lacking the overall brutality that Beelzebub's sheer size gave him. A third eye sat in the center of his forehead, blinking as he reached the bottom of the stairs and embraced Beelzebub in a firm hug. The two men laughed until Belphegor pulled back, studying Beelzebub's face intently. "You missed me so much you had to come home?" he asked, pulling away slowly.

Beelzebub patted his brother's cheek condescendingly. "Keep dreaming. How could I possibly miss a little shit like you?"

"Why else would you be here?" he asked, turning his attention to me. "And why would you have brought me such a lovely gift?"

I sighed when he took my hand in his, leaning down to press his lips to the back of my hand. That eye at the center of his forehead remained fixed on me even as his others looked down at the hand he kissed. It was unnerving to have something so unblinking fixated on me, and it was only Beelzebub's warning growl that ended the moment when Belphegor lingered too long. "Not a gift," he grunted, tugging me by the waist. The growl lacked the venom he'd had with the other demons who'd made comments toward me, displaying his trust in his brother.

At least once he had made his intentions clear.

Belphegor's eye widened, a broad smile at his mouth hinting at trouble to come, but whereas the trouble we'd faced thus far felt dangerous, this was of the teasing kind.

"*Oh*," he said, nodding along in agreement. "Well, welcome to the family, random woman I've never met. I see my brother works fast, but I have just one question before I approve."

I flushed, the word *family* drawing up all the horrible hangups I had with my own. Family wasn't something I'd wanted to find; it was a bond that had never been anything but inconvenient for me. "What's the question?" I asked, letting Belphegor guide me out of the foyer and into a sitting room off to the side. He guided me down onto the sofa, taking the seat next to me as he grabbed a deck of cards off the coffee table and shuffled them in midair.

"How are you at Siege?"

36

MARGOT

I slapped my hand down on the table, stealing the cards out from under Belphegor as soon as he placed a fourth card down. The demon laughed in delight when his hand came down on top of mine a second too late and I hoarded the stack of four to myself.

He and Beelzebub had played a round of Siege while I watched, observing the way the game worked. The trick to learning was that they swore up and down they couldn't tell me the rules and that I had to learn by observation.

The point of the game was to collect all the cards in the deck by creating sequences of numbers and passing cards back and forth on each turn. There were four piles of ascending cards being worked on at any given moment, and in order to claim the stack after the last card was added, I needed to be the first to slap my hand down on top of it.

I started a new pile on the next turn, watching in fascination when Belphegor drew from the deck. He pursed his lips in thought as he studied the piles, eventually sliding a card to my hand when he couldn't make a play.

I added it to the pile in my hand, not the pile of sequences I'd gathered separately. Those cards were out of play once they'd been used, a fact I was very grateful for since I did not have to wield them all at once.

"She's kicking your ass." Beelzebub laughed, standing behind me. His hands came down on my shoulders in a soft and soothing massage, leaving me to study the cards before me carefully.

I played a four on top of the sequence of two and three, readying myself for the moment Belphegor might put down a five. In order to play the final card, he would have to draw his hand back to his cards before slapping the sequence, the same as I would have needed to. Otherwise it would have been impossible for me to get to the sequence before him.

"Beginner's luck," he grunted, drawing from the deck and studying his cards. The game continued on as he went through his hand, searching for a card he could play and eventually discarding one to me instead. "You haven't told me about Crystal Hollow. Was it everything you were expecting it to be?" he asked, but the question was posed for Beelzebub and not me, so I kept my focus on the game before me.

"What's it matter to you, worm?" Beelzebub asked with a laugh. "You've never had any interest in the surface. You've been adamant that it wasn't for you."

"That doesn't mean I can't wonder what it was like," Belphegor said as I played my hand, studying the cards before him for the briefest of moments before he made his play. "I'm fond of Heresy and content to remain in the only home that was ever meant for me, but I know you've always had greater aspirations."

"It was far from what I expected actually," Beelzebub answered, lowering himself into the chair at my side finally. He placed his elbow on the table between us, leaning into it with his chin on his hand and stifling a yawn. "The Coven is corrupt, but there are some attempting to bring it back to the natural order that the Source had always intended."

"The Source," Belphegor scoffed, the bitterness in it shocking me. I'd never heard the demon sound anything but pleasant and jovial, so his disdain for the very magic that had created him came as a shock.

"Enough," Beelzebub warned, scolding the other demon like the slightly older brother he was. Belphegor rolled his eyes but completed a sequence, growling when I slapped my hand down on it before he could.

"*How* are you so fast, witch?" he asked, his tone lighter than it had been only a moment before.

"Probably a question for the Source," I asked, my body nearly vibrating with the energy flowing through me. It was a new feeling, bolstering me in a way that I'd never experienced. I understood why Willow was so in tune with her magic now, how the feeling of the give-and-take with the world around her made her feel energized and braver. What could hurt you when you had the very magic of the world at your fingertips?

"We do not have the privilege of speaking to her, so I guess that will remain unanswered," Belphegor said, handing me the final card in his hand. "But you should thank her for your victory. I cannot remember the last time I lost a game of Siege."

"Don't be such a poor loser." Beelzebub laughed, standing from the table at the same moment Belphegor did.

He clapped his brother on the shoulder, the movement jarring the younger demon slightly. I stood as well, my body feeling fluid like water as I stepped away from my chair and looked to the pillars and cathedral-style ceiling that surrounded us. I'd expected a more intimate setting with a fire when the two suggested a card game after Beelzebub and I had eaten more food than I cared to admit.

But it quickly became clear that there was nothing small or intimate about Belphegor's home.

"Not a poor loser at all, it just means that we'll need a rematch tomorrow night," Belphegor said, a bright smile lighting his face. My heart fell at the joy in it, Beelzebub's sad expression coming to me for a moment.

"We'll have to save the rematch for another time," Beelzebub said as I made my way to his side. "We need to leave at first light. We're on our way to the Ninth Circle so that I can get Margot home."

"You're going to use the lake to speak with Him," Belphegor said, his eyes sliding sideways to me. "You're planning to return to the surface?"

"Making Crystal Hollow my home has always been my plan. You know that," Beelzebub said, his voice laced with notes of sadness. I knew without a doubt that he'd likely tried to convince Belphegor to come with him, but it was clear from the way he clung to his home that he wouldn't leave it so easily.

"I'd hoped something had changed after it didn't live up to your expectations," Belphegor said.

"The Coven may not be perfect, but Crystal Hollow is where Margot belongs. The living do not belong here with the damned." He paused, reaching out to take my hand in his. He raised it to his mouth, pressing a lingering kiss to the back of it. "She's my home now, so I belong wherever she is."

I stilled, hating the way Belphegor's eyes slid to mine in accusation. "You could come with us," I said, offering the only solution I could find. I couldn't remain here, especially not when Beelzebub didn't even seem inclined to it. It might have warranted a conversation if he hadn't intended to live in Crystal Hollow before meeting me, but we were united in that goal.

But the notion that we were discussing where we would live together so casually was enough to make my head spin. I was suddenly grateful that Willow had been the first one to establish a relationship with one of the demons, because hopefully it would be slightly less jarring if I returned with Beelzebub at my side.

Fuck my life.

"No, a town full of witches is not for me, I'm afraid," he said, smiling through the words as if they weren't laced with judgment. "There was a time not long ago that I'd thought it wouldn't be for you, either." He turned the force of his glare on Beelzebub, leaving me to wonder what that meant exactly.

Beelzebub had actively chosen to leave Hell in favor of Crystal Hollow, fully knowing that it was a town filled with witches. I knew he'd had his prejudice against us when he came, he'd made that much clear, but this felt like something more.

"Things change," Beelzebub said, shrugging casually as he guided me toward the stairs that would lead to the bedroom he'd claimed as ours when we arrived.

"What was that about?" I whispered as we made our way into the room and Beelzebub closed the door behind him.

"It's no secret that our kind have hated one another for centuries," he said, taking a seat in the chair beside the bed. He stripped his boots and socks off, keeping his eyes on mine while he did.

"Then why did you all choose to come to Crystal Hollow in the first place? Why not stay here?" I asked, trying to make sense of that choice.

"That is a question that we should save for when we are both ready to share the skeletons in our closets. You said that Susannah allowed Itan to touch you when you saw her in the cemetery. What did you mean?" he asked, crossing his arms over his chest as I kicked off my own boots and debated taking a shower before crawling into bed.

I sighed, finally, wanting to hear his truth and knowing I would only get it by giving my own. "Itan was the only one who could do a binding ritual to cut off the heirs to the Tribunal from the Source. I only found out about it just before Michael found me on the stairs. I was on my way to warn Willow about what it had done to us. I never got the chance," I admitted, keeping out most of the details about what that had meant.

But Beelzebub saw right through the worst of the offenses, standing and making his way to me. "The Covenant knew what he would do to you and still allowed it?" he asked.

"The Covenant knew as well as our parents. They decided it was worth the cause of starving the Source and magic and in turn . . ."

"The Vessels," Beelzebub said, filling the gaps. "And these are the people you are so desperate to return to?"

"No," I said, shaking my head sharply. I didn't care what happened to my mother or to ever see her again after what I'd learned, but that didn't mean that everyone in Crystal Hollow was bad. "I'm desperate to get back to Willow and those who would turn the Coven back to the ways of tradition. I want to see it become a better place. I want to know what it looks like when magic flows freely and the witches are in harmony with their conduits. I want to know what it was always meant to be."

"I do, too," Beelzebub said finally, nodding his head in agreement. He ran his tongue over his bottom lip thoughtfully before he answered the question I had asked before he'd turned it on me, not expecting me to open up.

But keeping this a secret felt foolish with all that Beelzebub already knew.

"There was a time when some of us were resolved not to share Crystal Hollow with the witches who called it home. Their involvement mattered little to us, but that has clearly changed now that Lucifer is in love with Willow. He would never try to take her home from her," he said, and I nodded. It made sense, and I couldn't even fault them for it really.

The witches would have done the same if given the first opportunity.

"I'm going to go shower before bed," I said, needing some time and space to be alone with my thoughts and process all that had happened.

37

MARGOT

The portal to Violence was a traumatic experience, striking far too close to home. The memory of how Willow described the ritual Gray had performed to open the gate hung over me, the violence involved in magic like that serving as a reminder that not all magic was used for good. That the magic held within blood could be used for something beautiful or adapted to something cruel and hideous.

Atrocities were committed when people claimed the ends justified the means, the loss of life somehow erased as irrelevant as long as the ending was a favorable one when all was said and done.

The altar rested atop a set of stairs that ascended toward the sky, ending abruptly as green flames danced behind the stone table. Beelzebub kept my hand within his, holding me tightly as we ascended them slowly. A single dagger rested on the stone beside a bowl, waiting for me to make my offering to the portal and see if it would permit me passage into the circle of Violence. Since the archdemon for Violence had yet to be properly made, the portal hadn't given up enough control for Belphegor to give us his blessing and allow us passage to the next circle.

The payment for Violence was blood.

We stopped before the table as Beelzebub wrapped hesitant fingers around the hilt of the blade, holding my hand out over the bowl as he stared down at me and waited for my permission. I wished there were another way to pass through, but the alternative would have meant two days' walk to the boundary itself, the circle of Heresy a vast network of tombstones and the suffering dead, and we'd be forced to listen to their muffled screams as they drowned each night and tried to claw their way out of their graves, only to be washed back in by morning and reburied by the force of the tide.

"It's alright," I said, splaying my fingers wide to give Beelzebub easy access to my palm. He leaned down, running his nose along the side of mine as the tip of the knife touched my skin. He pressed it deep, cutting through the skin and muscle to draw a straight line across my palm. I turned my hand over, letting the blood drip onto the stones waiting at the bottom of the bowl. They hissed with steam as they absorbed the blood, Beelzebub dropping the dagger beside the table to use both hands to bend my fingers back, forcing more blood from the wound. I knew that while he'd cut me deeply, he'd cut me more shallowly than he should have for the offering.

He hadn't wanted me to be wounded as we fought our way through the circle known for physical pain, preparing us to battle our way out the other side.

"I'm right here. Always, songbird," he said, his voice gentle. It felt like a warning of what was to come, as if he could feel the fear consuming me. Something was wrong, a premonition I felt in my gut.

Violence would ruin me.

I tucked myself into his chest as a torrent of air surrounded us, whipping my hair about my shoulders with the force of a tornado. It formed a swirling vortex, surrounding us in a tunnel of wind that destroyed the altar beside us, whipping the stone through the air. The sound of it crashing into the platform where we stood made me burrow into his chest, shutting out the world around me and the fear that I might die before we could even reach the Ninth Circle.

The wind tore Beelzebub's hand from mine, earning a scream from me as his form disappeared from in front of me. His chest was gone, leaving me to stumble forward as darkness descended upon me. Reaching for him, I called his name in desperation. "Beelzebub!"

Only the wind answered, the deafening sound of it surrounding me as I fell through time and space. I landed in a pit of black, a complete void of light as hearing returned. The wind vanished, making the air feel too still suddenly as I looked around for something, anything that might answer what had happened. "Beelzebub?" I asked, my voice far quieter.

There was no answer, only that eternal darkness that made my breathing quake. My chest shook with the force of it; a barrage of shallow breaths couldn't draw in enough air. I'd had enough panic attacks to know the makings of one forming in my heart, clutching at the organ when it couldn't get enough oxygen. My head went light as the memory of darkened nights in my childhood bedroom filled my head. Of wandering hands on my skin and far worse things I refused to name even in my mind.

Just when I thought I might lose consciousness, stumbling to the side, lights illuminated the pit in front of me.

There.

I made my way toward the fairy lights, the small twinkle of them surrounding an intricate silver border. The mirror was so like the gate to Hell, with the figure of a woman carved into the metalwork at the top. A filigree of feathers and scales comprised the rest of the border as I came to a stop in front of it. At first there was only darkness on the other side, and I paused as I wondered if it was a pathway.

"Beelzebub?" I asked again, spinning as I searched for the archdemon who belonged at my side. There was no sign of him or his hulking form, only silence as I approached the border in front of me. Reaching out with trembling fingers, I touched the cool surface of glass that cut through it, the warmth of my fingers leaving a mark on what I realized must be a mirror.

But there was no reflection in the glass, only darkness waiting on the other side.

I pressed at it more fully, contemplating breaking through the surface when a flash of movement came from the other end of the tunnel on the other side. A flicker of light came from a torch as it approached, with a child's delicate fingers wrapped around the body. I followed them up the arm that came into view as she came closer, her small frame looking so tiny in the width of the hall that expanded out behind her.

She stopped only when she could press a free hand to the other side of the mirror, deep mahogany eyes staring at me blankly as my heart stalled completely. I watched her for a moment, unable to stop the sob that made my throat close. The younger version of myself remained perfectly still, studying me as if trying to understand how I had come to be the way I was. She looked deep into my soul, seeing straight through me in a way that no child should ever be able to.

Her favorite nightgown was intact, the innocence that had been taken from her staring me in the face for a brief moment before her mouth spread into a cruel, sardonic smile.

She screamed, the sound tearing through the air and shattering the glass of the mirror. I hurried to bend down, shielding my face as I curled away, covering my ears with my hands in a desperate attempt to shut out the sound. Stabbing into my head, drawing a matching scream from my own mouth, I was oblivious to the shadows arcing through the air after the glass. The girl took a step forward, toward the threshold as I finally pulled my head from my knees and looked to her. Blood dripped down her ears, sliding down her neck as moisture coated my own hands. Her scream stopped as shadows played in the hint of light from the twinkling vines on the border of what remained of the mirror, leaving me to pull my hands from my head finally and stare down in horror at the blood that covered them.

I took a step back as the girl lifted her nightgown to show the bruises covering her thighs as she did. She crossed the threshold, emerging into the pit with a roll of her neck. The shadows that had swirled about in the light moved, striking me in the chest and knocking me airborne. I struck the wall on the other side of the narrow abyss, my teeth rattling in my chest before I fell to my knees in the dirt beneath me. Tiny stones cut into my palms, embedding themselves in the slash that had gained me entry to Violence.

I'd expected a war. I'd expected pain.

I hadn't expected the circle to use my worst memories against me, to make me face the fingerprint-shaped bruises on the thighs of my childhood self.

I sobbed, gasping for air as shadowy tendrils grabbed me by the arms, flipping me over and pinning me to the dirt. My legs thrashed, a fight I remembered all too well, moving my muscles as the girl came to stand before me. She was perfectly calm as she looked down at me, an empty shell of a child where joy should have been. "You let him touch me," she said, swiping her hand through the air.

A shadow followed her motion, slicing through my thigh so sharply I screamed in pain. I stared down at it, the deep gash to the muscle of my leg where her bruises had been. It disappeared from her body as others emerged, covering her form by the markers of years of abuse.

"No, I didn't. I swear," I said, pleading with her to see reason. I hadn't let him do anything, hadn't wanted him to come to my room at night.

She vanished from my sight as the shadows surrounded me, cutting into my skin in every place I'd ever hurt. Marking me with each bruise, bleeding me and reopening those wounds all over again. I whimpered through the pain, but it wasn't the sharp pain of open wounds I felt. It was the dull throb of bruising hands, of fists and violence that had made me hate myself.

"I'm sorry!" I screamed, my fingers breaking beneath the force of a boot. "I'm so sorry."

"You became everything we hate. You became a monster just like him," the child's voice said, soft and smooth and unmarred by the emotion threatening to consume me. I couldn't breathe through the weight of the shadows, so like the weight that had covered me, making me feel like I might be better off buried alive.

"I'm not like him," I protested, shaking my head as those shadowed hands clawed at my skin, tearing my bicep open and letting my blood soak the ground beneath me.

"You can't control it forever, and then what will you be? Another rapist, taking what isn't yours from those who wouldn't give it if not for your magic?"

I couldn't deny the warning, couldn't shove away the knowledge that it would happen one day. They'd all warned me what the consequences of withholding would be, and I'd be ready to end it before that time could come.

The girl knew that resignation, knew the choice I'd made when I was barely older than her. I would never allow myself to be like him, never let it get that far.

The shadows circled back, retreating as the girl stepped closer. I fought my way to my feet, wheezing through the pain as fresh blood pumped onto the floor. Something glimmered in her hand, sparking in the light from the mirror behind her. I stood before her, towering over her small frame as she raised her hand and opened her palm, revealing the jagged shard of glass she held within.

I shook my head, already knowing where this path led. "It's time," she said, her voice softening as I took a step back. "This is how you make it right. This is how you fix what you've become. You save all the people you'll hurt if you end it."

I reached out with trembling fingers, taking the piece of glass from her hand. It cut into the wound on my palm, reminding me of the archdemon who'd said he would be with me.

But he wasn't. He'd left me alone, left me to face this demon on my own.

I raised the glass to my throat, pressing it against the carotid artery that would offer me a quick death. A mercy I didn't deserve for what I was, and I stared at that little girl who had lost everything.

The one Itan had taken everything from. Her mahogany eyes were warm and familiar as she watched me, filled with sympathy and understanding.

I remembered her vividly in my mind, but I wasn't her anymore. I didn't hate myself with the same visceral violence she did, didn't want to die.

He didn't get to take that from me, too.

"No," I said, taking back my power with the word that hadn't been heard. It hadn't stopped him, but I knew it would stop *this*. I stumbled back a step as my lungs filled with a sudden shock of air, cooling my too-warm insides as I dropped the glass to the ground. It shattered on impact, the vision of the girl fading away as she lunged for me in horror.

And it all faded away in a sudden shock of light, cutting through the darkness and surrounding me with warmth.

38

BEELZEBUB

Margot slept.

Her face was blank, as expressionless as the girl's was in the pit. But whereas the girl had been filled with the emptiness that came from trauma, Margot seemed to have finally found a little bit of peace. She didn't so much as twitch when I leaned forward in my chair beside her bed, sitting vigil until she awoke from the aftermath of the visions.

I wanted her to wake. Wanted her to know without a doubt that the violence of the Seventh Circle had fully released her from its grasp.

I ran a hand over her smooth, unscarred arm, remembering the way her flesh had torn open beneath the weight of her own self-hatred. The mirror served as a reflection for the worst of our violence, pitting us against our worst enemies. Whatever it was that drove that violence was what we faced in attempting to overcome, and I'd long had the sinking suspicion that it would be herself that Margot had to face.

I hadn't been able to bear to tell her the truth, to tell her that she would need to face her own demons in order to reach the Ninth Circle. She'd already been so combative about coming with me because of her fear of the Second Circle. Telling her there was a chance that she might need to find a way to forgive herself would have doomed the mission from the start.

She'd have sat in her anxiety and fixated on it, letting it stew within her in a way that would have been far more detrimental to her mental health than just facing the challenge when it came.

"Come on, songbird," I murmured, brushing a lock of blond hair back from her face. It wasn't uncommon for people to take some time to wake after emerging from the pit. While the injuries sustained there may not have been real, the torture they inflicted on the mind was every bit as real as I was. "It's time for you to wake up."

She remained still, her head tipped toward me—drawn to me even in the depths of sleep. I watched her chest rise and fall, counting the movements to reassure myself she was still alive.

I'd come so close to losing her. To having to stand by and watch her lose the battle with her own self-violence. I'd known she was suffering, but never had she made me realize just how deep the fear of what she was capable of was. It had sunken into the depths of her soul, etched itself onto her very bones in a way that she hadn't thought to escape. She'd planned to die before she could hurt others the way she'd been hurt.

She'd planned to strip the world of her beauty, of the kind of selflessness that came with a person willing to make that sacrifice for people she didn't even know.

She could never have been the monster she saw when she looked in the mirror. She wasn't capable of it, no matter what her magic could do.

I hung my head forward, dropping it into my hands where they remained clasping hers. They were the fingers she'd broken in the pit, the ones I'd heard snap in the illusion that was created for her benefit. I ran my fingers over hers, feeling the rightness in them. The lack of breaks reminded me that she was okay, that the trauma she'd had to re-experience was horrible, but she'd wake up.

She had to fucking wake up.

"Violence is cruel. It takes the very thing we hate the most in our lives and makes us face it, where most people spend their entire existence avoiding it except for small transgressions over the course of years. To pass through violence, you have to take it all on at once and come out the other side without committing murder," I said with a laugh, thinking back to my first time passing through the Seventh Circle. The demon I'd had to face had been my greatest competition for my place at Lucifer's side, a practice for a battle that would one day come to pass.

I'd let Satanus live in the vision, and later on I'd allowed him to continue being free at Lucifer's behest. It was a fact I still regretted to this day, believing the smug bastard would be far better suited to the prison that now housed Michael the archangel.

Instead, he'd saved my life. If he hadn't been there, Margot and I might have been dead. Maybe Lucifer had known I would need him one day, or maybe He hadn't. But between that and the mercy Margot had shown herself, I had to think there was something to be said for overcoming one's own violence.

"Beel?" Margot's soft voice said, making my head snap up. I looked to her as she blinked back the sleep in her eyes, centering her focus on my face for a moment before it dropped to her uninjured hand. "I don't understand. What happened?"

"You won," I said with a gentle smile. "You made it out of the vision without hurting yourself."

"It wasn't real? It was an illusion?" she asked, and I watched the thoughts churn in her head. The realization that she'd suffered for something that wasn't actually happening, and her attempt to wash away the conclusion she'd come to in her moments of fear.

I touched the side of her head with one hand and her heart with another, letting her feel the weight of me. "It was real in here. That's all that matters," I said, waiting for her nod of acceptance.

Her lips twisted like she might cry, and I hoped more than anything she wouldn't. I'd seen her tears more often than I cared to in such a short time knowing her, and I'd have done anything to erase them permanently. "You left me," she said, her voice cracking.

"Just because you couldn't see me doesn't mean I wasn't right there, songbird. I was with you the whole time," I said. Even if it had been torture to watch, to have to witness and be trapped on the sidelines and unable to intervene without condemning her to being stuck in the Seventh Circle. Unable to progress, unable to move through Hell as she pleased.

"You saw?" she asked, the caution in that voice giving me pause.

"I saw," I said, agreeing even when it would have been easier to lie. To tell her only she'd been privy to the details of her experience.

"You must think I'm pathetic," she said with a scoff, the laughter betraying a new annoyance with herself.

"I think you're strong, Margot. I think it took immense strength to overcome that. There was nothing pathetic about it," I scolded, reaching down and squeezing her hand in reassurance.

She sat in silence for a moment and I let her, allowing the quiet of the room to give her the space to process all that she'd experienced. When she finally spoke, it was with glowing eyes of fire and a newfound determination in her voice. "I don't want to just exist anymore. I want to *live*," she said, voice catching as she snagged her bottom lip between her teeth.

I smiled, tucking her hair behind her ear as I leaned in. With one hand braced on her other side, I kept my weight suspended over hers, not touching her anywhere but that beautiful face. "Then that is exactly what you'll do."

39

MARGOT

We made our way out of the circle of Violence early the next morning. I had no intentions of staying in that hellish place any longer than necessary, even if the truths I had been forced to face to accept myself as I was would be valuable in the end.

They might have been something that I'd needed, a long overdue forgiveness I hadn't seen a way toward finding, but that didn't mean I didn't hate the path the circle had chosen to give me that forgiveness in myself.

My acceptance had come at a cost, and it felt like the desire to avenge that little girl had been the one to be sacrificed. It felt like I'd had to let go of making sure that never happened to anyone else in order to find my own peace.

The stormy cliffside was a force of wind against my face as we approached, a sudden drop down to the sandy beach below. Waves crashed into the shore, a narrow passageway on the beach before the drop-off plunged into the depths of an ocean.

My hair blew about my face, making me long for something to tie it back as Beelzebub led me right up to the edge. He peered down over it, staring at that narrow passageway of sand below.

"Give the wind a lie when you jump. You won't be able to speak it, not with the way the wind will steal the breath from your lungs. The lie is your payment for entering Fraud, so make sure you keep it at the forefront of your mind," he said, turning his back to the cliff. He faced me fully, making me watch in horror as he took a single step back.

He toppled over the side, his body angling away from me as one foot stayed planted against the cliff for a second that felt like an eternity. He pitched back until he was parallel with the earth itself.

Then he fell, plummeting toward the sand below. I lost sight of him in the swirling winds of a storm that swept him up, entwining around him. Staring after him, I watched for the moment he would appear on the sand below. Waiting for him to either stand triumphant at the bottom or fall to his death.

My heart was in my throat as I waited, and waited, and waited.

He never reappeared, as if he'd simply vanished out of thin air. I swallowed hoarsely, toying with the edges of a lie in my mind. I had every intention of considering my past, of taking that plunge with the lie of a happy childhood in my mind. Erotes families went to great pains to maintain the illusion of happiness, of the perfect family in spite of the pressures they tended to place on their offspring.

Run faster to be thinner. Sing louder. Take more care with your appearance to increase natural appeal.

But as I took that step off the edge, my heart racing so harshly I felt its beat in every corner of my body, that wasn't the lie that danced at the forefront of my mind.

That was a lie I told to protect my family, to play into the narrative they'd chosen to write. My greatest secret was the one I kept to protect myself, and the lie I told to cover up the truth.

I'm not in love.

The thought was a distinctive, tangible thing with weight that felt like it, too, helped gravity pull me down toward the sand. I plummeted feetfirst, my hair blowing up past my head and my arms raised from the force of my fall. I wished there was a way to get him off my mind, but he'd begun to occupy it eternally. There was little freedom from him and his assault on my senses, little reprieve in any corner of my mind.

Wind enrobed me, wrapping itself around me like a cold embrace. I spun in the circle of its current, twisting and twining as the sand neared, and then I slid right through it.

The grains of it surrounded me, swirling around like a vortex as I plunged into a cool, blue-gray place that reminded me of water except for the dryness of the air.

When I finally landed on the sand, it was another beach entirely. This was the freedom that came with the searing heat of the sun in the sky, with the summer humidity in the air.

The wind faded out, vanishing from around me. I lay upon the sand, feeling each individual grain where it clung to my dry skin. The tide lapped against the shore softly, touching my toes as a broad shadow interfered with the sunshine on my skin. I peeled open my eyes slowly, blinded from the brightness as the shadow held out a hand, an offering to pull me to my feet.

The temptation to remain right here, to linger in this place of warmth and tropical beauty, was strong, nearly overwhelmingly so. I wanted nothing more than to stay here, but the sanctuary felt false.

Like it was too good to be true.

I placed my hand within the shadow's, allowing him to pull me to my feet slowly. With the sun no longer at the forefront of my eyes, Beelzebub's face slowly came into view. His soft smile as he gazed out at the crystalline blue ocean was an echo of what I felt myself. A desire to stay that we both knew was impossible.

Stairs curved up the cliffside at our backs, embedded into the rock with the intricacy I'd come to expect of the nine manors of Hell. The top of the cliff was less moody than it had been when we'd jumped, a garden of flowers planted into the cliffside. Plumeria bloomed in splashes of yellow and pink on trees beside the white marble of the building, wisteria planted farther past the gardens with a mix of red and purple flowers cascading over the ground.

Vines of roses climbed up the columns of the building that seemed to have been built out of the cliffside itself, lending an ethereal sense to the building that felt like it belonged on the Greek seaside. It was beautiful, a vacation home that no one would be able to pass up. Even though my personal taste leant more toward the moody, gothic structure of Hollow's Grove and Beelzebub's manor, even I wouldn't have objected to spending a great deal of time in this place.

It was a haven, a sanctuary by the sea.

As Beel led me to the stairs and we started our ascent, I couldn't help that nagging feeling that it was a trap. That maybe what we saw before us wasn't the reality. Deception wasn't something I thought you could feel around you, and yet here it felt like I could taste it. Like the bitter end that followed the sweetness of dark chocolate, it cloyed the senses. The floral scent was like incense clinging to the air, fresh and thick. It only grew stronger as we neared the top of the stairs, my hand dragging over the surface of the stone wall at the edge.

"This place is all a lie, isn't it?" I asked, stilling before we could approach the manor.

Beel smiled, the look resembling something of pride. "Not exactly," he said, but the tone of his voice seemed to defy the statement. He drew out the last word slowly. "Everything is as real here as it is in any of the other circles. It comes down to something more along the lines of not being able to trust what is in front of you. A beautiful home on the outside can hold a prison within. A rose can hide thorns sharp enough to bleed. A handsome man can be the devil in disguise. Pretty lies on the surface often hide the ugliest truths deep within."

His last example was given with a smirk, knowing that while Lucifer had fooled Willow and deceived her greatly to get what

He needed from her, He'd lived among the rest of us in Crystal Hollow for centuries. I'd known Him most of my life, and while it hadn't been under any greatly personal circumstances, I'd never even begun to think about Him as more than just another run-of-the-mill demon.

"Am I about to walk into a prison?" I asked as he guided me toward the front door to the manor. My voice was light, attempting to keep the darker conversations at bay.

"You're already in one," he replied with a soft laugh, swinging his free hand out in a circle before him. "All Hell is a prison. Each circle is just a different cell."

Those words struck deep, making me gape up at him. I'd known as much, but hadn't thought an archdemon would think that way about the only home he'd ever known. His face was carefully blank as he pulled open the door, gesturing me into the manor with a nod of his head. I passed him as I made my way in, all too aware of the brush of his body against my shoulder as I did so. He was oddly quiet as we entered, but I had to brush it off as we came face-to-face with a single woman.

Incandescent purple eyes stared out of her face, accentuated by sharp features that felt almost batlike. Her nose was thin and pointed, her ears tipped like wings. Atop her head were four horns of varying sizes, standing straight up toward the ceiling of the grand foyer as she lingered beneath the chandelier.

"Lord Beelzebub," she said, her voice a purr as sharp teeth peeked out the corners of her mouth. With another woman, I might have thought it seductive, but with this demon in particular, she seemed far more inclined to eat him than fuck him.

"Legion," Beelzebub said, stepping forward. He left me to approach her—touching his forehead to hers and murmuring something beneath his breath. A moment seemed to pass between them, an unspoken communication I wasn't privy to. I couldn't hear the words, not over the thundering of my heart in my ears. His proximity to her set every bit of jealousy within me on fire, made me want nothing more than to confront him for the falsehoods he would have had to give me in order for him to have a relationship this intimate with this woman.

She opened her mouth slowly, a thin, forked tongue sneaking out to drag over Beelzebub's cheek. She licked him slowly, as if tasting him, and let out a shuddering gasp as he pulled away and stood to the side.

"Margot," she said, turning that eerie purple stare toward me. I watched in horror as she took her first step, closing the distance between us and leaning in. Her tongue scraped across my cheek in the same way it had Beelzebub's, rough and coarse like a cat's. "You must be very special to him indeed for him to ask that he be permitted to pay your debt of truth."

"I don't understand," I said looking back and forth between the two of them. I would have sworn that I hadn't seen either of their lips moving when they were close, and I certainly hadn't heard Beelzebub speak to ask to pay my debt.

Legion pressed her forehead to mine, mimicking Beelzebub's posture from before. She was taller than me, making her the one to curl her upper spine and neck over me. The moment her skin touched mine, I couldn't take my eyes from her vivid purple. My own memories flashed before my mind, like the shuffling of a tarot deck, as if someone was searching for something.

Unfortunately for him, I think I am far more interested in finding your truth than his. Her voice slid through my mind, wrapping itself around a memory as she pulled it from the deck. The image of her fingers toying with the card imprinted itself on my brain, her smile wide and gleeful as she pulled back and stared at it. Her fingers tapped the card, nails painted a vivid purple as she turned it to face me.

A picture of Beelzebub and me embracing graced the front, the word scrawled into the bottom of the card a direct contradiction to the lie I'd given to gain access to the circle of Fraud.

Lovers.

I swallowed, staring up into those purple eyes as she toyed about in my mind. I was both inside my brain and outside of it, staring up into her eyes and watching her rifle through my memories like she belonged there, but she never released that card. She kept it pinched between two fingers for safekeeping, and it was only when she took a step back that I allowed myself to let go of the hope that she would choose something else. *Anything* else.

You're in love with the archdemon, she said in my head. Her lips curled around pointed fangs that pierced her tongue as she ran it over the surface. *This truth is not mine to keep, little liar.*

"No," I said, my voice sounding too loud in the silence that followed as she retreated from me. Her forehead left mine, severing the connection between us as she stepped back, that card somehow still held within her hand. She clutched it to her chest, keeping the image hidden from Beelzebub as she backed away. She danced as she went, swaying her hips and almost skipping her legs, as if my panic brought her joy. "You have your truth."

"And it is up to me what I do with it! So rarely do I get to have both the holder of the truth and the recipient of the truth in one place!" she said, grabbing Beelzebub by the hand. He let her lead him to stand in front of me, pausing only when she put him in place. He remained perfectly still as he waited, watching me as tears welled in my eyes. To give him this truth would be to condemn him to a life with me, even knowing he would probably be better off without me. It would be to dive off the cliff and be willing to take a chance with the man I'd sworn I would keep away from. "I do not suffer a liar!" Legion said, her voice rising as if frustrated that I hadn't simply outed myself.

"Come on, songbird. Just tell me whatever it is, and we can move on," he said. His voice started out gentle, but it turned pleading and panicked as he cast a glance at Legion over his shoulder. At the way she'd begun to fidget, her fingers tapping on the card rapidly.

"I can't—" I said, swallowing down the surge of emotion in

my throat. It stung, making it feel too tight to voice the words even if I'd wanted to.

"You will not leave here as a liar," Legion said, stepping up beside us. Beelzebub reached out, taking my hand in his and opening his mouth to speak. There was a warning in his wide eyes, a plea for me to give what I couldn't. Legion cut him off with a tear at the edge of the card, the sound splitting the air as Beelzebub groaned and pressed his hand to his chest. He dropped to his knee, nearly pulling me down with him as I looked down at him in horror.

"What did you do to him?" I asked, my hair flying to the side as I whirled on Legion.

"Either you give him your truth, or I make it so it is no longer true," she said, tearing at the card once more. The tiny tear at the edge was the start of splitting the card down the middle, and I felt that second pull somewhere deep within me. Like muscle tearing from bones, like a soul ripped from a body, it was the hint of an agony I couldn't begin to fathom. I swayed on my feet, nearly falling over as Beelzebub worked to keep me steady. "The choice is yours to make."

"I—I . . ." I broke off, pinching my eyes closed to shut out the red of Beelzebub's stare, the patience in it even though the pain of that first pull had been enough to drive him to his knees. He stayed there, as if expecting a third tear that would drive him back down if he tried to stand. "I have feelings for you," I said quickly, unable to face him. They felt like a weakness, like admitting there was a way to hurt me when I'd spent so long building up my armor.

Legion pulled again, the tear rending through the air. My eyes flung wide as Beelzebub pulled at my hand, squeezing it in a viselike grip. "Not good enough! A half-truth won't help you here," Legion said, her voice raking over my skin like nails on a chalkboard. Every part of me tensed in preparation for the pain if she tore through it again, if she tried to sever our bond.

I realized that what I'd felt splitting was the love between us being torn from one another. A few days prior, I would have welcomed it.

Now, the thought of not having it anymore filled me with panic. My breathing quickened in my lungs; my heart raced in my chest. Before Beelzebub, I'd known exactly who I was. I'd known I was barely surviving and hanging on by a thread. Now, it felt like I had a future, but I didn't know what it looked like without him.

Legion tugged again when I hesitated, tearing the card to the halfway mark. I dropped to my knees before Beel as that pain tore through me, too, taking both his hands in mine. His stare was apologetic, filled with sympathy as he kept quiet. Allowing me to make the choice for what happened from here, I realized. This was my chance to set him free and he would let me, because at the end of the day this thing between us meant nothing if I didn't choose it, too.

He'd chosen it even with the possibility that my magic would take from him. How could I not respond in kind?

"I want to have a future," I said, watching from the corner of my eye as Legion paused before completing the tear. My voice shook with the words, emotion clogging my throat and tears stinging my eyes. "And I want to have it with you. I don't know what it looks like. All I know is that I'm in love with you, and I can't let you go." My voice broke at the end, and Beelzebub lunged forward as the card vanished from Legion's hand. She stepped away, seeming satisfied with my confession as Beel's hands wrapped around my cheeks and he touched his mouth to mine.

It was everything soft and gentle, soothing the hurt that only vulnerability could bring. That warmth and comfort within me mended, sewing itself back into my bones as he held me still. I knew it had to be love, because anything else would have been a lie and Fraud would have known. Still kneeling on the ground, he drew me into his arms and surrounded me with his warmth, chasing away the chill that fear of rejection brought.

"I love you, too, songbird, and I know exactly what my future looks like," he said, guiding me to my feet. He took me away from Legion's waiting presence, taking me up the stairs to the upper story of the manor.

"What does it look like?" I asked, my voice quieter than I could remember it being. Beelzebub made me feel bold. He made me feel like someone who fought for what she wanted, when I'd always thought of myself as someone who waited for life to happen to her. His hand at my back bolstered me, even as we approached the bedroom at the top of the stairs. There was no fear in what might come next, because I knew without a doubt it would be my choice.

With Beelzebub, it would always be my choice.

"It looks like you," he said, pausing in the doorway. "You are my future, songbird. That's all I need." He cupped my cheek in his hand, the gentleness of that rough skin solidifying the decision forming in my mind. He paused on the threshold, made no assumptions about what I would want. I knew this room could be a sanctuary to wait out the vulnerability and just be together.

Or it could be something more.

I took his hand, peeling it off my cheek and tucking it into my side as I turned and stepped into the bedroom.

Taking Beelzebub into our future with me.

40

MARGOT

I made my way toward the bed at my back, sitting on the edge and taking Beelzebub with me. He sat beside me, looking at me with nothing but patience. It was such a stark contrast from the man I'd assumed him to be at first, with his glowing red eyes that seemed to radiate the evils of Hell. While I'd found the legends to be true in some ways, there were also some people I'd met along the way who had made me believe that maybe not everyone was filled with pure cruelty in spite of this place. The Source had proven to be kind to Willow in her own way, though she'd also been pragmatic about doing whatever was necessary.

He was so different from what I'd expected him to be, more patient with me than any human male who'd attempted to get close to me.

I lifted his hand from the bed where he'd rested it, placing it on my chest just above my breast. His fingers splayed over it, covering the entirety of my collarbone with the breadth of his hand. "I don't have any expectations, Margot," he said, his voice gentle as he watched me. His hand didn't so much as move to shift the fabric of my shirt, didn't drop to the breasts that were right there for the taking. "You having feelings for me and you being ready for this are two entirely different things."

"I know I don't have to do this," I said, smiling at him as the truth in those words warmed me from the inside. After everything we'd been confronted with, even with all the lust that pumped through my veins and must have constantly affected him, his priority was still making sure I was taken care of. "But I want to."

Beelzebub studied me for a moment, his stare roaming over my face from my eyes to my mouth. "Are you sure?" He searched me for any sign of hesitation, any second thoughts that might have disastrous effects if we tried this before I was ready. When I nodded, he stood from the bed and towered over me, the dominance in that stance making things inside me tighten—not with fear, but with interest. "If you want something, then I need you to use your words, songbird."

I swallowed, staring up at him in surprise. "I'm sure," I said, the words coming out more quietly than I'd intended. I cleared my throat, shoving off the nerves I felt over what he may think once he'd had this from me. It was easy to say he wanted me before he'd had me, easy to imagine the Red witch as some natural at all things sex, but what if I couldn't live up to that expectation? I'd never been with a man, never touched or engaged with one. "I'm sure," I said, forcing more certainty into my voice.

Beelzebub nodded as if he could sense the determination in me, holding out a hand for me. "Then come with me," he said, and I placed my hand into his in confusion. He guided me to the bathroom at the corner of the room, leading me into the space. He didn't waste any time before he reached into the shower and turned the knob to hot, the sound filling the space around us.

Self-doubts crept in. Did he think I was dirty? Did he think I needed to be cleaned before he could touch me? It would have been a lie to say that I hadn't spent countless nights scrubbing my skin raw in the shower in a desperate bid to erase the unwanted touch, but it had been so long. I opened my mouth to ask the question, unable to find the words to communicate it. If the answer wasn't one I wanted, I didn't know that I would be able to recover from that.

"Hey," he said, catching my chin and pushing my mouth

closed. I realized it had been hanging open as I fumbled for the words. "I don't want to risk you feeling trapped beneath me in the bed, and I don't want you to have to take the reins for your first time," he said, and the thoughtfulness filled me with guilt. That I'd thought him capable of thinking I was dirty, that I'd let my own insecurities tarnish his goodness all over again.

"Oh," I said quietly, the sound quiet compared to the water plunging down from the ceiling. The rain-shower head was at the center of the shower covered in dark gray tiles, sparks of purple glimmering within the stone like stars in the night sky. He couldn't know that the different setting also helped remove me from the familiarity of the bed, from the situation being too similar and becoming a trigger for me in itself.

"Just breathe, songbird," he said, cupping the nape of my neck and leaning over me. He kissed me, soft and slow, no sense of urgency within the touch. He explored me like he hadn't already gotten to know my mouth, like this was different entirely and we both knew it. He angled his head, using his hold to guide me where he wanted me, turning me this way and that as the urgency built slowly—moving in time with the arousal he stoked within my core with nothing more than his mouth. When I moaned into his mouth, he raised his free hand to the hem of my shirt, toying with it where it brushed against my hip. I wrapped a hand around his neck, pulling the elastic out and letting his hair fall down to his shoulders. He groaned into my mouth as his hand wandered higher, sliding beneath the fabric of my shirt to splay over my belly.

The muscles there contracted, a shiver running through me at his touch as he ran a single finger over the skin, tickling me as he drew a path up from my hip to my belly button. He continued higher as I whimpered into his mouth, that finger coming to rest in the valley between my breasts. I tugged away from him suddenly and his hand dropped without hesitation, falling out from my shirt as he stared down at me. He wasn't angry with me for stopping him, only concerned that he might have pushed too far.

I grinned up at him as I grabbed the hem of my shirt, tugging it over my head and tossing it to the side. He stared at me with a smirk that was feral and all dominance, stepping toward me as I mirrored the motion. His hand rose to my breast without hesitation this time, cupping it and testing its weight. He kneaded the flesh lightly, running his thumb over my nipple and the piercing I'd given myself strictly because I knew the Coven wouldn't approve.

A pang of heat shot straight from my breast to my core as I tossed my head back with a moan, his mouth dragging from the corner of my mouth to the side of my neck. Nipping me there, he ran his thumb over my nipple again and smiled when I whimpered.

"So sensitive," he murmured, working his way in a path over my throat and collarbone. He bent at the waist to grasp me around my thighs, lifting me up onto the bathroom vanity and setting me atop it. His mouth continued his exploration of my collarbone, his tongue dipping into the hollow groove where it met my shoulder. He switched his hand to my other breast, giving it the same attention he had the previous one as his breath trailed down over the swell. "These piercings will be the death of me," he murmured as he gazed up at me. I placed my hands on the counter behind me, leaning back into them. The movement put my breasts on display, allowing me to watch as he wrapped his lips around my nipple. His tongue toyed with the edges of the barbell, making me quiver as I watched him. Those red eyes held mine as he worked it over, gliding his hand down over my stomach. I writhed as he trailed a path, tormenting me with each and every moment of touch until he found the waistband of my pants. He released my breast as he dragged my pants down as far as he could, lifting a brow at me when I didn't move. "Lift," he ordered, and I leaned farther back into my hands as I raised my hips off the counter.

Tugging my pants down slowly, he watched the muscles of my stomach work as I fought to keep my ass raised. When he'd finally cleared the swell of my ass, I sat back down and shivered at the feeling of the cold counter against my bare skin. He'd taken my panties with my pants, and dragged them down my legs until he reached my boots. He rid me of both as he kicked off his own boots and socks, shoving everything to the corner by the door so it was out of his way.

When that heated gaze landed on me once again, he trailed it over me from head to toe in a slow, languid study. He touched a hand to my chest beneath my throat, his thumb and forefinger brushing against either side as he cupped it in the webbed part between them. I swallowed against the touch, but couldn't deny the way my breathing quickened in response. Beelzebub tipped his head to the side as he used his free hand to shove my legs apart, gliding his body into the gap he created. He raised his other hand a fraction higher, encircling the front of my neck in his hand. There was no pressure to the touch yet, just a promise of what was to come if I could take it.

And I wanted to take it. I wanted to take anything he would give me, give him anything he wanted. The desire to please him was overwhelming, threatening to consume me if I wasn't careful.

He trailed that free hand between my breasts as he squeezed my throat lightly, slid it over my quivering stomach to touch the light dusting of blond hair at the apex of my thighs. He moved slowly, watching my face as he moved his hand lower, slipping it between my lips to find me wet and wanting. He growled as he dropped his forehead to mine, circling my clit with two fingers as the hand at my throat tightened. My pussy tightened around nothing, a spasm coming to my core as I responded to the touch.

His grin was satisfied as he released me, dragging his mouth over my stomach in the same path his hand had taken. He lowered himself to his knees on the floor before the counter, sliding his arms beneath my upper thighs and yanking me to the very edge of the counter. "What are you doing?" I asked, a note of panic creeping in. Beel seemed to know it wasn't the kind of panic that came from trauma but from embarrassment when my legs closed around his head, trying to shut him out.

He forced them wider, baring me to his gaze as he stared at me. He spread my pussy open, taking in every detail as I heaved a sigh. "So fucking pretty," he murmured, the affirmation soothing the frayed edges of my nerves. "Even here." With that, he leaned in, dragging his tongue through my slit in a slow glide that set all my nerve endings on fire. My hips bucked toward him from the intensity of it, earning a chuckle from him as he pressed a hand to the top of my lower belly, pinning me still as he circled my clit with barely there brushes of his tongue.

"This is cruel," I hissed when he lowered and slid his tongue inside me, fucking me with it when I wanted something *more*. He laughed into me as he slid a finger into me alongside his tongue, drawing a strangled, raw sound from my throat.

He continued with his torment, exploring every inch of my pussy with his tongue like he was committing it to memory. That finger worked in and out of me slowly, making me writhe as I watched him between my legs. I reached down, tangling my fingers in his dark head of hair as he added a second finger to my entrance, gliding it inside slowly. I felt impossibly full as he worked them, scissoring them apart to spread me open.

Given what I'd seen the day he touched himself, I'd need it.

He worked my clit more aggressively, giving it his undivided attention. It didn't take long for the heat of an orgasm to build within me, for the sounds of my breathing to come more rapidly. He groaned into me as I clenched around him, my climax stealing the breath from my lungs. He continued to finger me through it, his tongue making gentle passes over my clit until I shoved him away. "Too much," I whimpered, earning a satisfied bark of laughter from him as he rose from his knees. He kissed me sweetly, the taste of me on his mouth making something possessive light within me.

A determination to make him smell like me all the time, to make it known who he belonged to in the most primal way possible.

He grasped me at the waist and glided me down over the edge of the counter, dragging me down over the ridge of his cock where it was still trapped inside his pants. I reached a tentative hand between us to stroke him.

He groaned, grabbing me at the nape of my neck as he guided me backward. "Get in the fucking shower, songbird," he murmured, releasing me. I stepped back, watching as I plunged beneath the cascade of water. I tipped my head back, letting the spray fall over my head and down my back as I spun to face the wall.

I hummed to myself as I let the warmth fill me, my song only cutting off as Beelzebub stepped in behind me. Water splashed off him and sprayed against me as he dragged a hand down the tattoo on my spine, pulling back and slapping my ass. I squeaked as I turned to face him, letting him back me into the wall.

There was a bench beside me, and Beelzebub didn't hesitate to reach down and grasp me under the thigh. Raising my leg, he positioned my foot on top of it and spread me open all over again. I was still too short compared to him, but he bent his knees deep enough to drag the head of his cock through my pussy. I whimpered as I looked up at him, feeling the weight of that gaze and the silent question.

Reaching between us, I wrapped my hand around his where he held himself, guiding him down to my entrance with a ragged breath. He kissed me as I pulled my hand away, letting him push forward to slide inside. I parted for him, his head slipping in easily. He groaned as he pulled back and pushed deeper, giving me shallow, slow glides to get inside me. He gave up on the bench with a growl, lifting my leg so that he rested my calf on his shoulder, bending me in half as he worked in deeper. I leaned back into the shower wall, panting for breath as he kissed me. I couldn't close my eyes, couldn't shut out the visual of him moving inside me.

Needed the reminder that it was Beelzebub, that I *wanted* this as heat built within me. He got deeper and deeper, until he filled me completely. He stayed there, planted deep as he kissed me, running his hands over my body, the slick glide of him over my wet skin soothing the ache that I felt deep within me.

So deep it seemed impossible.

"Please, Beel," I begged, and he picked up his motions. The slow glide of him dragged over the most sensitive part inside me, making my eyes roll back in my head. He was too good to be true, filling me with warmth with his lovemaking. It was everything I needed my first time to be, but as he stoked that heat higher and higher, I needed more. "Please," I repeated, my voice higher than I cared to admit.

"Tell me what you want, songbird," he said, his voice gentle. As if he wasn't as affected by the feeling of me wrapped around him as I was feeling him inside me. I had a moment of doubt, a moment where I wondered if this was more for me than it was for him and if I could really take what I would be asking for. "I need the words."

I shuddered, blinking up at him as I rested my head against the shower wall. "I want you to fuck me," I said, scanning his face the moment the words reached him. He stilled inside me, studying me, and it bolstered me, letting me see the strain on his muscles as he fought for control. He wasn't unaffected by me.

He was holding back.

"You don't know what you're asking for," he said, shaking his head and kissing me gently. It was the sweetness I should have wanted, the gentleness I wanted to want. But all I wanted was to see Beelzebub unrestrained, to take the shackles off and feel the way he wanted me.

Maybe I was broken, but in that moment, I wanted to be broken in his arms.

"I don't want you to hold back. I want to be everything you want," I said, and the vulnerable admission must have clicked with his unwillingness to give me what I asked for.

"You already are," he murmured, the gentle ease bolstering me. He'd gone to such lengths to make me comfortable, to let me know I was safe with him.

Now I could put that to the test. "Now, Beel," I ordered, sliding my leg over his shoulder and down his arm to rest on the floor so I stood before him. He curled a brow at me as he waited. "You told me to use my words and I did, now give me what I fucking—"

He spun me to face the wall so suddenly my palms slapped against the tile, the sound reverberating through the enclosed space. He drove inside me from behind before I could take a breath, slamming into me with a force that shoved the air out of my lungs. "Fuck!" I screamed, looking over my shoulder at him. He stayed planted for a moment, giving me time to change my mind before he withdrew and set a hard, punishing rhythm. Each drive into me brought a whimper from my mouth, the pitch rising higher and higher. He wrapped a hand around the front of my throat, arching my back as I fought to maintain my hold against the slippery tile. "Oh God," I gasped.

"You're in Hell, songbird. God can't help you now," he growled, sliding his other hand around my hip to stroke my clit while he fucked me. I groaned, the sound long and deep as I tightened around him. My magic pulsed out of me in a wave, bringing him over the edge with me. I fed the Source and Beelzebub fed me, and nothing had ever felt so harmonious before that moment.

His own groan came with his orgasm, as the warmth of him finishing inside me filled me. It dragged me over the edge with a scream that clawed its way up my throat, his hand vibrating against me with the force of it.

"Fuck," Beelzebub sighed, pulling out of me slowly as he spun me to look at me. He tucked me into his chest as I swayed, my legs feeling like jelly beneath me. "Did I hurt you?"

I just smiled. I could feel the heat of his release slipping down my thighs, and my body was covered in the marks he'd left behind.

But it had never felt more like mine.

41

BEELZEBUB

Margot still slept when I lifted her from the bed and clothed her. Her exhaustion was potent, sinking deep into her bones. Between the physical violence of the Seventh Circle and the emotional turmoil of the Eighth, she needed a long, hard sleep. I'd given her a sleeping tonic when we'd found our way into bed finally, and she'd been too sleepy to protest.

Maybe it was a betrayal to do it with the intention of speaking with Lucifer alone. Maybe she would have wanted to be there for that conversation.

But things moved quickly in war, and I had no way of knowing what had come of Hollow's Grove after they'd repelled Michael. Another archangel could have easily been sent to take his place since we'd been gone and made it so there was nothing safe to return to. I didn't know what I would do if Lucifer needed me to return to help Him in the latest war. I'd never questioned my loyalty to Him, never hesitated to lead His armies in the past.

But if they put Margot in danger . . .

I swallowed as I finished tugging a long-sleeve tunic over her head. It hung low on her hips, cascading over the fleece-lined pants I'd dragged up her legs. The circle of Treachery was a freezing landscape of cold and ice, a stark contrast to the heat and seasonal weather of the other circles. Legend said that Lucifer's rage burned like frostbite when He'd been cast out of Heaven, that it had changed the landscape of the original circle forever. The Source had taken in that rage and made it a part of herself, leaving Lucifer to be the more calm, callous man I'd come to know when they created me later on.

I tugged pants onto Margot's body, shoving socks onto her feet before I lifted her into my arms. What she would view as a betrayal would serve as her payment to enter the Ninth Circle, the cost of which was either betraying something or someone or being the one betrayed. It may take her time to see it as the kindness it was, but I hoped that eventually she would.

She was light in my arms as I strode out the door to the bedroom we'd claimed as our own for a few hours, ignoring Legion's arrogant face. She knew better than most what the cost could be of love; the consequences of taking the bond of marriage were very real for demons. It was why I'd been so shocked to find that Lucifer had married the witch who had never been more than a means to an end, that He'd been willing to share Himself and His power source with her. Not only strengthening a woman who could have very easily decided she'd much rather remain His enemy, but weakening Himself in doing so.

I'd never even considered marrying, never wanted to see my mark on a woman's skin, but now I found myself staring down at Margot's collarbone as I walked. I could already imagine how my mark would look curled around the back of her neck, the edges showing at the front of her shoulders.

I could feel the way she would shiver in my arms when I ran my tongue over it, the heat of her skin scalding me.

I was so fucking screwed.

I sighed as I left the manor of Fraud, making my way to the cliffside. A fence surrounded a circle of roses that were frozen over, trapped in a moment of time at the rear of the manor. I approached them slowly as I opened the gate and paused at the edge of the flowers. Looking down at Margot's sleeping face, I hoped the tonic would be strong enough to keep her pulled under the spell of peaceful oblivion. The entrance into Treachery was terrifying enough when being awake to make the jump, but to wake up in the middle of the plunge would be horrible.

I tightened my grip on her as I stepped over the roses, my heels resting on the edge before the circular hole in the ground. The tunnel extended impossibly far, feeling bottomless beneath me as I tucked Margot's head into my chin to protect her and stepped off the edge.

The feeling of weightlessness was immediate as we plummeted down through the pit, surrounded by complete darkness. Margot began to stir in my arms but I shushed her, trying to encourage her to fall back asleep. I wasn't sure it would be enough, what with the intensity of the feeling as darkness gave way to the bright gleam of snow beneath us, but she settled just long enough for me to land in the snowbank below. I took the brunt of the landing, cradling her the best I could, immensely grateful for the strength of the tonic Legion had given me.

The cold of the snow immediately penetrated through my pants, sinking into my bones as I hurried to stand and make my way into the manor of Treachery. Lucifer's home was more a palace than a manor, carved out of snow and ice itself.

The Lake of Coccidus sprawled out before it, the surface frozen over eternally. It was said to have been formed from the tears He'd shed in the first century after His exile, pleading for the man He had viewed as a father to take Him back into Heaven's embrace. It had frozen over only after His tears had stopped, only after He no longer sought his father's approval.

A grand stairway curved up to the palace as I made my way up the shallow steps that were somehow harder to transcend than steep ones. The front of the palace was covered in arched windows of ice, the structure of the building crafted out of packed white snow. I'd often wondered if there was *any* sort of structure to the building outside of something that would melt without his icy rage, but it seemed to hold even in his absence.

Spires reached for the sky, the sheen of sunlight gleaming off their tips. There wasn't a cloud in the sky overhead, a perfectly clear, sunny winter day that made the bitterness of the cold seem even stronger. The center tower and spire were taller than the others, belonging to Lucifer Himself. To the right was the spire that connected to the bedroom that belonged to me, and to the left was Zepar's—the demon Lucifer had chosen to rule over Treachery in His absence.

In the time it took me to ascend the stairs, Margot's nose had already turned red, her cheeks pink as I shoved open the grand front door. The palace of ice burned me as I touched it, cold sinking bone-deep as I stepped into the somehow comforting warmth within.

A fire blazed in an iced-over fireplace in the great room to the right of the foyer, the magic keeping it from melting. I bypassed it and headed up the stairs for the bedroom that belonged to me when I came to discuss business matters with Lucifer. Margot settled as we made our way up the three stories of stairs to the spire at the right of the building, the warmth soothing away the chill that might have been enough to wake her. The door to my room was already open, allowing me to bring her in and rest her on the edge of the bed as I yanked back the covers. I settled her beneath them, tucking her in gently and kissing her forehead before I turned and made my way back outdoors.

While I suspected I still had hours before she woke, I didn't want to risk her waking up and finding me in the lake. She wouldn't be able to come without serious consequences to her more frail, living body, and that would only piss her off on top of discovering me taking this step without her.

The frozen lake was perfectly still as I approached, my boots crunching over the snow that had frozen at the edge. I took off my boots, stepping onto the top of the ice with bare feet. I took nine steps toward the center, stopping and allowing the cold to sink into my toes through my socks. They burned with the bite of frost that would cost any human the digits in the end, but the lake warmed beneath me as the ice melted away.

It cracked, extending out through the water to reach the shore.

It caved beneath me, plunging me into the depths of icy water. It surrounded me, penetrating my lungs as my body refused to move, freezing within the waters.

Only when my eyes closed did Lucifer's face finally fill my vision, His voice playing on repeat in my mind as He answered the call. "It fucking took you long enough," He grated with impatience.

42

MARGOT

My face stung.

It existed only in the fringes of awareness, the haze of sleep clinging to me and refusing to let me go. I didn't remember falling asleep, only remembered tucking myself into Beel's chest and enjoying the feeling of his warmth pressed against mine. The safe cocoon of his wings wrapped around us had been a haven as my eyes drifted closed.

He'd pressed something to my lips, murmuring something about it helping me sleep and healing any soreness our *activities* had left me with. He'd promised I'd be feeling up to exploring more when I woke, so why did I feel like I'd downed an entire gallon of wine?

I peeled my eyes open as my other cheek stung, a blaze of flame kissing it as I raised a sluggish hand to touch it.

Satanus stared down at me, his eyes blazing within his cruel face. His red skin seemed deeper than it had the last time I'd seen him, his horns sharpened like weapons. His body was covered in a black armor that hinted at wartime, stained with blood, and he grunted in satisfaction when I stared up at him. "Get up. We need to go," he barked, leaving me to look around me.

I forced myself to sit, clutching the blankets to my chest in confusion. I didn't remember much about the room I'd fallen asleep in, but it hadn't been this one. This one had dark furnishings against bright white walls, a floor made from snow as I stared down over the edge of the bed. Satanus thrust a pair of boots into my chest, the force knocking the air from my lungs. I swayed, shaking off the sleep the tonic kept at the edges of my mind. "Where are we?" I asked, cradling the boots. I couldn't bring myself to leave the safety of the bed. I'd been tucked in with care, the pillows arranged just the way I liked them.

There was no reality in which Satanus had been the one to put me here. There was no reality in which Beelzebub hadn't been the one to do this.

"Treachery," Satanus grunted as if my question was an inconvenience. He snatched one of the boots from my hand, pivoting me in the bed. My legs splayed out over the edge, emerging from the blankets as he shoved the boot onto my foot. "Beelzebub brought you here while you were sleeping and went to talk to Lucifer. A rebellion broke out. They're trying to seal the gateway from the inside."

Panic made me stand. While I slept, demons had tried to take away any hope I had of ever returning home. Any hope of seeing my friends again, of facing my family and telling them what I thought of their treachery, telling them that I would never be like them.

It wasn't something I'd realized I wanted until that moment, but suddenly the chance of never getting the opportunity was a stark reminder of all the things I'd never lived.

I couldn't be trapped here in this place of death.

"Where's Beelzebub?" I asked, hurrying to my feet as quickly as I could. I scanned the room and went to the bathroom as if he might be in there, as if he would have ever allowed Satanus to be the one to wake me unless . . . "I need to see him."

"He's speaking with Lucifer in the lake, formulating a plan. He asked me to take you to Gluttony where you'll be safe while he deals with this," Satanus said, grasping me by the forearm. He guided me toward the door, all but dragging me as I dug my heels in and refused to move. The memory of Beelzebub's distrust of Satanus was like poison in my veins, sitting heavy as a warning. Of all the demons he could have sent to escort me somewhere safe, Satanus was the *last* one he would have chosen.

If this had been what Beelzebub wanted, he'd have sent Belphegor for me.

"I'm not going anywhere until I see him," I snapped, grabbing onto the blankets as he pulled me harder. They tore from the bed, falling to the floor as I reached for anything within my grasp. "No!" I screamed, stomping on Satanus's foot. He shouted as his hold loosened, allowing me to get free as I sprinted for the bathroom and the door I hoped I could lock. I never reached it, grabbing the edge of a console table beside the door when Satanus wrapped his arms around my waist and pulled.

The table crashed to the floor, its contents spilling over it. A vase shattered as it landed, spraying glass over my boots, and candles rolled through the room. Some disappeared under the bed as I struggled to get free, kicking out in my struggle. My foot caught the mosaic hanging on the wall, sending it careening sideways until the frame dented against the packed snow floor.

I screamed again, determined that there had to be *someone* in this place who could hear me. There had to be someone who would find Beelzebub and tell him I needed him.

Tears streamed down my face when Satanus covered my mouth with his hand, leaning in to whisper in my ear, *"Anything."* I froze in his hold, the word erupting through me like a command. I couldn't move as horror dawned on me; I couldn't fight anymore. His mouth widened into a smile against my neck, his hand parting my lips open as he slid his finger into my mouth. The metallic taste of blood washed over my senses, spreading over my tongue and filling my mouth until he pulled his finger back and released me.

Anything.

I shook my head, trying to shut out the word as his blood

seemed to warm me from the inside. I felt the path of it as it slid down my throat, winding its way through my body until no part of it felt like mine anymore. It didn't belong to me, primed for the command he would utter to get the payment he was owed.

"I—I thought—" I stuttered, trying to wrap my head around the trap that I'd walked myself right into.

"That I would want to fuck you?" Satanus asked, barking a cruel laugh at my expense. "Hardly. You're worth far more to me dead than you are in my bed."

I blinked up at him as he drew a small dagger from his pocket, running his thumb over the surface affectionately. It grew beneath his touch, forming a curved short sword that he held at his side. The weapon matched the words, the threat spoken so casually I'd almost missed it. If it hadn't been for the gleam of his blade in the light shining through the windows, I might have thought I'd misheard him.

"Why?" I asked, shaking my head as I tried to understand. I hadn't done anything to him, hadn't earned a death at his hands.

"It's a shame you had to go and fall in love with him. Didn't they ever warn you that love was weakness?" he asked, stepping closer to me. I couldn't move away to fight, couldn't do anything to protect myself as he pressed the tip of the curved blade to the hollow in the center of my chest. "It's nothing personal, little witch. You are merely a means to an end." There was something wistful about his voice, some part of him that softened as he stared down at me. A red hand rose to cup my cheek, its thumb wiping away the tear found there.

His blade pierced my skin, cutting through the thin line of muscle there with ease. He paused when he met the resistance of my sternum, his head tilting to the side. "Was it worth it? Trading your life for his in the end?" he asked, waiting for my answer. I knew what would happen when I gave it, knew that these were my final moments. I turned to look toward the ice window at the back of the room, searching the ground below for any sign of Beelzebub.

But there was none, and I was alone all over again.

Still . . .

"Yes," I said with a nod as I turned to look at Satanus once more. "He's worth it."

Satanus nodded, clasping a hand atop my shoulder as he pressed that blade in sharply. It cut through me, splitting my bone in half. I bent over as I fought for breath, staring down at the hilt where it protruded from my middle. Satanus tightened his grip on the handle, pulling it back. A surge of blood followed, pumping out of my heart and making a squelching sound as it splashed against the floor.

I followed, landing on my knees as I touched my hands to the hole and tried to stem the bleeding. My breath was wet, rattling about in my lungs as I slipped and swayed to the side. I didn't let myself fall, clinging to the hope that Beelzebub would find me before my last breath.

"Let go, little witch. It is time to pay your debt," he said, staring down at me. He kicked me to the side, sending me toppling over onto the floor. My hands slid off my wound, blood pooling around me to stain the snow a macabre shade of red that left little doubt. There was so much of it.

I'd lived haunted by the color, and it seemed only fitting that I died in it, too.

"I thought this was my debt," I said with a wheeze, my eyes feeling heavy.

Satanus stood over me, his red face and horns the last thing I saw before my eyes drifted shut for the final time. They would not open again. My body lay limp as it lost all facets of life. His voice was a murmur above me, a warning of what awaited me.

"No, little witch. Death is only your beginning."

ACKNOWLEDGMENTS

First and foremost, thank you to the readers who have loved this series and asked to continue on in the world of Hollow's Grove. Your passion for the characters and setting and willingness to take a chance on them has been my greatest inspiration, and I have thoroughly enjoyed getting to explore another legacy house with Margot.

Thank you to my children, who have taught me more about unconditional love and understanding than I could have dreamed. You are my entire reason for being, and I love you to the moon and back.

To my team of staff and alpha readers for supporting me in all my more eccentric habits and writing rituals, as well as listening to all the rambling voice memos when the muse hits.

To Justin the first, for sharing your wife with me. I mean, let's face it, the bestie comes first anyway. Caitlen, I love you. I'll refrain from making you cry this time around.

To Justin the second, for always believing in me and making me feel a little less eccentric when I go on a creative spiral and pull out the sticky notes. Thank you for treating my writing like it has value and is a point of pride, instead of looking at it as an obstacle you need to overcome. Thank you for standing outside a bookstore on release days and bragging about my books to everyone who will listen.

To my team at Bramble, thank you for believing in these characters and doing everything necessary to allow them to shine. Thank you for continuing to take a chance on me.

AUTHOR'S NOTE

According to RAINN's website: an American is sexually assaulted every sixty-eight seconds. Every nine minutes, that victim is a child.

You're not alone.

If you or a loved one has experienced sexual assault, please contact the National Sexual Assault Hotline or chat with RAINN online.

1-800-656-HOPE
https://rainn.org/

ABOUT THE AUTHOR

HARPER L. WOODS is the *USA Today* and *New York Times* bestselling fantasy romance alter ego for Adelaide Forrest. Raised in small-town Vermont, her passion for reading was born during long winters spent with her face buried between the pages of a book. She began to pass the time by writing short stories that quickly turned into full-length fiction. Since that time, she has published over thirty books and has plans for many more. When she isn't writing, Woods can be found spending time with her two young kids, curling up with her dog, dreaming about travel to distant lands, or designing book covers she'll never have enough time to use.